A SHINING
IMAGE

A SHINING IMAGE

HOLLY M. PFEIFFER

ABOOKS

Alive Book Publishing

Additional copies may be ordered from the publisher for
educational, business, promotional or premium use.
For information, contact ALIVE Book Publishing at:
alivebookpublishing.com, or call (925) 837-7303.

This is a work of fiction. Names, characters, places and incidents are
either products of the author's imagination or are used fictitiously.
Any resemblance to actual events, locales or persons,
living or dead, is entirely coincidental.

Book Design by Alex Johnson

ISBN 13
978-1-63132-102-3

Library of Congress Control Number: 2020915230

Library of Congress Cataloging-in-Publication Data
is available upon request.

First Edition

Published in the United States of America by ALIVE Book Publishing
and ALIVE Publishing Group, imprints of Advanced Publishing LLC
3200 A Danville Blvd., Suite 204, Alamo, California 94507
alivebookpublishing.com

PRINTED IN THE UNITED STATES OF AMERICA

10 9 8 7 6 5 4 3 2 1

Dedicated to Sweetpea, my cat.
You've literally been by my side all along.

CHAPTER 1

Hope is a distraction. I gave up on that wretched emotion nine years ago, right after the passing of my mother and father, the sovereigns of Andria. I only gave up my precious hope because it was hurting me, eating me up inside and making me go insane. It made me wish to see my parents again, it made me think that there was a chance that they were still alive somehow, somewhere. I would grasp onto every little thread of the loathsome hope, no strong thread amidst the lot. I found myself restless at night with thoughts of the way life had been before it all. I loved them, just as any normal five-year-old child would love their parents. Now I think the way I loved them was the wrong way to live. I was a child, but I decided not to let childish thoughts affect me any longer.

My name is Alexander. I could tell you my full Christian name, but that would be a waste of time for me. I don't believe in wasting time that could be spent in more important ways. Every second of life counts, so if I can add a few more seconds to my life by refraining from telling others my full name, I most certainly will. I'm fourteen years old as of today, but I turn fifteen on the eighth of October, just a few months from now.

I stare out the window, pondering what else I could add to the already interminably long poem, written on the parchment curling against my desk. I've been working on it for quite a few months at this point. I know that nobody will read it, but it's been consuming my unscheduled time and I'm very grateful for that. Sometimes rhyming until I fall asleep is a good way to distract from moments that cause the blackest of fears to emerge.

I've lit candles and placed them on every surface in my study. They illuminate the paintings of past kings from hundreds of years ago. All of these stiff-looking old men seem to stare down at me with the most judgmental eyes. It's hard to believe that they were once fourteen like myself. The candles I've lit are burning close and the shadows around the rapidly darkening room have made themselves more pressing. The sky's too dark and grey to write without the meager light provided by the dribbling stubs.

The significance of today is the king, my brother's, wedding. I wouldn't attend the supposed celebration if it wasn't mandatory. I have to, being the second prince and all of that. He doesn't even know the woman he's going to marry. My parents arranged this marriage when Edward was young and he had no say in it. He's to be wed to bring peace to Andria, and isn't that what marriage is for? It's to end wars and bring peace. In fairytales, the protagonist of the ditzy tale marries for *love* and *self-fulfillment*. That's another lie. I can only hope to learn to love the person that my brother decides to pair me with. I squirm at the thought of it.

Twenty-four is a late age to marry, but my brother put off the inevitable to make right the needs of our previously forsaken kingdom. He's a distant person, always lost in his own realm. He doesn't like to be around people. I don't blame him. I suppose another world would be a better place to live than where he is now. I don't have enough courage to call him a recluse, but I haven't seen him for months. Simple man.

After the death of the king and queen, he would visit me each and every Sunday to check up on me, although that was more for his own consolation. We would play in one of Palace Andria's various gardens until his duties pulled him away. He needed me more then, for I was all he had left of our deceased parents. But a year after their passing, he would only visit me once a month. He needed me less then, for he decided to plunge into the venerable role of king and such at only fourteen. Now I only see him on holidays. He wouldn't see me at all if he didn't have to keep his image perfect. I'm just a reminder of his past. Last year I only saw him once. See, he's made quite the descent into darkness.

He's drowning in troubles caused by the current war with Walsia. Our countrymen usually are tall, slim, blonde people. Godly looking. We are known for our beauty. I turned out differently, though I don't know why. In fact, I look more Walsian than Andrian. I am still slim, but I'm quite short for my age. I have wavy, ebony-colored hair that falls just below my ears. I'm in desperate need of a haircut and my curls hang into my blue eyes, clouding my vision in place of the tears I have never cried. If I had brown eyes, I'd be mistaken for a Walsian! That would be awful. I've never even considered employing someone to trim my hair for me.

I believe my brother is marrying a Walsian to try to make peace. The sovereigns arranged this union and I'm proud of them for orchestrating the end of a twenty-year war. Deep in thought, I'm suddenly broken out of my trance as I hear a slight, hesitant knock at the tall, gilded door. Just the right amount of detached politeness implemented. I would know a knock like that anywhere. Standing in the shadows of the doorway is my brother who only calls himself Edward. I could also tell you his full Christian name, but again, I don't like to waste my time on trivial things such as that. He looks down at his feet stoically, letting his shining crown slip down to one side of his head. Astonishment envelopes me as I gaze into his eyes. He can stop by my wing of the palace before one of the most important days of his life, but he cannot find time to do so on an average day. How terribly interesting.

"Hello, brother. I haven't had the pleasure of your presence in quite some time." I stutter in spite of all my efforts to remain nonchalant and composed. This is a surprise indeed. I wasn't expecting to see him until after the ceremony at least. I half expected not to even speak personally to him on such an important date. "You should have called ahead so I would have had time to make the proper arrangements for the king of Andria and her many regions," I add in a falsely bored and uninterested tone to make him aware of my resentment of this little visit.

"Yes, I should have," he replies solemnly, with a dark tone of superiority in his voice. I haven't heard a tone quite like that in the chorus of my brother's voice before. I step away from the large entryway to let him through, but the look he gives me tells me he could have crushed me to get through the doorway if he so desired.

He stretches across my chair comfortably, although he was not invited to do so, and motions for me to sit in the stiff, dark green chair across the way. I comply, but I let a little anger seep into my expression as I unwillingly oblige. His eyes flicker to the expanse of my leather notebook. It's splayed across my dark-paneled desk. My heart thuds against my ribs. I should have closed the leatherbound volume as soon as I heard a knock. Angst fills me. I wonder what his thoughts are on the second prince, meant to be an ambassador, writing poetry?

"She liked to write poetry," he notes in a barely audible tone, pulling his hand across his forehead.

"Who?" I ask, perplexed. I straighten my jacket and ruffle my hair a bit, for I'm sure he's going to make the answer seem prominent, therefore making me feel lesser than him. I at least wish to look my best if that's the case. Even though he barely speaks to me anymore, I still know his actions before he acts. I suppose that's the bond brothers share. Who am I kidding, it's intuition and only that.

"Our mother," he replies sternly with a frown, as if I should have known that immediately. Our mother: I barely remember her. How would I have acquired the knowledge that she likes poetry? His eyebrows turn down as he appraises my handwriting. They land on a small drabble I formed off to the side of the main stanza of the poem. Oh Lord, that's not something I wish for him to read.

The sky is grey,
Come what may,
You cannot change the day,
No matter how you pray.

"Not excited about my wedding, are you," he states with a look of dismay. I nod hesitantly after a moment, not knowing if my nod would offend him or not. He sighs and shakes his head in response to my small gesture.

"I'm not all that excited either, Alexander. I don't even know this woman and I have to spend the rest of my life with her. I have seen her portrait and she is … beautiful. She has wavy dark hair and the most intriguing eyes, but that is not a substitute for real love. The love that is described by great poets. Not in the slightest," he adds.

I look down at my polished shoes, not wanting to return his icy gaze. "I heard she's Walsian," I reply, my eyebrows climbing slightly. I rub the spot between my eyes, trying to alleviate a rapidly growing headache. I thought this day wouldn't hold so much angst. He beams at me, trying to reassure me that he's all right through his actions.

"Yes, that's the one good thing about this arrangement. It'll end the twenty-year war once and for all."

I chuckle heartily, pulling my hands over my eyes. Yes, he's the perfect king. Always putting the wellbeing of his subjects before his own. I hate to admit it, but I most certainly would not be able to do a thing such as that. His charming smile grows empty as I pull my head up to look at him again. The expression within his eyes is amiable, but his eyes are full of fear.

"You should know that I'm proud of you, Edward. You will now face a lifetime of companionship with the woman you are going to marry later this day. Chances are that the two of you will fall in love with each other." I try to console him with hopeful words of whimsical things, but those phrases feel so awkward and unknown to my lips. The encouragement spills out mechanically.

"She's the best I'll find. They're all the same to me. I don't believe anymore in such ideas as true love, at least for the monarchy," he replies, squaring his shoulders with the masculinity of his words. Only moments ago he spoke of poetic true love. He contradicts his own words to assuage his own pain. We sit in a heavy silence. It isn't awkward or strange; we only sit together, enjoying the company of the one we've missed. He abruptly stands with an emphatic grunt, buttoning his suit jacket once again in a resolute way. He stops to admire himself in the gilded mirror propped up against a shadowy wall.

"I'll see you next year, maybe we'll briefly talk about politics in some meeting before that," I say to myself dryly as he leaves the study. I hear his footsteps growing ever quieter against the paneled floorboards. Before too long, I rise to my feet with a sigh. What an interesting event. I stack the papers I was busy with precariously atop one another before exiting in the same manner my brother had, buttoning my suit jacket the same as he had done. I must prepare for the wedding. This will certainly be a long evening.

I arrive at my bedchamber half an hour later. I was dragging my feet, for I'm not looking forward to this. I can't say that the hallways are short here. Each corridor seems to span miles the first time you tread through one. The red carpeting and priceless pieces of art that were meant to brighten the dimly lit hall get so dreadfully boring after just minutes of admiring them. Despite the dullness, I spend time attending to each and every one of them to deter the inevitable.

I dunk my head into a bucket of icy water and scrub my unruly locks with lavender foam, a soap I enjoy. If I could just manage to keep my hair out of my eyes for one night, then maybe I would be able to appreciate the mindless festivities. No matter how fiercely I scrub, the hair lays flat in my eyes. The moment I brush the stygian curls away, they fall back into my face. I manage to allow myself minimal vision through some act of God. The raven strands only remain over one eye and I'm able to peer through the other.

The part of the preparation that I'm looking forward to least is the part about the cravat. The short, wide strip of fabric is even more of a nemesis than my unruly hair. Honestly, those objects are the devil wrapped around your neck, threatening to squeeze the life out of you at any second. I'm very passionate about this issue. I also hate the bright royal blue I will have to wear for this miserable meeting. The garment is a long coat with many buttons that don't appeal to me in the least. It's the kind of thing that will make you swelteringly hot in the cold of winter. The cravat, also known as a noose, sticks out in such a flamboyant way. Andrian people have an affinity for bright colors. That is another way I am different from my kind. The colors remind me far too much of the panicked feeling one gets in their chest when fear comes. I have to go along with it, though, to keep my image pristine and untarnished for the kingdom. I can just *imagine the uproar* if I wore dark blue instead of light blue to this event! So outlandish!

My skin is scrubbed clean after a brief sponge bath. I dress in the ridiculous uniform before struggling to shove the outrageous cravat into place without choking myself to death. I stare at myself and nod in an unsure manner at a large mirror next to the doorway. I'm determined to be respected. I'm determined to be feared. I'm determined to keep my image perfect. With one last shuffle of the terrible cravat, I march out of the dressing room.

I can see that the day is quite grey, as I suspected it to be. The clouds swirl overhead, popping out against the dark green of the wind-crafted fields. The shapes they make are something you would see in your deepest state of dreaming. It looks as if heaven is being revealed for human life to see. A light rain falls, coating everything in sparkles. Indeed it looks like something from a wonderful dream, but I'm sure the servants will get their buttons in a bunch about the slight inconveniences the rain brings after weeks of preparations. I personally think it's rather nice.

I lumber into the courtyard, saving every bit of time alone I can while preserving my punctuality. I may have to make small talk with Walsian nobles the entire wedding reception, so I'm savoring this small free period I've found. I've heard tales of strange Walsian customs before and for that reason I'm on edge—more than usual, at least.

"Ah, there you are Prince Alexander C—"

"I would prefer it if you would only address me as Alexander. I don't need to waste my time by listening to my full Christian name be spoken," I reply snappily to the girl.

Her name is Mary. She's not my favorite person in this world, as others can tell. She's planned this wedding down to the smallest detail and the fact that I'm slightly late to the ceremony is her worst nightmare. Her face turns crimson and she grasps my arm tightly, pulling me to the front and violently shoving me into my seat. I recover from the painful chide swiftly. A rather large man who might be a great uncle stares at me as if I'm a fly on his dinner plate. His small rat-like eyes seem to bore into my soul with judgment. I smile back at him nervously, trying to ease the tension.

"Hello," I mumble to him, trying to recall some of my fat great uncles' names. He might be called Rupert, but if I were to call him the wrong name he would be deeply offended and I would never hear the end of it from a manners instructor that my brother would inevitably hire to tutor me if he heard of this incident. My time alone would be up for auction. I must remember this man's name.

"Hello Prince Alexander, *second* to the throne," he spits. The man puts an emphasis on the word "second" with a little gesture towards me as if I'm trash he's ordered a servant to pick up. I sigh and shake his hand firmly, glaring into his eyes. I'm much shorter than the man, but there isn't much muscle under those rolls of fat. I squeeze his hand with bone-crushing strength. He pretends not to notice, but he nurses it when he believes I'm not observing any longer. The unpleasant look that appears on his face is enough to satisfy my unrequited need to throttle him. Suddenly, music begins to blast. I stumble in bewilderment. The intense strings play a wedding melody traditional for the strange Walsians. The sound emanating from the royal orchestra is dark, yet also melodious. The melody has many different layers and each one is delectable.

A woman saunters down the rich black carpet laid out before her. I hear her heels clacking tackily against the wood hidden beneath it. The wood laid under the carpet was shaped in such a way to only be for this wedding, a waste. It practically begs to be walked upon. What a strange notion. Used for only one purpose.

My brother stands near me, an expression of worry crossing his face. The woman is hopelessly short compared to my brother. I can see her dark hair through the creamy white veil hiding her face. A magnificent train is attached to her dress. It's carried by at least ten beautiful Walsian girls. Their dresses are brilliant sapphire blue. The Andrian court must have made that decision. Such a bright color! They are almost groaning from the weight of the train, yet they still smile as brightly as one could imagine.

Philosophers from many hundreds of thousands of years ago say that the eyes are a window to the soul. I catch a slight glimpse of the bride's eyes through the side of her veil. They aren't what I would expect the eyes of a bride to be. They're frigid and purposeful, nebulous. As dark as I expect the soil in hell to be. There are flecks of gold in her eyes. They illuminate her eyes like stars do the night sky. Her indifferently beautiful face astonishes me. My brother lifts the veil as if he's lifting a priceless artifact off of a pedestal. She smiles with *genuine happiness*. Is she actually pleased to marry one that she does not love, nor has she ever met?

My fingernails dig into my soft, white flesh. A vault of rage stored in the pit of my chest opens suddenly, blurring my fake expression into one of fury. I close my eyes, trying to regain control of myself as the ceremony proceeds. How could she possibly be joyful? How could she be at all pleased with this unbearable arrangement? What does she gain from something such as this? After taking a few shaky breathes, I open my eyes again and plaster a false yet assured smile on my face. I won't know her intentions and I suppose I'll just have to accept that for my own sanity.

Her stride is courageous, beautifully crafted, so that all who've attended believe she's putting on a brave face and that she's legitimately upset by this. Manipulative is an adjective that describes her well. My smile wavers slightly like a blade of grass in a soft but sudden zephyr. I shake my head, trying to convince myself that all that I've seen through her celestial eyes and confident stride doesn't prove her intentions. Yes, I shouldn't judge someone by their eyes despite what some philosophers say. She's most likely only had to act her entire life, much like myself. She's so used to pretending to be jovial that it comes naturally to her. I take a shallow breath in an attempt to make my plane of vision wane. I need to regain composure. Before I can fully retract the idea from my brain, a thought too valuable to forget flashes across my mind and I grab a tiny leather notebook that's always stowed protectively in my right pocket.

To see, but not to touch,
The eyes are windows, but don't see too much,
A shining image, protected by lies,
You can see it, but not with eyes.

It's an offense to be mocked with her jubilant smile. It's an offense that I'm letting this simple expression of happiness toy with my insecure mind. My palms will begin bleeding if I clench my fists any tighter. I take more consoling breaths and consider whether or not I should erase the small creation. The verse burns a hole in my pocket as the ceremony continues on placidly. Nobody knows my recent, intense thought. I sigh one last time before directing my attention to my poor brother again.

The clouds I saw before are darkening with my mood and I know a downpour will reach us soon. I'm standing up straight, my back arched and my chest puffed out, projecting the image of someone with no flaws while staring at the flawed ceremony. The priest chants something to ensure that a love that never existed will last forever. All lies. I try to believe the words he speaks and keep up my visage for a little longer, just until I can be by myself again. My fingers are itching to write a longer work about this event. Words float through my mind. It troubles me that I'm becoming bothered by something as plain as this. I'm strong enough to ignore it. That's what I should've done from the beginning.

My brother gazes up towards the clouds. He's probably wondering if he'll ever see them the same way again. He's wondering if marriage changes the person he's become, or whether the new Walsian queen will only be a new elective added to many. I see that same brick-like expression on his face that I'm so used to seeing return after his short moment of contemplation. Am I really to end up like him? Marrying a flimsy-minded noble from another land for the benefit of the great kingdom of Andria? Am I going to be one of those men who always wears cravats? Am I really to have nothing but my own thoughts to myself? This should be the best day of his life, but instead, it seems like his royal position has chained him to someone he's never even met for the rest of his life. Best day of his life my arse.

"I pronounce you husband and wife, sovereigns of Andria," the royal priest pronounces in the loudest, fullest of voices. This is to ensure that everyone who's attended hears the proclamation and cannot claim that this event never occurred.

The rain's messed up my brother's customarily flawless hair that most definitely took hours to prepare, and the bride is carrying at least twenty gallons of rainwater on her bulky, pale dress. My brother pecks her quickly to make the marriage official although the priest hasn't uttered the command for him to do so yet. I feel myself clenching my hands into fists again, but soon relieve the pain-inducing pressure. I cannot let this influence me. I cannot note that this is the first time they've kissed each other and it was only a brief peck.

Nobles in the back rows hurriedly begin to venture inside, praying no one else will notice their disrespect. They don't want to get their hand-made gold-threaded clothing damp as well as their dainty little hats. They don't care even slightly for my brother. They're only here for the prestige of the event and the benefits that come after. Lightning webs its way through the sky and thunder rumbles deafeningly. I hear an array of shouts echo throughout the crowd. Makeup runs from the faces of maidens as they lunge for shelter. They're so incredulously frightened of those around them seeing the beauty hidden beneath their masks of powder.

Finally, my brother and his bride rush inside with the rest. I make a move to follow them, but a voice inside me tells me that I shouldn't bother. It tells me that it isn't as if they're going to care for my absence. It isn't as if they've ever legitimately cared. They won't miss me if I stand out here for a few moments.

Moments grow longer than moments should. Not a single soul has come for me just as the voice told me. I'm still standing as straight as I possibly can as if someone is watching me.

How pitiful, Alexander, just go inside, the voice whispers, contradicting its previous words. I shouldn't waste my time on a matter as trivial as this. I refuse to waste my time on it. In the end, nobody will care. Nobody will remember it. I usually write these thoughts down on sheets of parchment and there they are, perfectly preserved on parchment that will age and age and crumble away into the wind someday. This notion gives me the silly foolish hope I so desperately avoid that maybe, maybe someone will read my work and someone will care. I lift the little leather notebook out of my pocket along with the small pen. Water rushes against it, but I don't care.

Standing up,
Emotions erupt,
I cannot see,
What happened to me,
For if I do,
I might shoot through.

An ode to life. No, this—this isn't life. It's far too surreal, standing in the rain with only the ink of a pen to console me. At least the ink allows me to leave this place. It helps a lot more than those mindless breathing techniques. It's a mode of contemplation, I suppose. If I speak on this matter anymore, then I'm sure it will be a bore. I scribble in the little leather notebook. My miniscule pen travels down page after page at a furious pace as I write frightening thoughts that've been bouncing around the walls of my head all day. I close my eyes as I scratch at the paper. I'm sure my writing will come out in a terrible form, but I don't particularly care much about that. The page is already drenched and my only concern is to empty the madness into the pages before I empty it in a less acceptable manner.

I'm afraid if I look at the sky now I'll drown like a turkey. My hair is a black, wet mess, distorting my vision. My breathing has not steadied but become faster and more panicked. I'm sure the ratio of oxygen to rain won't be enough to sustain my rapid breathing. My vision gains a few dark spots and everything seems to start running left. My fingers look as if they're trying to escape my plane of vision. Suddenly, I feel a hand on my shoulder. Her hand is a soft hand that I know in ways I haven't any other. I'm shivering and she knows it for she pulls my coat over my shoulders in a kind manner. I immediately feel my breath return to normal.

"Alexander, the ceremony was over an hour ago. The reception is continuing on right as we speak."

My spine stiffens, but my hands fall back at my sides. I slowly loosen all of my muscles enough not to waver uncontrollably.

"Lizbeth," I reply tersely.

"Yes, it's me," she responds in a blank manner.

With a quaking hand, I try to brush the sopping wet hair out of my frozen face.

She looks at me with her verdigris green eyes, a concerned display written all over her face. An unnerving sensation builds in my chest and I attempt to swallow it as I would an ordinary lump. I don't wish for Lizbeth to be concerned for me. She was employed on my behalf, though. That simple statement brings my level of guilt towards the clouds. She deserves to be free. I wish I could set her free. That can only be done by my brother, though.

"I'm all right," I add solemnly, trying to conceal my former breakdown.

She smiles in a melancholy manner, but the concerned look stubbornly remains on her face.

"You don't have to focus your consternation on me. I'm

perfectly fine, I was just taking a bit of time to myself," I add, endeavoring further to pass this off nonchalantly.

She shakes her head to herself and sighs annoyedly. "You must have caught your death out here, though. You insist on making day-to-day life harder for me."

I put up a quaking hand.

"Oh, are you sure you're alright? Your hands are shaking. I've never seen you like this before," she adds, a little more than human decency slipping into her tone. It's true that she hasn't seen me like this before. She hasn't because I've kept to myself and kept myself in check. I've hidden this side of myself for nine years. She's never once seen me distraught.

She comes from a land known as Hyvern, where mountains most certainly go into the heavens. You would never see the realm beyond though, for the tips are always shrouded with extraordinarily thickened clouds. It's always misty and unclear in that enigmatically beautiful land. I'm sure Lizbeth misses it. Hyvern is a very insignificant country wedged in between Andria and Walsia. For both Andria and Walsia, Hyvern is a scapegoat. Slaves are taken from the country brutally and forced to serve in either land. I seal my eyes shut at the thought of Lizbeth being taken anywhere against her will. Lizbeth, like many others, was obviously taken to Andria. How else could she be here? She would be a house slave customarily if it wasn't for her bright blue-green eyes. Brightest things I've ever seen in my entire life and I've been inside the Royal Andrian treasury before. Andrians thought she was a magical being for how suffocatingly green they are. They look like pieces of polished jade and blades of new spring grass at the same time. Her eyes are quite enchanting. My brother was looking for a companion for me at the time because I was . . . How do I say this? I wasn't like the rest after my parent's passing. I didn't attempt to speak to anyone. I just sat silently and played with my own dreams. He heard about her enchanted eyes and thought they would bring me some sort of good fortune if I was around her. My brother has always been rather superstitious. He carries our father's cutlass for good luck even though that man was the most wretched being I've ever met. I'm embarrassed to be his spawn.

"I certainly don't want you to get sick, so we should both go inside now," I return, venturing to transfer the blame off of myself. She crosses her arms and shakes her head nonchalantly.

"Don't patronize me, Alexander," she says in a low tone. She marches forward without waiting for me. I realize that my heart rate has returned to its customary rhythm and I've ceased quivering. What a curious event, curious indeed. I'd let something like that bother me? I sigh, realizing I don't know what I'd do without her assistance. Actually, I know exactly what I would be doing without her right now. I would be still standing in the pouring rain shaking profusely over a marriage that would exist without my existence. All I had to do was stand there in a ridiculous suit and look pleasant. I start running after her with a newfound smile splayed across my face, a genuine one at that.

Hours later, I'm alone in my study again, just like I was before the ceremony. The silence is heavy and all-consuming. My mind returns to that moment when Lizbeth rescued me from myself. I gazed deep within her verdigris eyes and lied that all was well in the world. Why does this moment out of all the disarray matter? Why do I care so deeply about this?

He sits,
He sighs,
Thinking of her eyes,
There are no lies.

CHAPTER 2

Graveyards are silly, useless things in my not so humble opinion. Of course, it's somewhere you go to remember a loved one who has passed, but isn't that just kind of depressing and counterintuitive? Just think, you've finally gotten over the death of a loved one who was very dear to your heart. Then you go back to the place where their corpse lays to rot. You read the date they passed on. You remember how it happened. You see the lump in the ground. After a while of standing there silently and respectfully, you hear their voices. Tears threaten to flow from your eyes.

Graveyard memorials are a silly, useless thing indeed. They can drive someone to insanity when they should be emerging from that dark place where everyone goes at least once in their short lives. Yes, memorials are to remember, but why remember something you're trying desperately to forget? It's hope that brings you to the wretched place. Hope that your loved one is still there somehow, still with you. Your mind plays tricks on you as you stand in the mist. Your mind makes you hear those voices and sometimes even see a faint glimpse. A crunch of a small twig breaking under your foot can turn into some sort of deep and meaningful sign from the deceased. That is the truth and the whole truth. Your loved one is actually gone forever. Forever until you go and rot in the ground, making someone else ache for you. If I recognize this simple truth already, then why am I standing over my mother's gravestone memorial? Why do I visit here when I know these things as a fact?

It's a foggy day with a foul outlook to it. "Sunday" is an ironic name to me because not every Sunday has fair weather. Yes, I am standing over my mother's grave as I do every Sunday with foul weather, for she loved this type of weather although I don't understand why. I like a sprinkle of rain every once in a while, but not a complete downpour. I grip the bouquet of white roses in my hands as I wait for the reason for my coming here to appear. My love for her died long ago, almost a year after she herself died. I guess it just got easier after that. I believe I remember the night that it happened. I was sitting up on that balcony. It was around sunset and nobody could pull me from that chair she used to sit in to watch the sun rise and set. No. I cannot remember that night. Nor any night before that. No tears have been shed since then. No more tears will ever be shed.

The reason I'm here is to keep my image perfect and venerable as can be. Ah yes, a shining image protected and defended by lies. A good prince would always visit his mother's gravestone memorial. A good prince would bring her flowers to please her soul. I remember the flowers she used to pick. A good prince would look back at her quiet, short, empty life, letting her weak memory live on. A good prince would swear to avenge her untimely death. I'm just "maintaining appearances," as some would say. This is so that nobody thinks any less of me than they already do.

I kneel down before the tombstone and run my fingertips over the freshly polished stone, tracing the letters of her name. My finger soon becomes dusted with the dirt in the grooves. I drop my hand from the rock.

"If somehow you are actually listening despite all logic," I address the grave hopelessly, "please tell me if I'll be given the answers. Please, just bequeath me a sign if your existence itself wasn't erased when you passed on." I wait respectfully for a dull moment or two. The air feels like a heavy burden on my shoulders. The only sound I hear is my breathing and the squawk of a few listless crows who have nothing better to do with themselves. And the whistle of the wind through the tight-knit wrought iron fences of the gaunt graveyard.

An ornately dressed nobleman strides into the memorial's grounds hurriedly with his nose up, holding an arm full of blooming begonias. He's dressed in a weighty black overcoat and black necktie. I can see that he's used his wealth to get the garment perfectly tailored to his form. His hair is combed back, trying to conceal a growing bald spot. I whip my head sharply at the sound of his leather boots crunching against the autumn leaves that sprinkle the dirt path. We glance briefly at each other. He attempts to look away but is captivated when I continue to stare into his almond-colored eyes. His expression flickers to that of recognition rapidly before a terrified expression takes its place. I frown tiredly at him and saunter over to the patch of dirt on which he stands. Before I reach him, his frightened expression flickers to one of superiority.

"Prince Alexander C—" He whispers politely. I cut him off by raising my slender hand. His mouth closes.

"Please, I'd rather not have you waste my time by reciting my full Christian name," I respond in an aggravated and equally aggravating tone. He stares at me with his nose turned up for a second. I feel my stomach flip multiple times. Such disrespect, I haven't seen anything like it since years ago. I have proven my worth since those times and I don't have the slightest idea why he's under the impression that I have the mind of a four-year-old. I feel the need to tell him that I'm not as incompetent as he believes me to be.

"I was just bringing these flowers to your dear father," he states pretentiously, as if I am not worth his time. Now I've discovered another conundrum. Every denizen of this hateful kingdom knows of the woebegone horrors my father committed. I myself petitioned for his grave to be put in another melancholy hole of misery away from everyone else, but sadly my request was denied. Well, the effort worked in part. My petition is the reason he's buried on the opposite end of the graveyard from my mother.

"He doesn't deserve such an honor as these fronds. Why do you waste your meager amount of time on such prospects as honoring that ghastly man's soul, may it burn in hell with his body, with a gift such as this? We all understand what his crimes are." I speak harshly, staring even deeper into his eyes as if the glare will draw a suitable answer out of the man. My hostility towards him is very apparent, especially now that I've seen him doing something as criminal as this.

"Well, I just thought..." he retorts. I straighten myself up to my full height in an attempt to intimidate him further. I'm still a foot shorter than him.

"I know what you thought, Sir. Are you Walsian?" I ask the man. After all, I was the one who approached him in the first place. The silence was beginning to grow tiresome, so I found a way to entertain myself. The only reason he would come and honor my father is if he didn't know his dastardly crimes. If he came with the new queen here from Walsia, he wouldn't know of the suffering the former sovereign's crimes caused.

"You read me like a book, Prince Alexander."

I begin to feel the hairs on the back of my neck curl up straight like stiff arrows. I now notice his somehow faint yet prominent Walsian accent as he tries to appease me. His charming smile is filled with an indulgence that would be effective on a child.

"Do I have to demand you again not to address me with my full Christian name, wasting my time even further than you already have?" I ask the now apparently Walsian man sternly. "And don't flatter me!" I add somewhat childishly.

I should have noticed with his black hair and bright eyes, which are noticeably similar to my own features. He could be an older version of myself! The only difference is that he is Walsian and I am Andrian. He moves his head quickly, taking a defensive step backward again. But all the while, he has a coy smile on his face as if this entire situation is immensely entertaining to him. I am not a performer in the circus. It's growing increasingly more difficult to look down on the enraging Walsian. It's hard in the first place because he is much taller than I am. I can't quite understand the reason I've been so perturbed by small things as of late.

"My point was, prince, that you have such an ability for reading situations. I'd like to congratulate you on that. How did you know?" he asks with mock interest, attempting to flatter me again despite the fact that his previous attempt failed miserably. This level of animosity is uncommon for me. I'm customarily so very serene.

"Stop pretending to worship the ground I stand upon. You are a noble, right? Aren't Walsian nobles supposed to be proud?" I press harder, trying to get him to cut the garbage coming from his lips. He cannot appease me, so, therefore, he should stop.

"Ah, yes of course, prince," he responds in a soft voice, the kind of voice you would use to reason with a selfish child. "Just like the fairytales say, I am a proud Walsian noble." He whispers under his breath, probably believing I cannot hear him. The comfortable, amused smirk on his face vanishes and in its place forms a look of mild annoyance and discomfort. His thick eyebrows knit together and he tries to avoid eye contact. It looks as if he is in deep thought. I think I've pushed him to the point where he's actually distressed. I must have finally daunted him. A small gratifying look spreads across my face as he proceeds to stare down at his boots. Guilt trickles through me along with the gratification. I should make an apology. Our countries have been at war for my entire life and now we have made amends. I should act as such.

"Well then, don't come back here ever again to see my father's gravestone. Obey and you will be able to keep your head," I say in a low tone essential for intimidation, a skill that

I have mastered over the last year or so. My eyes narrow as I stare into his chocolate-colored pair. We stand in a deep, warm silence. The silence isn't at all pleasant. The words that came from my lips were not the ones floating around in my head. The prejudice is intense. He honors my father, and I mock his reasons for doing so. My heels dig into the ground as I wait for him to look away and in doing so ease the tension. Minutes seem like hours. Finally, his gaze drops to his own fur-clad boots again.

"I'm deeply sorry again, my prince. If I have your permission, I will be taking my leave now," he whispers, deciding to make the wise decision to heed my advice and not take the route of patronizing me further. His voice sounds just as soft and as smooth as it did when he first spoke. His voice sounds like the golden color the foothills turn during summer. It makes me shiver that he has such ease in speaking. He speaks like he doesn't care about his own death and I'm very envious. This man must have heard something about me.

"Permission granted," I respond roughly, trying to mimic his tone despite myself. He bows low to the ground and pretends to stumble out of the memorial site as if my power is causing him fright. This act is pure foolishness. Both of us already know that he's not daunted. I shake my head in disbelief at the rueful display. I never did believe that anyone could act at ease around royalty. I may be a bit self-righteous, but I am genuinely astonished by this behavior since I've never observed it before. I'm frightened by how swiftly he shifted from at ease and charismatic to listless and hostile. The strangest thing was how he remained charismatic after our stare off. It was as if he remembered himself. Why isn't he scared like the rest? Not the kind of fear that you fake to flatter someone, the kind of fear that makes you do anything to escape. They either fear me or they attack.

People have been behaving in an eccentric way since the

wedding of my brother and the Walsian woman. I've heard chuckles and sighs as I pass through the halls every day. Almost every Walsian nobleman chuckled when I proposed a long-term plan to re-monetize our trading with primitive tribes wandering through the wilderness territory in Andria. I don't have the slightest understanding of why it was so hilarious. The plan was very solid and I didn't stutter once. I even heard them jesting about how I should join those same primitive tribes we were discussing. They said something about how I would be better off presenting my ideas to people who didn't understand my language then proposing my idea to them. I was very insulted of course, but also intrigued. Nothing of the sort had ever happened before. I eavesdropped further, standing just slightly behind a large marble column. Their laughter echoed and bounced off every structure in the large courtyard. All but one voice became silent. A few moments later the joke came. His deep voice had a tone of dark arrogance and valor to it. The voice was also clad with a prominent Walsian accent.

"But we cannot let the *second* prince know what has been said about him. Rumors only grow and spiral, but no matter the size of these, he must not know. He would be outraged, and he has more power than us, to be frank. We must remember our positions here. The fact that he is just a young man makes him more dangerous. Young men are eager and tend to have short tempers. All of you will be relieved of your positions and your heads the second he discovers what we have been discussing."

"Of course, Jakob. We would never endanger ourselves in such a way," another male voice replied. I attained a sense for the order of power in the conversation. Jakob made the mood shift from lighthearted and amusing to somber before you could say die. I had the urge to make my presence known and inform them that what Jakob said was the truth and they would not be allowed to remain with their heads.

I've never sentenced anyone to death before. I want to know

who is responsible for this rampant rumor. That man at my father's gravestone was probably involved in it. He was scared at first though. At least I still have the element of surprise. The only asset I have is the element of surprise.

I spit on the former king's memorial bitterly. I watch the saliva slowly dissipate into nothingness on the surface of the coarse dirt. The dirt only just conceals the dead body of my father, probably just bones now though. The reason for this poor burial site is that a shallow grave is a sign of disrespect. I remember his eyes, deep icy blue, lighter than my own. The only difference between my eyes and his was that there appeared to be nothing at all in his. You couldn't see a thing through those windows. Philosophers were wrong about seeing the soul through the eyes and they would know that if they looked deep into the eyes of my father. They could venture and venture, but they wouldn't find a soul. I reach into the right pocket of my jacket and pull out my little leather notebook and the pen that rests beside it.

Rumors grow,
Rumors thrive,
But how can they survive?
How do they live?
What do they give?

I chuckle at my own work miserably, wondering why I'm even bothering to loiter around this melancholy memorial site yet again. Yes, why am I in this silly place that humans crafted from their greatest hopes and sorrows? Hopefulness will not help me, nor will be staying here. I shove my notebook and pen back where they were and where they will remain. I give one last good kick to the pile of dirt that represents the former king before I walk in the general direction of the gateway, following the footsteps of the strange man who thought himself greater than I.

Merlot-colored leaves drift easily to the ground as I walk in the direction of the main ballroom where I have an engagement party to attend. Some nobleman that my brother trusts is getting married. Because I am the second prince, I have to attend the event. So many prospects these days are bothering me. Last year, I was barely troubled with anything other than a few stray lessons. The only thing I was required to attend was some adventitious banquet in honor of a knight fallen in battle. I couldn't bring myself to shed a tear for the lifeless man. This was seen as disrespectful to his soul, so I wasn't bothered for the rest of the year. I suppose they just didn't want me to embarrass them with my disrespectfulness again. My pulse quickens as I check my silver wristwatch, trying to gauge how quickly I'll have to move to arrive on time. My pace quickens as I realize I'll be quite late if I don't pick my feet up.

I only wish I could take my time and enjoy a stroll through sweet autumn. Andria really is splendid this time of year. The tall briers are the most beautiful on the continent, at least that's what I've heard. Reds and yellows mix together in the lethargic, dappled light. Choruses of both laughter and whispers can be heard from any patch of ground occupied by friends and lovers. The trees and other foliage are aware that they are to wither away, so they wither away as noticeably as possible. I see the endeavor as successful. Blades of grass are at their greenest, mimicking the other plant life's decision before the deceased leaves drown them. I would love residing in Andria if it weren't for the constant turmoil and the ghosts that follow me. I shouldn't blame the land for all the terrors I've endured. The ground on which I walk hasn't harmed me. Only the others who walk upon this ground.

I push open large, dark wooden doors that lead to an intricate maze of passages and corridors. This is a lengthened journey for this reason, but I've had far too much free time as of last year. In my year of silence, I've committed the route to almost anywhere on the palace grounds to memory. I have a feeling of forewarning. I know that this knowledge will help me in the future in a less trivial way than finding a route to a gathering. I frighten a sleek, black cat half to death as I barrel around a corner at my new, hurried pace, but stop abruptly as she weaves across my path. My mind flickers to an old superstition that states that letting a black cat cross your path is lousy luck. My brother would admonish my behavior if he knew of this. This engagement gathering won't be my best performance. That fact doesn't trouble me. Few things have gone well for me as of late. It won't make much of a difference. Never mind these thoughts, I must arrive soon in order to spare my reputation for punctuality.

I'm peeling down a winding corridor as fast as a racehorse to reach the room on time. With all these rumors circulating through royal Andria's blood stream, it would definitely not be acceptable if I arrived late. Not with even the greatest of excuses such as, "I was visiting my mother's grave." I don't want to tarnish my reputation further despite this occurrence being inevitable. This newfound rumor has done enough tarnishing for a year of my antics and I don't have the knowledge of what it's referring to. The laces of my polished, leather boots are undone. The threads pat against the ground in a distracting rhythm. I peer at my watch despondently. There's no way I won't be late.

I hurriedly straighten my uproariously tight necktie as I wrestle with the handle of the large, gilded door of the meeting hall. Just when all hope of ever entering leaves me, someone miraculously hears my struggle from the humming hall and comes to my aid. The man who opened the door for me has a face that would make a wolf turn tame and lay at your feet. Yes, my brother can be quite frightening at times. His teeth are gritted together tightly as if he is trying to form a smile, but can't bring himself to do so. He isn't as trained as I am in the art of concealing anger.

"Ah, my brother has arrived at last. Everyone who hasn't had the pleasure of meeting him, his name is Alexander C -" The king introduces me in a deafening tone. He allows a hint of jubilance to fall delicately into his demanding tone. It seems to work, for everyone falls quiet after his first word. Before I can silence myself, my lips open and my first name spills out. Oh Lord, if there was any time to correct my brother, now isn't it.

"Alexander!" I finish regretfully as I realize the extent of my embarrassment. My brother's grimace deepens and he appears to age five years in only moments. I cringe briefly. My brother's feeble facade has fallen entirely. His pale eyes penetrate mine like a sword does the body of an adversary. This rumor will last longer than it would have if I had dealt with this stance formally. I sigh deeply with dissatisfaction. My brother mimics my actions. The bewildered audience returns to its mindless chatter seconds later.

"Added to your lateness, this is a great offense!" He whispers to me as his mechanical smile returns. I follow suit and plaster a false smile on my own face. All I need to do is smile, that's all. My mask-crafting abilities may not be as great as I assumed them to be. He pats my back amiably as a display of brotherly kinship, but I have to admit that the gesture is more painful than amiable. I feel myself cringe at the pain. A few still stare at our shameful display although the man and woman of honor have beckoned the attention of all others and taken their seats at a grand, gilded table. I gaze around the star-dusted room. Candles flicker from every surface as if the celestial sky has been brought to this room. They seem to imperil the room with the red and gold streamers hung so close to them. In the center of the grandeur, an overblown cherry cake sits balanced precariously atop a pedestal.

"C-congratulations!" I yell to the betrothed pair, endeavoring to compensate for my previous offense. I realize all too late that I shouldn't have. What an astonishment. I didn't take heed to my last humiliation and caused myself to receive further shame. Everyone sips their goblets politely in an unwieldy silence. The orchestra begins to play a melody again, but even they look daunted by the recent series of events. I've addled my own reputation. My brother will search tirelessly until he discovers a way to end my life and make it seem as if it's a mistake. I won't be perturbed when those around me begin to ignore my presence. I seal my eyes shut and study the miserable night ahead. I'll have to flatter an outrageous amount for my societal standing to even be a husk of its former glory. These thoughts might be a bit embellished, but everything is a bit bolder when you're alone in the middle of a gathering. I hold my breath and push myself into the party, trying to recall the names and interests of the dull nobles I am to appease. All I have to know about when speaking to the men will most definitely be drinking and hunting. I believe it's to note that I've never drunk alcohol before and I rarely hunt, although I have studied the process of winemaking and know the right vintages.

The rest of the dismal evening is refreshingly uneventful. That's somewhat true, for me at least. It's a quiet affair until the groom drinks himself into a stupor (called it) off of the expensive bottle of champagne everyone is supposed to share as a final toast. The poor fool drinks the entire bottle! It looks as if someone isn't looking forward to his marriage. I wouldn't be either if I was marrying someone I could care less about. I'm pleased with this simple distraction, for it gives me a short moment to breathe and try to make my supposedly joyful smile feel authentic on my sullen features. But even then, with the outrageousness of the situation, the loudest sound is only a small gasp from a petite elderly woman dressed in an obnoxious shade of rosy pink. Her horrendous makeup runs down her wrinkled face in the same manner rain does as a few tears fall from her eyes. The rest of them have seen it all before and decide to pretend as if it hadn't happened. It's easier that way. His words may have been slurred during the speech he gave on behalf of his future bride, but every one of us just pretend not to notice. This is the customary scene at these soirees. The truth is that this man is alone in this room, just as my brother was at his wedding. I'm not implying I'm here for other reasons than the benefits that come after. I have many facets, but not one of them includes any form of hypocrisy.

I've found myself in a rhythm of discussing the same topic with different nobles every other moment. I feel a slight tap on my suit-clad shoulder. I turn around exuberantly to appraise whoever I am to deal with next, but instead of a blonde man with deer-breathe, it's Lizbeth. She smiles politely at the group of noblemen and noblewomen behind me. I nod at her in bemusement. Why is she here?

"Alexander, who is this?" a woman from behind me murmurs in a heart-sickening voice. The putrid sweetness of her tone is enough to turn the stomach of anyone. I turn back to her with a sugared grin. Lizbeth taps me on the shoulder in a slightly more intense manner. I can't ignore her this time. The noblewoman indulges herself with another sip of champagne and her nose becomes ever redder.

"Lizbeth, what a pleasant occurrence! What are you doing here?" I ask her hurriedly, half turning back to the noblewoman. Her illuminated expression forces me to give her my full attention, though. She looks over my stiff form wearily with her marvelous green eyes. She appears quite abashed. The emotion most prominent on her pale face, though, is none other than guilt.

"I need to tell you something, Alexander," she exclaims in a secretive tone, a knowing look appearing on her face. Her breathing is rapid and forced. She smells of sweat and angst. The knot in which her hair was tied has come undone. Her searing crimson curls cascade down to the small of her back like a forest fire. She's quite captivating with tendrils of her hair encircling her face, but I can't be distracted from the guilt in her eyes. I've never seen Lizbeth this upset before. The last time she was surprised was when I remembered her birthday and gave her a locket of silver. She nearly cried, but contained herself before she could. That was a pleasant sort of surprise. This surprise radiating from her is most certainly the inferior sort of shock. The shock you acquire when you have seen a ghost.

"Can it wait?" I ask her halfheartedly, as one of the men puts his meaty hand on my shoulder. I cringe inwardly as he does so. I don't appreciate the touch of such vile individuals. With every ounce of my being, I want to leave with her now and escape this disagreeable situation, but my standing will grow increasingly worse if I don't play my part in the monarchy. I pause and wait for her response.

"No," she answers breathlessly, to my delight. She grabs my cold hand without warning and pulls me ferociously through the sea of minglers, not stopping once to allow a brief bout of banter. She barrels over all in her warpath. By the end of this, there'll be a pile of fallen people outraged by our disrespect. I fall over the heels of anyone we pass, shouting barely understandable apologies to them. We're already out of the hall by the time I can even register what happened. I feel as if I'm going to faint, but she doesn't allow me to rest once out the door despite my pathetic pleas. She keeps a firm grip on my upper arm as our pace finally slows to an enhanced walk. I still feel quivery and sickened, noting that I probably shouldn't have indulged myself with so much sparkling cider.

"If you don't mind me asking, where are we going?" I ask, half bitingly, half politely. The polite half of my voice is most definitely leftover from having to speak with all of the royal partygoers. I raise my eyebrows as she gives me one enraged look before focusing back on her unknown course again. We pass by sprawling paintings and tapestries that stretch as far as the eye can see, to the end of the hallway. It takes me a moment to realize that the tapestry ends just around the bend. I only wish I could pass through one of those pieces and take a rest on a starlit beach. It takes me a few moments to realize we've stopped. I hold my breath and glance at my surroundings. A door stands before us, different from any of its kind. This opening is worn, crafted from the darkest wood. I imagine the tree that was used to create this door was found in the deepest part of a fen. There are a few holes, just large enough to make the door look dilapidated but too small to see through. It looks as if the bottom part of the decrepit arch had something green spilled upon it. The silver handle is rusted and reddish-brown.

Another odd aspect I notice after I regain a sense for my surroundings is the temperature. It's absolutely numbing. Nearly the most frigid cold I've ever felt, only second to when my brother threw me outside in only my nightshirt during the middle of a blizzard as a cruel jest to entertain a few of his older friends. That's the coldest I've ever been. I would be shivering if I didn't have my fur-lined suit jacket. I'm glad I chose it over a beautifully made silky suit jacket that wouldn't come to benefit me in this situation. I turn my attention to Lizbeth. Her face cloaks her anguish, but her body can't. She shivers and her breath leaves her lips in great clouds.

"Here," I whisper to her, reluctantly pulling off my warm, comfortable jacket. When I say reluctantly, I mean thoughtlessly. If I were a perfect gentleman, I would totally give her my jacket without a second thought. I have to refrain from sighing. Ah, the things I'll do for Lizbeth. I forget everything as she gives me a gloriously warming smile, followed by a simper at my intense gaze. Her bright eyes ignite my heart and suddenly I don't feel as miserable as I did before.

"You didn't have to do that," she replies softly. I let a gentle smile seep onto my features. We stand placidly for a second, her small hands on my shivering shoulders. We stare deeply into each other's eyes. Her red lips are pursed in distress as if trying to remember why she's brought me here.

"Why are we here, Lizbeth?" I ask her in a soft voice, not caring for what she has to say. I need her to speak in order to distract me from my own wishes. I wish to kiss her. The unlawfulness of that statement doesn't perturb me in this moment and it should. I breathe in her buttercream scent and stare into her eyes, which are the color copper turns over time. It seems as if time himself shaped her eyes with his own fingers.

Why am I here?
She is near,
That is why I'm here.
She is a ray,
Brighter than day,
Brighter than the sun,
My heart is won.

"Alright," she whispers to me hurriedly, clasping her hands together tightly. Worry crosses her gentle features before she opens her red lips to speak again. "I wish I could have you sit down for this." She plays with her hair agitatedly. My brow knits together in a look of deep concern. Why is she so troubled? Tears threaten to trickle down her cheeks as she grabs one of my hands in hers tightly. I can't help but feel myself become rosy as she does so.

"What is it?" I ask, letting extra honey left over from the gathering seep into my voice. She looks up at me and chews on her lip cautiously, another bout of worry overwhelming her features.

"You are going to absolutely loathe me. I'm about to show you something that will make you loathe me. Don't be scared, Alexander. I'll clarify everything to you if that is what you so desire."

My eyes round slightly as I listen. This sounds rather dire. Her tone daunts me. Lizbeth hasn't acted in this manner before me in all our years of companionship. She looks to be a wreck over this unknown trouble. I can't fathom how this single door could make her lose composure so rapidly. I hate to say it, but I'm sure I'll break down from curiosity if I don't view what's behind that door soon. She loses all composure when she even glances at the entryway.

"I could never ever hate you. Never," I promise her. I craft a guise of my sincerity on my features, for I don't know how to create one naturally. I let my stygian curls be pushed behind my ears by Lizbeth's free hand. Having my hair out of my eyes is rather outlandish for me, but again, I'll do anything Lizbeth ever demands of me.

"Are you... Are you sure?" she replies hesitantly. In the middle of her final phrase, her voice falls. Her tone is so sorrowful. I have to refrain from wrapping her in a consoling embrace.

"S-sure," I confirm, fully shaken now. She grabs my other hand even more tightly than the first and takes a step towards the ominous door, pulling me along with her all the while. My hair falls in my eyes yet again, but I don't bother to lock it behind my ear again. I grit my teeth, wondering what could be hidden behind the enigmatic entryway.

But when Lizbeth opens the door, all my theories look like a halloween costume compared to a ghost. A loud creak rings throughout the hollow halls of the deepest part of the palace. Nobody heard it, save those who reside on this level. The sight makes me feel as if I'm being torn limb from tortured limb. The ghost before me smiles grimly in introduction. He's a phantom, a past memory I've tried so desperately to bury. He was buried. He was dead. Now he stands before me alive, in the flesh.

"H-h-ho-ho-how..." I manage somehow as I stare into his

eyes. Void of soul. What I thought before was truly a halloween costume compared to a ghost. A ghost of my past.

"It's been quite some time since I've been here. I was hoping that I would get to see you," he whispers in a low tone, awe shining from his time-ignored face.

CHAPTER 3

My greatest fear is standing before me. I'm physically facing it. But I can promise that in no way will this help me overcome it. I'm sure that this hasn't happened to anyone but me and a small handful of others before. At least, nobody with as great a fear as this. I can feel my soul knocking against my chest in a desperate attempt to escape this vulnerable body of mine as I stare at the man who murdered my mother in cold blood. I close my eyes very briefly to calm myself, honestly just wanting his cruel face out of my sight. He's almost identical to an older version of my brother. The only difference is in his eyes. His cold, calculating blue eyes.

All my senses seem to dim a bit like a how a room with an open window does when a cool gust travels through it, causing all of its candles to flicker briefly. I feel numbed and dazed by this. I can hear a few sharp, echoey footsteps. Lizbeth must be leaving. Liquid seems to fill my lungs. She was in front of me, but she left. Why is she leaving me? She said she would explain it all. I want to call after her, but I feel too tired to make an effort. I've felt this before. This is omnipotent shock, the sort of all-powerful astonishment in which your senses are eliminated and you drown in fresh air. I can't breathe, let alone move.

"You think I did some sort of evil, don't you?" I hear faintly. His words waver in my stream of understanding as I try to make sense of them. The man who I once called father and sovereign claims innocence? I can hardly name his words. My vision dims, but I compel myself to stay conscious. The last thing I want is to be left defenseless in the presence of a murderer.

"You did," I whisper defiantly, staring at him with a deep sort of fury. I don't know how I managed to speak. If there's one single thing I know about this man I used to call father, it's that he absolutely hates being interrupted or disturbed. I've heard terrible stories. When my mother was beginning my older brother's labor, my father had the maiden who made him aware of it tortured within an inch of her life. He was busy with paperwork. Truly a lunatic of a man.

I try to take deep, long breaths to keep my heart from thumping out of control. This has no effect on my dancing heart. It's quite difficult to stop wheezing like a maniac when your father comes back from the dead. My mind overloads with questions as I try hysterically to find any sort of answer. I was there at his funeral. It was an open casket funeral as well. I saw his cold, rigid face, not a trace of life left in it. I was six or seven when I peered over the edge of his ebony resting case. Someone with a keen eye would notice the wind lashings on his face carefully hidden under a layer of powder. I surely noticed them, but yet I wasn't bothered by them. I was old enough, even then, to know the extent of what my father had done.

I didn't appear upset by the event either. I imitated my brother's customary expression of ease. Despite my efforts to appear undaunted by the occasion, my family and those who knew him still gave my brother and I regretful, arrogant glances and forlorn pats atop our heads. Edward was sniveling and shaking in frigid air with the heartache he felt, his usual confidence absent. He clung to me and cried for not just one of our parents. I just stood there and let him.

The memory of it is mollifying. The memory of his lifeless body consoles me, for that moment when I saw him, I knew he was gone for good. He seems to be alive now. I can't quite fathom that. With the slowing of my tiresome breathing, I can make out his words a bit better. His customarily cold and unfeeling tone is gentle. The least I can say is that I'm astonished by this act. I look into his eyes and a slice of angst sears through me. I try to see past the iris, but I can't. A dark blue ripples around his pupils.

"Wait, Alexander! I'm not who you think I am. You aren't who you think you are either!" he shouts in a desperate attempt to prevent me from leaving.

My hand is locked on the firm handle of the door. I look into his eyes yet again and see a drab sort of pain. The hand that rests on the knob of the door goes slack and drops as the sense of understanding continues. His lips curl slightly at the edge of his mouth. He sees he's gained my attention.

"Leave me, phantom!" I plead in a quiet tone. My spine crashes against the rough wall behind. I claw around to regain a grip on the handle. I can't read the emotions portrayed in his face. I don't know if he's furious or calm. I don't know if he's going to end me or try to make amends. He takes a step back in compromise, a reassuring expression falling upon his features. His step echoes around the domed room.

"It's locked. Your friend locked it. I have the key. Now, we've wasted enough time on your thick-witted thoughts. They're all wrong anyways. I'm not your father. The man you thought to be your father is dead. I did not commit the crimes towards your mother and the kingdom of Andria that you believe I did. The past sovereign still did those things, but I assure you, that man is dead." He pauses a bit to collect himself. He was speaking very urgently. I take a deep breath and let my back slide down the wall. I let my agitated fingers run through the lines in between the cobblestones. I've placed myself in a vulnerable position, but I'd fall anyways if I was on my feet for much longer. I hold the sides of my head as if I'm shoving the two respective halves together.

"Are you his brother?" I ask hesitantly, not daring to meet his harsh gaze again. He snaps his fingers without warning, making me flinch away. He chuckles to himself and holds up a hand in apology. Why would he do such a thing? Only moments ago he was imploring me for my attention.

"I'm your brother. The rightful heir," he whispers, a far-flung flicker in his eyes. My mind flashes to my brother who's probably pouring over a stack of papers next to a few dying candles as of now. Ruling a nation is a difficult line of work, difficult in the finest sense. Work such as that can also reap great rewards if one is willing to do the job. This man could be a fraud, my father, my brother playing a trick on me, another brother who wasn't aware of, or an insane man who fancies himself the king of Andria. The possibilities are endless.

"How come I've never heard of you then?" I say, raising my voice ever so slightly. I find it hard to compose myself. He rests an arm against one of the bleak walls and allows a smug smile to seep onto his features. My nails dig into the flesh of my wrist. The pain is delayed a couple seconds. My arms are crossed against my chest as if I could protect myself in this position. Countless possibilities flicker through my mindscape. My thoughts fill to the brim with prospects. Is he illegitimate? Did my father have an affair? Was it my mother? No, it couldn't have been her. Not her, with her sweet smile and constant philanthropic attitude. She gave grace and happiness to all she passed. No, it can't be her.

"My father cast me out when I was fourteen. My little brother was a young child at that time. How is Edward, by the way?" he asks in an astonishingly genuine manner. He cocks his head to one side as my brother does when he asks me something. The level of importance attached to each inquiry doesn't matter. His head-cocking doesn't discriminate. This supposed stranger is starting to feel a bit familiar. But none of these actions matter because of one word. That word is "my." Why did he say "my father" instead of "our father?"

"Why did you say 'my' instead of 'our'?" I ask him, diverting away from his previous question. His eyebrow twitches ever so slightly. Another one of my brother's characteristics. A reserved facet trickles onto his face as we allow a quiet moment to pass.

"You're more intelligent than I believed you to be," he whispers almost to himself in a condescending voice. I open my mouth to speak, but he holds up a pale hand to stop me. "No worries, Alexander, I'll explain everything to you. I know you must be confused right now. I would be if I were in your situation."

This fool's words are becoming quite annoying. Now he won't tell me anything, asking me to wait as if he has the right to request anything of me. I pull myself to my feet.

"Great! Don't explain anything to me! I like wondering!" I yell at the man. He smiles and mumbles something to himself. "Can you stop doing that?" I ask him in an irritated tone. His stuttering crawls atop my nerves. If he could only speak clearly, maybe I'd have the slightest clue as to what he means.

"Okay Alexander, I'm going to start over. This's gone wrong far too quickly. We haven't even gotten to the most troubling truth. You've most likely been granted a death warrant by all this stress," he explains placidly, clasping his long fingers together. I feel my ears turning red with something other than petty anger, but rage and chagrin. How dare he even speak in such a manner to me, sovereign of Andria? My dreams are remarkably frightening, but never have I had an angering dream. This can't be reality though.

"Go on then, start your story I guess..." I reply, trying to return my stature to one of composure and ease in hopes that it will affect my inward feelings. I unclasp my arms and arch my back as if bracing myself for pain. He repositions himself in his chair and parts his lips to speak.

"Our mother was with another man before she was wed to our father. Well, not your father, I believe."

I cough lightly and swallow a bout of angst. What does he mean by "not your father?" What is he claiming?

"His name was Aaron. She had intimate relations with this man."

Aaron. Is he claiming that this Aaron is my father? How dare he make such accusations. This cannot be true. But yet again, my Christian name is Alexander Aerabella Aaron Mattias. I always wondered where the Aaron in my name came from.

"How is he my father?" I inquire, my words interrupting him as he begins another phrase. He coughs a bit, but smiles charmingly, looking back up at me. Before he can utter another word of explanation, we both hear a loud crack rumble throughout the bones of the building as if someone's whacked the door. The ease drops from his pale face as the sound rings out through the pressing silence again. The pounding becomes constant.

"Oh, bother, someone must've recognized me and tipped off the guards. Alexander, I have to get out of here!" he shouts to me. He pulls himself to his full height. I follow suit and spring away from the door. A spiraling crack circles throughout the molded wood. It looks as if it's about to burst. The guard? Whatever did he do to cause such commotion?

"Why are the guards here?" I ask. He gives me an animalistic look and my mouth closes abruptly. The former sovereign threw him out and it was illegal for him to return here. I know that someone must've informed the royal guard of his location. I hear a groan shared between the troops as a small chunk of wood heaves away. The squadron cries out once before a peeling noise conquers my senses. The heavy door shatters on final impact and pieces of wood, both large and small, hurtle through the air in the same manner asteroids do. The agility of my vision falters. For a moment, everything's entirely still. I know that the impending future is approaching more hurriedly than visible. I feel it coursing through my veins, foreboding. Pure fervor towers over me. I stumble backward as a hunk of wood from the door makes contact with my stomach. I feel fiery pain rip up my abdomen on impact. The piece was dislodged with such great force that it feasibly tore through my side. I can't hear myself screaming. In fact, I can't hear anything at all. I can only feel. Feel the vibrations against my throat from my invisible screams. Feel the piece burrowing deeper beneath my flesh. The splintery chunks deviate against one another as my pale shirt turns a dark crimson. My mind faintly scolds me for not stepping more prudently. If I had only been quicker.

I cower in the wake of Andrian troops and a large, suspicious battering ram. I observe it all faintly as if a milky film has been pressed over my eyes. My body spreads itself across the cool ground. I turn my neck delicately, for fear of losing consciousness, in order to see the man and all his exploits. I feel the tremors of footsteps against the palms of my hands. The scrawny recruits abandon the battering ram next to my quaking form. The top of the dense instrument nearly lands atop my arm. My sight wanes as I feel my own blood pooling around one of my legs. The wood turns again in its cavity, leaving me to let out another sharp gasp of anguish. I reach towards the spot in my chest where the wood is most certainly lodged. My blurred vision manages to pick up the sight of the dark wood standing erect. I run my long fingers across my abdomen, trying to find the source. My fingertips become wet and red. It feels surreal to see my own fingers stained by my own blood. My vision blurs slightly as I see the man who called himself my brother grappling roughly against the grip of the burliest recruit. His eyes flicker grimly as I stare up at him. He looks so much like Angel of Andria, former sovereign and the man I believed to be my father. His name in battle was the Angel of War.

He claws at the eyes of another who joins the scuffle and throws me a smile. "Peter," he mouths above chaos. Whatever does he mean by that name? Is that his name? My abdomen becomes numb and a boy with orange hair and simple brown eyes bends into my waning vision. His lips move in a hurried rhythm as if he's tripping over them. This guard fears for his life, I can see it in his eyes. If Peter doesn't have his head first, my brother will. He despises mistakes such as these and wishes to abolish them. My last thought is comical: Prince Alexander of Andria, fatally injured by a door.

Third Person Perspective

The girl watched the raven-haired prince sleep. His eyelids were closed placidly over his sapphire blue eyes. He looked just so tranquil, none of the pain he'd been bequeathed throughout his life was visible while in the clutches of sleep. In fact, Lizbeth had never seen Alexander appear more at ease before. To be fair, she hadn't made it a habit of watching him sleep despite her current actions. It would become one, though. The prince's arms hung clumsily like wings away from his torso, his light skin spattered with bloody droplets that the medics and nurses were too petty to wipe away. One of her fiery eyebrows twitched slightly with displeasure at the thought. If only they could see him the way she saw him. Maybe then the world would be perfect. But sadly the world is not perfect, nor will it ever be. Nobody would ever see Alexander the way she did.

Lizbeth looked towards the large timepiece at the end of the infirmary, the two ebony hands ticking away. During one of those ticks, Alexander would awaken. She knew that tick would be soon. His eyelids would flutter open to reveal his deep blue eyes and that familiar look of joylessness would corrupt his princely features yet again. He would remember his earthly restraints and duties. The pressure would shove him back into a neat little trunk and he would no longer be the immaculate individual before her. The monarchy didn't care for him. If they did, they would let him become the person he was meant to be. Lord, if they cared for Alexander, they'd give him some proper medicinal herbs for the pain.

Lizbeth stood in solitude, the others inhabiting the room either rushing around or lying in beds in the manner of Alexander. Those who rested in a room such as this one customarily wouldn't have people who would wish to visit them. They placed the sovereign Alexander with servants and soldiers with minor injuries. These mere wraiths were given better treatment than Alexander. Lizbeth had observed that Alexander's bandages had been crafted out of leftover cloth, whereas these disreputables were given fresh bandages that were intended to be bandages in the first place. Footsteps echoed around her against the hard, stone floors and she knew that she should be moving around like those who could stand in the room. She knew she needed to be leaving Alexander. She needed to tear her eyes from him, but she felt as if magnets were pulling her back towards him. She would look suspicious if she stood there all alone for much longer. They would discover that Lizbeth was a servant, even if she was a high-ranking servant meant to serve the prince alone. Finally, she pulled herself from his persuasive gravity. Now her footsteps echoed throughout the hall like the others.

Alexander's Perspective

Light hits my eyelids suddenly, despite it being rather dim. Is this the truth of the whimsical tale that everyone tells about "seeing the light" and such? Is that tale a solid fact? Well, this light is most definitely brighter than my future in Andria. A chuckle forms in my throat at the thought. Impossible that I would get past the gates of heaven. My faith is always wavering and I have committed many crimes in my short number of years. I'm sure that the creator would not appreciate either of those things. This must mean that I'm still alive and breathing, also implausible. I was sure that the twig had punctured my lung or something of that sort. Whatever it was, it was certainly painful.

With the thought of pain, an unpleasant ache settles in my side. The small ache grows into the same vicious pain that tortured me at the moment of impact. A small gasp escapes my chapped lips as I realize the situation I've found myself in. I have a sudden urge to slap myself across the face, but I refrain from doing so in fear that my side will become more painful than it already is. I should have never left that dismal party. I should have sighed my way through all of those empty people. Couldn't I have just stayed within the line of what's considered normal only once? No, I was tired of appeasing those pigs, so I ran off to my own demise with Lizbeth, the girl who left me when I most needed her. I acted in the manner of a child. The frustration hits me harder than the pain did. I'm the one who's at fault for this unfortunate injury. I can't believe that that complete thought was formed only moments after I awoke.

"Hello?" I croak into the muted room, which I've realized is an infirmary for mere servants. I see. This is how they see me now. Once I'm out of this mess, I'll have to jump at the opportunity to attend those dull dinner parties and falsely joyful events to regain the honorable reputation I had attained before the wedding. Yes, it'll certainly take a lot of gatherings to be up to par with the nobles of Andria, but I'll do what it takes. This is the way my life was meant to be, after all.

"Hello there," another voice replies. I was not ready for anyone to reply to my call. I shuffle a bit. The pain that follows this slight movement makes me cringe. The dim lighting fixtures of the bleak chamber dance as the figure of a man rises from the shadows at the opposing end of the room. I've heard his voice many times before, for he is my brother. The sovereign visiting me in a servant's infirmary. What a pleasant surprise.

"Edward?" I query as he approaches me, stepping further into the meager light. His footsteps echo all around us. The room has a rounded roof, making it impossible for any sound to lay flat.

"I had to order all those little medics to clear out so I could speak to you privately. It was really quite a pain." Yes, it's Edward. He lifts a hand to massage his temples as if the act of speaking to me causes him angst. I wouldn't be surprised if it did though, seeing the previous events were quite strenuous for both me and all who had to keep it a secret. The kingdom certainly wouldn't want the general public to discover that the maniacal illegitimate son of the even more maniacal former sovereign had returned against all odds. The king would most definitely be involved in a cover-up of that caliber.

"I'm sorry that it caused you trouble," I reply, trying hopelessly to match his audacious tone. I've never heard my brother speak with that sharp an edge of anger in his silken voice. His royal features twitch as he hears my almost mocking tone. He twists his lips into a frown and takes another daunting step towards me.

"I bet you are," he responds to my insult in a low tone. The blue tie he wore at the party hangs loosely on his neat yellow shirt. His matching blue suit jacket is unbuttoned despite him standing. He usually buttons it every time he stands, for it's a common rule of male conduct. I do the same. This ordeal must have caused him a considerable amount of stress. Well, his glossy hair is still perfectly coiffed. That counts for something at least. His hair is much different than mine. His remarkable golden locks stay perfect even when not gelled or messed with. I certainly did not inherit that gene. My hair is unruly and a loathsome raven color. It's uncommon for Andrians to have dark hair so therefore it's frowned upon. We stare into each other's eyes for a moment, waiting to see which one of us will be courageous enough to speak.

"So, what brings you to my little corner of hell?" I question him in what I try to make a daunting voice. A small smirk plays at his brick-like face. The mood just became a little more hostile if possible. A wave of sweat hits me as I cringe into an extremely uncomfortable sitting position. I wish to appear as robust and able-bodied as I can while in a situation such as this one. The dim candle light flickers in harmony with my jittery movements. Just sitting places a large strain on my body. I must seem so feeble to him despite my efforts. He stands as tall as he can. At his full height of around seven feet, he is quite intimidating. He stares down at me from above like a looming giant from the clouds. I'm just a crippled boy without any form of protection. It's a vulnerable feeling, to say the least. My confident visage crumbles under his intense stare.

"Business. Also, your wording was wrong. This *place* is not a corner of hell, for if it was then the rest of Andria would be hell. I'm striving for that to be a lie, although you're making it quite difficult with your childish antics as of late." He spits at me, fury crowning his regal features. The evil streak in him shines with the heat of his anger and his eyebrow twitches erratically. I smile back at him.

"I believe it's hell here and I shall say what I believe unless your endeavors as ruler of Andria have taken my freedom of speech from me. I wouldn't be surprised though," I counter in a strangled voice as I try yet again to prop myself up into a more professional bearing. Moving and speaking are becoming far too much to deal with in my weakened state, but I must continue. I am not going to be foolish enough to lose this verbal battle. I'll pray it doesn't become physical, then I'll really be in hell.

"You have no right to judge *my* nation, Alexander. You shouldn't even hold sovereignty in Andria. Hell, you shouldn't even be a denizen!" he fires back at me, a cruel sort of pleasure appearing in his bright eyes as I process his strange words.

"Pardon?" I ask him in a soft, shaky voice as he starts to pace back and forth across the stone floor. Every one of his echoey footsteps ring in my ears. My thoughts travel back to Peter and all he claimed about my parentage and his own. A quiet laugh escapes Edward's lips as his pacing slows. A harsh northern wind rattles the small building we occupy. Leaves blow silently past the decrepit windows.

"Don't you see it?" he asks me in an uncommonly fearful voice. He wavers a bit at the end of his sentence and turns his back from me. I shiver uncomfortably by his side, afraid of what he is to say next. I dread his words of confirmation. His lips will speak those words. Another wound will be added to many. It's inevitable, yes indeed, but I still dread those words.

"S-see what?" I ask him slowly, wrestling to pacify my rapidly beating heart. A small part of me wants it only to stop beating for a moment so that I can hear my own words. Edward turns leisurely on the balls of his polished leather boots. Every inch he moves scars itself into my mind like a burn. His face frightens me more than his impending words. His eyes are rounded and a crazed grin is etched into his usually serene features. I haven't seen him smile with any genuine emotion in years. Tears fall freely down his rosy cheeks as he looks down upon me.

"Not even you are truly my brother. Y-you don't care. You're like the rest of 'em. You're fake!" he shrieks with pure anguish, throwing his fists into the air without a single care as to where they'll land. Words form on my lips just to be silenced by doubts and untruths. My mouth shapes those words over and over again but to no avail. At this moment, I see him as his younger self again. A terrified fourteen-year-old much like myself with no fathomable way to deal with such a loss as the loss of your parents. He's searching desperately for something to latch onto, but it all falls away in the end. He's completely and utterly alone. We both are, we just hadn't realized until this moment. The epiphany is only how I knew it would be, another wound to my collection.

"I'm just the bastard son of our mother, am I not?" I confirm in a flat tone. A hint of wavering gives up my level of distress. We stare into each other's eyes for a brief moment. In that time, his face returns to the same, monotonous expression he always wears. The tears from just seconds ago roll away, leaving his face entirely blank.

"Yes, that seems to be the truth. I had almost forgotten about Peter until this day. He left us when I was young because *my* father thought him illegitimate like yourself, despite him not being so. He confirmed your parentage. Your father is the same man my father feared to be Peter's father," Edward explains resolutely, bowing his head as to not have to look me in the eyes.

"Well then… What shall we do with my power in the court?" I ask him almost indifferently. A flicker of disbelief crosses his face before clearing his throat calmly.

"We will discuss such things in later days. It would be a waste of time to decide theoretical things. You may not live through this, God forbid," he replies, feigning worry for my injury. A clever way to hide an insult. A clever way indeed.

Edward nods at me composedly, turning to leave. I notice his gallant form shaking uncharacteristically as he staggers off in the direction of the door. His footsteps echo yet again, but this time it appears that it's he who is daunted more by the sound. I lean back against the stiff cot, the pain increasing through my back with the sudden movement. It seems like nothing next to the array of unpleasant emotions plaguing me at this time. The wind batters the sides of the small enclosure as I settle into the warm uncomfortableness of the scratchy covering. The disturbing conversation leaves me tired and I soon succumb to a sleep nearly as terrible as the event previous to the sleep.

CHAPTER 4

The sad truth of my parentage has been spread around the palace and lands within the gate like a nasty thread of plague. Everyone on royal grounds knows of it, but they've chosen not to share the truth with those who dwell outside of the gates, the general public if you will. I am still of value to them, even if it's just to control the population's beliefs of a strong monarchy guiding them into the future with an even stronger hand. They're really just being lulled into a false sense of security. I'm ashamed to be a part of something such as that. At least I'm not being burned at the stake or sent away like that man Peter had been all those years ago. Honestly, at this point, I'm sort of praying that the monarchy will decide to do either one of the things I just mentioned. I'd either be free from the chain that my brother holds around my neck, or I'd be free from living and all of these wounds would be gone.

Not a single medical professional has deigned to assist me since the night I saw Edward cry. I no longer have the right to blame them anymore, though. It isn't an obligation of theirs to offer help to someone who isn't a part of the royal family or who serves them. It's difficult to understand why they won't show even some human compassion to a bleeding boy lying pathetically at their mercy. My situation is infuriating, but I'm more desperate than infuriated. This is the reason why I've chosen not to express my anger publicly. Perhaps if I act both equally polite and pitiful, someone will give me some clean dressing for my wound and something, anything for the pain. The ache in my side has worsened in past days, but my body just barely killed off the deep infection given to me by that hunk of wood. I would have died if that were not the case. I need to be enthusiastic if I'm ever going to escape this strange realm of pain and the ignorance of others towards my pain. I refuse to remain in this limbo forever, so therefore I will endeavor to leave this place as soon as I am able.

In the hours after the king took his leave, I spoke to a doctor about my care. In all truth, it wasn't really about my care, it was about cutting off my care due to my origins. It wasn't much of a discussion either, for I wasn't allowed to speak back to him. I wasn't even able to see his face. It was buried in his various journals and medical documents. I only ever saw his eyes dart up to stare at the blank wall behind me. At least the knowledge he seemed to tell the blank wall was useful. He said that I could leave as soon as I "feel fit" or something of that sort. Fear took hold of me as soon as the man had scurried off in the other direction. I would never feel fit. I would more than likely cross over to the other side before that. I haven't eaten or drank anything for three days. I spent that day, yesterday, suppressing tears of cowardice. I came to the decision then that I must leave for my own survival. I cannot remain deprived of sustenance for much longer. I won't survive another day without water.

My clothes are folded neatly on the floor next to my small, uncomfortable cot. The first step to leaving this miserable place will be to dress myself. They are still stained in my blood from three days ago. The memory of the event crosses my mind at the sight and pain rips through my side. The fragile scab that's formed over the wound will most certainly leave a scar. The stitching they did that first night was removed quite roughly, breaking the first scab. They could have at least bothered to provide me with clothes that aren't soaked in blood. I'll look like some sort of monster leaving here. I suppose that's what I am to everyone anyways. I wince in pain as I remember my previous attempt at moving to speak to my brother. I remember the raging blue flames of the pain that licked up and down my side. I remember all of it. And I'm terrified of that helpless feeling. If I don't leave soon I'll most certainly die and that means I have to move. They wouldn't let me die, would they? This thought is a disturbing one because the more I think on the prospect, the more it seems it would be possible that they would let me die here in this bed. My last moments would be filled with my own wretched screaming until death finally came to silence me. Nobody would notice, nor would they care. They'd only notice I was dead when the stench started to take hold of the small room. I wouldn't have a proper funeral either. They would bury me far, far away from the rest of my family since they weren't my real blood. They would spit on my grave as they did the man who I thought to be father. I was seven when he was executed, two years after my mother died. Even I spit on the mound of dirt he was buried under.

These thoughts are enough negative motivation for my first attempt at moving. I start slowly with a slight movement of my arm. The ache of sore muscles brings me to another realization. Lying in a moist, dim room for three days has made all of my muscles sore. This transition to walking is going to be even more challenging than I first thought it would be. If I take into account malnutrition, injury, and sore muscles, this will nearly be impossible. I grimace at these dark thoughts. Lord, even grimacing is painful.

I push myself up ever so slowly into a crass sitting position. My posture is just awful. If only Edward could see me now. My arms have the most strength out of my other limbs, so it's them that the load falls upon. Just seconds later, my arms begin shaking like leaves in a windstorm. My breathing becomes wheezed and my raw throat demands fluid. The fear takes hold of me yet again. My bravery disappears almost completely and I feel as if I'm just a child yet again. I cannot call out to my mother though. She won't ever come again. I've come to the conclusion that I'm invisible. Why won't anyone help me? Many masses of people have passed me by, but none will help me even if I dare to call out to them. If one walked into a room and someone, anyone begged you for water, that person would give them water if they knew how. Correct? I would. After this experience I certainly would. My pride slowly seeps away into the cracks of my discomfort and dolorousness.

Now, this thought encourages me even further to make progress on my current situation. I'm trying to brace myself to button up my formerly white-collared shirt that I was wearing at that man's engagement party. That man getting engaged set all of this in motion. This shirt used to be white, but now it looks like an artist specializing in the abstract approach painted all over it with my own blood. Like I mentioned before, nobody bothered to get me a clean set of clothing. I'll probably frighten a few noble children on my way out of here, seeing I look like a mangled ghost. Or better yet, the grim reaper himself. That is, if I even make it out of here alive. I might collapse once I stand up. I would just lay there on the floor and nobody would notice me. They only wouldn't care. They would laugh at my unfortunate position, in fact. I would just be there, waiting for the last beat of my heart to come before I succumb to death, everyone's soulmate.

I decide that the best move after painstakingly buttoning my ruined shirt is to pull on the formal black jacket I wore that night. It's quite strange. I could've sworn that I'd given it to Lizbeth before I met Peter. She wasn't down here in the infirmary, at least not to my knowledge. I'm quite thankful for its sudden appearance though, for it will help cover the blood stains. My reputation is all but dead, but old habits die hard and if there's even a chance that I can regain my previous stance, I will choose the most aggressive options in order to do so. I lift a shaking arm up and into the silky sleeve of the midnight black jacket. The usually comforting material does all but bring me comfort. An array of pain spirals through me as I make my first attempt at clothing myself. Finally, after what seems to be thousands of years, I'm fully dressed in what I wore that night of the incident.

The pressure on my side is unbearable with the old blood-stained dressing still strapped to my side underneath the ensanguined shirt. The coat doesn't help the pain at all. My crude sitting position wavers as I desperately endeavor to stay conscious. I have attained a small amount of attention through my loud gasping and erratic shifting. The ruffians who rest around me in the small, cramped room crane their necks to see the newfound entertainment my struggle provides. The wretched creatures cackle as a small cry escapes my lips. Shame floods my system along with an array of other emotions, the most prominent of the others being rage. If only I still had the power that used to be so customary for me. Everyone in this room would be out of my sight.

My breathing becomes steady after a while and keeping my back straight isn't as difficult as it was before. The pain that'll come with transitioning to my feet will be all-encompassing, so I'm thankful for this brief quiescence. I ponder laying back down again and allowing death to lay claim to my soul. I try to erase those alluring thoughts from my mind and instead focus on how painful it would be to die in such a way. The cot creaks as I stand, drawing more attention to my deplorable stance. Whoops of laughter come from a small group of scrawny soldiers attending to a member of their ranks. The sound of my teeth grinding against one another echoes throughout my entire strengthless body as I push myself to my feet. I don't appear very impressive to the onlookers, but standing on my own feet counts for something. The fiery, all-consuming pain attacks my fragile form and a loud yelp escapes me. The uproarious laughter that follows makes me cringe. Every single person in this room is against me. It feels as if I've been forced to the bottom of the ocean, the blackest depths of the murky water pressing in against my insignificant airway. I bite down against my lip to ease the pain. A small, crazed smile spreads across my sickly features.

"He won't make it a single step!" A soldier cries out amongst the laughter and merriment happening at my disposal. The jeering somehow fills me with an adrenaline-like emotion. The hunger, the longing to prove the incompetent fool wrong. I will go as far as it takes, I'll climb over many mountains, I'll go to the moon and back if I could only prove him wrong. I'll prove them all wrong. I'll uncover every lie, dig up every secret if it only means I'm free from such a languid position. Everyone who stands before me now will pay for all of their despicable transgressions. As I've said many times before, this place is a shining image protected by lies. That image will be shattered, if not by my hands, then by the hands of another, more capable individual.

My plain of vision crumbles around me as I plant one foot in front of the other. I've already vanquished any doubt that I'd make it a single step, for I just did. A flood of confidence overwhelms the pain for a brief moment, allowing me to take another step out into the center aisle of the room. The small audience whispers amongst themselves as my progress continues. Each one of their dastardly faces twist into grotesque glares as I make a start on my third step in what appears to be many. Fortunately for me, none of the cowards make an attempt to stop me. If one of them even breathed heavily against me, I'd fall over.

The rims of my eyes grow wet. I take my seventh step in the direction of the exit. I still have such a long journey ahead of me. A great number of things could go wrong during this time. My body grows more faint with each moment. My breathing grows more ragged as well. In contempt of all these things, I will keep going. There's such a vast contrast between the day of the wedding and this unfavorable day. I allow a yelp to escape my lips in lieu of tears. It's better than abandoning control.

I hear a chorus of laughter after my unfortunate cry. They take this as a manner of entertainment while I slowly crumble into a husk of my former self. By the end of this I'll either be dead, thrown out like Peter had been, or alone and safe back in my study with the least amount of status I've ever possessed. The only constant in the universe is change though, so I'm going to have to become accustomed to it. I take another small step in the direction of the grand doors leading out of the infirmary. Another seemingly constant thing in the universe was Lizbeth. I don't ever leave my rooms unless I'm needed for an important matter, so I barely eat unless food is brought to me. Soup somehow appears on my desk while I sort through important papers or something of that sort. I suspect that it's Lizbeth who brings me the meals every day when I'm gone for too long. It may be another servant. In that case, I'm all but doomed. I'm praying, hoping, begging that I'll find some leftovers that I can nourish myself with.

Lizbeth has proven to be another change in the universe. Both she and I always thought I was the legitimate prince of Andria, but Edward confirmed that my legitimacy is false. She may cross over to the other side and join forces with those who loathe me for not being Andrian. It would be hypocritical though, since those who dislike me because of my parentage are mostly Hyvernian. I'll allow them to dislike me though, they certainly have that right.

Slowly but surely, I take bungling steps towards my goal. My side aches like the flames of hell itself. I stumble and stutter on some of the most painful steps, much to the amusement of those around me. They even have the foolhardy audacity to make bets with the meager amount of money they possess on how far I'll make it. I wheeze for a breath of air and pay no mind to their cruel comments. I pity them. They don't have sharp enough minds to comprehend the willpower I possess. Every atom of my being screams at me to stop moving. Death seems to be an easy comparison to giving up and falling to my knees. My throat is raw and dry. My stomach is all but full. My energy is at its lowest level. The only thing that keeps me moving is the fear of failure I possess.

I no longer have the ability to move just a few steps from the exit. I can see those who walk on the other side. I understand that it's a miracle that I can still stand, but I'm so furiously close to my goal. If only I could make it even a few steps closer, if only I could reach that gilded handle. A few of the mystical beings who dwell just outside of this dank room look in through the nearly translucent glass of the door just to look away again. The voices behind me fade into oblivion as I focus on preserving my own shallow breathing. I only require a few more moments of rest. I'll make it to that door.

My legs buckle under me without warning and I fall against the rough stone floor, my face smashing into a particularly pointed stone. An angry pain shimmers behind my eyes as I shift to a point where the pressure is off my most certainly broken nose. The feeling of complete and utter despair fills me, all of me. It overwhelms the feelings of pain that used to dominate me. I give up. I can't push my way through it all in the end. I'll die right here and right now. For all the suffering I've endured, it's plausible won't make it to a better place. I'll go somewhere where the fiery pain is caused by actual scorching flames and my very soul burns from my body. Death will come to take me soon I'm sure.

I turn over to face the sky above me. I'm not met with the soft, comforting blue of the sky outside; I'm instead met with a stony archway. My breaths become too tiring to maintain and I hear somewhat of a rattle in my throat. Is this what they call the death rattle? Is this my last breath? Before I can fully slip into a peaceful unconsciousness, a bright-red-haired girl enters my plain of vision. Her equally bright green eyes penetrate my own eyes. Is Lizbeth the angel of death? A look of consternation spreads across her graceful features and I find my own face twisting into an unfortunate smile. The great love story I imagined for the two of us long ago will never come to pass. She'll never read what I've written for her, she'll probably be put to death if they don't find a use for her as well. There's only one difference between our fates. Lizbeth will go to heaven and most certainly become an angel. As I said before, I will be tortured and burned in hell. The last inkling of light disappears as I sink into a black, inky pool. I cannot see the bottom, nor can I see anything at all.

Lizbeth's Perspective

Alexander falls to the ground before me. His face is surprisingly twisted into a broken sort of smile as he makes contact with the hard, stony ground. I heard the sickening snap of a brittle bone as his face smashed against the ground. His twitching form turns slightly to stare up at me. The smile remains plastered upon his dying features to my horror. I clap a hand over my own mouth to keep a strangled scream from escaping my lips. Dread fills my heart as it drops down to my stomach. I shouldn't have left him for so long. I shouldn't have left him at all! Now the love of my life will die before me in such an unholy manner. His eyes flutter closed and I can tell he's shifting in and out of consciousness. The poor boy doesn't have long to live, at least, not if I don't provide him with sustenance within the next few hours.

I fall on my knees beside his shaking form. I lift a trembling hand above his mouth and feel a calming wind coming from his lips. He's still breathing, thank the Lord. I didn't intend for the consequences of my actions to be so severe, especially in the case of Alexander. In a perfect world, Alexander would've been able to retain all the same respect and power he had before, but the world is not perfect, nor will it ever be. All we can do as humans is try to improve it and sculpt it to our liking. Trust me Alexander, this is all for the best. The chains you bear will be snapped as soon as my long-coming plan reaches its climax. I run my long fingers through his greasy black hair as our audience stares in disbelief at an individual actually making an effort to help the poor dying boy on the floor. Crude whispers circle around the narrow room as I check his pulse. The dull thud of his heart is evident yet slow. More fear adds itself to my load at this. I must bring him to safety. I hate myself. I absolutely loathe my own existence for putting him through this, the one person who's ever even slightly cared for me.

I understand that if he doesn't awaken to eat and drink soon, he'll most certainly die. He's become a lot thinner in our time apart. He was already small for his age, or maybe I'm just rather large. I am a lot taller than he is. I suppose it's in my Hyvernian blood. I wish I was of Alexander's kind. The Walsian people are so beautiful. I'm biased in that matter though because Alexander is of Walsian descent and everything about him is absolute perfection. I worship the ground he walks on, despite him not having knowledge of my little obsession. His pulse slows more as I check it in the next few moments. There's only one way to get him to safety. I shall carry him, although this will tarnish his name more. It will be quite embarrassing since he always tries to put up a manly facade.

I pull him to his feet and sling his arm around my shoulders. His knees go slack underneath him despite his consciousness returning slightly. He mumbles something. A wild look appears on his face as he looks around at our scenery as I pull him from the wretched place. He never deserved to be in such a place. He tries to shove me away from himself weakly, trying to form words through his fatigue. I hold steady though, not daring to say a word to him. We trudge past a few guards patrolling the area and they offer us a few suspicious looks. They turn almost immediately though when they see Alexander's bloodied face. Recognition flashes in their eyes before they hastily speed away. I bite my lip with angst as Alexander fades back out of consciousness. What an odd sight. A female supporting a male. Imagine if Alexander's half-brother were to see this. I almost chuckle at the thought before realizing we've finally arrived at Alexander's chambers. We clamor through his gilded doorway as he protests weakly, now conscious yet again. He's thoroughly confused and endeavors to make that fact apparent. I can't form the correct words of comfort in my mouth, so I simply remain silent and watch him struggle.

I place him down onto the massive four-poster bed, trying desperately to restore his composure. The overt pain in his side causes him to fall out of reality yet again. I must have pressed too hard against him. The shame envelopes me yet again as I watch his sleeping form. I sprint to fetch him something to eat and drink, knowing I left him some soup the night of the gathering. It'll have to do for now. He won't be able to survive another hour without something to nourish his dying body. I won't let him leave this world without the completion of our great love story. I will never relent.

Alexander's eyes flip open yet again as I grasp the forgotten saucer of cold stew he'd ignored days before. I left it on the hearth for a reason. If someone had bothered to restore the fire to its former glory, the issue of heat wouldn't be relevant at the moment. Alexander stares down at his bloodied garments, horror traced all over his pale face. He breathes in harshly, most certainly trying to calm himself down.

"Wh-what? Liz-Lizbeth?" he croaks frantically, gasping at the pain of his own words.

I cringe yet again at the pain my plan had caused him. I pray he'll forgive me at the end of this ordeal. I won't survive if he revokes me. Why, he's all I have and all I'll ever have. He's the world. If the world rejects me, I'll be trapped in the void of emptiness where the universe decided to lay its roots. I cannot, will not be there again. I gently pull Alexander up to a position in which his back rests against pillow upon pillow. He's still frantically searching for an answer to all the chaos. I rest my hands softly on his broad shoulders, diving deep into his sapphire blue eyes with a wordless message of asylum. He stares back into my own verdigris green eyes, a tortured expression displayed on his face. Slowly but surely, he regains himself. He commands himself to breathe passively although his eyes dart around the two of us erratically. Finally, we're both entirely calm and he can lift his own spoon without shaking. A small smile graces his lips as he looks at me. Conviction hits me as I'm reminded of a smile much like this one.

It was a blustery day four years ago when I saw him smile. Alexander only enjoys days of darkness and rain for the sole reason that his mother enjoyed them. It's surprising how many little things Alexander remembers of his mother, how much he knows about a person he knew for less than a third of his current years. His mother told him that rain was God mourning for all of his creations that had died since the last rains. The notion comforts Alexander and makes him feel as if God really does care for the universe he created and that we aren't just a hindrance to him. Makes him feel that maybe, maybe, he has a hope that someday, somewhere, he'll be alright.

Back to that day. My responsibilities towards him and his well-being weren't as important as they are now, since Alexander had completely rejected most interactions with me in previous years. His older brother was beginning to become worried about him, because he hadn't emerged from his chambers since his tenth birthday. I was the closest thing he had to a friend or an acquaintance who wasn't over thirty, so I was sent to console him. I absolutely hated being around brooding boy. He never made an effort to speak to me, although he was quite polite. I dragged my feet across the red carpets of the halls as I made my way to him that day, dreading the peculiar silence I would have to endure. There he was, sitting all alone in his study. There was no fire lit in the fireplace and a chill had wrapped itself around the candlelit room. It was as if I'd stepped into a coffin. He might as well have been dead, just sitting there all alone in the dim light. I greeted him formally as per usual and he actually responded with a cordial greeting. He struck up a conversation moments later after I'd busied myself with fiddling as I had expected to. The rain had inspired him to speak to me about his family and his mother's philosophies about the rain.

I in return was inspired to share some of my personal memories with him as well, since I had felt an odd sort of shiver run up my spine. It was a sensation, a feeling. It was so foreign and new that I thought I was about to die. But then, it passed and I was back to my hollow self again. I wanted more of that *feeling*. I told him of the day I was taken. My mother's tears. My father's lifeless eyes open wide. The muddy cage. And then his brother. Alexander was absolutely appalled by my treatment. He apologized time upon time for the ordeal. Then he showed me a poem he'd written about a Hyvernian group he'd once met with.

Their souls are sold,
Their families taken,
It seems as if…
They have been forsaken.
A great force, it's unseen,
It has left them,
And so have we.

Alexander turned to me, the ghost of past sorrows possessing his ten-year-old body for a brief moment as he stared into my eyes. I wondered how someone of such a young age could depict the suffering of a people so profoundly. And there it was again, the sensation. He took a pale arm and wrapped it around me as I sat, a blank expression plastered across my face. Another spark of emotion hit me, then another. This new awareness was tantalizing and addicting, making me crave more and more of it. It was as if a switch had flipped when I stared into his eyes. Whenever I looked away from him, the world was cold and empty. There was no point to living.

There were downsides to this newfound emotion though. Jealousy, possessiveness, worry, fear, rage—all of these things now plague me. The addiction is too strong to break now. He's already firmly rooted himself in my heart and I'll never let him go, so long as I live. His smile, that smile is my life blood. I saw him three months ago this very day at a ball. A girl our age was dancing with him. She had beautiful blond curls that cascaded down her back in an ornate manner. Her eyes were chocolate-colored and enticing, drawing Alexander closer to her. Her slight frame was parallel to my own strong stature. *Jealousy.* He twirled her around him, a broad smile forming on his face as the dainty girl leaned closer to him. *Rage.* His hand shifted slightly downward on her powder blue gown. A blush formed on her high cheekbones. *Possessiveness.* They spoke the whole night. *Worry, fear.*

"Lizbeth?" Alexander whispers agitatedly, taking me from the distant memory. I breathe in, not letting these hateful thoughts consume me. "Are you alright?" he asks me yet again.

"Am I alright? I'm the one who should be asking you that!" I exclaim, not having anything else to say. Well, he's alright now. I leave, taking my shame, worry, guilt, fear, and anger with me. He doesn't call after me. The sweet words he spoke to me replay in my mind over and over...

CHAPTER 5

Lizbeth leaves the room hurriedly, not bothering to look back. Bewilderment is my most prominent emotion, although the anguish is right up there too. The world is too silent, far too silent. I became accustomed to this way of living long ago, but after just a couple days of noise, this soft silence is astonishing. I owe my life to Lizbeth. If it weren't for her heroic actions earlier this day, I wouldn't be conscious. She walked me through the halls and gave me the sustenance I needed to keep living. My stomach is still in knots from the seemingly large quantity of food, but it's much better than dying from lack of nutrition. I'm just so relieved I didn't have to die there all alone and ridiculed. The words of the cruel men still echo in my ears. It frightens me, for I believe that they're in the room with me again. I'm afraid they wouldn't stop at words if they were here now. I'm blessed with the fact that my fear is soon drowned in the exhaustion of the burdensome campaign. My eyes no longer have the energy to remain open. I shiver unpleasantly, burrowing my way into the soft sheets. Echoes and enemies cannot disturb me now. Death has been chasing me for some time. I say if he's going to take me, he'd do it in one of the more appropriate times that have presented themselves over the past few days. This thought comforts me slightly as I sink into an uneasy sleep.

Sadly for me, sleep doesn't come without dreams. I absolutely despise my own dreams. Every moment of every dream seems absolutely real to me, down to the detail of each blade of grass. Sometimes I can't tell the difference between real life and my dreams. I always realize I'm in a dream before I awaken though. My adventure goes downhill from that moment. Terrifying things infringe on the peaceful world my mind has crafted for me. Ghosts of people I don't recognize. Strange structures. And almost certainly a void of blackness destroying all of the beautiful dream realm at the end of the night. Most would call these nightmares, but life would also be a nightmare in that case. Ghastly ghosts that haunt our lives, whether they be people or past events are common. Strange structures and things that make no sense are also common. Black voids are most common in day-to-day life. Your entire being slowly ebbs away into this dark abyss over the span of your life. I've had countless hours to contemplate things such as these, hours that would traditionally be spent sleeping. That brings us full circle, for my fear of my own dreams is the issue keeping me from sleeping. When I do attempt to sleep, it's quite easy.

I find myself standing in the dream realm yet again. I bend down to examine the blades of grass on which I stand. The color of the blades is made darker by the swirling clouds above. As I slowly stand to my feet, I realize that this is the courtyard on the day of the wedding. Everything down to the cursed cravat is the same. A feeling of deep dread fills my heart. This is the day everything fell down. This event began those treacherous rumors, although I don't know how.

I can't tell why my mind has chosen to process something such as this. I've certainly thought a lot on the subject. I would think that my brain would have sorted the memories into the proper places by now, yet here I am. They call this lucid dreaming and it's apparently quite rare, but it's all I ever do. I know that I'm dreaming, but I cannot wake until it's finished. If this is a lucid dream, I can manipulate my surroundings to my advantage. I don't have to follow the same course of action that I did that day. I don't have to attend the doomed marriage. I don't have to stand alone, holding my tears back in the rain. I can escape my sad fate this time. I begin to walk, but soon my feet are lifted off of the dewy ground by a soft southern wind. I follow its path as if climbing a stairway to heaven. I see a break in the ominous clouds above me, making that my target. I want to see the angelic blue of midmorning sky.

I spread my arms out beside me, feeling a cool northern breeze brush along them. A tickle in my bones gives me a rush of spontaneity. I throw my formal blue coat into another patch of wind, the dreadful cravat on its heels. All I'm wearing is a button-down shirt and trousers. The wind blows against me, erasing all feelings of turmoil and angst. I'm only a bird, flying freely next to the sun. I've broken through the perilous clouds. I've watched the lightning form within them. Now the clouds look like an amorous ocean of unknown shapes and creatures. I see the faint twinkling of stars above me, but I understand that those are too far out of my reach. I'm content in my current position, unable to view the grand Andrian palace or the wedding or any of it. I can't see the vast rolling green hills. All there is is sky.

I wish to stay in this ecstatic state forever and ever. Nobody can hurt me, nobody can leave me, nobody can die. The fearful earthly thoughts are unable to hit me up here. Nobody can abandon me up here because I'm already alone. This is a better life, a better way of living even if my thoughts never grow complicated again.

I close my eyes for a brief second, allowing myself to breathe in the upper atmosphere. I crash into something, sending a shock of pain through my body. I've run into one of the ominous clouds. I didn't know clouds were solid. Terror rips through my veins and I let out a cry of despair. My eyes open wide again, scanning my surroundings for something, anything to grab onto. The wind no longer carries me. I had the foolish thought that nothing could abandon me up here, but I've just been abandoned by the wind. It's almost ironic and the situation would be comical if I wasn't falling. I fall back through the lurid wisps of clouds, this time being struck by all the little electric shocks of lightning. The ground is all I can see now. Andria has disappeared around me and I can only see a stony patch where I'll land.

As I fall the last few feet, my descent slows significantly. I shrink as I drop as well. I'm only a child now at the mere age of five. Foreboding rocks my small body. A psychic sense fills me and I'm suddenly aware of my current place in time. It's that day. That day. Panic fries my senses. It's that day. She died today. She died on my account today. In fact I watched her die. I watched her die at the hands of my father and at my own small hands, although I didn't physically harm her. Imminent fear captures me in the moment as I view my surroundings. Marble pillars rise high above me, higher than they normally would. The world is so much larger.

"It's only a dream," I tell myself in desperation. I lift a hand in front of my face to see if it's shaking. The familiar jittering is apparent on my fist. Turns out I can shake in my dreams. This is why I dread them so much. Moments like these are why I'll put off inevitable sleep for as long as I possibly can. The emerald-colored sky is now clear from what I can see from a small upper aperture, proving the difference in time.

Not even a split second after these thoughts are processed, my small feet start moving without my permission. I crane my neck, trying to turn myself about, but I'm not able to. It's as if my feet aren't my own any longer. I move down the dimly lit hall in the direction of a faint crying. Memories flood into my head, memories that I've only ever tried to lock away. Whole chambers of my mind open as the words become clearer. The words that he's screaming. The pleas she's throwing back at him. The begging for my life and for her own.

I see an archway up ahead. I remember gripping that archway for support years ago. I remember the exact events that happened just through that archway. I'm closer to the climax of the dream than I thought I was. Every fiber of my soul screams at my legs to stop moving. I'm pleading with myself, begging not to see the things I've seen. I don't have control of my own mind anymore. *Please, please don't make me.*

The cries grow louder and I lurch into the same position I was in nine years ago. There she is in that graceful white dressing gown. Her blonde hair falls down her back, a soft blue ribbon keeping it in place so that she can remove her makeup without interruption. There he is, that man who I convinced myself was my father. His crown still rests atop his head. I know it'll fall by the end of this ordeal. The pure rage in his soulless eyes proves his absolute insanity. He's got the sick idea that she has to atone with her death.

"He is not my son, Aerabella! We've gone through this with Peter before, yet you've done it again! This time I won't be so kind as to allow him to leave with a small chance of survival. He's an abomination and he must die, for he is not my son! He's a bastard, illegitimate!" my father screeches, glaring down at my mother's slight figure. She's fallen before him, agony etched in her deep blue eyes. Concern is written on her young face. She possessed angelic beauty until the very end.

"Alexander's innocent! The child shouldn't be blamed for his parentage! It's solely my fault. Allow him to live! Offer him life! Take me in his place. Destroy me in his stead." She says the last few phrases calmly despite the tears rushing down her pale cheeks. She's made up her mind about my life and her own life. She'll die in my place, much like the savior except she was never perfect. She had committed many sins in her time. Her words are stained red, for she is bleeding internally with the burdensome sin.

My father's face is deadly calm as he stares down at her. No emotion, no humanity on his face. His skin is wrapped so tightly around his jaw that you can see the color of his yellowing bones.

His light hair slicked back against his skull. His piercing blue eyes look towards me only seconds before the slaughter. I scream a vicious plea at him, the tears of my past flooding down my cheeks. He smiles gravely. An ornate cutlass rests in his hand. Blue precious stones adorn the handle. I know what is to come from that knife. A scream shatters my surroundings, the last sound my mother ever made.

I'm my actual age again and I have regained full control of my body. I rush over to the woman, falling on my knees in front of her. Her white dressing gown stained red. She's no longer screaming, but I am. I shake her roughly, trying to resuscitate her. *No, no, no!* I collapse on top of her, the blood staining my shirt and fingers. I cry out in complete despair. All of the wounds I've tried so hard to heal have been ripped open again, this is only but a dream. I'm back to the position I was in all those years ago. Why must my own mind torture me in such a way? The cacophony in my head has calmed slightly and I take a moment to stare into her lifeless eyes. Her mouth is hanging open slightly, the ghost of her last scream on her face. More sorrow fills me as this image is captured in my mind.

I don't notice her killer kneeling down beside me as he did so many years ago. I can only tell from the sickly smell of his cologne. I know the words he'll speak next. I know what he'll say will scar me more than any of the previous events. These words will be the hardest to fight off. He breathes out and I feel his hot breath on the back of my pale neck. I close my lips in acceptance. I have nowhere left to run, no more layers to protect myself.

"I hope you understand that it's you who's responsible for her death, not me," he whispers solemnly. I hear the smile in his voice and I feel his maniacal eyes on my back. He's deriving pleasure from this, I can feel it. Suddenly, the ground starts to rumble. The walls crumble and collapse into rubble, only leaving a cruel darkness around me. The laughter of the evil one echoes throughout the darkness. I try to cover my mother's corpse as the sky begins to fall in pieces. Instead of rushing up towards the sky, the sky is rushing down towards me. The dream has completed a full orbit and it's coming to an end. The inevitable void I spoke about is slowly consuming the realm around me and soon all that's left is me and a corpse, sitting alone in the darkness.

My eyes flutter open and I gasp for even the slightest hint of a breath. Somehow I'm awake and have escaped from the suffocating darkness that tried to envelope me. I'm alive. I'm alright. I'm alone now in my massive bedroom. The blue curtains are drawn shut and only embers remain of the fire Lizbeth set. My sheets and coverings are splayed across the red carpeted floors. Every detail of the dream remains with me. Maybe I'll call this one a nightmare. This experience was far worse than any I've ever had to endure. I'll now be trapped with an idea until I can force myself to forget. She traded her life for my own meaningless life.

CHAPTER 6

A few weeks have passed since the incident. My dreams are still torturous and haunted, but I'm alive. I've been recovering quite nicely despite the extent of my injuries. I've been able to walk half a mile without passing out. My energy levels are still extremely low, but that's to be expected. Maybe I'll be able to pull myself out of this abysmal pit. The words the former king spoke still echo in my eardrums as I go about my life. Lizbeth brings me a meal every day. Whenever I'm occupied with another matter, Lizbeth enters and exits my chamber tersely. She doesn't doddle or stop to chat. She's supposedly become busier as of late. I'm unaware of the reason why she's suddenly so preoccupied.

It seems I haven't been made aware of many important things as of late. I was limping around an unpopular courtyard a week ago to stretch out my sore limbs. I hobbled past two lavishly dressed noblemen. They spoke of an imperative war meeting. They raved about how they were to be in the presence of the king himself. The purpose of this conclave is still shrouded for me. That truth is quite unnerving to me. I would have been invited to something of such great import a month or two ago. The prejudice is almost surreal seeing that the queen herself is Walsian. I would have at least been notified of such an event if my parentage was still fully Andrian. If my hair was even a shade lighter or my height an inch taller, maybe I would have been accepted for something other than my biology.

I've realized that this solitude isn't the best for my mental health. I enjoyed having the time to stare out the window for hour upon hour before, but now my many wounds have been reopened and the customary fear is beginning to infringe on my mundane attitude. The sound of silence turns into something more. Sounds that aren't in existence are heard through my ears. I hear him whisper to me. I see her. Her body on the floor in front of me every time I turn around. The reddish color the sun turns when it falls just slightly below the horizon makes my mind turn to darker things, associating this usually exquisite sight to something more morose, such as the color her blood was when it first started to spill from her neck. That's not the end of this torture. The slightest sound or movement is him behind me. I begin to sweat at the slightest disturbance. I don't know what's wrong with me. Am I infirm? Am I going insane? My contemplations die down after a while as I stare out of the same dirty window that I have been this entire day. Even those who clean the windows have been notified to stop their duties in my area of the palace.

My senses perk up when I hear a slight knock from the main entryway of my chambers. There it is, the cold sweating and shivering. There she is, lying on the floor before me. There he is, standing in the corner of the room, his pale eyes staring into my own. His soullessness makes me shiver. I stand weakly to my feet, the pain from exertion still present. Curiosity sets in as I walk past dusty shelves of treatises and manuscripts penned by great Andrian poets. My interest in poetry has peaked in the last few years seeing that I've exhausted all other forms of entertainment. I even tried knitting for a brief bout. I arrived at my destination a little under ten minutes later. I got distracted by the alluring pages of a large hardback I was browsing earlier this week. The man standing before me has a tall narrow form and a fake smile plastered across his face. It's more of a smirk now that I think of it.

"Greetings, Alexander." His greeting is light and airy as if to cover the noticeable act of disrespect he has displayed. He stares

down at me, the unnerving smile still slapped on his face. I try
to keep my expression similar to his despite the disrespectful
action. He must have forgotten my position of power in Andria.
He should have added the word "prince" before his greeting.
He could have at least addressed me with "sir" or something
equal to that. He used my first name and that's inexcusable. But
I should become accustomed to such things. I must remember
that my position of power has been suspended because of the
scandalous truths that have made themselves evident. He is
perfectly entitled to call me what he pleases. I must remember
that.

"Greetings sir. May I ask, why are you here? It's the middle
of the night." I add a hint of buttercream to my tone in an
attempt to educate him on my absolute politeness and kindness.
He may be a friend or a foe. I don't know which he is, but I shall
treat everyone I meet as a friend from now on. I certainly wish
they would do the same. His smile abruptly snaps into a frown.

"Yes. It's the middle of the night. I by no means want to be
here. I did not wish to *disrupt* you. It's just—the royal queen of
Andria has decreed that I send a message to you. You see,
Alexander, she wants to invite you to a banquet tomorrow
afternoon at four hours past the noon hour. She even noted that
she 'hates the family being apart.' That is why she sent me." He
explains in a stern tone, a slight edge of annoyance in his high
voice. He's probably just aggravated that *he* has to talk to the
famously illegitimate prince. He'll be a complete pariah now in
front of his friends and allies. I've never spoken to the queen
personally before. When I last saw her she was hidden under a
veil. This could be interesting. Before the series of unfortunate
events, I would have asked if this event was mandatory. Now I
see this as a fine opportunity to gain some knowledge and social
standing in this hostile environment.

I could find answers with this event, indeed I could, but I
may already know all the answers. I'm just unaware of the

questions they're paired with. I know this debacle has something to do with me and my parentage, but what made the question come up in the first place? Who coaxed this scandal to light? And finally, what does this scandal truly entail? I wish to ask these questions without seeming too pernicious. It may even be too risky to ask these questions on the first meeting. I'll have to ponder it more. I'll have to charm the queen to gain her favor enough to invite me back into her presence.

"Excuse me, but why did she send you in the middle of the night?" I say to him, restating my previous question. His narrow face turns red at the inquiry, a slight frown settling on his features. An odd reaction for a mere servant. Quite strange indeed. I lean back and forth, anxiety setting in. An awkward silence fills the room as the two of us absentmindedly fiddle with whatever we kind find. He messes with his long black coattails. They make him look like a nasty old crow. Maybe they're a Walsian custom. I do notice the slight curl of his words. He speaks them with a hesitant sort of Walsian accent as if he's trying really hard to suppress it.

"Er, she was a bit delirious with sleep loss." The man looked away from my intense gaze, his face turning a deeper shade of red, the color of Bing cherries. "She's a night owl," he added, desperately trying to save his dignity. The remembrance of whatever came to pass with the queen must've been an exhilarating experience for the crow-like man. I nearly snicker at the comedic thought.

"Oh. Well excuse me for asking," I reply, letting a bit of the past harshness slip into my layers of buttercream. "You're excused, have a *superb* night sir," I whisper, looking him directly in the eyes. I even let a ghastly smile plant itself on my face. His coattails seem very crooked... This is another question I must ask when I see the queen. But, as I said before, I wouldn't want to seem pernicious after this glorious opening was handed to me from a nasty old crow.

"Very well, sir," he says, nodding curtly as he turns towards the exit. A question flashes through my mind as his hand is on the door knob. Maybe I could do a bit more investigation before the night has come to an end.

"Wait. Where is the king of Andria tonight?" I ask in a low voice. He coughs loudly and turns to me. He tries to seem immaculate, allowing no blame to seep into his eyes. He explains to me in words I can barely understand that my half-brother is away tonight. The door slams shut with an ample amount of anger. I sigh. I walk expeditiously down all the corridors I previously strolled down. Every shelf I loitered at, I now avoid. Finally, I'm back before the blank roll of parchment I sat before earlier in the evening. Inspiration hasn't struck me like this in weeks. I now have something to ponder, something to fill my mind. This will help me greatly. The contemplation fills me with words and phrases as if a geyser has opened up beneath me, a geyser of delicious, glorious words.

Every snowy night,
At the time before the light,
She comes.
She comes and tries many things,
She comes and does anything.

Many more like this come flowing from my hand, my penmanship growing increasingly worse as my hands grow more and more exerted. I'm most likely out of practice, but I'll do my best to get back to the spot I was in before. Even my chosen pastime has become difficult for me to enjoy. I'll have to do my absolute best to be who I was previously.

My hands keep scribbling away as my mind grows further and further away. My brother is a noble man who knows what chivalry is. He would never step out of line, nor would he break the mold. He abides by any set of rules laid over him. He has been groomed to be the perfect king and husband. But from what I've heard so far, his wife isn't up to his level with perfection. The perfect blood son of Andria is surrounded by shameful Walsian maniacs who have nothing better to do than bedhop and write dismal poetry. I don't know if the queen would do such a thing. Who would be daring enough to be with the queen of Andria? My life was so predictable before. I never had to leave my room for anything, save a few banquets and war meetings. Now, my life is anything but predictable. The spontaneity of disaster is frightening to me. In the past month or two, my life has become a dark contrast to the splendors of the beforetime. I could order the death of anyone that merely looked at me wrong before. One of the many holes in me was filled with that power. I filled my holes with many pastes such as that. Now I have nothing left to fill them with. I would make the joke of me being holy, but I feel too empty for that at the moment.

The previous king of Andria did many sick things, far too many. I've done a few sick things, but I didn't cover them as well as he did. His ending, an execution before all of Andria, almost seems like a better ending than mine will be. I'll most likely die in a private execution in a few months' time, or I'll die alone many years from now. The cause would be old age or something I inflicted on myself.

I mustn't jump to conclusions about my own ending or what it'll be like. For all I know, God will start the rapture tomorrow and I'll either ascend with all of those who're holy, or I'll go to burn in hell. I won't jump to conclusions about the acts of us Walsians either. The queen may just have been up late. That may have just been the end of it. I, however, am most certainly writing the most dismal form of poetry anyone's ever read. I'll set aside the topic of the queen's purity for tomorrow. I'll also set aside this ink and parchment for tomorrow. It feels incredible to have my fingers stained red again with the wine-colored ink.

As I gaze down at my hands yet again, I see them as I did in the dream. My quill drops to the wooden floor with a slight tap. There she is now, her lifeless eyes staring at my own. I feel the phantom of a hand on my shoulder and I turn to see the former king of Andria. A satisfied smile is plastered across his inhuman features. My bloodstained hands lay before me and I feel an awful sort of shame build within me. An overwhelming sense of downheartedness washes over me like the biting waves of a lake. I let myself go limp, my hands falling to my sides.

I walk almost mechanically out of the room, his torturous whispers growing more faint with every step I take. He can't follow me forever, can he? It's impossible for a spirit to roam the Earth for this long a period of time—is it? I barely notice when I'm in my sleeping chambers again. I stand there, heaving breaths rushing over my shaking figure. The memory of the wet hour I spent outside after the wedding comes back to me.

I finally collapse on my large four-poster bed. The hollow feeling of loneliness sinks into me as I lean back into the cushiony pillows. The position soon becomes uncomfortable and I hug my knees to my chest. I wish Lizbeth would stop avoiding me. She was my only friend. Now she doesn't care either. After hours of tossing and turning restlessly at this thought, I finally sink into a light and disturbed slumber.

Lizbeth's Perspective

I stare at him as he sleeps. Tonight he doesn't look as peaceful. He rolls over every few moments and groans mournfully at something in his dreams. A few times he cries out for something. A terrible feeling fills my chest as I realize I am the one who caused him such pain. The feeling is soon replaced with purpose, and I'm more stimulated with the prospect of us riding off into the sunset together, nobody following us. It will all be worth it then. He will never know it was me and all this damage will be repaired.

Alexander's Perspective

I awaken with a strange feeling in the pit of my stomach. I feel the light of day hit my closed eyelids as I slowly pull myself into a sitting position. The strange feeling is unmistakable. I was being watched. The most frustrating part of it's that I feel as if I've just missed the one who's invaded my privacy. I clearly forgot to lock the doors when that man left last night. Whoever it was could have been plotting to end my life. The fear I feel is somewhat dull now. Such a big deal. They could have killed me.

That feeling is soon forgotten. I realize all too late that the sun is not where it's supposed to be in the sky. The large yellow circle is on the left side of my opaque glass windows. That's quite odd. I push the pillow away from me as I get up from the still neatly-made bed. I'm still wearing the rumpled clothes I was wearing before as well. As I approach the window, I can see that the bright looming giant is sinking instead of rising. A pang of shock rises in my chest and my breathing quickens.

Absolute panic possesses me as I run my long fingers through locks of knotted raven-colored hair. I glance quickly over to the stately clock propped up on my wooden nightstand. To my horror, the clock reads half past three. I woke only a half hour before the banquet. I stand, frozen in time. My feet are glued to the carpeted floors until I realize that it's important I move.

I clutch a comb in one hand, a large bucket of water in the other. I must make my hair presentable for the queen of Andria. I will if it's the last thing I do. It may very well be. I've never seen my hair in any state but positively loathsome. The rat's nest atop my head will never be acceptable in society and I suppose I should just learn to deal with it. I check the clock again after a couple minutes of struggling. I have only seventeen minutes until the meeting. I cannot be late to *this* of all things! The wedding had more leeway for me to be late! This is life and death for me. I may have just given up my life by staying awake too late. I suppose yesterday's clothing will have to do if I am to make it on time.

I brush off the crimson button-up shirt and khaki pants I wore yesterday. No, not formal enough! To my horror, I find my hands snaking their way towards a dark green V-neck sweater and, wait for it, a *cravat* of all things. I still appear slightly disheveled, but it will have to do. My leather loafers pad against the red carpets of the palace as I make my way to the impossible destination. I've been eyeing my wristwatch for a while now and it seems as if time is moving faster than it usually does. I pass all of the tapestries and paintings I'm so familiar with in slow motion. I won't be able to beat the clock this time around.

The entire venture seems hopeless now, for I'm five minutes past the time I was expected to arrive. My wild hair flaps in my eyes quite uncomfortably as I skid around corridors and hallways, trying desperately to find the meeting hall. Disgruntled noblemen and noblewomen brace themselves against walls as I scurry past them. I'll laugh at their horrified facial expressions later when I'm out of trouble.

It seems as if I've been running since the wedding. To that banquet, with Lizbeth, from the miserable infirmary, and finally, from myself. I'm running yet again to another meeting much like that awful banquet. I can only pray that the cycle doesn't repeat itself once I'm in the presence of my brother. All this running and hiding exhausts my soul, drying out my reserves of attention. I'll need to use my last little bit of that for this matter. After that, I won't be able to provide those around me with the proper amount of attention they desire. I'll just be too tired.

Lizbeth's Perspective

The plate in my hands crashes to the floor as he rushes past me. He barely glances at me, uttering a brief apology before returning to his rampage. Why is Alexander running? Is he safe? My subconscious notes that he's running and that's a good thing. I was worried that he wouldn't ever be able to gain back enough strength to run. I'm sure he didn't recognize me. He was moving far too fast to take a good look at his surroundings. If this little jog of his aggravates the injuries he endured, then I'll be quite upset. I've been focusing on my other duties around the palace as of late. The place is understaffed. The meager amount of laborers can hardly cover the amount of chores there are to do around here, so I was a welcome addition.

I crave Alexander's presence, but I've realized what that would do to me and my intentions. The guilt I feel when around him is absolutely suffocating. It consumes all ideas of a happy ending. It seems to wreck the very purpose of this engagement I've prepared. For the good of both me and Alexander, I'll refrain from being with him until the very final moments. Despite my longing and anxiety to be with him, I'll stay away. The only thing that will get me through this sudden drought period is the fact that someday he'll be happy. Someday he'll be all right again. I'll be the one to fix him.

Alexander's Perspective

I curse my deft ability to sleep for extended periods of time. My legs grow tired soon enough, but I won't allow myself the luxury of taking a rest. It's my own fault that I'm so late to this event. I've already horrified countless people today. This isn't the stupendous start to my career that I was praying for. I check my wristwatch yet again, squinting to see the tiny second hand

ticking away. I'm a quarter hour past the meeting time now, but
lucky for me, the hall is just up ahead. Just a few more turns until
I arrive. Just a few more frightened people I'll have to pass before
I can finally sit down again. The strain on my feeble body is
evident. I won't make it much longer until my vision goes blurry
as it has so many times before. I should have prepared myself
better for this.

I try to picture the face of the queen in my mind, but I can't
seem to do so. I've only ever seen her once in person before. That
was nearly three months ago. Many things have occurred since
then and my mind's been overflowing with new information. I
think I should be allowed a little mercy on this subject. Another
burden is placed on my shoulders as I try to remember how to
properly greet someone of higher rank. That greeting has been
performed so many times towards me. Even if I do remember
how to properly greet the queen, I may address the wrong
person as the queen of Andria. If I bow down to a lowly servant
girl, I'll be shunned and shamed.

I've finally reached the door. The tall entrance is framed with
gilded candelabrum to show the importance of the room. I eye
the wide aperture wearily. The dark wooden paneling is similar
to that of the godforsaken door that decided to wedge itself in
my side. My heart rate quickens, if that's even possible. I'm sure
my heart might stop all together if I was to put more strain on
it. I look down at my side. I blink in utter confusion at the sight.
Blood is seeping through my shirt and onto my green sweater. I
don't feel any pain, though. The sight of blood seems to make
all calm thoughts rupture and die away. It takes me a few more
moments to realize that my shirt isn't actually bloodied. It's my
newfound insanity. I shake my head, forcing myself not to look
down and to instead enter the room awaiting me. I reach out a
shaking hand to the steel door handle, gripping it timidly.

Before I open it, I decide that it's appropriate if I knock. I eye
the heavy knocker. The steel is the shape of a dragon's head. The

fixture's pupil-less eyes glare into my own as if in warning. I grit my teeth, pulling up on the steel. I let it drop with a satisfying thud. The sound seems to echo through the very bones of the old building. I'm filled with a sense of new beginning, although foresight also comes with the sense. This beginning is a grave one, as if I'm entering the start of a real conflict. Everything I've done as of late has resulted in some form of conflict, so I'm not surprised, nor am I frightened. If the universe is so desperate to end me, so be it. I'll fight with all I have. I'll fight for the sake of my mother who died for me.

CHAPTER 7

The quiet chatter from inside the hall stops abruptly. I hear the shuffling of feet before all noise ceases. I wait for a few moments before realizing that my brother and the queen must expect me to open the large door myself since I'm of lesser status than them. Yes, I must remember myself now. I've got to make the best impression I possibly can, especially because of the rudeness of my lack of punctuality.

It takes two of my shaking hands to open the large door. It's quite the journey for my compromised arms and I have to breathe in deeply once the creaky door is fully open. The first sound I hear once I open the door is the sound of a modest string orchestra playing from a corner. There are only four men, so I suppose I must call them a string quartet. The song they play is a Walsian tune. The dark yet melodious chords speak to the refined parts of me. The sound is food for the soul. This slight melody is meant to background noise, a small addition to the ambience of the exuberant hall, but it captures the attention of all who hear it. This is true, although the sound fits in perfectly with the atmosphere of the midnight purple furniture and stained-glass window.

I turn my head slightly when I hear a voice speak over the strings, but I'm blinded by the sun filtering through the cold-toned stained-glass windows.

"Hello Alexander! What a pleasure to see you!" an enthusiastic voice says loudly.

I squint to make out a slight figure silhouetted by the gleaming sun.

"You're quite right, Edward. He is always late, isn't he…" the voice says in a lower tone. She obviously meant to be quiet enough for me not to hear, but that doesn't seem to be in her nature.

I finally step out of the bright shard of sunlight and into the cool shadows of the hall. I nearly trip over a few logs next to a large furnace. The heat from the blue flames within makes my face burn. I finally catch a glimpse of the queen. Her beauty hits me with full force.

Both her eyes and hair are the color of shining piano keys, ebony. She stands near a golden bureau on the other side of the room, but I can still see every detail of her magnificent eyes. It seems as if the souls of those damned to hell are contained within them. A trait such as that would usually repulse someone, but the voices of the deceased call to me in a somewhat musical tone. I'm drawn to her glowing orbs.

There is a hint of something else within the vast abyss of her eyes. Tiny flecks of golden starlight are spattered all throughout them. The pattern reminds me that without light, there cannot be darkness. The woman is thin, but not fragile. I can see her carefully outlined curves through the powder blue dress she's chosen to wear. Her lips are painted red, making the darkness within her pop. Her lips themselves are beautiful and heart shaped. She purses them in anticipation before smiling a smile that I would usually assume would belong to some otherworldly being. She moves to greet me and I realize just exactly how short she is. She's nearly a foot shorter than me and I'm really quite average for my age.

"Alexander? Are you in there?" she asks in a soft tone, walking closer to me. I'm broken away from my ogling and I blush deeply in distress. I catch a whiff of her perfume. She smells blood roses and white chocolate. She's either an angel or a demon. I'm not quite sure yet. I try to find words to say to the creature in front of me, but it takes me a while to even open my mouth. Her smile grows wider at my apparent foolishness. Her teeth are slightly gapped in the middle, adding a small bit of endearment to her regal face.

"Yes, your highness. Tha-thank you for allowing my presence in your majestic domain," I say in what I hope is a confident tone. Maybe she won't see through my guise if I act in this manner. I didn't have to deal with making a mistake in greeting her. I had no trouble recognizing her as queen, none at all. She appraises my form, probably noting that I'm shaking slightly. An unrecognizable look crosses her features as she stares at me. She allows the smile on her perfect face to drop ever so slightly as she does so. I should be smiling back at her, should I not? I try to place a confident smile on my face, but it comes out as more of a cringe.

"So, you're my brother-in-law?" she says in a questioning tone.

I was wrong about the string quartet. The only thing in this room that could hold me in frozen time is her eyes.

"He really is quite a silent man, isn't he, Edward? He only seems to speak when spoken to. Almost like a child…" She turns to my brother and stares at him in the manner she did to me, eyes scraping up and down his form. He nods somewhat stiffly at her, a grimace of distress crossing his features. His eyes flit to where I stand. He gives me a searing look of warning. His bright eyes seem colder as he does so. At this moment, I realize what that look in her eyes suggested. Flirtation. Maybe even lust.

"Uh, yes. I really do prefer to keep silent," I answer truthfully. I'm fully aware that those words of truth shouldn't have been more than a mere thought, but somehow her words get me to empty the reserves of my senses. It feels as if truth serum has been injected into my heart.

"You've dressed quite casually for the occasion. I appreciate your audacity. Eddy, you weren't a good example as you said you were!" she says lethargically, allowing a bit of her strong

Walsian accent to slip in her last phrase. She lazily rests one of her pale hands atop a wide hip before turning to my brother. He looks straight at me, his piercing glare penetrating whatever wits I have left. I've been immobilized and tortured by a few forlorn gazes and greetings. I've never been affected in such a way. There it is again, the pull to speak the truth.

"I was up quite late last night. I was scribbling away until the early hours of the morning, in fact, trying to make sense of your request. I was perturbed by the suddenness of it," I explain in a loud voice that doesn't feel like my own.

This experience is quite bewitching. I'm bewildered by my own truth, to say the least. I bow low to the ground, allowing my knees to drop before her. I look up to see a satisfied smirk plastered on her graceful features. I leave the cold ground and stand again. To my astonishment, she lets out a glorious giggle at my ostensible discomfort. I'm thoroughly confused by this new challenge.

"I'm jesting, Alexander. The man can't take a joke, can he?" she says, pointing her thumb back towards me as my brother makes himself comfortable at the long table in the center of the chamber. "You do look rather scruffy, though. I didn't expect that of you, especially after how you dressed at the wedding. I do wish I got to speak to you that day, but I just couldn't find you at the reception." Her tone becomes a bit darker.

Her face shifts slightly into a scowl of sorts. Still, a scowl pleasing to the eye. Her high cheekbones and heart-shaped lips disguise her distress deftly. "I forgive you for your disrespect though. I'm merciful, lucky for you. I'm only pleased you made an appearance here today," she adds lightly. The string quartet's music ceases as she lifts a hand up.

The power she holds in that hand. I crave to have power such as that again. This meeting is a step in the right direction. I hear her heels clack across the floors as she moves closer to me, a knowing smile in her eyes. I look down at her, allowing my messy curls to fall yet again into my eyes. I'm frozen, unable to move as she comes closer to me. Her form entices me, but she belongs to my brother. Right as she's about to take my hand in forgiveness, my brother speaks for the first time.

"Oh, I don't believe he's worthy of our trust and respect, a second chance as you say it," Edward says slowly, slippery words slipping from his sly lips. Obviously he is one I'll never be able to trust again. "He's deceived us for far too long, my dear Cordella. He's only half of what I am," Edward whispers, putting the emphasis of half.

She's about to speak in protest, but he holds up a patronizing hand. Her lips close over her gleaming teeth slowly, a look of fury coming over her usually placid features. "After all my dear," Edward says, forcing us to listen and take note of every little word that escapes his mouth, "he is the cause of my mother's death." He's using his perfect hypnotic voice to convince her of things that aren't true.

"Don't be rude, Edward. You do understand the reason I called you both here, correct? I explained it in great detail. Last night before you left. I hope you remember that," she says, pivoting yet again to look at my brother. She bites her lip as he ignores her comment. I know that feeling. His icy stare is still fixed on me as if I've wronged him again somehow. I turn my attention back to the queen. She looks somewhat despaired. My brother continually ignores what she says. She doesn't deserve that kind of treatment. It may be the way the relationship works between them. I'm just too captivated with her surreal beauty. She looks like a creature from an ancient myth, maybe even a goddess, although it may be my bias.

"Brother, listen to what she has to say," I implore my brother without thinking. The words fall from my tongue without my consent. I stare calmly into his bright eyes as his temper flares. He lets his teeth part slightly in a cruel grimace of rage. His teeth seem to be jagged and sharp like the teeth of a demon dog.

"Do not call me brother. You aren't my brother. You are brother to no man," he retorts. He's apparently disoriented with his own rage. He leans back in the upholstered chair allowing some comfort to seep into his troubled form. The queen makes a move to seat herself across from him in another one of the midnight purple seats. The rich red candles cast an eerie sort of glow from the gilded chandelier above the pair. I can see newly formed wrinkles on my brother's immaculate bow. His grimace deepens into an all-out scowl as he turns his attention to Cordella. I nod in resolution. There's nothing I can do to convince him of my loyalty. There's nothing he can do to convince me of his either. I take a few small steps across the mahogany paneled floors to the long table. The queen clears her throat in an attempt to regain our attention. She already has mine. She'll have mine forever as long as she's in a room with me.

"I haven't brought you together just so that you can argue. You people are my closest relatives in this new nation. I want us to be civil when I announce what I've been meaning to announce the entire time." She pauses to regain composure and I see tears in her entrancing eyes. Her red lips are pursed together in a grim sort of smile. "Alexander, you are to be an uncle. Edward, you are to be a father. I'm anticipating a child."

Her eyes shoot to Edward, a brief look of utter hatred crossing her regal features. Edward stares back at her, his strong eyebrows shooting up his face in a brutally amused expression. He breaks his posture and fully leans back into his stiff seat. The feeble chair creaks as he crosses his arms. I'm still standing. I cough nervously, allowing the brief sound to resonate throughout the grand room. The stiff string quartet in the corner of the room gawks at her misfortune. You would think this statement would diminish at least some of the attraction I feel for her, but it's as if her words sink right through me. I'm not affected by them.

"Cordella. Cordella, Cordella, Cordella. You are far too young to be carrying a child. You are not fit to be a mother, you're only sixteen, my dear. I say we should visit an herbalist and find you the proper mixture to end the pregnancy comfortably," Edward suggests in a dark tone, allowing the ghost of a sarcastic smile to fit onto his grim face.

Horror floods my senses at his words. A crushed look comes over Cordella's face as she stares at Edward's face. He corrects his posture as if he hadn't just uttered those soul-releasing words. A lone tear rolls down Cordella's soft cheeks before she speaks her next words. I satisfy myself by taking a seat as far away from the pair as I possibly can. This is quite a lot for me to process. I've already taken in a lot of information as of late. Her lips tremble slightly as if she's nervous to speak. My brother sighs, annoyed with her.

"Y-you married me, Edward. You consummated our marriage with me. We've been together many times. Is this not what you expected would come of it?" she inquires, a broken glare fixed on her face. Tears fall freely down her face. Her dark eyelashes seem to be elongated with the dewy drops. Even her tears are alluring when most tears are ugly. The strings on the corner notch begin to play a dulcet tune, but it's I who hold up my hand this time. I know the correct times to act. I clasp my hands together solemnly and prepare to watch the altercation. A ray of stifled light falls upon my fingertips from the stained-glass windows of the chamber.

Thoughts flood my mind as I cower in their increasingly toxic wake. She just had her sixteenth birthday but a month ago. She was fifteen years of age when she married my brother. I'm going to turn fifteen in four weeks. My brother married someone who's nearly my age and she's carrying his child. Or maybe it isn't his. I do have my suspicions about her promiscuity, although I view her as a perfect angel while in her presence.

I shouldn't contemplate things. I'll give her the benefit of the doubt as I should with all ladies. I stare at the table, memorizing the intricate patterns in the dark wood. I try not to relive the snippets I remember of the former king and my mother's arguments. I try not to jump back into one of my crystal-clear dreams. Despite my best efforts, the two worlds meld together and I'm trapped in a perilous limbo between the pair. Shouts from either side enter my ears. I restrain myself from blocking my hearing with my hands. Finally a single phrase pulls me out of the unhealthy trance.

"You actually believe the bastard son of my mother will take your side? The fool has no sense and will therefore remain silent like he should. I would silence him indefinitely if the court would allow me to!" the king cries furiously.

A dagger runs straight through my fragile heart at his bitter words. Cordella is silent. The tears still fall from her macrocosm-like eyes. Her bright red lips still tremble slightly. Indescribable anger and pain writes itself on my face. Edward glances directly at me as the words leave his usually silver tongue. An ugly smirk finds its way onto his face as he realizes the profound discomfort he's caused me. I let the emotion drop off my face and into my fists. I want to murder him. He wants me to be murdered. The feeling is now mutual. He threatens to silence me. I want him to be silenced. I want to cut out his tongue and then his cold, black heart. "As for you," Edward says, fresh power in his detestable voice. He turns to Cordella. "You and *your* child can go to hell," he finishes, a childish look of gratification crowning his insane face.

I stand to my feet curtly with an unreadable expression finding its way onto my face. The chair slides forcefully away from my back, scraping its way across the shining mahogany floors. It topples over against the notch where the string quartet stands. One of the hapless men begins to sob loudly. I let my curls fall into my eyes intimidatingly. Edward's atrocious smile only grows as he stares at my stiff figure.

"*Brother,*" I say haughtily, "we do not treat ladies that way. You are far better than to fall into temptations such as that. Now, the queen is expecting your child. There is nothing you can do to help that, lest you want to *kill* her, God forbid. It's fitting that you support her since the child is yours."

I say nothing more about our previous confrontation. I've controlled my temper for far worse offenses. I don't have the power to end him yet, but I will someday. Cordella stares up at me with deep admiration and gratitude in her eyes. She nods, more silent tears falling. She stands as I am, allowing her chair to topple as well.

Edward looks into my eyes, purest hatred encircling his irises. I allow a brief smirk to cross my face as I stare at the hopelessly indignant man below me. He's always been the example of all that's perfect and true. All things pure and serene. Now I've done one thing better and more fairly than he has. I must admit that this is extremely pleasing to me. I'll treasure this moment until my dying breath. That may actually be quite soon because of the superior words I've just spoken.

Cordella can no longer hold back her noises. She cries out in forlorn agony. Cordella kicks off her black heel and heaves them in all directions, a look of utter distaste forming on her beautiful features. She sprints as fast as she can across the hall. Her light footsteps echo and ricochet off of the domed roof. A lone servant rushes to pull open the large wooden doors, but she shoves him aside with a gasp of rage. She grabs each of the steel handles and lugs the wooden entrance open with brute force. My brother appears shocked at her indelicate actions. I'm equally as surprised as he is. I didn't realize she possessed such strength.

My brother stares at me murderously. His breathing is incredibly intense, so much so that I don't know if any oxygen will be left for me in the room. He looks like a rabid wolf, just about ready to sink his razor-sharp teeth into my soft, vulnerable skin. He may even start snarling like one as well. Fear, now a familiar emotion, takes its usual spot in my chest. I don't allow myself to show the wolf that I fear him at all though. I stare down the long table at the man-dog. He glares right back at me. I wait for him to leave and go console his wife, but after ten minutes of this contest, I lose all hope that he will. The queen deserves far better than this filthy human being.

"Go, console your wife. I give up," I admit matter-of-factly. I let my hands fall lightly on the table as he grits his teeth. He's probably trying to hold back some sort of growl.

"No," he replies simply. He glances back at me, wondering why I'm still in his presence as if it's obvious I should leave. I suppose it's my job to go assuage the queen's sadness, not the job of her husband. My brother grabs the jewel-adorned crown from atop his golden head and lobs it recklessly in my direction. The hunk of gold misses me by an inch and crashes into the delicately placed floorboards. It leaves a sizable hole in the fragile wood. He stands up, pounding his fists into the table with inhuman rage. If I don't run now, I'll never run again. The sound of my pounding footsteps ricochet around the domed hall as I flee in the same manner Cordella did. Now all members of the lugubrious string quartet sob, allowing the bows of their various instruments to sag into less robust positions. They're all grown men. It's quite strange that they're perturbed by this.

The regretful thing about this domicile is how strong the acoustics are, even in the matter of speech and sounds in general. I can hear her mournful cries as soon as the massive, gilded doors of the hall open. Awful cries and moans waft from all the collective halls surrounding me. The cries are faint yet prominent. These cries were probably voiced moments ago, but I'm only now hearing them because of the echo effect. They've been floating through the corridors since then. A servant slams the door behind me. He's only fulfilling my brother's orders. I won't hold a grudge for that. The sound deters me from my mission and I lose my sense of direction. I curse under my breath, deciding I'll go left past a row of gleaming Andrian knight statues. The cries meld together in my head, but I don't allow the memories of weaker moments to come back to me. This is far too imperative for me to concede to the growing madness within me. I'm not a lunatic yet, so I will not act as one. This rhythm of self-control grows more and more difficult to maintain as the sobbing gets louder. That should be a good sign. I'm getting closer to the unknown destination where the queen has hidden herself. The sounds are just another factor that makes this mission more formidable. It's easier to ignore my growing madness by looking at the ordeal in this manner. Just factors, only factors. Nothing more, nothing less.

I find myself stumbling through a small entryway and into a sparsely ornamented room. Two armchairs sit by a slowly dying hearth. A slight bookshelf waits in one of the corners of the tiny room. A ragged little green carpet sits on the floor underneath the rosy armchairs. I didn't know a humble room existed in the vast palace grounds of Andria. There isn't a single status-equipped painting adorning the peeling wallpaper. The awe is apparent on my pale face. There she is! She sits upon a small window seat next to a curtained window. A small bit of grey light shines through, but it wouldn't be enough light to illuminate the pages of a novel. Cordella doesn't notice my presence in the room. She's too busy with her own tears. I slowly approach her, making an effort not to disturb her yet. The floorboards squeak despite my best endeavors and she looks up at me brightly. Her eyes dull when she realizes I'm not her husband. I rest my hand on the door frame, allowing myself to appraise the sight before me. Quite an odd one indeed.

"Er, are you alright highness?" I ask softly, moving closer to her. I'm wary that she'll run off. It's as if I'm disturbing a sleeping dragon. A rather gorgeous dragon I dare say. She tries to force a shining smile onto her readied features, but she can't muster the energy to. I nod calmingly back at her, trying to force a similar smile onto my own face. She's presented herself brilliantly. She projected the image of someone who has no flaws. Her guise was deceitful, a lie. Something that both Andrians and Walsians have in common are their hatred for lies and liars. Anything less than the truth is despicable. That's somewhat ironic in my humble opinion. Their entire fortunes, their entire histories are built on lies. In Walsia, someone proven to have lied is strung between two ropes in the street. Chicken's eggs and rotten vegetables are thrown at the proven deceivers. Hypocrisy in the finest sense.

"I would prefer it if you refrained from addressing me so formally, Alexander. It gives me the feeling of being captured, held in place or something of that sort," she explains, lifting a hand to wipe iridescent tears from her enrapturing eyes. I have the strong urge to reach out and touch the place where those tears once flowed, but it's against my values to do something such as that. The smile on her face grows just slightly more palpable as I stand silently. Finally I figure out the proper words to say in response. Friendly, platonic words.

"As you wish, Ella." I slap a hand over my ludicrous lips at my own horrifying words. I just called her Ella instead of Cordella, like a nickname of sorts. I really shouldn't have done that. That singular word was an immense mistake. A reddish hue appears on my face as she starts to giggle at my misfortune. She utters a few words of forgiveness before lifting her hand and motioning to the spot next to her on the bench. Is she—Is she beckoning for me to sit next to her? Am I really to sit so near to the queen? That's unlawful. I shouldn't think of the simple gesture in such a manner. She only wants to grow closer to me as a brother-in-law. That's all. This act is no sin.

I oblige involuntarily, taking as much time as possible before squeezing into the seat next to hers. I control my breathing with a significant amount of effort, thank the Lord. She turns to me and smiles, showing the adorable gap in between her teeth. Her nebulous eyes still radiate in the meager light as if they possess light magic of their own. My hard work is undone and my heart begins to thud heavily in my chest. We sit in silence for a while as tears begin to fall from her eyes yet again. She couldn't maintain the smile for very long.

"I never did want to have a child," she admits slowly. All I can do is stare at her uncomfortably as she speaks. To my dismay, her body grows closer to mine as she fills the tiny space in between us. My body grows tense as I try not to reciprocate the warm signal. I try to move away to give my pureness of mind a chance at continuance, but there is no more room to move away. I'm so desperately close to an angel. A very seductive and seemingly unchaste angel at that. Her dark perfume overpowers whatever senses I have remaining.

"I never did want to be put in a cage such as this. I'm all alone here despite being surrounded by so many people. All of them are much older than me. None of them ask me how I am, all they attempt to do is find flaws in me. It's quite grueling being an impeccable queen all hours of the day," she says.

Deep compassion floods me as I realize how similar a situation we're in. I've had to act in such a manner since I was eight years of age. I admit this fact to her and she smiles a curious smile in my direction. Few words are exchanged between the two of us as we sit together. She tries to close the small space between us increasingly, but I'm attempting to do the opposite. It's unlawful for us to even be speaking for long, yet she appears to want more. More than I want. I only longed for an amicable relationship with someone of status. The way she rests the palm of her hand on my thigh is an indication that the relationship she requires is a romantic instead of platonic. Events such as these don't occur in real life. Her face is quite close to mine. I feel her hot breath on my neck and I close my eyes. My breathing is now noticeably heavier. It's a herculean effort to refrain from grabbing her and pressing my lips against her skin. The gravity between us threatens to push our bodies together.

"This is quite strange," I state in a nervous tone, forcing my back against the window behind us in a final attempt to move away from her. These advances are very flattering and she is very attractive, but she's also pregnant and married. Married to my brother, of all people. Well, my half-brother. The man who threatened to silence me indefinitely. The man who believed that it was the right choice to denounce me and cast me out of the royal court. The man who all but abandoned me. I could screw him over this way, just as he screwed me over. No teenage boy gets an opportunity such as this on a daily basis. My morals shove those unruly thoughts out of my mind.

"What's strange? This feels completely natural to me. It's all I ever even do anymore." I can see tears welling up in her eyes. I stand up. I tower over the poor girl. She looks up at me innocently. She can't deceive me, though. Everything, every aspect of this situation is incorrect. Her next action puts me in an irrevocable state of anxiety. She stands as well, placing her soft hands on my waist and pulling me closer to her. She smiles up at me, tears falling down her cheeks. The mood can change rather quickly with her, can't it?

The corners of her mouth waver as she tries to press her body into mine. My arms hang limply at my sides as I watch her feeble attempts. With each push or grab, the tears in her eyes grow. The mask on her face melts away. She throws herself desperately at me in the small, hot room, but all I can see on her face is the sorrow of so many years of torture. All I see are all those who have left her, forsaken her in the past. She's thrown herself at those men as well. Even now when her crying continues she presses furious kisses against my cold lips. She's begged them, pleaded with them to love her. To give her some attention for all her efforts. And for a short period of time her needs were satiated with empty promises and words with no meanings. She

was only just an object to them. That and only that. I see it with
clarity now. I nod at the now screaming girl. All she wanted was
attention.

I wrap her in a tight embrace, pulling her shaking form closer
to me. I feel her waves of emotions crash onto my chest as she
holds me tighter. I close my eyes and whisper soothing words
of peace over her. I won't leave her like those other men did. She
doesn't need a romantic relationship with anyone other than my
brother. What she does need is a friend. I am also in desperate
need of a friend. I pull her body from mine and stare into her
eyes.

"You don't deserve the way he treats you. You don't deserve
to be used for your charms either," I state in restitution. I lift a
hand and wipe the tears from her glistening eyes. She looks up
at me with wonder at this gesture.

"But—" she says confusedly.

"I'll be here for you if you'll be here for me," I explain to her
simply. There's only one emotion present on her face at this time.
Hope. But we all know hope is a distraction.

CHAPTER 8

Three weeks have passed since the banquet. Three weeks. Those weeks would usually feel like ages for me. The days slow incredibly when all your time is spent alone. These weeks have not gone by at their usual sluggish rate but have instead flown past me. Each day feels like a separate moment. The reason for this sudden increase is Cordella, the queen, although she allows me to call her Ella by some grace of God. The two of us have been alone for so long with nobody to talk to. This was our first chance to speak to another soul on the same level. The conversation was stagnant at first, seeing that the both of us were still healing from our first awkward confrontation. Then the conversation began to flow like a stream. There were trickles of words here and there that nourished our collective thirst for company. We began to speak more freely and the stream transformed into a powerful river, then an ocean. A vast sea filled with complicated subjects and endless possibilities for discussion. I've never had such a long conversation with anyone in my life, neither has she. We were both extremely surprised by this.

The first topic we discussed was her life back in Walsia. It was hard to speak of such things, seeing that our nations have opposed one another for so very long, longer than both of our lives put together. In Walsia, nobody wants to forget the past and all who breathe have grudges they still hold. The government isn't as centralized in some parts. There are vast forested areas of wild jungle that have yet to be cultivated. There could be anything within those leafy green forests. She told me this with fascination as if she wished to explore such places. A real sparkle came into her eyes as she told me this. It was genuine and not false.

She also told me about the cities in Walsia. Cities in Walsia are always built around the underlying crags of mountains so that all who live in the city can spend the entire day working in the shade of such cliffs. It's extremely hot in Walsia, so this is a useful strategy. Cordella was surprised by the biting cold when she traveled to Andria. She had never once experienced the season of winter, never once seen white powdery snow fluttering down from a rapidly blackening sky. She'd never seen the grand evergreens of Andria that I'm so used to. It's the same for me with Walsia. I've never experienced the passionate heat of their eternal summers or seen their monstrous jungle fronds.

She then told me of her family. She only ever spoke to her father once each year on her birthday. He always returned from his conquests to visit his only daughter and tell her of all the grand cities under his powerful rule. Each city's buildings were as dark as night and the palace house in each of them even darker. He would stay in each city for extended periods of time and flatten out each and every curved line and every denizen who dared to step out of those newly flattened lines. She would always long for him to return and protect her from those who hurt her. She would pray to the Lord each and every night for his safe return. Her way of Christianity is a lot less stark than mine, which allowed her to become more committed to it. I'm fascinated by her philosophies on this topic.

I told her of how different Andria is from Walsia. We avoid mountains because of their treacherous cliffs and the immense shade they cast over our lands when we need the sun more than ever. The wind in winter could sear through the skin of one who's unprotected. They used to send criminals out to die in this slashing wind. It's the worst manner of death in my opinion. I saw my father die in such a way. I was only seven then. I've never gone outside since then without a simple coat or sweater just in case I'm overtaken by a sudden windstorm.

The government is quite centralized in Andria. There is no uncontrolled territory, yet each city has a governor appointed and is not solely ruled by the king. All the cities are colorful and vast. Andrians do not celebrate the past and instead try to look towards the future. The colors symbolize a new Andria, brighter than how past Andria acted. I recall a speech that my brother gave when he took the throne at age 14.

This is a terrible time for our grand nation, it really is. The ground shakes with unsureness in the future all of Andria is to endure. The mountains in Walsia loom higher than ours do. These days feel like the end times, the rapture that was prophesied about. But I assure you Andrian people, this is not the end of times. This is in fact the beginning of something far greater than mountains or earthquakes. Under my rule, Andria will become the greatest nation there ever was. Walsia will easily submit to us and we will be sole rulers of the known world, you and I together. So come Andria, let us forget of times past and focus on all the splendors we'll be blessed with in the future. That is all I wish for you to hear, my beautiful nation.

I recited this to Cordella and she noted how right I was. Andria was bright and forgetful, Walsia dark and rich with retrospection. I had a good laugh at this. I've never once forgotten anything, but I suppose I'm part Walsian. That's still difficult for me to think about despite my newfound comrade.

We spoke of many other things, such as poetry and our philosophies about Christianity and life in general, but our opposing nations were the most intriguing to discuss and therefore the most prominent part of our discussion. I've learned almost everything about her culture through her words and she's learned much about mine through my own words.

"Oh, if they only let me marry you, Alexander, our life would be so fulfilling and grand," she said to me one day. A smidge of concern filled me at this thought. I'm not at all grand. I'm not at all fulfilling. I create the visage of being both of those things with beautiful words. I'm great at painting the picture of such things, but I'm not at all. If she knew of my past, she wouldn't be meeting with me all hours of these empty days to learn about what a life would be like with me.

I'm far too selfish to let her go, though. Once I experienced the sensation of having someone, I'll never be able to go back to my desolate hours of silence and contemplation of my own death. It seems far too morbid now that I have the shining light of her eyes illuminating what life should really be like.

Last night I brought her up to an unpopular parapet soldiers no longer patrol. I showed her the scene I love the most in Andria. It was just around twilight. In Andria, the sky turns a curiously green color before it sets below the many lakes and cities of the palace grounds of Andria. The twinkling stars that emerge from the nebulous purple sky of deep night remind me of her eyes and I told her this. I made her smile and her eyes shone true even in the suffocating blackness and cold of an Andrian night. I stared into her eyes and realized for the first time since I was five years of age that I wasn't alone.

Cordella's Perspective

Alexander has told me many things about life and Andria. He's filled my time with the beautiful sound of his voice. He's compelled me to speak about my life and Walsia. He's very charismatic despite his own opinions of himself. This is a strange occurrence for me. I've never been refused anything but happiness in my life. Now he's refused me a romantic relationship and instead given me a platonic relationship. I didn't know men were good for anything but a temporary fill of false satisfaction.

I know of my own beauty so this is quite odd indeed. It's as if we're having an affair because it's still unlawful for us to speak for extended periods of time as we do. We still have to find secret places to meet and secret times to meet as I have with all the other men I've seen in my time in Andria. It's exactly the same, save the fact that I feel no pain.

Andria is a far greater place than Walsia. I'm certain of this. In all my time in Walsia, I've never seen the color vermillion. The reddish orange tones of the entrancing color are particularly captivating in my opinion. Alexander described to me the concept of a *favorite color*, favoring one color over all the rest of the many seemingly otherworldly colors. If I had to choose a color I favor above all others, vermillion would be that color. As soon as I discovered this, I visited the royal seamstress. She is a tall, thin woman with bright eyes and golden hair just as most fully Andrian people I've seen. She wore a gown that contained all colors imaginable, even grody colors such as brown and grey. I'm enamored with Andria's love of color. It's such a foreign idea for me, though. Alexander loathes the fact that he must wear such glorious colors. He would be welcome in Walsia with that attitude.

Despite all the wondrous aspects of life with color and Alexander, Andria still has its defects. The strident temperatures slice any chance of a warm day to pieces. My husband is just as cold and unfeeling as the temperature. He leaves me during the daytime to go sit upon a throne all alone and hold a court for all those who've done wrong or right in Andria. He doesn't take a break to ever see me. I'm sure I've said less than two hundred words to him since the day we were wed. He's a deep contrast to his brother. Words flow like a waterfall with Alexander. The words we've spoken to one another are countless.

I do see quite a lot of Edward after dark though. He's tense from such a long day of being king of Andria. He never speaks. He only ever—well, I will not dwell on Andrian imperfections. I will focus on all that's good and right in this place. I will trick my mind into believing this frigid unfeeling place is paradisiacal.

It becomes *so* easy to dwell on moments though. His moments of passion are reserved for the blackest, coldest of nights. He reserves his love for moments when I will not consent to receive it. I believed that I would fall in love with him eventually, but I don't think I could *ever* learn to love a man of his character, nearly abandoning the child he put in my womb. I stole an old journal from Alexander. Each and every page was filled with the same melodious voice that leaves his lips. Words about life and the war and his brother and a red-haired girl and anything at all.

Do you want me, do you hear me?
Do you want me, are you near me?
What is this life I was meant to live?
Is this where I'm meant to take and not give?
Each of these questions has its own meaning,
And to an unknown God I will be kneeling

CHAPTER 9

The room's filled to the brim with countless court members. Everyone who has been on the court in the past and everyone who will be on the court in the future occupy this room, all but Alexander, for the decision which we will be making decides his fate and I as king don't believe that it's Alexander's right to be in control of anything, let alone his fate. He's not worthy of such an honor as to know his future. The room's completely silent and nobody dares to make even the slightest sound while in the king of Andria's omnipresent presence. Those who deign to even cough are thrown dirty looks and scolded for their misbehavior. I'm well aware of the dangerous amount of power I possess. In fact, it's really quite addicting. The power to snuff the life out of an individual with a word. I'm also well aware of the sunbeam directed at the back of my head to make me appear as if I have a halo. That was carefully orchestrated by the architects who painstakingly crafted every glorious inch of this court hall. This crucial spot is where my father stood and where his father before him stood. The construction was meant to be a metaphor for how all-powerful the Andrian king is, for even the sun submits to him.

It's rather an epic moment. I'm practically announcing my half-brother's death. Only a fool would turn against the king. I clear my throat subtly to grasp the attention of the few wayward watchers who allowed their attention to slip.

"Greetings, distinguished Andrian tribunal," I declare loudly. My voice resonates throughout the entire hall, even the far reaches of the back row can hear it clearly. Suddenly everyone in the room stares towards me attentively. All backs are arched and all heads are raised. The silence is abundantly more imposing than it was before. Cordella is seated at my right hand. Her lavish throne is adorned with the most extraordinary jewels I could obtain. Those who have the pleasure of viewing such jewels could be blinded if they gazed upon the glinting rocks for too long. The gemstones were extracted from the famed eastern mines of Hyvern. Hyvern is most known for its affinity for precious stones and its great ability to find such stones. I can only assume Cordella's pleased with such a gift because she smiles every time her eyes fall upon one of the luminous gems.

I heed that the gorgeous girl doesn't appear pleased at the moment when I sneak a glance at her. Opalescent tears have formed at the corners of her dusky eyes. The reflection of the jewels seem to paint her tears in color. She gazes to my left at the empty seat that Alexander would usually attend if he was called to the royal court for whatever reason. It's off-putting to see her mourning a boy she's only ever conversed with twice. That impudent boy shouldn't concern her. In fact, this entire event shouldn't concern her. I wouldn't allow her to be here if it weren't required for me to have someone of an equal station in my court if such a person exists.

"We have come together to decide the fate of Prince Alexander Aerabella Aaron Matthais of Andria." He hates it when I say his full Christian name. A smirk plays at my lips. "Collectively we will decide if he is worthy to live longer than the fourteen years he's already so graciously been permitted to live. You see, he's quite blessed to have gained those years of his life, for he shouldn't have been born at all." My voice becomes dark at the end of my statement to add an angry effect to my speech. The array of court members cannot hide their astonishment at my bold words, but they do try to out of some piteous form of respect. I allow a charming smile to slip onto my handsome features. My leader-like face will nudge them into a further belief of Alexander's great number of sins.

I scan the seats before me with a glint of satisfaction in my eyes. Alexander and my closest known relatives occupy the first block of the chestnut church-like-pews. I wouldn't be surprised if this room was once a part of a grand cathedral. I never did care much for Andrian history. I take after the rest of the nation and try to forget as much of Andria's dark past as I possibly can. Our family's eyes are fixed on my slightly shaking body. I feel drunk with the power I hold. Such power is unheard of in humans. The power of life and death is only known to God. I lick my lips in anticipation as I prepare for my victory. If nobody speaks in the next couple of moments, Alexander will most certainly die. There's no emotion in my loyal subjects' bright eyes, just purpose and willingness to do my bidding. Alexander and I share the same opinion about nobles and their power. I'm just a lot less self-righteous about it. I've learned during my ten years in this majestic position to use these fools to my advantage. The gracious smile on my face wavers slightly at this thought.

Not a single voice has spoken in objection yet. I know that nobody will, I'm sure of it. Yet why do I hesitate to call out my victory? I casually stroll across the stand towards the chair in which Alexander would sit. His throne is sparsely decorated compared to Cordella's prism-like seat. The chair has a simple iron frame with golden lining adorning the interior. He enjoys the simplicity of the backing and the luxury of the alloy. The poor fool's just so simple. He'll be gone soon and I won't have to worry about this chair's modesty ruining the decor of my venerable courtroom. Servants scurry around with pitchers of either water or wine. I'm sure the majority of the crowd will choose to enjoy wine from Andria's finest vineyards on this momentous occasion. I'm cleansing Andria of the last remnants of shame my mother left behind. I grip the opaque glass in my hand. I take generous swigs of the scarlet liquid in an attempt to calm my bizarre agitation. My conscience tells me not to go on with this dastardly deed, but my mind says otherwise. All Andrian logic tells me to move forward and end that abomination who called himself my brother. My mind and logic are certainly the right voices to listen to. Far more credible than the delirious, wavering voice of my past memories.

My eyes travel to the back of the interminably long hall to the glimmering green eyes of a servant girl. She holds a tray of tinged goblets filled with both wine and water, yet she hasn't moved to serve the refreshments. It's as if she's rooted to the spot by some unknown force. Her fiery red hair tucks itself away from her soft features in a somewhat severe manner so that nobody who gazes upon her can avoid the intensity of her eyes. She seems to stare into the very chamber of my thoughts. The unnerving feeling fills me further as I break the odd stare. The servant girl seems quite familiar, but I can't recall where I've met her before.

I raise my ornate glass towards the rounded ceiling in a toast to all who rest within the room. They all hastily raise their glasses in return, afraid to be the last to do so. "The second prince is a torment to all that's good and true in Andria. He's the embodiment of a lie. Lies are something that we all detest, Walsians and Andrians alike."

Cordella's mouth hangs open slightly at my words. She blinks back her beautiful tears and her red lips begin to tremble slightly. I grit my teeth in defiance to this inexplicable behavior. Can she not control her emotions for less than a moment? The damn woman can't hold it in, can she? "He's the son of Aaron, a Walsian man, and Aerabella, the former queen of Andria. My mother was committed to the former king of Andria at the time and her actions are therefore a sin. The second prince is the product of sin and must die," I proclaim, satisfied by my convincing choice of words. I allow a pleasing smile onto my lips as the trustees talk amongst themselves. I think I've won them over. Now all I have to do is call for a vote.

"Ezekiel verses 18 through 20," A voice rich with a melancholy sort of fervor states. My head snaps to Cordella's throne, but she's no longer seated upon it. She is instead kneeling before me, tears flowing freely down her smooth skin as they always seem to be. All she ever does is sob, therefore, filling my days with the sound of her dreadful wailing. Rage fills me at the audacity of the sound of her voice. I only register her words seconds after she's spoken them.

"Pardon?" I nearly growl at her. I let my smile become more pained. "Do you *dare* to speak?" I ask her loudly, making an effort to sound as pleasant as I can possibly allow. My attempts are futile. The sound of my voice is intimidating rather than jovial as I intended it to be.

"Y-yes. I would like to take the opposing stance," Cordella says in the ghost of a whisper. Her body shakes as she speaks. Her figure quivers so intensely that her words are slurred. I can barely decipher their meaning. It's hard to believe she possesses the foolhardiness to speak out against my wishes in this manner. It's hardly anything to worry about though. I still have the fear factor on my side. I will certainly be victorious in this case. My smile grows slightly more reassured as I turn my attention back to the gathering before us.

"Proceed," I command harshly, ready for the slightly entertaining attempt to cease. She gingerly leaves the floor and plants her feet on the ground firmly.

"The person who sins will die. The son will not bear the punishment for the father's iniquity, nor will the father bear the punishment for the son's iniquity; the righteousness of the righteous will be upon himself, and the wickedness of the wicked will be upon himself. That's what Ezekiel verses 18 through 20 states. I believe all in this room have put their faith in the Lord, have they not?" she asks the population before us. Some of them nod their heads sharply, others glance around anxiously to copy the movements of those more confident in the crowd. It's almost entertaining to see worry crossing the faces of the elite class for once in their privileged lives. I'd be a hypocrite if I said my life wasn't privileged, it's just that none of them have ever had to cure Andria of past sins by ending their own brothers. I believe that I would win a war of pity if we focused on that aspect.

"I believe they do," I answer for them hollowly. My conscience screams that the verse is correct. Alexander is innocent of his parents' unlawfulness. But he is still the product of such complete and utter evilness. I'm horrified by it. I'm horrified by his very creation. All those in the vast crowd of court members nod their heads idly in agreement to my sharp words. They all have put their faith in the God of nations from many hundreds of thousands of years ago. The room eventually goes silent again. Silent enough for me to hear the smashing of crystal glasses in the back of the monstrous hall. The green-eyed girl has dropped her platters of refreshments. I ignore this alarming fact so that I can focus on the imperative matter at hand. Cordella's plea is weak and easy to overturn and I will do just that. What other evidence does she possess? This is a fluke and a crime to try and disperse the king of Andria's efforts.

I scan the room to see if there are any other defectors. Not a single soul dares to move and stand with my wife. Nobody dares to utter a single word of resistance. My immense power would crush their bodies if they moved in protest. My power would strangle their words as they left their tongues. All appointed as court members are far too wise. They value their own lives over Alexander's life. I cross my arms over my orange cravat aggressively. Cordella won't hear the end of it later tonight. Of course, I'll find some way she could *atone* for her transgressions. I can't exactly have my pregnant wife executed. That would be just as vengeful as my mother's death and I certainly don't want to be similar to my father. He was a demon from the depths of hell, I'm sure of that. He animated an entire chapter of shame in my life. I would put an end to him all over again if he still lived.

"Queen, you cannot continue with your case if nobody agrees with it. A singular rock cannot withstand the weathering the ocean brings. One stick cannot hold back what a dam is capable of," I explain theatrically, to put on a show for my loyal subjects. Some of them nod along with my striking words. I hear an array of gasps crash through the contemplative stillness. A feeling of dread embeds itself in the pit of my stomach. I turn deliberately to where the majority of the sound centers itself. A small, blonde priestess pushes herself onto her feet with God-given morale. A plaintive look settles on her chaste features.

"I-I agree with the bible and the queen," she ventures in a falsetto. She toys heavily with the brilliant cross dangling from her slender neck. "S-she can continue her case now, can't she?" The priestess urges wildly. She concludes her feeble speech with a redundant bow. I've seen so many guilty bows such as hers in my lifetime. It becomes tiresome to view the same attempt at gaining grace over and over again. I can see why my father went insane.

The gaudy candelabrum that cling to the walls illuminates a scene that can only be described as unpredictable. More brave souls begin to stand with the priestess and my wife. A shadow casts itself over all of their grave faces. My great uncle Rupert stands to his feet, tears framing his watery eyes. He straightens his suit jacket in a self-important manner and nods at me in an impartial manner. The rest of the few who stand are members of the church most definitely. Still, their candle is only twenty amongst five hundred in the room. They're a small beam in the impending blackness. Those who've stood will most certainly not have their heads by morning.

The servants move to draw the red curtains of the wide lunette windows as night approaches. Night comes early as winter approaches, especially in Andria. The green-eyed servant still refuses to move. She stands as still as a statue in the very back next to her crippled pile of dishes. Her eyes are still fixed on my own in the most menacing manner. The sensation of her eyes raking into my skin is quite disheartening. Her hands clasp themselves together as if in prayer, but her eyes are wide open. How incredibly peculiar this situation is. I was not expecting the judgment of a servant or this feeble uprising either. This is beginning to grow hysterically amusing.

"I have another verse I would like to state as counterevidence," Cordella murmurs. All eyes transition to Cordella. She wears a vermillion dress that accentuates her figure perfectly. She's had all her gowns made in that color as of late. I haven't found the time to ask her the reason for this and frankly, I don't care very much. Vermillion looks just as fair as all other colors do on her. I'm actually quite glad she's becoming accustomed to Andrian culture seeing that she will remain here for the rest of her life, however long or short a period of time that may be.

"Proceed," I drawl in an even more animalistic tone than I had previously. I see the beginnings of fear forming in her exquisite eyes. That oddly enhances her glowing viewpoints as almost every emotion in her repertoire does. I love every nuance of those eyes. A mixture of both indignation and lust fills me as I continue to gaze upon her. This feeling is unprecedented at a time such as this and with the memories of her past misdemeanors filling my mind. Her comeliness is to die for though, so I suppose that turning rage into passion is expected around a person of this caliber.

"Let all that you do be done in love," she states decidedly. Her stance becomes slightly more confident as she utters those theological words. "That originates from 1 Corinthians verses 14 through 16," she adds, a husk of a smile finding its way onto her sublime lips. "Show love to the illegitimate prince. He is not responsible for his father and mother's crimes. Be like our Lord and Savior," she implores, devotion seeping into her musical voice. I grit my teeth in response to her insubordination. I know of her past crimes. I know of all her unfaithfulness to the book before she was wed to me. At least she isn't being hypocritical. At least she's speaking of forgiveness in a way that doesn't display her as holier than the rest of us. Her disrespect is unheard of still in spite of all this.

"Does the bastard son really deserve love? Is he really one of us?" I ask the gathering before me in a surreptitiously maniacal tone. My voice sounds exactly as my father's voice did when he conveyed an idea to a crowd. I allow my disgust with myself to be ignored as I continue with the harangue. "Just think Andrians, does he really deserve such grace from us?" Whatever I have to do to make that reminder of past traumas die. Whatever I have to do. I hear murmurs of disillusion in the audience. Panicked court members chatter quietly amongst themselves. I'm quite aghast by such confusion infecting the greatest class of people. At the beginning of this meeting, I chose to believe that these chosen ones are more astute than the general population, but I suppose I'm incorrect.

"Remember what our Lord said, my king," a quiet voice from behind me says. I whip my head around to see the green-eyed girl with fiery red hair looming in the shadows of the red curtains. She gives me a wry smile before gesturing towards the gathering before me. Around a quarter of the room is standing in agreement with the queen at this point and I'm beginning to sweat. Not only am I frightened of the outcome of this event, but I'm also frightened of the girl fixed only inches behind me. She's oh so recognizable, but I can't remember where I've seen her before. I feel her eyes on my back. Her gaze creeps up my spine as I search for some desperate words of protest against the gradually rising masses.

"I wish to state another bible verse," a voice from the crowd calls. Panic fills my lungs and breathing becomes somewhat difficult. My plane of vision wanes slightly with the effort. I can still see Rupert clearly standing before me though. It was he who spoke. I thought he absolutely loathed Alexander. He was one of the first to stand and now he even possesses the boldness to speak out in court. This is quite a shock. A surprise indeed. I can now see how great a disadvantage I have. I must say something to salvage my abating point of argument.

"Above all, keep loving one another earnestly, since love covers a multitude of sins," Rupert suggests in an airy tone as if he were about to lose consciousness. He looks the part too, for his saggy face pales at the sight of me. "That is First Peter verses 4 through 8," he finally finishes. The room grows uproariously louder at these words. I feel the beginnings of a torturous migraine in my temples at the acute din.

"If I may, king, I agree with this man's words," Cordella remarks, agreeing with Rupert's statements. The minuscule smile bridging her lips grows wider as she speaks. I nearly snarl at her in anger, but I remember myself. The world around me seems to swirl as the noise levels increase gradually. The leering girl behind me doesn't help the outrageousness of the situation. I place my large hands on my cutlass adorned hips as a gesture of confidence. I'm painfully aware of the blade hanging near my thigh. I could brandish it and lunge the razor into Cordella or the enigmatic green-eyed girl without a moment for each of them to take their last breaths. I must refrain from doing so, for that would be far too morbid, even for an Andrian crowd. The gem-adorned scabbard is heavier at this thought. It's so tempting to give in to these malicious thoughts.

Cordella recites more verses from the holy book with my regretful permission and many more ascend to their feet. Tears flow from some of the most passionate Andrians' eyes. They're all holding out for a useless, sickly fourteen-year-old abomination. I just don't understand the meaning of this shameful display. Cordella throws her hands in the air as she chants verse after verse of love and mercy. The naked eye can almost view the holy spirit flowing through her mind and heart, compelling her to continue with her shameful activity. The previous amount of standing Andrians nearly triples itself as this persists and I know now that there is nothing I can do to end Alexander, absolutely nothing. At least for today. The feeling of failure echoes throughout my hollow soul. My usually impeccable posture slumps and I stare towards the grand entryway, wishing to leave this mortifying mess in the past.

Just as I do, my eyes pick up the same fourteen-year-old I've been trying to end this entire time leaning against the back embankment of pews. He's dressed in a formal blue suit, save the cravat. Cravats are something the boy hates so dearly. He refuses to wear them unless the action is mandatory. A grim smile plasters itself across his sharp features as he stares into my eyes. He saw it all. He heard it all. His sable curls hang low around his sapphire blue eyes casting a shadow over his gaunt cheeks. He mouths a few words to me. *Nice try, brother. It's my turn now and you'll regret this, that's a sure thing. I suppose I've been saved by the grace of God, haven't I?* My mouth twists into an unruly glower as his smile changes into a righteous smirk. I wish I could pull the teeth that make up that smirk out of his mouth and grind them to bits. I clench my fists as my migraine progresses. I've lost the battle, but I haven't lost the war. Just because grace saved him this time doesn't mean destiny cannot end him. I will make sure destiny comes faster than Alexander would prefer it to. When destiny strikes, Alexander will not be allowed the peaceful, contemplative death that he's so hoped for.

Alexander's Perspective

So Edward decided to hold court to execute me, didn't he? I didn't expect my evil adversary to act so rapidly. I expected at least a few more months until he was royally pissed enough to act on his determined anger. The whole process was just so succinct. You can't really ever count on anything in life, can you? One moment you're the stoic prince of Andria and the next you're the illegitimate prince of Andria whose brother is trying to murder and will beg for any connection he can acquire. The only constant in the universe is change. I shouldn't have become so accustomed to a cushy, trouble-free life. In peace, prepare for war.

What was even more unexpected than the campaign to end my life was the fact that Lizbeth stood behind my brother the entire time. She was practically breathing down his neck, which was reddened with his immense fury. She had a dangerous expression on her face as well. Even now as I stand here she looms behind my devastated foe. That means that maybe she does care for me, even just slightly. Maybe I misread her sudden absence in my life. And maybe I'm just telling myself such things to bring me through a desperately painful day. Some part of me believed that my previously beloved brother would never act on his cruel words. I didn't believe that gentle, distant Edward would become a nefarious nemesis of mine. If someone told me this only a month ago, I wouldn't believe that individual.

In the end, what saved me was Christianity and those in the room who believe in the religion, that being practically all Andrians. Cordella sang out verses of the bible on my behalf and it influenced the usually rigid decisions of the Royal Andrian court. That's highly implausible. Those ancient verses and sayings are the very thing that saved my life. I'm quite thankful for that. Cordella and all her heartfelt audacity saved me as well. If it were anyone else who wed my brother, I would be on my way to my demise right now. I lick my lips deftly before slipping out a little leather notebook and pen.

I just viewed disaster,
My life should end much faster,
it's drawn out because of things such as this,
I was just saved from the abyss.

I look forward to our impending competition and the day of
my birth, only two days from now.

CHAPTER 10

I stumbled the long distance back to my quarters after I was sure I hadn't heard the plea to save my life incorrectly. The residual shock stayed with me. It was nearly inconceivable that my brother, the only person I have, no, had left would betray me in such a way. God only knows how I was able to keep my composure in that hall. The room felt as if it were spinning when I saw that soulless expression on his handsome features. I'm not afraid to admit that that experience was the most painful out of the recent events that have befallen me. I feel absolutely sequestered from my own life. Whatever ties to past Alexander's life had been sliced. The chill of the approaching winter didn't bother me as I went down each corridor. The stares of looming nobles didn't bother me either. Those two ailments have a contrary effect on me in most cases.

As I sat alone in my chamber later that night, unable to fall asleep, I only wondered what I could do in return to make Edward endure the same pain I had. I certainly couldn't kill the man. He's the king of Andria after all. Don't think I didn't consider sneaking into his chamber at midnight with my most potent of knives. Then I thought of Cordella. That sweet girl would be asleep while I slashed his throat open as ruthlessly as his words had cut into my own. She would wake up and find the blood from his veins splattered all over her nightgown and the silken sheets that the two of them had previously slept upon. She would find that some of his blood had splattered onto her face because of his restless struggles. She would sob against his corpse because he would have died alone in spite of his best efforts to wake her. Despite his wickedness, she would mourn him honorably as one should and I would have to put on yet another mask and play the part of a mourning brother when I would be just the opposite. I would be celebrating his demise. This series of thoughts was almost too gruesome for me to stomach.

Murder was out of the question. Murder indeed. It seems almost comical that I would even consider such a reckless idea. I'm far shrewder than to ruin my chances with an overly masculine solvent such as murder. The thought of Cordella sobbing on my account was already trapped in my swirling mind at that point and sleeping was out of the question. I unbuttoned my shirt gingerly in an attempt to keep the ever-present burning sensation in my side under control as my thoughts wandered farther and farther away from any form of brightness. The burning becomes worse every time my mind happens to fall on an aphotic subject such as what I previously plotted. I sat atop my neatly made bed, trying to ignore the nonexistent pain. Trying to ignore my own insanity. I instead focused on the moonbeams from my open windows. The night was clear and bright. The snapping cold was abated by wrought iron heat casters adorning every opening. I traced the moonbeams with my perspective-enhanced fingers until I could no longer see their silver tails. I created new constellations in my mind. Hell, I even attempted to count all the stars visible from my small windows. None of these actions aided in the ceasing of my mental turmoil. All the night sky reminded me of was her eyes. Her aster eyes would have tears in them if I had decided to act in the boorish manner my brother does. Shame engulfed me.

A thought struck me like an asteroid. My back became rigid and my arms began to shake again, but at least the uncanny pain left me. The righteous and unrighteous half of my consciousness fought against each other, leaving me petrified and unable to move. Every single thought that included Cordella was lustful and entrancing. I thought of how my chest becomes tight whenever I'm in her presence. My emotions are emboldened and every action is meant to please her. I would do anything if it would only make her smile. *Her* with her cherry red lips and chocolate scent. I felt the air condense around me as a decision finally began to form in my recollection.

I could kill two birds with a single, well-aimed stone.

I really could. I did promise my brother a good show in response to his crimes.

This plot would be devious, a worse fate than death for my brother. His pride would be shattered and mine would become inflamed with the remnants of his broken smile. I could take Cordella as mine. It would be effortless and simple. The spark between Cordella and I is impossible to miss. Those moments of passion between us would be oh so easy to procure and then she would be mine and mine alone. I won't forsake her like my brother does on a daily basis. I won't forsake her like those other men did, for I know nearly everything about the seemingly nebulous girl. My brother knows close to nothing about her, I'm assured of that. I felt my hands curl into fists with the outrage the thought of my brother brings me.

I woke from my trance to find myself pacing the frigid floors of my abundantly-furnished chambers. The wind whistled past my window as I decided on my plan and the righteous half of me let out a strangled cry and fell away. The protest within me died off and the pros began to outweigh the cons. Now I'm here, relaying the pros and cons once again. Yes, there is the slight possibility Cordella could refuse my advances or suffer in the midst of my plot, but that's only if I ever abandon her, which I'm certain won't happen. Edward scored a scar right on my heart, larger than any scar I've received in all my miserable time spent enduring lashes from those around me. The instinctual human reaction is to hurt the one who hurt you. I'm a simple man. I've never believed that violence and deceit were the answers, but there is nothing else I can do but retaliate in this situation if I'm to keep on living.

Edward will be damaged beyond repair. Our mother had an affair with a Walsian man and died when Edward most needed her. I'm the product of that affair and it would be as if his family's past shames were coming back to bite him. I am the embodiment of our family's past shame, after all. This action is the most prominent shame he awakens to every morning and his greatest regret, as if he could have stopped her from following what she loved. He's ignorant in having that futile belief. If I were to coerce Cordella into repeating the same behavior with me, I could figuratively scar his heart as he did to me. I could make him hurt. I could make him feel the miserable pain that I suffered on his account. I could end all the happiness of his life as he attempted to do to me. I could do all of it just by loving someone whom I already love very dearly. It's as if this opportunity has been delivered to me on a silver platter.

I lean back onto my lustrous covers in a satisfied manner. My aspirations will be completed on my fifteenth birthday. I don't bother to pull the blankets over me, nor do I bother to close the curtains across the silvery moon. I simply fall asleep, an action usually quite daunting to me. My dreams are misty and undecipherable. My only dream is standing in an everlasting downpour of rain. I'm drenched and cold, beaten senseless by each heavy drop of rainwater. This is much prefered to my usually gruesome dreams. It's refreshing to suffer in a way other than re-living physical traumas of the past. Just the constant beat of rain on a cloud concealed cliff overlooking a sea of nothing at all. So very peaceful. And painful.

* * *

I wake up on yesterday's tomorrow purposeful and

ambitious. I'm no longer fueled by beautiful words and ideas kept to myself, I'm fueled by complete and utter rage and longing for her, all of her. I want the part of her tied behind her back by Edward as well. Clouds cover the once clear sky and I'm positive that the impending rain will most definitely turn to a harsh snow. The silver moon last night had a luminous ring around it, hinting of a raucous storm. I shiver uncomfortably in anticipation of the day's events. They'll either be rueful or glorious.

I dress myself quickly in a stiff, white collared shirt and an uproariously bright purple embroidered jacket. A look of disgust crosses my face as I appraise myself in the mirror by the door. It seems as if every day I gain more and more hatred for Andrian casual wear. My royal blue trousers are tight in all the wrong places, but I suppose that's also the standard in Andria. At least I look halfway decent. I would look decent in anything though. A new sense of confidence comes with the assuredness of my plan. I don't even bother trying to fix my unruly curls in an acceptable way. I just leave them hanging limply where they'd naturally be without my constant fussing. I don't care very much about my hair at a moment as impactful as this one. This moment will be the culmination of all my efforts to thwart my brother.

I refuse to be late today. I am to meet Cordella for tea in one of our secluded meeting places. I arranged this to thank her profusely for saving my soul and to invite her to spend the night of my birthday at a hunting lodge on Royal Andrian grounds. I dash down the halls at a less lethargic pace than I would usually. The future seems so bright when you know of its many opportunities and splendors. I'm energetic today because this isn't the day I die. It's the day I seize the future by the collar and make it mine. Today, God feels real for other reasons that aren't factual. For those who don't understand how warm and comforting that is, I'll explain it. It feels as if your hand has been taken by an invisible spirit who guides you along the path that you're meant to be on. I know my path; indeed I know it. I know it like I know the back of my own hand. My path is to take a nonviolent revenge. To repay that man for all his crimes in a way that will break him.

Before I reach the main corridor filled with my most prized artifacts, I pat my right pocket gently to assure my little leather notebook is tucked in place. I don't know what I'd do if I didn't have the familiar, comforting heaviness of the small volume in my pocket. I would have cried the day of the wedding, that's what I would have done. I would have told Lizbeth my feelings before entering that room to meet Peter. I would have made a spectacle of myself the day I saw my brother attempt my murder. The notebook is a buffer for my emotions. My sigh of relief is genuine as I check my golden wristwatch. I don't have to run this time. I may never have to run again if my brother evaporates in a pool of his own despair when Cordella begins to pull further and further away from him. It's the very least I can do in return for his crimes. I could do much worse to him, but I'm feeling quite generous. I chuckle at my own sentiment.

Our meeting place is peculiar. There's an empty building on palace grounds. It used to be a church in which servants attended services and got married, but there was a fire that burned away half of the building. I've heard stories of how the searing flames were a violent shade of purple. It seemed surreal to all who observed the strange occurrence. Nobody knows how the fire came to be, but servants create the most wretched of rumors. They say that a demon came and set it ablaze. Some of them even testify to have seen the dark arsonist lighting the first flame with a scratch of its long, black fingernails. I don't believe in such rumors and neither does Cordella. The church was rebuilt long ago, but hardly anyone enters. There's a wooden staircase with a large landing. Cordella and I discovered it while patrolling the palace grounds the other day. The emptiness of the building was ideal for us. She brought in some lavish furniture for us to lounge on. It's become one of our private meeting places. We watch the warm, vibrant colors from the stained-glass windows transform into cool, enigmatic colors as evening begins to take hold of the Andrian landscape. She marvels over the ever-changing spectrum of colors. Her eyes fill with wonder each time a brighter beam of light hits a patch of vermillion. I'm acutely aware of those colors, for I've been forced to live with them all my life. The fascinating expressions on her face are the only reason I agree to meet in a place so colorful.

I'm broken out of my thoughts when the church appears before me. I'm a bit apprehensive about entering through doors that are a color darker than mahogany as of late. The dark wood of the door makes my heart rate quicken substantially. The entryway is a similar color to the wood that decided to wedge itself in my side. The splitting pain erupts into my senses as I take heed of my memories. The strangled sunlight pops in and out through the clouds, making me quite disoriented. At least the blood hasn't appeared this time. Sometimes it even flows from my lips. At least that isn't happening. I shove the aggravating insanity to the back of my mind before confidently pulling the golden handle of the door open before me.

The light is even more strangled in here. I wouldn't be able to see anything at all in the gloom of the bottom story if it weren't for the many candles lit around the large space. Cordella and I have been snatching unwanted candles from anywhere and everywhere for the past week. The candles are all different colors, much to Cordella's delight and to my distaste. Sea blues and magenta purple fill up my vision as my footsteps begin to echo across the languid floorboards. Cordella sits in a mismatched armchair on the large landing with an elated smile adorning her features. Her imminent happiness is quite contagious. I allow a small smile of my own to sneak onto my usually barren features as I capture her face in my memory. I wish to remember moments such as this one. Moments where you're truly happy are quite rare in this life, so commit them to memory whenever you can.

"You've added more carpet," I note quietly. It's vermillion, no surprise. She's draped it across the dilapidated stairway. The pale light from the gap in between the curtains of the lower story shines upon the stairway as if beckoning me to climb to the far reaches of where Cordella sits.

"I thought that you deserved the grandest of entrances. It's almost your birthday. You will live to be fifteen!" she cries happily, a genuine smile filling her face. I try to change my attitude to one of celebration, but all I can muster are thoughts of my own death. She may have just jinxed my good fortune. I won't say that though. She's made quite the effort, hasn't she? I force my smile to grow.

"Thank you. Thank you very much. Cordella, I owe you my life. It's because of you that I'll be able to see the day I turn fifteen," I acknowledge solemnly, allowing my smile to grow slightly larger. My pace quickens as I race up the stairs to be with her. The newly-minted carpet feels soft under my heeled boots. Cordella wraps me in a warm embrace as soon as I pull myself up the last step. I eagerly accept her arms. I feel as if I haven't hugged someone in a long time. I'll take all the affection I can handle. She's the first person I've felt a connection to other than Lizbeth. And she and I barely spoke as much as Cordella and I do. I feel a pang of worry in my heart as I ponder what I'm about to propose. Will she refuse? It's possible. Still, I'm fazed with the audacity of my own proposition.

Cordella pulls me carefully behind a weathered copper console she brought in for me to write at. The strange beryl color it has turned is quite stimulating. All of these mismatched pieces are quite impressive. I had no part in decorating this previously empty space. It was all Ella's doing. We'll have to abandon this spot soon though, just as we did the small room in which

Cordella and I had our first real conversation. It would be worse for both of us if Edward somehow found out we're still corresponding with each other. He would have a legitimate reason to end me. His previous logic was as illegitimate as my parentage.

I feel another pang in my heart, but with it comes the fury my brother brought me. This fire within me is all-consuming. Fires burn away sunken villages that contain ugly, evil people, but they also incinerate righteous cities filled with golden people. I bite my lip in irritation at my ever-shifting thoughts. Sometimes I wish I was a simple-minded person who didn't think of such things and could act on impulse without questioning every step. I would rather act on my concerns than live through this unbearable shame though.

"I brought winter apples and honey," I say with a small smile, holding up a metal container. I picked them on the way. The dark skin of the fruits was particularly bitter, so I snagged the honey from the east dining hall. I had to duck behind crates and racks of various poultry in order to not be seen. The cooking staff would make me beseech my way out. They most likely would have thrown their knives at me. The ostracized prince stealing honey. Such gossip that would be. They would scoff at my discomfort as I bled out on their kitchen floor. A grim smirk sneaks onto my face.

"I've never tried winter apples," Cordella states suspiciously as I pull the swollen fruits out of the vessel. I rest the container on the console with a gentle smile. I hope my newfound expression takes the edge off of my cruel smirk.

"You're in for a treat."

Cordella takes a seat at the rickety old chair across from mine wearily. She slowly uncurls her finger to accept the bulbous apple. She raises her eyebrows as she dips the foreign fruit in the rich honey. She slowly sinks her teeth into its flesh, a look of pleasure crossing her features as her mouth finally separates the skin. I watch her in anticipation of her inevitably positive response.

"You're quite correct, Alexander," she notes as she finishes chewing.

I can't help it now. An authentic smile takes over my sullen features. "I'm glad you like it. It's the very least I can do for you." My heart cries to me desperately. *Don't ruin another good thing, Alexander. Don't ruin your only good thing, Alexander.* These phrases repeat themselves in my head as Cordella stands to take a pot of boiling water off of a miniature gas fireplace in the corner of the forgotten landing. Cordella pours us both a small cup of ginger tea, Walsian poise on her fingertips. I watch each of her actions attentively, memorizing each of her swift movements in my mind.

I take a ready sip of the scalding hot tea, allowing the liquid to burn my tongue. My agitation numbs the searing pain in my throat. "Cordella I-I want to take you somewhere tomorrow. Just the two of us, away from the palace. I've hired a servant to take us there and he's sworn his confidence. I've traded our secret for a secret of his own as a contingency plan, so you need not worry about false pledges," I blurt anxiously, looking down at my cup to take another agonizing sip of the liquid.

"Alexander, I'd love to!" Cordella answers enthusiastically. "Where are we going?" she asks me animatedly. I look up with a bright smile crowning my features. Surprise is the prominent emotion on my face. A rosy blush forms on her features as she sees my full, genuine smile. Her eyes crinkle at the corners as a smile similar to my own shimmers into existence on her face. Her eyes twinkle in the light of the candles.

"Uh-um, really? Endless gratitude. You were there at that engagement ball a month or so back, were you not?" I ask her, shivering at the memory of the events that took place after that gathering. His icy eyes blaze into my consciousness. The familiar pain in my side returns subtly. I try to ignore these hindrances and continue.

"Yes, I was there. It was only a week or so after the wedding." She bites her lip in contemplation before looking back up towards me. "Funny how we never met," she adds quietly, a fervent smile finding its way onto her face. The intensity of her gaze is beginning to burn through my carefully crafted guise.

"I left early," I say quickly. She gives me a strange look before turning her attention back to her ginger tea, a small smile gracing her features. "Anyways, my great uncle Rupert spoke of a hunting lodge he would be going to in the summer months. It's on Royal Andrian grounds, but it's a few miles out and completely empty, for we're on the verge of winter. It would be devilishly cold though."

Cordella's eyes light up at the prospect of a trip.

"We would spend the night there and leave in the morning," I add hesitantly, a hopeful look in my eyes.

"That sounds absolutely splendid, but we won't be able to go outdoors because of the dreadful storm that'll take hold on your birthday," she notes calmly. I nod silently, trying to find the right words to say next. The light of the stained-glass skylights filters down ambiently, illuminating the seemingly golden dust particles floating listlessly through the cold air. She watches me with a thoughtful expression on her face.

"We'll stay inside and chat or read poetry or something of that sort," I suggest happily, a new smile bridging my features. "I've been to that particular hunting lodge once before and there's a great hearth in which we can light a roaring fire. You'll be warm. The cold won't be as devilish as I first thought," I continue hastily. My nerves are showing through the prominent optimism I feel.

"Well then, it's set. We will leave early tomorrow morning for the lodge with that secretive servant of yours."

Cordella and I chat mindlessly about everything and nothing as we always do. She continues to tell me beautiful things about her mind and soul that I'll never be able to forget. Her lilting smile captures me. I have to say, this isn't just about revenge any longer. This is for my own personal feelings for her. I'm strong enough to call it love. I've known her for only six weeks at this point, but love grows fast. Before you even realize it, love's vines have already snaked their way around your throat, threatening to squeeze the life out of you at any moment. Love is a treacherous concept. I wrote a poem to present to Cordella tomorrow, a poem that allows my feelings to show through proper words instead of relying on intense eye contact and physical gestures as most others do. Through my words I will show just how confident I am in my love for her.

> Love is good, love is true,
> But it's nothing if I don't have you.
> I'm not content watching and waiting,
> Hoping that my feelings will begin abating.
> I want to have you,
> I want to hold you,
> The cup I refused once before,
> I will not refuse once more.
> If you'd only offer it to me,
> your attempt would not be in vain,
> I will drain your cup again and again.

I love her and I hate my brother. I want her and she doesn't want my brother. I need her when my brother would opt to throw her away if it was possible. He doesn't want anything but power, not even his own child. He'll cast his child out like he's cast me out. My heart stops screaming and the pangs cease. I'm done with my own excuses. I'm done listening to the pleas of weakness. I will silence that voice just as my brother attempted to silence my own.

Third Person Perspective

What Alexander doesn't know was that the queen has reasons of her own for hating his brother. Deep, evil reasons. Just a week before Alexander's decision, Cordella endured something absolutely despicable. Something that only the devil would condone. It planted a newfound darkness in the queen's ripe heart. Something just as twisty as Alexander's past. If Alexander was in the room with Cordella that night, he would've seen something like this:

The queen sits in her chambers alone. Her husband has a late meeting he *so desperately* needs to attend. He watched her bleeding on the bed covers and he left. At only ten weeks, Cordella is having her baby. The baby won't be born alive though. Blood soaks the silken covers of the massive bed. Tears roll down Cordella's cheeks as she watches the blood spread and begin to stain her legs. The acute pain in her stomach is nothing compared to the rage and abandonment running rampant in her mind. She feels so alone, completely and utterly alone. The bleeding would stop by midnight and the child would be gone.

Edward had left her. He hadn't called a medic or a nurse. He left his sobbing wife alone, for she was always crying. Always crying. He no longer cared, for he had grown so accustomed to the sound. He didn't have a meeting, he just felt as if he would be on the verge of insanity if he saw the blood and heard her cries. Those who've gone insane do not know they're insane. Edward had already bridged that gap. He didn't speak to anyone that he didn't have to. He tried to end his brother's life. And now, he left his wife alone as their child was miscarried.

All Cordella could think of was how to get revenge on this evil man for hurting her so badly. A plan similar to Alexander's formed in her head as she stared motionlessly at the opposite wall. She was done crying. Now she had to do something. Now she had to repay that terrible man for leaving her in the time when she needed him the most.

CHAPTER 11

I squint into the darkness at my silver watch, trying to read the ebony hour hand accurately. The watch is off my wrist and the straps hang limply from each side of its center. I watch the dim light from a few dying stars cascade over each rivulet in the time piece's links. It really is quite an exquisite watch, but I hate it. It belonged to the former king. He gave it to me right before his execution. I suppose I haven't had the heart to rid myself of it. It's quite valuable. Finally, the time is clear. It's a quarter hour before midnight. A quarter hour left of my fourteenth year. The past few months of this year have been particularly disturbing and I'm happy that they will be coming to an end, possibly with the many troubles I've accumulated.

I allow the collar of my plain nightshirt to become rumpled as I turn from my side to my back, holding the watch directly over my face. My eyes are strained from staring at the tiny hands for so long, but I won't allow my harsh gaze to relent for even a second before the clock strikes midnight. I re-wrap the bedraggled sheets of my bed clothes around my bare legs in order to keep them from freezing in the subtle chill of the drafty room. An hour or so ago I opened my blinds and windows in order to provide some light other than the dim candle flickering in and out of existence on my nightstand. Only a fool would waste time watching time go by, but I reserve the right to be a little foolish after all the schtick I've had to put up with as of late. So I will remain as I am, staring at a timepiece and willing its hands to move a bit faster.

I have a little over ten minutes before midnight and I feel that familiar flying feeling of adrenaline rush to my head. Soon tomorrow will be today and fourteen will have been the amount of years I had lived yesterday. The number fifteen will forever mean something consequential to me. This number of years is what I lived despite the best efforts of my brother and oh so many others like him. Against all odds, I survived and I will continue to survive. I will survive twice as much as others, for I bear the responsibility of two names instead of one. I bear my mother's name and my own, for her life was cut short for my sake. Her name lives on through me. My love for her died many years ago, but I would wish that my son would do the same for me. I will act how I wish others would act towards me.

Tomorrow is the day that Cordella becomes mine and I seek imminent revenge. I've longed for this reprisal for such an interminable amount of time. My heart thuds in my ears. The constant rhythm drowns out any other noises emanating from the empty room. Yes, he'll be contrite and she'll be mine. The number fifteen will forever be a momentous reminder of how I overcame every challenge thrown at me by God and the universe. How I outlived every secret and every troublesome rumor that ever wounded me. A reminder of how I will retain this remarkable level of perseverance forevermore. I take in a startlingly difficult breath of frigid air before turning over yet again. *Tick. Tick. Tick.* The sound of the watch joins the thuds of my heart as I hold the timepiece close to my slowly broadening chest. My eyelids become considerably heavier as I grow more and more accustomed to this content rhythm. It's only a few moments before midnight. I must outlast the clock before drifting into an assuredly fitful sleep.

My heart beats slightly faster as I marvel over the gruesome dreams I'll most certainly have to endure. I can only pray that I won't relive past agony or something of that sort. The one time my insomnia would be useful. I can't believe the exhaustion of so many late nights betrays me now of all times. My eyelids fall closed as I submit to the impending nightmares. The timepiece is still clutched tightly in my trembling fingers.

Fear is forever in my subconsciousness and I feel the constant emotion become enhanced as I sink further into the lulling depths of sleep. Another world begins to form around me, the shining mist clearing out of my vision little by little. My breath catches in my throat as a sinister figure reveals himself. The individual is shaped like my brother. His lean form and triangular shoulders match my brother's angular figure perfectly. The royal blue uniform my brother always wears adorns the character's body as well. He even wears my brother's bejeweled crown on his perfectly coiffed hair in the same lopsided manner my brother does. The only difference between this figure and my brother is the fact that he doesn't have a face. My stomach flips as I observe this. Mist curls around the fingers and feet of the character as he's bending the substance to his will. The figure lays his hands out before him, gesturing for me to move closer. Despite the rapid beating of my heart, I oblige coolly and step closer to him. I know enough about these sorts of dreams to give in as quickly as I can. The pain only becomes worse if I attempt to resist. He cocks his head to one side playfully, allowing his grievously placed crown to slip into his other hand without much effort. The humanoid mist transforms itself into several more persons of the first one's kind. The master individual beckons me forward again, a hollow sort of laughter resonating from the empty face. The sound reminds me of rain being blown through an open window. I move closer yet again. I start to notice the crown quivering in his fingers. The jewels are losing their diversity. The rainbow of colors adorning the golden crown shifts to red, deep, bloody red. I feel a pang of residual pain in my side as I view the spectacle.

Suddenly, a face appears on the figure, the face of my brother as I suspected. The enraged face of my brother to be exact. His skin pulls itself firmly around his callous skull. The yellow color of his sharp jawbone shows through his translucent flesh and a vein pops out of his lined forehead. His sullen eyes stare back at mine indignantly. He lobs the crown in his hand directly at me as he did the day I met Cordella. The same furnishings appear around us, but something's different. I can no longer move.

A tidal wave of pure horror rushes through my slight form. The hostile headdress strikes me in the side and a familiar burning sensation returns. I feel one of the sharp points of the crown dig painfully into my flesh. The dark color of blood grows dense in my vision. The misty, faceless figures from earlier encircle my waning form. I put my hands up in an attempt to keep them from moving closer. The hollow laughter accompanies their advances, but I don't see where it could possibly come from. They have no mouths to utter those wretched cries with. A high, shrill shriek joins the chorus of disturbing sounds. That's Cordella's scream. Helplessness closes in.

The crown morphs into that loathsome piece of wood. The tight pain in my lungs grows more and more acute as the dark color finds its way onto the wood and my brother... My brother becomes... Peter. He becomes Peter. The icy man standing over me wears a cruel smirk. His pale eyes show something similar to pity, but the look is too malevolent to be compassion. His teeth glint in the meager light of the nearly empty chamber. The few candles piled up on indiscriminate pieces of furniture flicker in unison Peter's ever wavering eyebrows. The previous king had that quirk. The pain starts to become as monstrous as the first encounter. I grit my teeth but the ripping sensation of my raw flesh becomes all too much for me to endure, although I've relived and endured this pain many times over before now. Fear and pain are all I feel. I let out a horrific scream, but just as the first time, I can't hear myself. I only feel the lucid buzzing of the sound hitting my throat. I can hear only the laughter of the mist. The world around me begins to collapse. The disembodied monster begins to eat away at this dream realm's bounds yet again. Hopefully for the last time. But we all know by now that hope is merely a distraction. A distraction indeed. I hold my head in my hands limply as the darkness consumes me.

I bolt upright from the clutches of my smothering covers breathing intensely as I always do. I have to convince myself I'm not dead for the twelfth time this week. A drop of sweat rolls down my forehead as I finally regain control of my own body. It falls down my face until it reaches my cold lips. I lick the drop off of my own skin. The taste. I'm alive. I feel feverish and shaky, but a sincere smile infects my lips as soon as I remember myself. I'm fifteen as of today. I've survived. I've survived, I've survived, I've survived. The phrase repeats itself in my mind until it no longer has meaning. I lift my own pale fingers up to my face. I'm here. I feel a cool draft tug my hair back from my face as I begin to feel my body all over. *Sensation. Thoughts. Feelings.* These are all things I thought I'd never experience again. Overwhelming joy fills me. I turn my attention to the windows. The curtains hang listlessly around the wooden frames.

A white valley is visible through the viewpoint. Snowy crystals cling to each solid point on the frame. The miraculous sun shimmers through each beautiful crystal kaleidoscopically. Beyond the icy frame, the terrain is frozen. Not a single frosted tree even rustles. Not a single bird sings. All time has been petrified overnight, leaving an incredible display. I breathe in the chilled air slowly, another smile taking me by surprise. Yes, everything's frozen. The only sign of life is the gleaming sun slowly rising above the flat horizon. The beams it casts bounce across the tundra, making some particularly bright patches of ice shimmer enthusiastically. Everything is bathed in a rainbow of warm colors despite the frigid temperature. Ah, beautiful Andria. My heart swells with pride. If only she was freed from the monarchy.

A small bit of my previously foul disposition returns as I

contemplate the dilapidated state of the sovereignty. I pull myself out of the rhythm of slowly spiraling thoughts. I won't let the darkness take hold of me today. Any other day it can take me as violently and painfully as it pleases, but not today. Today is a celebration of my own zeal, my own zest for this cursed life I've been made to live. The panic of the dreams has worn off and I'm fully conscious now. A low chuckle hits my throat at the irony of the situation. Today would have been the day of my funeral, but it isn't.

I sense the timepiece still gripped in between my rigid fingers. The clock reads half past the fifth hour. I'm supposed to meet with Cordella at a particularly secluded back exit around the seventh hour. I actually have some time between to prepare myself. A grin forms on my features. I pull my disheveled nightshirt over my bare shoulder before slowly moving out of the bed. A twinge of fear hits me as I remember one of my many points of insanity. Getting out of a bed is still quite difficult for me. The simple task would be quite effortless for any other person, but whenever I try to plant my feet on the ground firmly, a flash of unwelcome memories of that wretched infirmary enter my consciousness and suddenly I'm lying on the ground breathing intensely. Today I grip the edge of my nightstand as insurance that I won't fall. I curse offensively under my breath as I do so. This absurdity is debilitating.

Only minutes later, I'm settling into a bath of freezing water. I drew it myself from the fountain of freshwater in the center of my suite. Oh Lord do I miss the days where a servant could fetch me warm water. If I could have a singular privilege back, I would choose the privilege of hot baths. I shiver uncontrollably as I force my bare skin against the frigid water. My teeth grind against one another as I wash myself with lavender foam. The iron vessel barely holds the water in as my shivering pushes it in small waves to the edges. While ornately welded, the tub could do with more practicality. In fact, every little lavish decoration in Andria could do with more practicality. I dunk my head under the water, scrubbing my hair with another palmful of lavender foam. My face is numb when I pull myself from the icy clutches of the water.

I complete the rest of my preparations for the coming day. The sun kisses me through a circular skylight and I lean into its embrace. My thoughts are consumed only by the fulfillment to come. My heart belongs only to Cordella. I dress myself swiftly in a pressed silver button-down shirt. The shiny black buttons fit nicely with my broad frame. I pull on a pair of formal black pants with a belt to match the buttons. My feet begin to regain some feeling as I tug on a pair of fur-adorned boots. Finally I slip my arms into a long black overcoat, folding the collar in an optimal way. Today, I wear the color I wish to wear and that color is black. Ebony. Jet. Ink. Raven. Whatever you wish to call it. As long as it's darker than a midnight sky in Hyvern.

I admire myself in the tall gilded mirror by the door of my personal washroom. Everything fits my frame perfectly. I look impressive, if I do say so myself. I clutch a small, black suitcase in my right hand and my notebook in the other. I smirk at the similar colors yet again. I'm ripe for the celebration to come.

Cordella's Perspective

The deserted corridor has an eerie apprehension about it. I press my back against the cold stonework walls and watch the light filter in from a small upper aperture. The day is absolutely gorgeous. It's as if God has opened up the sky for this occasion. I'm very grateful for that. The sun has now risen up to its early morning point, low above the horizon. The sky looks as if it has been bleached. Alexander is going to arrive any moment, I'm sure of it. He'll scare the devil out of me though, so I must remain calm. Alexander has a way of showing up somewhere without making his presence known. I've been trying desperately to develop a sense for it though, for we're going to be spending a lot more time together.

I won't fail to seduce him. Not this time after we've learned every aspect of each other. I love him. I've never been able to say that confidently before. I've never felt this way, not in even a single conquest of mine. This feeling isn't material. Most would feel guilt in a situation such as mine. Being with so many men before marriage and a few after as well. I'm not in the slightest sense guilty about these supposed "wrongdoings" or "sins" or whatever everyone's been saying for hundreds of thousands of years. Who ever said that it was a sin to fill your life with passion when it's so readily available for you to enjoy? Who ever said that? I think the person who came up with ideas such as that must have never experienced the feelings I've felt. Of course, there is the abandonment. That's the bad bit of it. But that even happens during the so-called *joy* of marriage. He left me when our baby died. I saw the child before that kind servant girl took it away from me. Its skin was so cold and dark. It was… it was so small. Lord I hate the cold. I hate it so dearly. I hate this cold Andria.

Alexander is the warmth. He's never stopped being warm since I've met him. He's never once done me wrong. He didn't use me. He didn't leave me, at least not yet. It's implausible that he would do either of these things. Despite the sullen visage he displays, he's far too kind. Too kind for his own good. I know he won't forsake me. My only worry is that I'll forsake him.

My heart stops as I hear footsteps echo down the hall. At first, I can't see his body through the gloom. The darkness cloaks him. He's only wearing black and silver, the tones of shadows. He steps into the meager light and all my responsible thoughts about marriage and being a mother disappear. I'm filled with that familiar sense of teenage lust. Lust for passion, lust for adventure, and lust for risk. His eyes are his one bright characteristic. They're so much different from his brother's eyes.

The king is so cold and unfeeling. When he kisses me, it feels like nothing. My soft lips meet only stone when I kiss him. Alexander's eyes are a heavy sort of blue and it's as if he looks right at you, not through you as everyone else seems to do. His eyes are as pure as a freshwater lake in summer. As warm as the sun on my back. I want to draw a glass of water from that lake and drink out of it until my thirst is quenched. Edward doesn't look human, nor does he feel human. I can't form the slightest connection with him, but I certainly can with Alexander.

The miscarriage rings in my ears and the pain of the years crashes down on me, but I have to do this and I have to do this today. I have no other choice if I ever want to get what I desire and what I need. If I ever want to get revenge on that demon and his deplorable actions. I'll do anything to make him suffer, and I'm sure Alexander would do the same.

Alexander grins at me and I see his eyes travel up and down my vermillion gown. I had it specially made for this occasion. He barely keeps his jaw from dropping. I bite my lip and allow a smile onto my noticeably attractive features. He opens his mouth to speak prematurely. It takes a while for actual sound to leave his lips.

"You look incredible," He worships idly. This simple phrase is all he can find in the vast array of words in his mind. I'm flattered by this fact. This was the reaction I hoped for and expected. There's nothing wrong with being confident.

"Can I give you your present now?" I ask him softly, ignoring the awestruck expression on his face as he takes in the detail I put into the outfit. He closes his mouth and attempts to compose himself briefly.

"I suppose," Alexander answers, finally looking me in the eyes. His expression melts when he does though. A brighter smile appears on his usually sullen features as if my eyes are the part of me he finds most attractive. I feel some of the agony in my heart subside at this thought. I pull a small black box from my bag. The velvety ribbon is slightly undone so that he can open the package easily. He takes the gift from my open hands gingerly and pulls the gilded ribbon with a simple sort of elegance.

"Hair clips?" he asks me, a look of surprise forming on his features. I've never seen Alexander with more than an adequate smile on his face. I've *never* seen this much emotion on his face before. My heart races as his lips curl to a point I didn't believe to be possible for him.

"Yes." I answer enthusiastically as I pull the vermillion clips from his shaky fingers. *He's always shaking. Always.* I take a great tuft of his ample raven hair in my hands and clip it behind his ears. An adorable blush forms on his cheeks as my finger brushes slightly against his ear. I put the other clip in as well. As I move closer to him, I notice that his cologne has a deep scent of wet wood and new grass. I breathe in deeply which makes him blush even more. The scent reminds me of the time when I traveled through Hyvern. The splendors of the fresh air and adequate rain enticed me. I begged my father to allow me to stay there instead of going to Andria to meet yet another suitor who was seduced by my grand beauty and regal features. I turn my attention to the taller man in front of me yet again, deciding not to be consumed by the melancholy moments I've experienced in the past. Maybe I'll be able to return there someday. Preferably with Alexander.

"Cordella, we should be on our way. The servant I've deemed worthy to be our travel guide is awaiting our arrival. His name is Forsythe. He's as tall as a tree, I swear, so don't be frightened," Alexander stutters nervously. His voice becomes a pitch higher after our seemingly suggestive encounter. I can make clipping someone's hair back evocative. Alexander offers me a trained arm for me to take in a manner that he's been taught. His adorable gallantry makes me smile.

"Alright then, if you insist. It's your birthday after all," I chide playfully. Alexander returns to his normal stature at this average banter. I won't let him get too comfortable though. We stroll to the small exitway and I feel Alexander tense as he grips the wooden handle of the dark-colored door. Becoming agitated at doorways is one of Alexander's aberrations. His imperfections are beautiful to me, probably because I have so many of my own and I wish that he would find them beautiful as well. I can usually refrain from acting on my romantic urges, but not this time. I could have been not refraining this entire time if it weren't for Alexander's kindness and Edwards' ability to mask his true evilness. I thought I owed it to Edward to at least try after Alexander attempted to place me on the correct path for a queen to follow. Truth is that I wasn't meant to follow any sort of monarchy sanctioned path. I follow the trail I've blazed.

We meet with Forsythe as planned, just outside the gates of a gravel path. Both of us stepped lightly over the small pebbles. The foreign sensation of rocks under our pampered feet was really quite unnerving. Alexander's easy smile doesn't waver at all, though. What's more is that his eyes were fixed on me the entire walk. Not at my body, on my own eyes. I would glance up at him every so often only to meet his intense gaze pared with the grandest smile I've ever laid eyes on. Forsythe is a burly fellow with dark brown hair and black eyes. He's as tall as a tree just as Alexander mentioned. He only spoke a single word to us which wasn't surprising seeing that his manner is so enigmatic. Alexander just kept smiling as if the entire world was burning and that's all he could do to comfort himself. I don't notice the cold any longer when I see the burning passion in his eyes.

We come up upon a simple, ebony carriage with gilded highlights. The cabin seems to be battered and aged despite its obvious polish. Our breath floats up in misty, luminous clouds as we gaze upon the carriage. A single, miserable looking black horse stands as still as possible in front of the carriage. The pitiful creature lifts its scrawny neck to look at us. Alexander grimaces, a look of pity finding its way onto his face. I merely stare back into the animal's eyes, keeping my expression neutral. I've eaten a beast very similar during my trip to Andria. It was all we had for food. The disadvantage of that is that my sympathy for most animals has disappeared.

Third Person Perspective

The carriage ride was silent. The only communication made was through fleeting glances. The bumps in the icy road didn't faze Alexander, nor did they faze Cordella. The quiet was almost impending, for the two eventual lovers knew what would occur once they reached the hunting lodge. Alexander knew he would be losing something and Cordella knew she would be gaining something. Cordella felt comfortable with the prospect of love. She was ready to give and accept the potent cocktail of both pleasure and sorrow. She had experience in that sense. She had already cried all her tears and enjoyed all of her significance. She was so desperately bored of hearing from others how she was meant to make herself feel those things again and she was convinced Alexander was the way to achieve this new goal of hers.

Alexander, on the other hand, was completely inexperienced in this field, but was also ready for the romance awaiting him at the secluded hunting lodge. He was ready to be with Cordella. The uncanny psychic connection between the pair's minds told Alexander that Cordella felt the same. He still clutched the suitcase in which his notebook sat. In that notebook was the poem. The poem that he prayed would display his true feelings in better words than he could speak in an unplanned manner. More than anything, more than gaining his manhood, more than being with the one he loved, more than adventure, Alexander was most excited for his great revenge. That was a fearsome thing for him. He felt like a wolf for an impactful moment. He felt like his brother.

Alexander gazed out the tiny window idly so that Cordella would not see his fixed blush. He began to think of his previous time at the hunting lodge. Snippets of shattered memories began to flow through his open mind. A beam of sunlight falling perfectly against a shaded pond, bathing everything in rainbows. His mother, her pale skin and blonde hair, the way it cascaded down her back. The mantle, his older brother's jokes, and the immense happiness he had felt in that moment.

There was a gaping cavity within the seemingly immaculate memory. That hole was the former king. The man didn't accompany them on the trip. In fact, he was the one who sent them on it so that he could endure one of his many episodes in solitude. He found the time to accompany them to church on Sundays though. But that was only to keep his image perfect, for murderers care little about what's beyond this life. That brought a small frown onto Alexander's face for the first time that day. He let himself focus on the sea of white slowly rolling by through the viewpoint instead of such memories. The one memory he assumed was untarnished became tarnished as he pieced it back together again.

His heart began to beat faster as the path began to thin and turn into a dirt road powdered with the remnants of snow that the groundskeepers had left behind during their midnight rounds. That's Royal Andria for you. Those in charge will strive to keep everything immaculate, even if it's a scarcely used path to get to a small hunting lodge abandoned during the winter months of heavy snowfall and little to no animal life. Pine trees began to spring up on either side of the carriage and Alexander steadied himself yet again by looking back inside the carriage. His eyes met Cordella's with a knowing look. She placed her icy fingers on top of his and he took her hand with surprising gentleness, despite his panicked state. He took a deep breath and a ghost of the same smile began to find its way onto his face again. Cordella knew of Alexander's trials and tribulations. She knew of the long scar that snaked its way up his side and how a piece of dark wood was once ensnared in that very spot. She knew of his mother. She knew how difficult it was for him to get out of his bed in the morning. She knew all of this and he knew all of her. For these reasons he began to calm down. Even after the brief moment of doubt, the two still grasped each other's hands. Cordella enjoyed the building warmth between their entwined fingers, for she was unaccustomed to such cold and Alexander was.

Few words more were exchanged during the trip. The only person who spoke was eerily Forsythe to himself. He spoke in the Hyvernian language. There were a series of harsh snaps in his phrases that were almost certainly curses. Alexander had heard Lizbeth curse in such a way after she had cut her finger. The carriage began to slow and Alexander's serenity began to grow. All was in place now and nobody could stop him from getting what he came to get. Cordella was equally as sure as Alexander was in that moment. Alexander was even so bold as to help Cordella out of the carriage. He placed a steady hand on her waist and gave her a strong gaze.

Cordella's legs felt shaky as she felt Alexander's hands on her. Her legs were also substantially cramped from the interminable carriage ride. They could've arrived faster if it weren't for the treacherous frost infringing on their path. Forsythe threw a heavy animal fur over the pathetic horse before nodding stoically at Alexander. Alexander only smiled back.

The pale blue clay walls of the ornate main building were covered in a dark green eternal ivy that couldn't be choked out. Rime ivy is what Andrians call it. Bright red flowers popped out of the sea of green here and there, contrasting with the lodge's color. All the columns and apertures were all the same pearly white color, almost as if the material used to make them was pearl itself. The roof was covered in sheets of ice. The frigidity extended to the awning of the roof. Treacherously large icicles hung down. The pathway up to the main entry was frozen and all the carefully manicured plants were frosted and petrified completely. The pair had to be weary of rocks jutting out of the deceptive ice. They had to hold each other for support. Alexander's happiness only grew despite this difficulty. He was closer to Cordella. The couple shared a good laugh when Alexander tripped right before they reached the welcoming steps of the small manor.

Finally, after the arduous trek, they stood on the small wraparound porch. Frost had found its way onto all the carefully covered furniture. The freeze had a devious way of finding a way to worm into everything and cover all viable surfaces. Anything that falls under its icy influence wouldn't return as brightly as it did previously once the bright sun of summer cured it once again. Alexander put a hand on Cordella's arm to stop her before they reached the doorway. Alexander looked down at her, a graceful smile curving his lips upwards. The clips held back his hair and she could see every perfect line in his face, every nuance of his princely features that she could rarely catch glimpses of. She most enjoyed gazing into his penetrating eyes. He had a way of looking right into someone, not at them or through them. It was as if he could see her very soul and judge its every characteristic and wrongdoing. The idea made her feel somewhat violated, but also understood, appreciated, and, most importantly, known.

Suddenly, Alexander placed his hands delicately on her waist and turned her towards him. She could feel his rapid pulse through his fingers and her breath caught in her throat. The assuredness in his eyes was just so captivating. All she could do was swim in the lake of his imagination. All she could do was fall deeper and deeper in love.

"Cordella," he said as if her name were a venerable goddess's name. He appraised her everything slowly, a moved expression on his face. "I have something I want to share with you," He whispered, squinting to sense even an ounce of the emotion she felt. She nodded slowly at him. "This is a poem that I can only hope will describe what I feel for you in the meager amount of words available for me to use."

Cordella could no longer breathe.

"Love is.. Love is good," he breathed amorously. He moved his body closer to hers so that their torsos pressed against each other. Now she could really feel his heart. Her heart began to beat in a rhythm similar to his own. She felt the warmth of his breath on her neck. The luminous sunlight emboldened the image of the young lovers embracing each other. "Love is true," he added strongly, pulling a hand from her waist to caress her cheek. She felt his cool fingertips trace her skin thoughtfully as he prepared to speak yet again. "But it's nothing," he dared, a look of pure wonder coming onto his face as Cordella pressed herself further into his embrace. "If I don't have you," he finished the phrase delicately. All they did was breathe for a few woeful moments.

The remaining words rang in Alexander's mind as new emotions and sensations he'd never had the pleasure to feel before that moment coursed through his icy veins. All he could do was feel and that was almost fearsome for one who was not accustomed or advised to feel anything at all. Alexander lifted both of his hands to cup her face in his palms. Her breath smelled of soft roses and her eyes were just as nebulous as ever. Just as rare and as bewitching as they forever would be. Alexander in that moment hoped that he would gaze upon those eyes for the rest of his life. Love does such strange things to the soul. "I'm not content, watching and waiting," he stated lustfully, the expression filling his entire body.

Cordella couldn't wait until he finished the passionate stanza. She moved her face closer to his with the intention of kissing his lips, but it was Alexander that pressed his lips against hers. He pulled her face towards his. Alexander's heart dropped as he felt the sensation he so longed for every time he had the contentment of gazing upon Cordella. Suddenly, Cordella deepened the kiss, giving her all to Alexander. It was harder, more urgent and more earnest than the other kiss. Alexander's hands fell to the small of Cordella's back and the pair stumbled backwards, evermore fervidity on their faces when they took fleeting breaths to gaze into one another's eyes. "Hoping that my feelings will begin abating," he whispered.

Cordella began to plant kisses down Alexander's reddening neck as he spoke again. Cordella moaned in appreciation as Alexander continued. His back was pressed against the door. "I want to have you, I want to hold you," he murmured into her ears as she returned to kissing his lips.

The desire was evident in Alexander's eyes as he realized he would never get enough of tasting her dark chocolate lips. He would never get enough of touching her soft skin or looking into those magnificent eyes. His need for this new passion, this new romance was so intense that another wave of fear washed over him as the moment took further hold of him.

"Continue," Cordella groaned against his lips. She felt him smile into the kiss. Bliss filled Alexander with that simple request. He kissed her one last time before continuing. He would miss her lips even if it was just a second he was without their warm embrace. "The cup I refused once before, I will not refuse once more," he said as she placed desperate kisses up and down his sharp jawline.

Cordella reached past him to the door handle as he kissed her neck voraciously. "If you'd—" Alexander was cut off by another sudden kiss from Cordella. He pulled her body into his and built on the kiss. "—only offer it to me, your attempt would not be in vain."

He finally pulled her face from his neck so that he could look at her, look directly into her as he finished the final phrase. His heart beat so incredibly fast that he could barely hear himself speak of the exciting din. "I will drain your cup again and again." An amorous smile hit Cordella's face as she pulled the door open after all her struggle.

Love is good, love is true,
But it's nothing if I don't have you.
I'm not content watching and waiting,
Hoping that my feelings will begin abating.
I want to have you,
I want to hold you,
The cup I refused once before,
I will not refuse once more.
If you'd only offer it to me,
your attempt would not be in vain,
I will drain your cup again and again.

The couple had no time to so much as glance at their surroundings. All that watched them were the sunken eyes of animal heads strung up on the peeling walls. The pair kissed in front of the carpets and honorable paintings that they were supposed to delicately gaze upon. They kissed through rare patches of sunlight from the heavily draped windows. They kissed until they found a suitable place to settle. The mantle upon which Alexander had played so many years ago with his mother and brother. The pair were on the bear fur carpet before the hearth. For a long time the only sounds were the sounds of skin touching skin and the mild sound of the dying fire. There was also the occasional garment of clothing thrown to the ground hastily or a gasp for air in between frenzied kisses. This passion continued through the night, even when the snow began to fall heavily against the paneled roof and the fire died out completely. Even when the only light was the light in the other's eyes.

CHAPTER 12

I had a difficult time finding sleep with someone lying next to me, at least, more so than usual. The constant breathing and moving of another person in that bed was unnerving and almost threatening. There was no light in the room to satiate my need to see. The foreign heaviness on the other side of the bed was odd to say the least. Biting wind whispered through the numerous cracks in the walls. I should've been quite pleased with myself. I had gained my manhood and my revenge all in one attempt. I asked and God gave to me what I wished for. But all I could think of was how utterly wrong it was, the way I went about it all. She gave me undeniable pleasure and love that I know I deserve and need. I enjoyed what we did very much, but the shame began to infringe on my satisfied state of mind when a tall grandfather clock in the crook of the room struck midnight. I love Cordella very dearly, but we made love for the wrong reason. Love should be made because of love, not because of mutual hatred towards another person.

I still wish to be with her, but I decided to apologize for my treacherously spontaneous actions. They were fueled by a now diffused rage. I decided to promise to be better for her and forget my animosity. My heart grew warm at these thoughts and I made another promise, but to myself. *Everything will be all right, Alexander*. I repeated that phrase over and over in my mind until I could no longer conceive anything else in my mind. Thoughts were meaningless and I had no choice but to fall into a gloriously dreamless sleep. The rarity of that occurrence is extreme. It was only the cosmos making up for what it had in store for me next.

Refrain from torturing Alexander in his sleep, torture him by daylight.
I can just imagine the perverse mockery I'm being made up
above.

I realized that only seconds ago when I heard a gravelly voice
whisper in my ear. That voice doesn't belong to Cordella, I'm
certain of that. I'm afraid to open my eyes and awaken to yet
another warped reality. "Wake up, Alexander. You certainly
have a lot ahead of you to endure."

I grit my teeth and slowly squint my eyes open. A shaft of
light falls across the room from an open window. I breathe in
the unique scent of cold air and my senses grow slightly
stronger. The familiar frigid sensation of the air prickles against
my bare skin and more warning bells ring in my mind. A man
stands before me fully clad in a long, leather coat. A smidge of
jealousy hits me as I begin to sense how desperately cold it is.

"I apologize for opening the window. I thought the constant
draft would help awaken you." The voice speaks again. His
thought was correct. This breeze really is stimulating. My vision
clears and I look to my left. Cordella isn't there. My heart beats
a bit faster at this thought although my head still feels full and
stagnant.

"Forsythe took her. You won't be seeing her for a while," he
says again as if he can read my very thoughts. I bolt upright as
the severity of this peculiar stance takes hold of me. I trusted
Forsythe. I have the secret of his father's death and he has mine.
A more potent sort of exasperation fills me.

At first the man before me looks to be Edward. His angular
form and perfectly coiffed hair hint towards Edward's usual
fashion. But then I notice that Edward's crown is missing. No
matter what, Edward always wears his crown. It's a rule for him.
A shortsighted rule if anyone would care to ask my opinion. I
have a crown myself. I don't enjoy wearing it purely because of
the inscription that repeats itself in the inner golden band of the
ornament. It's doleful if I do say so myself, being a doleful

individual and all that. *Don't shed tears when others could shed tears on your account* it says in a ridiculously formal sort of font. I can hardly read it. It's in a complicated sort of old Andrian that scholars call English. It adds to the second prince's visage of being impervious. I'm not impervious in the slightest sense, although sometimes it's easier to disguise myself as impenetrable as the inscription hints.

"Who are you?" I ask the man, an implication of fear slipping into my voice. I answer my own question before he has a chance to reply. If he isn't wearing my brother's crown, he's that man who calls himself Peter. My supposed brother as well. I associate this man with the beginning of my misfortune, for he was the man who revealed my descent to the king. I haven't seen that riotous fool in months. He didn't bother to pay me a visit until today. This manner of visit is quite unpleasant. He's evidently stolen Cordella away from me. I want to take a knife across his throat and watch the blood spill down his ever-paling neck. He ruined everything I had worked for in a matter of hours. I would be in a much more auspicious position right now if it weren't for his disruptiveness. I've only gained such ambition for power after I lost all of my existing jurisdiction.

"Peter. We've met before, although I can't say our first meeting was difficult to forget for you," he says, eyeing the poorly healed scar snaking its way up my bare chest in an eccentric pattern. I redden bitterly and clasp my hands over my chest, trying to mask as much of the flagrant disfigurement as I can. Peter bites his lip, worry on his face. Could he feel even the slightest bit of remorse for all he did to me?

"Where is Cordella?" I ask him, my voice shaking indignantly. I pull the silken sheets up to cover my torso in replacement for my hands. Scars are shameful materializations of past traumas and I wish nobody would gaze upon them, especially the man who caused the scar to form in the first place. Blast! He nearly ended my life. He would've if the wood wedged itself anywhere but the spot it did.

"You shouldn't worry about her any longer Alexander, worry about yourself," he threatens casually. The man bends down and grasps my trousers roughly before flinging them in my direction. I become painfully aware of my exposure and move to clothe myself.

"I suppose this is proof that you followed your mother's hateful path then," Peter states resolutely, a thin smile forming on his lips. I grimace grimly and choose not to respond. At that moment, the greyish sunlight glints across the silver handle of a pistol in Peter's pocket. I recoil at the sight of the weapon, fear striking me like a bullet. Peter's smile drops into a frown as he notices my further resentment. "Put on your pants before you become too fearful," he notes condescendingly. I sneer repugnantly at him. He rubs the stubble dotting his prominent jaw before pacing the floors almost menacingly. I comply and pull yesterday's trousers over my underclothes swiftly.

"Where is Cordella?" I repeat, reaching for my belt on the ground next to the lucent bed. He clears his throat as I buckle the shining strip in place hastily. I move my head to glare up at him as I do so. He only leers back at me as if I'm something he could easily crush if he so desired. A shiver runs down my spine. It's as if the emotion's been manually peeled away from his soul. A bleak, husk of a person with only a few key elements intact stands before me.

"I'm not going to answer that question," he retorts nonchalantly. I bare my teeth and glance around the baroque room for anything of use. The massive fireplace has a set of iron stokers to rekindle fires, but Peter's guarding them unknowingly. I could feasibly get around him if I only could think of a proper plan. I reach for my button-down shirt from amongst the untidy sheets and pull my arm through one of the silvery sleeves. I wince as I always do, the burning sensation becoming more prominent. "I never meant to hurt you through my advances. I only wished to meet you and for you to know the truth. In fact, I wouldn't have met with you if it was my choice in the matter. But morosely, my life is void of any decision making. My soul is sold." His cryptic words cast an uneasy atmosphere over the room and a wave of chagrin clouds my mind. Whatever does he mean by this nonsense? I choose to remain silent yet again. Solving riddles isn't a way to ensure Cordella's asylum and eventual freedom. I'll be damned if I'm responsible for another death. I'll have to bare more names if she perishes and I don't believe I could survive the guilt.

"Where is Cordella? Answer me," I demand, an edge more of hostility and turbulence finding its way into my voice. I pull on my leather boots carefully, making sure to keep my eyes trained on the offending figure before me. I don't want to be shot with my head down. It would be a dishonorable way to die and a dishonorable way for him to kill. My heart pounds in my chest as I sense another impending disaster. I promised myself that on my birthday no darkness would take me. Now it's no longer my birthday. I did say the darkness could take me as fiercely and painfully as it pleased. I suppose my thoughts are becoming physical reality. The passion I feel for Cordella shrouds my logic as I continue to ask Peter the same question. "Where is Cordella?" I stand slowly. I can't lose her. I refuse to.

"Listen! I'm not going to tell you anything about her. I could explain other things if you so desire, for example, the reason why so many calamitous events have befallen you. Why your life changed so very quickly and why you of all people have had to undergo so much suffering. Wouldn't you like to know that Alexander? I'm trying to be kind here, but I could be a lot less kind if you preferred." Peter's voice drops to a low, guttural growl during his last phrase.

I open my mouth to speak and I nearly choke on my furious words as they rapidly leave my throat. The anger usually collected within the pages of my notebook spill out. I reach dejectedly towards it, but the words materialize just as I grasp the leatherbound volume.

"I would absolutely love to know why. I would love to know why my brother forsake me and why he tried to kill me. I would love to know why the man I thought to be my father killed my mother instead of having common human decency. I would love to know why the wood hit me instead of you and why my one friend Lizbeth abandoned me when I most needed her. I would love to know why this all happened when you showed up from whatever pit of grime you lived in before. I would love even more than all of that, why you, someone who I don't know in the slightest decided to take the one person who made me even slightly less than despondent away from me and why you won't tell me why you did it or where you took her." I pause and regain a shaky breath. "I would love to know all those things and one more. Why does God hate me? He saved me for some reason, but at this moment, I'd rather I had not have been saved just so I wouldn't have to endure torture one more damned time. I thought it was done, but I was sorely mistaken."

I'm breathless yet again by the end of my miserable speech. I haven't spoken for that long since I was—I can't remember when. This is why I always have my notebook in my right pocket so I don't say these things out loud. The reassuring pages are a constant reminder to hide it all away. Keep the sinful words to myself. I feel tears threatening my usually dry eyes. I force the rage down inside of me and wait for his answer. My head aches with the agony of past memories. I gave them a voice with my very own words.

"Do you want to die, Alexander?" Peter asks after a long pause. A wry smile wraps itself around his face as if he found contentment within my frenzied phrases.

"I was almost at a point where I truly believed there was a reason I was born other than to kill my mother. You dissolved any remnants of that with your question," I reply irritably, placing my hands on my head and sitting down on the bed again.

"I can shoot you right now if that is what you seek. It would be quick. A bullet right through your brain. You wouldn't feel a thing and you wouldn't have to worry about anything any longer. Not about our mother, Edward, Cordella, or your scars. Not about your *many* deficiencies, your life stretched ahead of you, or even the truth which I could also reveal to you. It would cause you more pain than a simple, iron bullet through your mind." His words are seductive and tempting. The outline of the silver pistol against his black trousers is comforting instead of hostile and my mind goes blank. No words run through my stream of consciousness as they always do. Only an offer and two possible responses. Live or die. Survive or don't. Endure more agony or go to hell, which would most certainly be better than my dreams and losing those close to me again and again.

Then Cordella comes back to me. Her perfect face and her eyes. Oh, her eyes. I still haven't gotten to explore every nuance of those eyes, visit every star contained within them. We showed each other our souls last night and if that counts for anything, I will stay alive and save her from this disaster. If I save her, maybe it will compensate for the death of my mother. If there's even a pinprick of hope in this darkness, I'll strive to reach it. Cordella would want me to try to reach heaven and endeavor to be with her. I look out the window and watch the icy sunrise silently for a moment. A spiritual sort of calm fills me as Cordella's face dissipates from my mind and I decide not to choose death as a momentary solution. I feel God's presence within the room, watching, waiting for me to make the correct decision.

"I need to live," I reply in a monotone voice, looking down at my boot clad feet. Peter's eyes shimmer appreciatively as I look back at him. The smile breaks and he chuckles slightly. I feel the edge of my set lips twitching erratically with the discomfort of watching this man.

"Well then, would you like the long story or the short story?" he asks me idly, a pleasant smile finding its way again onto his handsome face. He drags a bountiful armchair away from the fireplace and sits across from me.

"Short story. Then explain what you want from me and why you're here." I answer him in the same tone. He leans back in the chair and makes himself comfortable. The chair groans under his ample body. I get up slowly so as to not raise any suspicion and trudge quickly to the massive fireplace to get the other armchair. I wretch at the deep cerulean color. So cheerful for this incidental occasion. I eye the stoker wearily. I could get my answers another way and leave. I grasp the tool in my hand and tuck it behind my back. "You will tell me where Cordella is, you nasty, deceiving vermin," I accuse heartily as I place the sharp stoker across his neck roughly from behind. A low chuckle comes from the man sitting with his back turned. Suddenly, a knife flashes into my view. I screech blatantly and bounce out of the way.

"You want to do this the hard way. All right. No answers for you," Peter says leisurely, a coy smile finding its way onto his face as he turns in his seat. I've dropped the stoker right into his lap with my reaction and apparently a lock of my hair as well. The knife he was concealing cut my long bangs to a point where they're just above my eyes. I can see. Another cosmic mockery. Peter stands casually to his feet, an amused expression plastered on his face. He unhooks the gun from his belt and loads it with a single round. I gradually place my hands on my head, unease enveloping me again. Peter ambles across the wooden floors to me, a broader smile on his face. "Put your arms down and come with me." There's no need to protest now, although I believe he's bringing me somewhere for a reason. He wants me alive, although he could shoot me somewhere non-vital like my arms or legs. More pain. I lower my arms carefully and walk towards him.

"Where is Cordella?" I ask him again, allowing a sardonic smile to slip onto my face. He frowns disapprovingly and the resemblance between him and Edward is uncanny. I can see his jawbone pressed up against his sallow skin tightly and that evil sort of hunger in his unfeeling eyes. The only difference in Peter's expression has a slightly more vain and desperate air to it, as if my compliance would ease his suffering greatly. Too bad my compliance won't remain accessible for much longer. I need to take my leave and find Cordella without another wound.

"You're lucky I enjoy conversing with you. You're an entertaining person despite your usual lack of speech. I suppose you'll get some answers after all, you ruddy bastard," He says in a joking tone, as if he didn't just offer to kill me for my own good only moments ago. I shake my head in disbelief, but repeat my question a few more times. This is all very disorienting.

"I'm taking you to Lizbeth. She's employed me to complete a few tasks for her, now that we're in the final stages."

I breathe in sharply, but show no other interest in the all too interesting subject. To my knowledge, Lizbeth has nothing to do with this seemingly connected web of scandals. Is Lizbeth a part of this? Peter pulls open the door and beckons for me to go before him. The hairs on the back of my neck stand up. He could shoot me in the back. I wouldn't have time to speak even a single last word if he decided on that course of action. I submit anyway and walk wearily before him. Once in the narrow, dimly lit hall, Peter begins to speak again. "Lizbeth trades in others' secrets. She started with a singular twisted rumor and climbed up the rope of deceit until she had at least one dealing with every noble. Her roots have entwined themselves around anyone and everyone, whether they feel the strain of her grip or not. She knows many of the interesting little deceptions Andria and all her denizens have concocted. She learned her first from you. She told me she heard you speak of it in a dream."

My interest is piqued. My stride becomes a bit unsteady. So I give her an opening.

"Is that so?" I encourage dryly. "Why does Lizbeth need me any longer then?"

"I'm getting to that," Peter explains harshly. His disembodied voice from behind me is beginning to grow more and more disconcerting, especially when passing by a shelf crowded with various animal organs. I'm nearly sure they're animal organs, although one heart looks to be quite human. The eerie atmosphere and peeling red wallpaper are reason enough to be scared without countless mutilated animals splayed across the walls. "She heard you speak of the former king's insanity which nobody knew about before. His psychotic episodes and such. She flung the secret out on a whim and gained more for it. Lizbeth is respected and known by nearly every noble. Only the immediate monarchy doesn't know of her exploits."

My pulse begins to fluctuate as I process the knowledge. Lizbeth, secret dealer. Awe hits me in the face like a bone-cracking blow.

"Lizbeth? But she's only a mere servant. If she is this great secret trader, what does she need me for exactly? Her goal is to take down the monarchy, correct?" I reply in a carefully controlled way. My emotions may be spiking, but I must heed my own warnings and remain calm until I find an out. If I keep him talking, maybe he'll reveal an edge of loose skin in which I can get underneath. This man seems as disturbed as I know myself to be. If I locate his point of most anxiety, I can disable him briefly. Peter guides me down a stairwell with rough commands every so often, breaking up his rambling speech.

"Alexander," Peter says in a soft voice. His tone feels like rain drops on my bare back. I shiver excitedly. The damp room has an air of impact within it. I feel as if something imperative is soon to be disclosed.

"Yes?" I ask when the sound of our footsteps begins to

become too loud in my mind. Peter hasn't spoken in a bit. My constant pressing is having an effect. Peter's breathing becomes slightly more rushed as he contemplates the decision he's about to make. Anticipation floods through my system like a tidal wave. I listen expectantly.

"Lizbeth is in love with you. I wouldn't even call it love, though. It's more of a certain infatuation or obsession. She's fixated on you. You're all she speaks of," Peter explains in an almost apprehensive tone. His words are almost slurred from fear. I've never known Lizbeth to be an intimidating person. For a second, I believe an actual bullet has struck me through the heart. Soon I realize a figurative bullet has. I stop in my tracks and so does Peter. Complete and utter silence consumes the air as I try to focus on his words.

Lizbeth. I have loved her forever, since I was ten years old. My feelings were only quelled because she left me as all others did. At least I expected her to leave me. An irregular piece of this grand puzzle finds its place in my mind. The constant feelings of foreboding when I awaken each morning, as if someone's been watching me without my permission. The flash of red hair when I regained consciousness in the infirmary and when I gave up consciousness by the exit of the infirmary. Lizbeth didn't leave me because she desired to. She left me because of these so-called *final stages* Peter's been mumbling nonsensically about. She was far too engaged with her secrets. Secrets involving me. The puzzle completes itself in my mind. The image displayed on the many pieces is horrific. Andria seared by flames. The buildings are all ashes blown away easily by the strong northern winds, not a trace left. All of this chaos is my doing.

"W-why is she trying to end Andrian monarchy then? I'm a part of it," I say in my most robust voice to hide my physical shaking. I already know the answer. The puzzle is complete. I push back my newfound haircut and turn to Peter recklessly, a look of pure bewilderment found on my face. Peter holds his gun erect as if I'm attempting to escape his icy clutches. I quickly place my hands on my head before inquiring in a more erratic tone despite my knowledge. "Why is she d-doing this, Peter? W-why?" I stammer. I know his next words by heart.

"You hate the monarchy Alexander, do you not? She wants you to be free from your royal duties so that you both can quote "ride off into the sunset" together. She wants your great love story to be blemishless and complete," Peter discloses in an interested tone, pistol pointed directly at my heart.

I rapidly remind myself of my previous plan. I need to leave here. I need to go, go away from all this despicable madness.

"How does she plan on doing that? Why are you a part of this?" I demand, anguish displayed clearly on my face. Lizbeth is behind my sudden misfortune. I always trusted her, but she's just as deranged as I am. She has the idea that the monarchy should be destroyed. I despise the monarchy just as she believes, but innocent denizens of Andria will be hurt in the hateful process of leveling every ounce of stability past rulers had worked for. I don't wish to see Andria broken and dilapidated like she was in her past days. I wish to see her standing tall and strong as she does now. I feel my lower lip trembling as I look directly into Peter's eyes. I see panic displayed within his frozen viewpoints. I see fear and forlornness fixed within him.

"I'm the only one who can claim the crown based on sovereignty," Peter replies in a solemn tone as he realizes the consequences of this conspiracy. Peter's come to destroy the legacy he was denied.

"You would be the heir if your father hadn't cast you out. The crown is meant to be yours, so you have every reason to claim it," I whisper more to myself as Lizbeth's contemptible connection with Peter materializes in my mind. "She wishes for you to destroy the monarchy once you're crowned king," I add incredulously. Peter nods ever so slowly, a single eyebrow raised as he appraises my obvious intellect. "What does she have over you that persuades you to commit such a ruinous deed?" I inquire, blackness consuming my thoughts. I feel my plan beginning to take hold.

"I hate the monarchy as well. My father abandoned me," Peter whispers, his cocked gun wavering in his single hand. The weapon lowers a bit and I feel my mouth opening slightly to allow a better airway. All of this pain, all of this turmoil on my account. The severity of my own existence is trying.

"Why would you even prefer to return to Andria after such an awful past?" I press further as the control of the conversation strays towards my shaking hands. I rein in my sorrow and shove onwards. I only need to escape and find Cordella.

"My children," Peter confides wildly, his eyes bulging in their sockets. "She murdered all but one of them."

My heart drops as the words fall out of his mouth. Lizbeth? A murderer. She killed those children to secure her own victory. She's void of a heart.

"S-she called in a favor with another secret dealer. They sent assassins to my homestead in Walsia and k-killed my children because I refused her first offer. They left one alive because she still needed leverage." The gun drops from his pale fingers and clatters to the floor. An echo of the loud noise bounces off the ground and walls of the corridor.

Peter falls to the floor himself as distinct memories flood his mind. The visions show through his eyes. He's probably trapped within a realm that displays only their cold, dead bodies. An inkling of empathy for the erratic man enters my senses and I approach him wearily. A blank expression plasters itself on his face as he slowly sinks further and further into the stygian pits of recollection and despair. I've visited that region many times before.

I kneel besides the empty man, trying to keep thoughts from overtaking my mind like they have Peter and focus on my objective ahead. I eye the metallic pistol a few aching feet away from us. Peter looks to be just as gone as a corpse, so I begin my attempt. I rub Peter's back calmly while reaching my arm painstakingly across the ground stressing inconspicuousness. My fingers curl around the foreign object uncomfortably. Peter is still lost within himself. I grimly congratulate myself for putting a man in a similar situation to my own in the same type of agony I suppress every day.

I've only ever held a gun once. I was in a distinguished meeting with my brother. He was twenty-two and I was twelve years of age. He became aggravated with a bald man at the opposite end of the table. I drowned out the yelling as best as I could as I sat there listlessly, but the sound of a gunshot brought me back to reality. My brother had drawn a small handgun much like this one and shot the man. There was a final, agonizing cry before the bald man fell lifelessly from his chair. I remember the quietness that followed the fall of his corpse and how servants rushed to remove the dead man from the venerable room. My brother set the gun on the table casually and returned to his business. I discretely took the gun off the table so that he would refrain from using it again, particularly on me. I learned that day that it's better to be the one with the gun locked in your fingers than to be the one with a bullet through your chest. I now assess this gun with an earnest expression on my face. Yes, this will assure my safety. There is only a single bullet contained within the gun and I'm afraid to check Peter's hollow body for more ammunition.

Suddenly, Peter's hand moves slightly and an inaudible mutter escapes his lips. His eyes roll towards me and his pupils dilate as he notices the gun grasped in my fingers. Fear strikes me as he awakens. I jump to my feet and point the gun directly at him, no intention to shoot. I've never shot a gun in my life, even when my brother employed an instructor. I hid for an entire week to avoid such a violent practice. I didn't enjoy weapons or brutality when I was a young boy. It reminded me of what happened to my mother. I suppressed that memory and successfully forgot it over time until a few months ago when it began plaguing me again.

"Stop, Alexander. Please! She'll take my only daughter and my wife if I don't bring you to her." Pain floods my chest as the words of beseeching escape his lips. I reply as calmly as I can muster despite my situation.

"I apologize Peter. You don't deserve such pain on my account. But the world isn't fair, Peter, and I made a promise to myself that I would honor my mother's memory. She would want it this way." I slowly back away from Peter. He calls out desperately a few more times, but I decide to ignore the hapless pleas.

I begin to sprint as soon as I round the corner. I run as fast and as far as I possibly can. Memories and recollections of past times blur in my mind as the looming duty ahead of me makes itself more prominent. My notebook weighs heavily in my pocket, but I grasp a gun in my hand instead of a pen. I begin speaking words in a hushed tone to myself as I dash down unknown corridors and dreary pathways.

"I trusted you, you butterfly. You made my heart sing, but now you make my want to cry. Cry out against the night, cry and escape to my personal starlight. That which you have taken from me, surely gone forever, never to see. You've taken her from me, you butterfly. I only wish you'd fly away from me," I mutter frantically to myself as I escape alone into the frigid Andrian night, not a jacket to cloth me or a lover to hold my hand. Darkness encroaches on me as the ice freezes my senses. "Surely gone forever, never to see," I repeat in a ghost of a whisper.

CHAPTER 13

I was Alexander's age when my father decided I was illegitimate and cast me out of the monarchy. I don't even remember how old Edward was when that horrid event occurred. I do remember the yelling and screaming as if it were only yesterday. The strident words still plague my mind to this day. Those harmful, destructive words. He used to tell me things: I'm not man enough. Or that the world is an awful place and it's very unlucky for me to be alive within it at this time. And it's true, this world is an awful place and I'm not man enough to forget that. My father was deranged, but he certainly did tell the truth. He was different from all others in the kingdom of Andria, at least at the end of my time with him he was. He no longer had a sense for the image he needed to protect. He no longer cared whether it was truth or lie that came from his lips. He was genuine, authentic. Genuinely evil and authentically cruel.

I was sent out of the gates with the clothes on my back, a few days' worth of food, and my favorite wooden practice sword. The king was gracious enough to allow me to bring my prized possession, which naturally was the sword. I clung to it for protection. He explained personally that I would be given five days to leave Andria once and for all and I would never be allowed back. If I wasn't gone by that time, he would kill me by hanging me at the public gallows. In fact, every denizen was told to end my life if I was seen anywhere within the kingdom. I remember considering it a grace if I was found by one of Andria's people. They would end me in a less painful, shameful way.

I was scrawny for my age, even more so than Alexander. I was equally frightened. I didn't understand why exactly my beloved father wished me either gone or dead. I didn't know the answers for a while. Answers are inevitable, though. Over time, I pieced together the story from smidgets of gossip. My mother had an affair with a Walsian man close to the time of my conception. She also had been with my father during that time, so nobody knew my real parentage. It was discovered in later times, after my father's death, that I was actually his child. Even then I was not invited back to the monarchy. My father could not fathom even the slightest hint of impure blood running through my veins. He even told me that himself. He knew full well I was his son and he cast me out anyway just for some sort of petty revenge. He was a scornful man and I'm glad the world has been rid of him.

I watched my father go insane little by little. His mind slipped away so gradually that some days it seemed to be normal. My mother knew what was going on as well. She gave me fleeting glances of consternation whenever I was in close proximity with him. I never understood the anguish. He was my dear father. The good he'd placed in my life outweighed the bad and I moved forward with that notion. The court and nobles knew of his growing madness as well, but they concealed this secret deftly. It was all to protect Andria's "shining image" as Alexander puts it in his many journals. Not even a drop of that secret was exposed to the general population. It may be disclosed to Hyvern or, God forbid, Walsia. Walsia, sworn enemy of Andria for so many decades.

I'm forever thankful to God that Alexander wasn't born at the time of my leaving. The act of what seemed to be abandonment would add more brokenness to a life already riddled with similar events. Edward was most definitely alive though. I remember what leaving him was like exactly. I resent the fact that I do. He wouldn't let go of my sleeve when I told him about my absence. His face, still graced with childish features at the time, twisted into that famous scowl he still displays today. Great big tears pooled in his eyes although he tried to restrain them, just as Father had taught us. I pulled him close to me and wrapped my arms around him, trying to console the soon to be sullen child. I allowed my tears to fall that day, but I cried in silence. Edward wouldn't let go once he saw my tears. I was always generally jubilant. I never once cried in front of Edward before that day. Precious time was wasting as he held onto me. I needed to leave and never come back. So I did a regrettable thing. I told him that he had misunderstood and I was only leaving him for a short time. Edward was pacified immediately. He simply nodded and smiled. His grin made my heart sink to my stomach. He then explained that he was off to go play in one of Royal Andria's many gardens. He would come back from playing to find that his brother had actually left him for good.

I still had to leave though, despite all that sadness. I still have to survive. There's no excuse for my death. I told myself those things over and over again as I left the gates. And again as my shoes began to wear out ten miles into the interminable trek. Shoes made by a royal cobbler are designed to be handsome and appropriate for polite dancing. The footwear was not durable, not in the slightest way. The laces came undone quite often, so I soon just pulled them out. The airy leather began to wear away rapidly and holes began to form. My toes nearly froze off because of the intense Andrian freeze. I told myself those phrases again as I huddled around a stranger's fire with a pack of older boys who didn't have names. *I still had to leave. I still have to survive. There is no excuse for me dying.* I should've known then that those setbacks were only just the beginning of the arduous journey ahead. I still use those phrases every single day to remind myself to be the most resilient cockroach that's ever prowled a filth-covered wall. That wall being Andria, of course.

I persevered, even when I almost bled to death on the bank of a dried-out old river during my journeys through Hyvern. An old fool decided that he was entitled to take my belongings from me by force. I definitely put up a nasty fight. I caught the man in the eye once or twice, but in the end my efforts were of no avail. That dirty man stole all my belongings. He took a threadbare coat I'd bought, my rations and supplies, and my old wooden practice sword. I stumbled to my feet to try and retrieve my inventory, but the man whipped around and stabbed me with the blade. The sword's wooden edge was dull, so it took him quite a long time to break my skin. Many of my ribs were broken in the process and I endured a great deal of unnecessary pain. I took a substantial beating previous to the stabbing, so I was far too weak to so much as call out or struggle. I just had to lay there trying not to lose consciousness from the tremendous strain. His hollow black eyes darted around as he committed the crime. He just seemed so... So empty. I didn't understand how one could become so empty. I understand that all too well now. *I still had to leave. I still have to survive. There is no excuse for me dying.* I repeated that again and again to myself as I stood painstakingly to my feet. I had to squint my way under the shallow Hyvernian sun because both of my arms were pressed over my wound as to keep myself from fading away. It was one of the most excruciating experiences I've had in my life, only second to the death of my children. I've endured many other unspeakable things during my travels, but the first wound was most definitely the worst. I found it amusing that Alexander had been ashamed of a singular scar when I could show him so many of my own. It seemed as if I was cursed to walk the Earth forever as the biblical figure Cane did as punishment for ending his brother Abel's life. The only difference from us is a few hundred thousand years and the fact that I am innocent of any crimes worthy of such an exile.

At last I found some peace when my journeys extended over

the Hyvernian border to Walsia. I was ready for the silken sun and mild breezes of Walsia by then, for I'd suffered the harsh, biting cold of Andria and the dewy darkness of Hyvern. I celebrated my twentieth birthday underneath a tree with a caravan of individuals I had never met. I became accustomed to this nomadic lifestyle and learned to deal with thievery and criminals. Every night I would fall asleep in some sort of temporary shelter put up by ugly, indistinguishable people. Those living in Royal Andria seemed just so divine compared to these people. I even groveled to be in the company of these commoners. I was humbled and shaped by these people and owe them my gratitude.

A fortuitous feeling filled my chest when I crossed the border to Walsia. I felt as if an impending miracle was to occur and that excited me. I didn't have a passport, nor any identification. For all anyone cared, I wasn't even a real person. I wouldn't be able to cross over to Walsia legally, so I did so illegally. I'm not guilty about this deed, it was a matter of finding tranquility. I only managed to enter Hyvern because the king of Andria sent ahead a letter of approval. My father wanted to erase my existence so badly that he created a way for him to do so and pushed me towards it. Imagine that.

It was the quietest part of midnight when I crossed over. I wasn't frightened, for this part of the Walsian border was only protected by a measly fence and not by the border guard. There was still a smidge of apprehension in my demeanor. I didn't enjoy getting hurt. Apprehension has an amusing way of growing. Apprehension spreads to your fingertips from your heart. Apprehension's darkness controls your actions and manipulates the way you view the world. For example, every rustle of a branch was an ambush. Every lone bird call was a soldier's grim song. Those figments would end my life if they were real, not apprehension planting its devious seeds. No matter how many times I repeated my phrases, I couldn't shake the feeling that I was being watched by something, someone. *I still had to leave though. I still have to survive. There is no excuse for me dying.* The vast jungles of Walsia felt impenetrable and dark at that moment.

The fence sat right before me. It was made of rotting oak wood, part of it hanging just over a narrow river marking the border. Frogs croaked mindlessly in the cool shade of the night. Moss strangled every part of the feeble structure. The plant life sucked all the purpose out of the fence. I suppose that years before my crossing, it might have actually served its purpose and kept invaders from illegally entering Walsia. In the time since the last maintenance, the fence had languished and aged significantly.

I took a step towards the dilapidated fence, but just as soon as I had, I heard a voice. A small, quiet voice. A voice I would learn to love.

"You shouldn't be here," the soft voice called from across the divide. My attention snapped to a girl leaning against a monstrous jungle tree. Her wavy brown hair fell all the way down to the small of her back. Her slight frame was draped in an ivory sleeping gown with a silvery tint to it. The dress hinted of transparency under the shrouded moon. Her feet were bare despite the bracken-covered ground and the numerous bugs.

"Why not?" I responded playfully, despite my bewilderment. A smooth moonbeam fell upon her and illuminated her reddish-brown hair and chocolate darkness of her cylindrical eyes. I could see her thin eyebrows dip down slightly as I spoke those words. I couldn't read her emotions though, for half of her face was concealed by the darkness of deep night in the fen.

"Because you could die," she answered in a dead tone, oblivious to my peculiar jesting. One of her crystal-like eyes closed in a wink before they crinkled at the ends in what I assumed to be a smile. A somewhat panicked shiver crawled its way down my spine, but I felt myself sauntering confidently closer to the edge of the quietly flowing river as if drawn by a siren's song. It appeared as if she could be a siren. She certainly had the winsomeness of a mythical creature.

"If that is so, then you shouldn't be here either," I retorted, trying to match her eerie tone. I found that my voice had an odd sort of protectiveness about it. I hadn't heard that tone in my own voice in many years. I had taught myself not to care. The beam of moonlight penetrating the dense canopy above us moved down towards her lips the closer I got. She was definitely smiling. Her smile had a sort of extraordinary intention in it. I could see her gapped teeth. Her warm smile was infectious enough to influence me to break into my own crooked smile. The divide between our respective sides didn't seem so large after the smiling and the brief banter. A foolhardy will took control of my body and I leapt over the treacherous stream with little fear despite the sounds of the rushing water below me, certain to break my fall in a lethal manner if I should fail.

By some act of God, I landed firmly, planting my feet on a large river rock with weathered edges. I could have quite feasibly slipped off the surface and into the abyss, but I was cautious as I moved to dry land. She appraised me with an unreadable expression. I felt an air of curiosity emanating from her slight form. Her eyebrows creased together as she perceived my fair hair and blue eyes. I in return observed her. A sudden breeze swept through the fen deafeningly and her hair blew backwards. Her hair was styled with bangs, but in no manner were her features childish. She had a certain poise to her eyes and chin that I couldn't match even at my obviously senior age. Her dark cherry-colored eyes bounced to the river behind us as if my silence was boring her. Youthful agitation flooded my senses.

"Why do you wish to cross?" she asked me tentatively in Walsian. I picked up a conversational style of Walsian when traveling with a few defectors. The strange look vanished from her mild features as I mustered the reserves of my mind to remember how to properly phrase in Walsian. I found the right words, but I didn't know if she was a friend or a foe. Well, I couldn't exactly tell her the truth. She could inform the Walsian government of my bearings and I would be in deep waters. While not nearly as centralized as the Andrian government, Walsia was more proficient at inflicting punishment on all who committed transgressions. I planned to settle here, so it wouldn't be the best idea to be caught. I needed to find tranquility and peace somewhere. My body couldn't handle the strain of journeying across Hyvern and back one more time. My mind couldn't handle the disappointment of being turned away and treated like a pariah again, either.

"My tale is a very long one. It's mine and mine alone. Could you turn a blind eye to a weary traveler just one?" I inquired in an equally gracious and desperate tone. I hoped she would oblige and allow me to pass through the night. I shouldn't have engaged with a strange individual during the most starless time of night. The reclusive response didn't daunt the girl. The blank look of questioning remained plastered upon her face.

"All I want to know is why a beautiful Andrian such as yourself would wish to enter a poverty-ridden country. The conditions are becoming even worse than Hyvern's at this point. It was not wise of you to travel here. You will not gain asylum when all but royal Walsians search for it," the girl snapped furiously, a resentful blush spreading across her graceful features. My mouth opened slightly before anger of my own filled me.

"I've been cast out from Andria and all who I've met in Hyvern have only caused me trouble in one way or another. I chose to seek refuge in the third great nation because the other two only left me beaten and battered. You can't possibly be so ignorant as to believe Hyvern and Andria don't have issues similar to your own," I chide recklessly, nearly revealing my past. The girl stared into my eyes contemplatively, a look of pure wonderment on her face. After her pondering was done, she simply nodded and prepared to speak again.

"I have another inquiry," the inquisitive girl stated placidly. I nodded acceptingly.

"What's your name, Andrian traveler?" she asked in the same calm tone she used previously. Another flare of rage filled me. She had requested personal information after only a few words exchanged. I learned during my endless travel never to ask such a thing or oblige to such an ask. I decided it was best to be polite in this new, foreign country.

"My name is Peter." Regretful thoughts of my full Christian name entered my mind and I chose not to introduce myself in that manner. Her eyes crinkled at the corners again as a small smile graced her lips. "What's your name?"

"My name is Euphemia," she replied, her smile only growing.

"That's an odd name," I noted idly, a small smile slipping onto my face.

"My father says it reminds him of the northern lights. I couldn't say the same about your name as well. Peter. It's so plain." A small chuckle escaped her lips after her response. All I could contemplate was the sound of her name and how easily it would flow from my mouth. It had a luminous elegance that I couldn't describe at the time. *Euphemia, Euphemia, Euphemia.* Beautiful, beautiful, beautiful. I saw something else within her as well. I saw an opportunity for happiness and the peace I had so desperately craved for a boundless number of years.

Nearly two years thereafter, Euphemia stood at an altar with me dressed in the second loveliest white gown I'd ever seen her in. The first being her pale nightgown the first night we had met. I traveled to Walsia to find elation and that's exactly what I'd done, at least for a decade or so I had.

Euphemia offered me a place to stay for the night when we first met. After the heavy silence following our introductions, she warned me of the Walsian wildlands. The jungles were ridden with thieves and bandits as well as perilous creatures. This drew up numerous questions, half of which I refrained from asking. We did have quite the conversation though which led to the invitation. I accepted eagerly. In all my travels, I was never once offered a place to stay. I always had to grovel. My reputation preceded me in Hyvern. That was one of the many reasons I left that half righteous nation.

I became further acquainted with Euphemia and her father later that night, but not her mother. She was taken by an unknown character at midnight two years previous to my arrival. He was a rather short man with a bald head. He had a braided jet-black beard that sunk all the way down to the collar of his shirt. He looked up at me and shook my sweaty hand firmly with both of his. His dark eyes seemed to bore into my soul as if warning me of something. I hadn't the slightest clue why he acted in such a manner, but years later he explained that he knew Euphemia would someday marry me.

We collectively decided I would help Ivan, Euphemia's father, with some repairs to an old barn that housed a couple of old cows and an even older mutt. The periodic rain swept swiftly through the roof, chilling the animals and soaking the fodder. I was pleased for a place to stay for a few extra days. After a few weeks of continued extensions of this offer, I was extended a permanent invitation to work. I accepted immediately and completed arduous day after arduous day, growing closer to Euphemia each day.

I never did learn why Euphemia was out in the wildlands that night. All I can offer is that I'm grateful for her being there. My life would've been much more dismal if I wasn't given that opportunity to stay with her. Those years I was able to spend with her were the best, most golden years of my life. I didn't realize that fact while I was living them. If I had known, I would've cherished every second tenfold. I would've dealt with each and every unnecessary matter. I would have endeavored to do anything and everything.

Our wedding was beautiful, at least that's what I was told. All I can remember from that day is the sensation of holding Euphemia in my arms, finally at peace after all the wretched suffering that was thrown at me. I cradle that moment deep in my heart and go to it in times when I feel the most turmoil. I have a faded picture of glistening tears sliding down her cheeks as we proclaimed our vows in that tiny church. I'm not a romantic, in fact most of my emotions are difficult to trigger. I can admit that I found my person. My "soulmate," as they say. After being alone for so very long, it was an immense relief for both of us. Those tears streaming freely down her soft cheeks were not tears of joy, but tears of reprieve. Don't misunderstand me, joy came in plentiful amounts during the length of that day. I've never seen Euphemia smile so brightly. Her gapped teeth were on full display for all of our neighbors to see.

All good things come to an end. That is inescapable. Every secret will be uncovered, every monarchy leveled. Every civilization will fall and every denizen will no longer bear such a title. Every mountain will sink back to the Earth's fiery depths and every desert will become a vast, blue ocean once again. That ocean will dry up and make room for another desert. It's inescapable. I learned that cold fact in a difficult manner. It started when my eyebrow began to twitch and ended with a threatening letter sent by a well-known secret dealer. Insanity is in my blood. It's a cruel inheritance passed down from my father before me. I watched what that madness made him become and denied that the same fate could ever befall me. My oddness could've stayed just a lazy twitch of an eyebrow, but it was provoked and it festered, just as my father's oddness did when stress laced itself into his day-to-day scenarios. Euphemia left me after my growing madness and the death of the children became all too much for her to handle. I will never see my Euphemia, my soulmate ever again, all because of a telltale letter. I will never see my one surviving daughter again either. She left with her in the night.

I couldn't create bounds on the love I felt for my children. They were half of me and half of the woman I love. I disliked my half more, if I may be terribly honest. I would do anything for them, give up my life if I was given an ultimatum. I always stood by that idea until I betrayed it with my own ignorance. I no longer had the option to do anything at all. I ripped the gilded option from my own hands.

Faye is my favorite. Anyone would look back on an event such as that as lucky, a blessing even. The fact that she lived instead of her brothers feels like a mockery now, as if an inaudible voice is laughing uproariously at me. I loathe myself even more because I could've sustained my ties with her and I chose not to. I lost my daughter to a tangled web that took the others from me when I could've kept her with me. I lost Euphemia to that web as well, but for a reason unknown to me, I'm not as ashamed about that fact. I loved Faye more than all the stars in the sky.

Faye was seven years of age when it happened. She was only seven years old when she had to see her brothers die. A letter arrived for us. It was brought to us by one of our neighbors who was told it arrived from Andria of all places. The name struck fear in the hearts of many in Walsia because of the imminent conflicts, but talk of Andria daunted me more than all others. I'm assured of that fact. I had experienced such treachery, such mistreatment there that even the slightest hint of that supposed "golden nation" trifled with me. Talk of Andria influenced long buried memories to dig themselves up.

I found the bravery to unfurl the letter after a shot of liquid courage the night after its arrival. The fire was burning low atop the hearth and Euphemia had a headache. She therefore retired early and allowed me some time to myself. I ripped the seal with my bare hands, not bothering to look up the meaning of the symbol imprinted upon the wax. The letter was made up of a beautiful, handwritten script scrawled on old, yellowing parchment. The intricate phrases impressed me when I first glanced at it, but over time I would come to despise those words with the blackest depths of my soul. I would obsessively dissect the meaning of each wordage after their deaths.

Dear Peter of Walsia,
I will begin by stating a fact. You will have many questions after you've completed this letter. All of those questions will most certainly be answered, but all in due time. I apologize for disrupting the seemingly superb Walsian life you've crafted for yourself. Your and your family's wellbeing won't be impacted any further if you choose the recommended option of cooperating with my interests. In fact, my interests are your interests, for we share a common stance on the Andrian monarchy I'm certain after all your tragic encounters.

Not all can be revealed on a sheet of parchment, but I shall attempt to display all the information you need to complete your task. The most prominent bit of knowledge I wish to enlighten you with is that you have another brother. He is formally your half-brother because of his Walsian illegitimacy, but he also dislikes the monarchy greatly despite being second prince. I believe we are all connected on that front. His name is Alexander Aerabella Aaron Mattias, although he prefers Alexander. I am hopelessly in love with him and I'm certain he feels similarly. I appear as a mere servant in Royal Andria, so I am not allowed to be with him. For that reason and that reason alone I decided to trade in the secrets of Andrian nobles and climb to a position of power from which I can level the Andrian monarchy. I will then be able to ride off into the sunset with Alexander and our great love story will be completed. You are going to assist me with that because my plans involve your involvement. That is, if you wish to keep your same quality of living.

My plan is very straightforward and my sources tell me that you value simplicity above all things. I agree with you. You are to travel across Hyvern to Andria. I have sent ahead to the border guard and told them that you would be arriving soon. You will then be escorted by carriage to Royal Andria and brought through the gates by a few comrades of mine. Their fellows in my trade. The climax of my plan is for you to challenge Edward Aerabella Angel Paul for his position as king of Andria and win. You will then receive further instruction on how to feasibly destroy the monarchy from within.

I understand that you have a beautiful family. I wish for you to understand something as well. I have bitten and killed for my blessed bearings and another death wouldn't be quite so important to me. I have connections all over the trinity of great nations and I will not fail to send them after you and your family. But if you so kindly comply with my generous offer, you have nothing to be worried about. Everyone will remain happy and healthy just as they've always been and you will be better for it, having gained a massive portion of Royal Andria's monetary reserves. I hope I've made myself understood in every way I possibly can and I expect your arrival four months from the date of this letter's arrival. My great love story will be completed, mark my words.

Best wishes, Lizbeth of Hyvern

That letter shook violently in my hands as I processed each and every distressing word. This looming dealer of secrets and seemingly many other black market items wanted me to challenge my beloved brother Edward who I had left all those years ago. I had another brother named Alexander whom Lizbeth, dealer of danger, was madly in love with. This treacherous character would corrupt an entire nation if it meant she could complete her great love story. I hastily counted on my fingers. If this Alexander figure really existed, he couldn't be more than fifteen or sixteen years of age, hardly the age to wed. A deranged teenager had gained enough power to dismantle an entire monarchy for her first love. I let that though sink in as I poured myself yet another glass of liquid courage. I couldn't take it. My heart felt as if it were about to explode and my mind soared with sordid thoughts. I cleansed my mind of such impurity and returned to my alcohol solemnly.

I crumpled the letter down to the softest of pulp and then burned it among the embers of the nearly dead fire. A lone tear slipped down my cheek as swirls and rushes of unwanted recollections passed through my consciousness. I strolled to bed numbly and lay awake until the witching hour. It was only then that I sunk into a fitful sleep. When I awoke that next morning, I decided it was best to rid my mind of that letter and simply neglect the fact that it ever even existed in the first place. I instead focused on my family. I watched idly as they smiled and laughed as they always did when in reality they were in harm's way.

The time she allowed passed swiftly. Not once did my mind recall the letter or any of the secrets disclosed amongst the pages. I look back now and curse myself for standing still as the world walked by me. My subconsciousness convinced me it was a figment of my warped mind, a dream of some sort. I found out all too late that I was all too wrong. In fact, the malicious deed was already done by the time I even realized it was the anniversary of the date I had received that hateful letter. I remember the sensation of my heart dropping to my stomach with horror as I discovered my grave misdemeanor.

Liam, Gavin and Noah decided they wanted to go play in a small meadow beside the barn I had worked on so many years before with Euphemia's now-deceased father. The children had done it countless times before so I assumed it would be just as harmless as it always was. Faye didn't want to. She told me that the trees had been looking at her and that she didn't wish to go back there again because of that seemingly irrational fear. I laughed it off and allowed her to stay with Euphemia and me. That childish fear saved Faye's precious life.

The boys did not arrive home for dinner as we had instructed. They didn't arrive the next hour, nor the next. That's when I remembered. I locked all the doors and windows and restrained Euphemia from going out to search. She protested greatly. I wouldn't relent though, for I knew she would most certainly be killed if she so much as stepped out the door. The children didn't return the next morning, nor the morning after that one. The next day, however, Euphemia and I received the dreadful news that only I had expected. Our children's bodies were found bloodied and beaten on the main road. The tortured expressions on their faces hinted of an indubitably unpleasant end.

A letter was left with their bodies. Euphemia read the godforsaken note before I found it. The strangled expression on her tear-stained face is permanently scarred in my mind. She didn't understand why this had happened, she only understood that it was my doing and my fault that our children had perished. The world felt as if it were sinking into the abyss as I stared into her eyes. I no longer saw love within them. They were cold and empty, obvious hatred displayed on her features. She screamed and yelled for me to leave her immediately. And so I did. I grabbed my bag and returned to the road, cast out yet again. The cycle repeated itself. I left Faye just as I did my brother.

I stained the letter with my own tears as I read it again and again. My footsteps disappeared as I sunk further and further into the shattering text. Another furious threat from the girl who had ruined the tranquil life I had built from nothing.

She has ruined me. Now I must oblige and follow her every command. She'll ravage the remnants of that broken life I once had if I don't follow her ever command. Now Faye and Euphemia will most certainly die, for I've failed to capture Alexander. I pull the crumpled piece of parchment from my coat pocket containing the same letter Lizbeth left on the bodies of my children.

Dear Peter of Walsia,

This will remain short and concise. I'm so terribly sorry that I had previously written a letter that only displayed respect and partnership to one who I neither respect nor wish to be partners with. I will make myself painfully clear this time. Almost as painful as the deaths of your children. You are a dog and disobedient dogs get kicked. I own you because I decided I wanted to. Now, do a few tricks and lick my shoes and maybe you will gain an inkling of the respect I would've given you if you had originally followed my orders. Get your rear, which I own, over here in four months. If not, Euphemia and Faye will die in a more painful, shameful manner than Liam, Gavin, and Noah.

Best wishes, Lizbeth of Hyvern

CHAPTER 14

I lost myself to the swirling snow moments after fleeing. The storm had stirred yet again and I was without my coat. It wouldn't have done me much good in the long run, but I could've lasted longer outdoors if I'd had it. Each individual snowflake wasn't as unique as I always thought them to be. I had no time for contemplations such as that, nor the space in my mind.

Thoughts of Cordella were all I could focus on. I had to save her. There was no other choice. Her death was certain if caught in either of two situations. If my brother discovered our unlawful relations, he would have Cordella silenced in the same manner our mother was. He would decorate a wall with her severed head as if it were some gruesome victory prize. I gritted my teeth against the cold and sprinted forward, fueled by fear. The thought of her head dangling from a wall balanced itself precariously on the precipice of my sanity. Another death because of my existence. A frigid drop of sweat rolled lethargically down my neck. Over time I felt the sweat slowly solidify into ice crystals. The feeling was unnerving to say the least.

Cordella could also perish if she was found in the clutches of Lizbeth. Peter hinted that Forsythe had taken her. Forsythe could either be a cog in Lizbeth's plot, or an agent employed by my brother to investigate whatever suspicious behavior Cordella and I had been displaying. I placed my chip on Lizbeth, for nearly everyone I'd spoken to recently seems to have ties with her in one way or another, whether they knew it or not. I was told that Lizbeth was plotting the destruction of Andria because of her immense yearning for me. That concept is rather hard for me to believe. The thought was also unnerving, even more so.

I'd read great epics based on the obsession and agony that follows love. In those twisted tales, individuals would do anything for the one they love. They would end lives or end their own in a violent manner. I tried to picture Lizbeth harming someone, anyone, but I just couldn't. I had never known Lizbeth to be anything less than passive.

The flurries of snow began to fall more thickly and the temperature dropped massively. A chill of forewarning settled over my body. I felt a tingling sensation spread across my thinly-veiled arms. After the tingling subsided, I felt nothing at all, almost as if my arms had disappeared. My arms had gone numb, but I still ran. I had the lurking feeling that Peter was following me. The reassuring outline of the gun along my belt gave me a meager sense of security, but I couldn't move my arms very much. The sensation in my legs failed after the tingling feeling in my arms was banished. The numbness was spreading. My pace slowed to the swiftest lope I could muster with my current range of motion.

I relied heavily on my own fear to keep propelling me forward. I couldn't feel the cool metal of the gun against my leg any longer. My person felt violently warm as if fire was encompassing my entire body. My vision grew foggy as the raging storm progressed around me. I couldn't see anything five feet before me, only a few desolate mounds of rock. Tenacious winds swept dangerously close. If I were caught within one of those gales of ice and snow, I certainly wouldn't make it out alive. I was caught in a vestigial moment of beauty before my body failed. Ice and snow spiraled around my stumbling form. The crystals of frozen water seemed to swirl slowly so that I could see each and every nuance, each unimaginable color captured within the ice. My knees gave out underneath me and

I began to crawl along the ground, attempting to quell my growing lack of consciousness.

Strange images began to materialize in my vision, as if it were one of my horrible dreams. A woman without a face, a child without a head, and a black mutt holding the child's severed head between his jaws. The snow curled around my face as a small building came into view. I thought it was another one of my delusions until I ran right into it with a deafening thump. The noise sounded echoey as if created inside of a tunnel of sorts. I knew that it was a side effect of my algidity. I rolled onto my back in a listless manner. A warm lethargy fell over me as I sunk into the snow. I couldn't feel my face any longer. My consciousness betrayed me and a comfortable silence blanketed my mind. The last thing that entered my plain of vision was the familiar face of a man.

Lizbeth's Perspective

Forsythe delivered the queen safely to me, although I wouldn't have minded much if he had hurt her slightly. He's a loyal servant and I'm impressed by his exceptional sacrifice. He betrayed his own nation in order to serve me. That kind of commitment tickles my heart strings. Of course, I will have to kill him for not securing Alexander's safety with Peter. The pair were supposed to arrive at the same time. I'm disappointed by that. Alexander's safety is of the utmost importance. Forsythe reclines stiffly in a chair opposing my own. I leer at him, expecting him to run off screaming. He stares right back into my eyes as if the idea of death doesn't daunt him as it would others. His eyes are like inky black pools. They're almost frightening if gazed on for an extended period of time. Bravery is a good quality. It makes for an honorable death. He won't call out when the silver-tipped axe falls.

Cordella sits on Forsythe's right side. The contrast between my opinion of their two souls is so great that my vision grows weary whenever my eyes happen to fall on her. Every ounce of my consciousness whispers and tickles my ears. *Take your knife and cut her skin.* Alexander made her his own. She made Alexander hers when he is mine and mine alone. She took him from me. I so desperately desire to end her like I do all my other insufferable controversies, but Alexander has a reason to pursue me if I hold this single-use wretch captive. I'll end her once he arrives without harm. I feel my lips curve downward as my vision falls upon her again.

Another figure I'm furious at is Peter. He enabled Alexander's escape with his own lack of emotional strength. And to think, I could've had Alexander where I wished him to be. I've taken a small, secluded section of the palace to use as my headquarters recently and he would have had asylum here. Hatred towards him is growing immensely, so much so that his own brother made an attempt on his life. I begrudgingly have Cordella to acknowledge for the preservation of Alexander's life. She spewed biblical phrases and all present were convinced to spare Alexander. The saving of his life doesn't make up for an inkling of all she's done to make an enemy of me, though.

"Who are you?" Cordella demands relentlessly. She's been asking the same question for an hour at least. Her persistence is inspiring. A glistening tear rolls down her cheek. I cock my head allowing a graceful smile to slip onto my lips. If she asks that tedious question one more time, I may be forced to tell her. I pour myself another glass of white wine and take a delicate sip. Forsythe's eyes narrow slightly as I pour him another as well. Cordella squirms against her restraints as I appraise her. I still can't discern her appeal. She has rather nice facial features, her eyes in particular, but I've never known Alexander to be attracted to physical beauty. He's always been more taken with the allure of impactful thoughts and words. Pleasure was always a second choice for him. This woman seems to be like the first pastry off the dish. Everyone touches her but nobody truly wants her. She becomes crummy and old after some time and gets thrown out by a servant with a wrinkled nose. Alexander is not the touching kind. "Please, I implore. Who are you?" she repeats, her voice breaking at the end. Forsythe turns his neck slowly to look at her. He has yet to take a sip of his wine. It may be the last he ever drinks.

"Would you like me to gag her?" Forsythe inquires in Hyvernian, to frighten her less. I shake my head and lick my teeth indecisively before speaking. The candles flicker as her horror thrives. Her perfect lips droop and waver childishly. Her eyes grow larger like weeds amongst new spring grass. The windowless room becomes more cramped as her dramatic reaction becomes a vacuum for all the oxygen. This woman is so burdensome. How could anyone stand her presence?

"Cordella. Picture the most awful thing you've ever seen and describe it to me while you still have the ability to describe ideas with that *pretty pretty* tongue of yours," I whisper in a threatening tone. Her breath catches in her throat as she attempts to form proper words. I indulge myself with another sip of wine.

"I-I was having dinner with my mother and father in royal Walsia. We were dining on the finest o-of roast duck. It was marinated in a deep, red wine. As I lifted my first bite to my mouth, m-my father explained that it wasn't wine that the dead duck m-marinated in. I-it was the blood of the servant who prepared it," she stammers, more tears flowing from her eyes as she looks heavenwards. I've acquired the knowledge that this woman always cries. Her behavior is so tiresome and predictable. Tears flow from her alluring eyes whenever she finds herself in even the slightest of predicaments. I nod my head deliberately, relishing the pure panic displayed on her features. I take another sip of the wine mindlessly before speaking again.

"Now, let me explain something to you. I am Lizbeth, the one who cooks with the blood of others and enjoys the taste. I am a dealer of secrets and other less innocuous ideas. And most importantly, I am the one with whom you have made an enemy by taking what was mine. I will not hesitate to end you because of this reason," I say harshly, slamming my fist against the table, spilling Forsythe's and my own wine. The liquid runs through the cracks of the table languidly before spilling over the edges. Cordella recoils, anguish overtaking her feasibly as many men have. I release my tight braid nonchalantly, allowing my fiery red hair to fall down my back in a less restrained manner. "So don't cross me," I add simply, boring deep into her opalescent eyes.

Alexander's Perspective

A croaking cry escapes my throat as I lean forward. My breathing calms after a short time and I wipe the remnants of another agonizing dream from my eyes. It was again related to my brother and figures without faces under his authority. I force myself into passiveness as I begin to hear muffled sounds. There's the slow battering of a blizzard-like storm against the building. Faint, hesitant footsteps, a slight voice. Dull light hits my eyes suddenly.

"You're awake," a disembodied voice states matter-of-factly. I feel like saying *you're jesting* in response, but my vocal cords ache with the thought of speaking. I feel a heavy blanket wrapped around my legs. My vision clears fully and I consider my surroundings. I'm sitting atop a small, twin sized bed made of what looks to be cherry wood. This bed is not mine. A spright of fear rings in my ears. The blanket is an odd plaid pattern. It looks to be crafted from an alternative material to cloth. What person in their right mind would use blue for a plaid set? "I heard a loud disturbance last night and I braved the storm to uncover the cause. That was you. You're very lucky I found you. You owe me your life," the voice spoke again, bringing a rather large migraine along with the explanation. I groan in my most appreciative tone, hoping that the man will know how much gratitude I feel in this moment. My neck feels all too sore as I turn it to examine the remaining part of the room and the man who I allegedly owe my life to.

Recognition flashes across my recollection as I stare at the man. His dark hair hangs a bit lower from when I last saw him and his bald spot has miraculously closed over, almost as if the strenuousness of his life has decreased inordinately. His eyes are still the same shade of caramel brown that they were formerly, save a miniscule reservoir of that ineffable dusk everyone gains over time. His suit is less tailored and he's let a small beard grow atop his chin. Andrian blues and reds look out of place on his irrevocably Walsian stature. A grim smile finds its way onto his lips.

"I've met you somewhere," I say in a soft tone. He nods pleasantly before turning his back again. His face is so familiar. But where have I met this man before? The sheer understanding of gazing into his magnificent eyes gave me a false sense of uncertainty.

"You have indeed," the man confirms in another idle tone. A halting Walsian accent reveals itself at the end of his phrase. He stops his pacing for a brief moment to provide his thoughts for my contemplation again. "But, you do not recall where you made my acquaintance, now do you, second prince," he declares in a slightly less pleased tone. I can hear the smile in his voice. I have made many enemies in my short time. I can only hope this man isn't one of them. Hope is a distraction though. He most definitely is one of my many rivals and I should focus on leaving here unscathed.

"Maybe you could remind me sir," I reply in the same hushed tone. The bulging headache springs with every word from either of our mouths. He moves towards me and I get a better sense for the room. A carpet of blue spreads itself beneath the bed on which I sit. A table set is propped up on the opposite side of the room which is only a few yards away. The various windows are covered with blue hangings and the main source of light is a small stove positioned in the corner of the meager room. Other than those sparse decorations, there's only a few other furniture pieces. The only item of luxury amidst the rest is an opulent mirror carved of dark wood and framed with the most reflective of glass. The pattern within the wood displays picturesque blue flowers laid along a flat countryside. I can't see what's beyond the mirror, for an eerie penumbra is cast across the rest of the assuredly small space. All I can decree from my observations is that this man has an obvious penchant for the color blue. Cordella's private chambers are colored in the same manner as this man's. She colored every article of furniture vermillion. My attention flares at my own mention of Cordella. I have to leave here immediately and find her. The man still hasn't replied to my inquiry, but I don't care for his words. I must find her. I stand abruptly to my feet only to fall over. The wave of nausea that hit me is crippling enough to send me toppling.

"Heed my warning and return to your previous bearings," the man requests in an astounded tone. I hear him take a step back. His caramel colored eyes stretch themselves wide as he watches me slowly crawl towards the door. His jaw clenched as he decided to intervene and pull me from my less than holy position.

"We met in a graveyard for the first time, Alexander. I knew your name but you didn't know mine," he begins animatedly in a manner to distract me from my goal.

I huff and lean against the wall behind the horizontally positioned bed. The man drags a chair across the floor with an annoying screech. My head screams and I curse under my breath. The man's brows furrow, but doesn't take any other action. "I decided to visit the woeful former king of Andria's gravestone. You reprimanded me for this and had me stripped of my noble position," he reminds me, a sinister smile gracing his thin lips. This man is an enemy. A memory materializes in my mind. That was the day in which a piece of wood lodged itself in my side. I wince in recollection. My side contracts that peculiar burning sensation as my memories progress.

"You were really quite disrespectful, visiting the grave of a man who caused many to feel morosely dejected," I explain quietly, closing my eyes to calm the quickening spiral of memories. I whisper to the whirlwind in my mind, imploring it to slow even slightly. I hear a low chuckle from the man. A vague sort of rage fills me as I massage my temples.

"That man was most definitely insane. He couldn't help his deplorable actions. I don't regret my own. Everyone deserves some sort of remembrance. And also, it's quite an entertaining experiment to see how others would react to a Walsian man playing the devil's advocate." His lilting words feel wretched and poisonous.

I grunt disapprovingly, more heated anger coming over me. "And what do you know of how his *deplorable actions* fueled by insanity affected Andria in whole? Did you have to endure it for so very long? Did you see the soul leave his eyes at a young age?" I retort with animosity. My words only choke more chuckles from the man. I look away for my own good. Speaking for too long persuades dizziness to enter my mind.

"I'm one of Lizbeth's colleagues. I know much about that man that you've only ever spoken about in your dreams," he states coolly, his curved accent slipping around his words triumphantly. A clench my fists weakly and bar words from leaving my lips.

"I've found myself in quite the incipient predicament," I note pathetically, regretting my harsh words dearly. I don't want to provoke this foe to the point where my death would be easier to deal with. He nods idly, a small smile finding its way onto his face as he recognizes the obvious agreement in my words.

"That you have. You escaped from one of us just to be found in the clutches of another," he replies in a satiated tone.

I nod and picture myself holding my gun to his head. I feel at my waist for the gun and my hands lock around the cool metal. I feel the man's eyes piercing me as I unbuckle the weapon. "What's your name?" I ask distractedly. He'd be a fool is he didn't recognize the fact that I was unsheathing a weapon. There's got to be a catch.

"My name is Elli. I know you have a gun, Alexander. I've already stripped it of anything even slightly potent. I considered taking it from you in whole for fear that you'd throw it at me, but your arms are far too feeble and I'm great at catching. Don't bother attempting."

I sigh and look back at the man. He sits comfortably on the scrawny chair. His intent gaze gives me a dolorous feeling. I wish he'd look at anything else in the small room. There's many blank walls he could easily stare at instead of my sniveling form.

"Tell me Elli, what did the court assign you to after I revoked your power?" I inquire blithely to fill the impending silence. I understand with full consciousness that leaving here would be immensely reckless in the middle of a fierce Andrian blizzard. I will instead abuse this man to the best of my abilities. I could shape him into an ally or use him for information as I did Peter. I just have to gain enough of his trust, or I could influence him to drink whatever alcohol he has stashed in this little lair of his. The latter seems more pertinent to my current standing.

"They sent me to oversee farmers of barley. It's a woebegone employment during the winter months. Everything is so very dreary. I have you to thank for providing me with entertainment until the blizzard quells. I haven't spoken to anyone in an interminably long time. All of the farmers only speak Hyvernian, a language I cannot fathom," the man gushes in a giddy tone. He takes a deep breath and regains his previous composure. A nervous laugh escapes his lips.

I place a carefully crafted grin on my face. I try to display as much curiosity as I possibly can. "I can't say I'm the most interesting person," I explain quietly in the most agreeable tone I can muster with a man who honored the loathsome man who I thought to be my father.

"Your hairstyle is most definitely interesting. Lizbeth won't like it this way. Dear me." The man trails off. His easy smile drops and the makings of panic are evident on his handsome features.

"Peter did this to me. I held a fire stoker to his neck in an attempt to gain more information. He drew a knife from his pocket and slashed at my face. He took a lock of my hair off."

The man grimaces as if my retelling causes him great pain. I probably shouldn't have disclosed quite so much of the story. I gave the man an example of how I didn't comply with the orders of another amongst his ranks.

"I'll have to cut your hair in a proper fashion. The hack job Peter gave you is not presentable. Lizbeth will end me if you show up like this. Peter is my comrade and he'll get hurt as well if Lizbeth discovers this. He's necessary though, so she'll spare him," Elli states hastily. His nonchalant facade wanes gradually as he inspects my haircut. I lean away from him as he moves closer to me. Lizbeth really seems to daunt this man. I'm still in awe of this newfound truth.

"Please don't touch my hair." I reply with a sharp edge fragileness. A crazed look comes onto Elli's face. My jaw goes slack as an epiphany strikes me. This man will die if my hair isn't trimmed properly.

"But she'll hurt him!" Elli yells, pausing to take a small breath of composure. "She'll certainly hurt me." His woeful horror is mightily plausible. Should I let this man cut my hair? I've only ever cut my own hair. He'd have a sharp tool near my eyes.

I shiver uncomfortably and pull the heavy blanket around

myself. I see the fear bouncing periodically through his system. Lizbeth seems to be an ultimate adversary from what I've heard so far. I hear the sound of labored breathing and turn back to the falsely collected man. His eyelids droop and his pupils round as he tried to rid his mind of the thoughts that were plaguing him. He would appear very composed to an indifferent observer. I've trained my eyes to search the very souls of those around me and have therefore amassed a great knowledge of outward signs of human panic. The enlargement of pupils, the tapping of a finger, and a different breathing pattern than usual moments. Those are only some of the intimations of a crumbling mind. I feel the side of my lip twitch into a vague smile as I ponder the beauty of such a skill as what I possess.

"Alright, Elli. I'll allow you to cut my hair if that is what you desire."

He lets out a small sigh of gratified resignation.

I button the top of my damp shirt before standing wearily. Elli also stands, a graceful smile playing at his thin mouth. He appears to have calmed substantially, but the remains of his previous emotions still flicker his round eyes. I feel my knees wobble under me and my lungs seize as I attempt to take a step. Vitality drains from my body as I let out a dazed gasp, trying to draw in as much oxygen as I can. I find myself stumbling towards the table. My hands grow white as I grasp the edge of it determinedly. Elli surveys my actions carefully, a semi-detached expression splayed on his face as if he only half cares if I fall and crush myself beneath the evidently quaking table.

"Be prudent with this situation and take a seat. You nearly died. Your face was blue and your feet had no blood flow. I didn't think I could save them, but a miracle occurred and the color returned to them," Elli says, as if the notion of escaping death was some great feat. I smile grimly to myself. He doesn't know half of the trepidation I've had to hack through as of late.

"You see Elli," I say, turning to look towards the awestruck man once again. The meager light rings itself around his caramel eyes and dishonestly at ease forms. "Death and I have been intimate acquaintances for some time now. I would even be so bold as to call him a friend. He's been making an effort to converse with me almost every day for some time now. I know all about him and he knows a similar allotment of information about me. I am *assured* he'll follow me for the rest of my time, forever chasing me." My volume diminishes at the end as I realize how somber my personification is. I'm so very alone. The only one who pursues me is death. Elli's jaw falls suspiciously as he processes my evident curiousness.

"Are you quite alright? Can I offer you a drink? It may not be what you're used to, seeing you live in the palace, but it's quite potent," Elli queries as he pulls a bottle of amber liquid from a wooden repository. The sinister liquid sloshes within the bottle. Elli pulls two simple glasses from another compartment within the repository. The chinking of the glasses against each other rings in my ears. These glasses have served the poison that does evil things to the minds of people.

"You're most gracious, but I don't drink," I deny politely, edging my way into the seat across from his.

He looks up curiously. "Oh, but I insist. You appear to be awfully tense. This will most definitely loosen your joints. Lizbeth doesn't enjoy your discomfort. In fact she blames herself for the pain you've already endured," Elli construes swiftly, pouring me a glass of alcohol.

I didn't consent to that cup. I don't enjoy dining on poison no matter how slowly it works itself into the crevices of my body. Even if my personage endures forty more years without the toxins inevitably ending me. He could also put any number of sedatives or sleep drafts in that cup. There are far too many dangerous possibilities to risk even the smallest of sips. I don't want to awaken in the company of a murderer.

Elli grabs a pair of shears along with the cups. I gape at the trimming tool with distaste. Does he actually plan to shear off my hair as if I'm some sort of animal? I suppose that I have to give my consent to that. He seemed legitimately fearful for his own life. I don't want to be held accountable for another death. A particularly loud whistle of the blizzard tempest catches the man by surprise and he drops the glasses emphatically. I cringe away from the spray of glass, but a piece catches me in the cheek. Pain explodes on the right side of my face.

"Agh!" I cry against the pain. I feel the crystalline piece sink deeper into my flesh as my facial muscles constrict around it. I hear another gasp of horror from Elli. His careful righteousness dies away as he views the blood rolling down my face. I stare daggers at him as I try to silence my own cries.

"Oh no, oh no, " Elli whispers, the shears still in his hands. I realize all too late how unbalanced this man's emotional state is. He's wavering on the edge of a breakdown and I failed to notice the half of it. A skilled actor he is.

"No, no, it's alright. I'm fine," I mumble through the spreading pain. A wave of nausea hits me as I catch the tip of the glass through my peripheral vision. The residual alcohol coating the glass stings in my skin and I let out a small gasp. I spoke of death as a friend and now I've gained a warning scar. How absolutely hilarious. How extremely amusing. This confrontation is so entertaining that I can't bring myself to laugh.

"Again? Another puncture?" I ridicule nobody in particular. Elli's flushed skin has acquired a deathly sort of paleness. I sigh heavily, rolling my eyes with exasperation. And to think I'm the one with blood soaking into my skin. I take a tarnished rag from the table and shove it into my mouth without a second thought. It'll heal better if the skin doesn't grow around it. I close my eyes and lift wavering hands to my face. A bloodcurdling sort of fear attacks me. I have the absolute worst luck. It's a fact. I thought it was done.

"Ahagh!" My thoughts are cut away by my own strangled

cry. The glass didn't reach as deep as I assumed it did. Blood pools in the open wound before dribbling out. "Do you have anything to wrap this with?" I ask in a desperate tone. A crazed lilt joins the chorus of emotions found in my voice.

Elli lobs another rag at me, pure terror etched on his prominent face. I press the dry cloth against my gash. I turn my face towards the heavens angrily. "The audacity!" I shout again at nobody in particular. Another harsh wave of wind slams against the slight building recklessly in response. "You're petty!" I cry again. Elli grows more and more distressed as he observes my unseemly actions. The man begins to sob madly into his own arms. I've got to deal with another scar, this time on the right side of my face, and this man gets to cry. "Shut it!" I scream, not caring for his sanity any longer.

"I'm as good as dead," he whispers, looking up at me pitifully. I wretch the shears from his hands so that he doesn't hurt himself. The man recoils from my touch and I sneer back at him unethically. I feel as if we've switched roles in this situation. I'm the intimidator and he's the one I'm intimidating.

"Pitiful fool," I mutter under my breath. My body fuels itself with adrenaline and I limp over to the mirror to appraise the damage. I always did rather like my face. I'm a beautiful human being, that's all I can say. I'm sure the scar will defame me further. Another fiery bout of pain takes hold of me and I cringe. The face I see when my eyes open again is not what I expected. I haven't intensely inspected my own features in a long time. I've only ever stolen quick glances at myself in mirrors. My jawline has become more prominent and my nose more slender. My brow has sunken and my eyes. My eyes have grown empty and sullen. The sapphire blue of the iris has only grown, but the meager happiness I had attained diminished in only weeks.

I let the rag drop from my hand and onto the floor. The blood rolls down my face in the same manner tears do. Yet another cosmic joke, I suppose. My bangs are cut jaggedly, but at least my plain of vision is clear. I ignore the singeing pain and take the instrument to the rough line of hair I was so generously gifted. With the crude shears I'm able to trim away every uneven edge and imperfection. I appear less shabby and forlorn now despite the blood spattered across my face. At least it's beginning to clot around the main injury. This pain pales in comparison to the slicing wood. The intimately familiar burning sensation intensifies as I move away from the mirror.

My customary stretch of adrenaline is through and the dim, beleaguered feeling settles upon me again. I snatch the rag from the floor and make my way to one of the flimsy chairs with my remaining stamina. The agony only increases as I apply pressure to my face. Lightheadedness sets in and I'm desperate for a distraction. The chair squeaks under my girth and I let out a long, mournful sigh. Another good thing gone in the blink of an eye. I unsheathe my notebook and record the unintended rhyme.

A long, mournful sigh,
Another good thing gone in the blink of an eye.

"Tell me Elli," I venture in a somewhat demure tone due to my aching facet. "What did Lizbeth tell you to make you so afraid?" I inquire. The sobbing stops abruptly and I hear rustling from the ground. I hear Elli brush off his ill-fitting suit with some effort.

"Lizbeth is—Lizbeth is a demoness," Elli manages wearily. I hear him huff and pull himself to the ground. He pulls the opposing chair away from its former position and places it across from me so that I can observe him with my affected range of vision.

"Go on," I encourage in a subtly interested tone. The sting abates slightly as I take in his words. He takes a deep breath and continues. The fear is now evident in his glossy eyes. He isn't bothering to keep this half of him latent any longer. I've already seen his worst. There's no reason to continue with the suave guise, no matter how impressive it was. I'm not sure he even has the energy to continue. He just looks so subdued.

"She particularly relishes picking others apart based on their most tragic m-memories. She then uses the information she's strained from her subject to torture them, promising to be tenfold whatever that poor soul endured," the man replies. His words are very descriptive, pleasing to the ear. I feel the blood around my wound begin to solidify further and I let out a strangled sigh.

"I learned how she handles her colleagues from Peter. I only wanted to hear your perspective on her cruelty since you're one of her many supposed equals," I explain furtively. He nods, his lower lip trembling. He grabs the bottle of amber alcohol from the repository and pops the cork easily as if he's done something similar many times before. Elli admits a shaky breath before taking a long swig of the liquid. Something changes in his eyes as he completes it.

"None of this would've happened if you hadn't engaged in that fling with the queen," he mutters through another gulp of drunkard's water.

"I love her," I admit to the soon to be drunken man. He squints and takes another gradually confident sip. My voice trails off in a whisper as I contemplate her incredible eloquence and intellect.

"You call it love. I call it a marred boyhood." Another fit of laughter follows the phrase. I sober the anger within me. "Ah, I'm far too lucky for my own good," he utters nonsensically. Half the previously full bottle is now empty. "She took the Walsians who came," he adds, a lazy smile finding its way onto his face. "I was taken from Walsia, no friends. Good guard for the queen." He seems confused by his own lack of articulation. He mutters another few phrases in slurred Walsian before advancing.

I tie the rag across my face to give my achingly cold arm a break. "She killed some, used others. I had met you and she didn't kill me for that reason. Only that." He frowns thoughtfully and takes another dimming sip. "You were graced by his presence!" he mimics accurately. "You love the queen, Lizbeth loves you. She has the queen. Bait as if she's—she's fishing for men."

My lips curl into a frown at his words. Elli takes one last swig. "Fishing for you in particular. She re—refuses to have any—anybody else," he finishes. The bottle drops and the final bit of liquid splashes against the floorboards. Elli's head drops onto the table.

The man who made me feel like an insecure child when I first met him is now passed out before me. I check his pulse with two of my fingers to determine whether he'll live. His pace is slow, but consistent. He'll be out for another day or so.

I make use of what food and drink I can find. I'll have to leave as soon as this storm lets up. I can only hope that the bursting winds quell and become gentle zephyrs. I have a long road ahead of me. Now I know where Cordella is and that she's still breathing. She's alive. That small knowledge lights a spark within me, a flicker I can follow until my entire world is bright and true again. I can still save her.

CHAPTER 15

The tepid river surges its way around Royal Andria in a majestic manner. Even in the darkest of winters, this river remains unfrozen and undaunted by each and every perilous blizzard. It seems fitting that only the monarchy and court would be allowed to savor such splendors as efficient travel and warm water to bathe in at their leisure while winter passes them by. Only those with brilliant eyes and golden souls are permitted to possess such exquisiteness. The inferno concealed within the depths of the Earth provides the majestic river with the heat it requires to remain perfectly temperate. Another fitting idea. A deep evilness possessing those in positions of authority could cause something as grand and as praise worthy as Andria to come into existence. I'm envious, for I've never had the opportunity to settle into a steaming, freshwater bath drawn from the accurately named Sun River and it's highly probable I never will. I wouldn't choose to anyways. Anything reaped from glorious Andria is not my birthright, seeing as I'm Hyvernian.

I have, however, once run my hand along the top of the silky stream while being escorted to my rendezvous point of choice. The Sun River has many intricate branches webbed around each other. Some of which are well known, some secluded, and even some with no map marking at all. I was traveling along an unmarked branch to arrive where I now reside with all my plans, a rather dilapidated part of Old Palace Andria. It's long deserted, the only feet that have graced the floors of this cloistered wing in twenty years are my own and a few of my preferred colleagues such as Jakob, another dealer of secrets who formerly owned a residence and undisclosed business in Walsia. Jakob observed better underground opportunities in Andria, so he accompanied the queen to Andria as many of her admirers, servants and guards had done. He gained free citizenship and a noble status. I would label that act as pure genius, although he is rather devious if I do say so myself. We soon discovered each other's existence. We decided to become partners because of our common trade and mutual plot. We're both rulers of our respective hills, so it seemed prudent we combine our shrouded forces. He'll provide me with his amassed aid so long as I leave him Andria's burnt remnants once I've devastated them. This is to make sure the monarchy is completely gone so that Alexander doesn't have a reason to return. His only option will be me.

I've called for an assemblage this evening and many have consented to join us who reside in the fallen palace. Soon, many more feet will have graced these sprawling corridors and many more vessels will have glided atop that hell-heated water. Soon Andria will fall and soon Alexander will be mine. Soon we will leave and soon we will shake the gilded dust of this pompous realm from our thoroughly ordinary shoes. Soon we will be happy and soon our great love story will be complete. Soon, soon, soon.

It's been a week since Alexander escaped our clutches for the second time. He hasn't come to save Cordella as of yet, so I've decided to request our plan be dragged forward despite the few inconveniences that come along with this sudden change. Alexander may just need a bit of help finding my hideaway, so I'll employ someone to send him a message declaring our whereabouts discreetly. I've already sent a letter to the monarchy about Cordella.

Dear Miserable Monarchs,
I would like to make you aware that your beloved queen is

safe. We will return her when we are ready and she has served her purpose. I should make you aware of another concept though. The queen has a paramour and that paramour was mine. She has broken and distorted far too many good, pure things, so if I may, I suggest you execute her. I would do it myself if it wouldn't crush the heart of her paramour, my one true love.

Coldest Regards,
Verdigris

It's rather concise, but it'll do. I was planning to end her life until Jakob convinced me otherwise. I'm somewhat upset about that. I enjoy my nom de plume. *Verdigris*. The exact shade of green as my eyes. The color copper bends to as it ages. An almost surreal color, if I was asked.

The king has seen me once before, but that bloke can't tell left from right so he most definitely won't make the connection. He presumably doesn't even know what the word verdigris means. I take a satiating sip from an herbal tea and try to soften my features. My neck feels tight and achy. I set the saucer down on a glass table in frustration before tying my scarlet hair into a knot as the nape of my slender neck. I already see enough red without my hair clouding my vision. An empty sort of anger has haunted me as of late. I haven't been with Alexander in far too long.

I take my mind off of the plot and escape to a place of peace. Hyvern, a land where I'll most certainly bring Alexander. We'll breathe in the unique scent of the mist. The vivid scent almost smells of mint with a tinge of something sweeter such as honey. Almost. I can't render the other scent contained within the mix. We'll scale the mountains and live among the many jewels crowning each peak. Every day will be bathed in rainbows reflected from those very same crystals. It will be just the two of us, away from this stiflingly miserable society and even away from the fragile resistance of reality. We'll live in a wooden cabin and we'll always keep the hearth lit and the candles flickering. We'll never have to dwell in the frigid darkness ever again. Alexander will never have to so much as think about all the horrors he's endured in his lifetime. We'll rid ourselves of Andria. We'll rid ourselves of the world as we know it.

Alexander's Perspective

I am thankful for many, many things. I have to be thankful; I have to offer my gratitude. If I refuse to, I'll gradually sink deeper and deeper into the abysmal hole of self-pity. I'm counting my good fortunes. I realize that I have a plentiful amount of blessings. I'm not dead. I've escaped death several times. I've experienced love. I'm not a hostage of any of my enemies or my one, grossly obsessed admirer. I escaped my admirer's clutches twice without being scathed too seriously. I've undergone many tragedies and I've only been endowed with two scars, one of which isn't even visible when I'm fully clothed.

I'm alive for a reason. It feels as if I'm being poked and prodded by an intangible hand. Whenever I stray from the obscure path the hand wishes for me to attend, I'm pushed back onto the path. Even if it feels as if I'm running a fool's errand, I have purpose, I have life. I may not know the reason for either of those things, but I have gratitude and I will try my hardest to act in that manner. God has a plan, even if it feels like a mockery.

The raging blizzard vanished as swiftly as it had come. I awoke the morning after I had been given the scar on the right side of my face to a beam of sunlight trickling through a gap between the austere blue hangings. I drank in the honey-colored light rapidly, overjoyed to have heat other than the man-made kind against my pale skin. It almost felt like the embrace of another person, although I hadn't felt an embrace as warm as the sun itself before. I felt a sudden yearning in my heart, a foreign ache that I was not accustomed to. This outlandish feeling would soon become common for me. The feeling was so odd that for a second I truly concluded that I had passed in my sleep from some unknown ailment. My heart beat in an unsteady rhythm, a palpitation. Soon I realized why. The light from the hastily-covered window had triggered an emotion. My first thought upon waking was how bright and zealous Cordella's eyes were. I identified the many stars and other, crepuscular worlds contained within her celestial eyes. Some of the blue ice had miraculously tempered off of my time-hardened heart. I sat motionlessly on the fragile cot for a moment, the epiphany hitting me harder than that chunk of wood. The sensation was bittersweet. A joyful forlornness. I had gained the knowledge of what it felt like to love someone and I had lost it in an instant. I should have considered how much pain loving Cordella would bring me. A delicious tinge of sadness found its way into my glossy soul.

I stood to my feet, forgetting about the weakness in my throbbing joints and thereupon crumbling to my knees. A loud curse escaped my lips as I pulled myself from the fetal position. I had to balance my weight so as to not fall again. The blue rag was tied around my head in a lopsided fashion, but it had held strong throughout my fitful sleep. An odd sleep it was. I remember the immense fear I endured, but I don't remember what exactly I was afraid of. I couldn't put a name to the face or a theme to the dream. Only shattered odysseys.

Snoring brought me away from my peculiar recollection. My sharp gaze fell upon hapless Elli. He lay in the same, woebegone position he subdued himself in the night before. The bottle of amber liquid lay on the wooden floorboards. The crash it made when it fell rung in my ears. What an awful thing the sinister liquid has done to the collected man.

I finally observed myself in the resplendent mirror propped in the shadowed half of the small hovel. I admired the flowers carved into the wood a concluding time before appraising the fresh gash. After a few moments, I was able to remove the rag fully without crying out in horror. The pain was intense and my teeth ground together. The unseemly cut had become a raised, plum-colored lump on my pale skin. There was a red hue at the point of entry, but the cut looked quite infected. Despite the glass being coated in alcohol, there must have been some sort of other residue on it. I should have cleaned it more thoroughly. My entire face appeared gaunt and sickly. I felt absolutely miserable. That's when I began counting the many blessings I've been given. A rather long snort from the wretch made me turn from my own reflection and take stock of my resources.

I rummaged through his repository and found some rations and more alcohol as well as a coat and multiple pairs of grey, woolen socks. I used a bit of the alcohol to clean the infected gash as best I could. Uproarious pain filled me as I did so. I had to put another rag between my lips. It was almost as dreadful as pulling the actual shard from my skin. I needed a coat and mine was gone, so I made do with Elli's coat. I admired the rich, chocolate brown color and placed it over my shivering shoulders immediately along with two of his other shirts. They were all about a size too large and not tailored to my slim form, but they were warm and that's all I cared about. I discovered a hand-knitted blue scarf in the depths of the large box and begrudgingly clothed myself with the ridiculous garment. It was almost as terrible as a cravat, but I was counting my blessings and considered this another gift.

I packed away the rations and alcohol in a leather bag I also found in the repository. I would need each of those things to overcome the journey ahead of me. I fell several times while packing. Resting another day in the warm comfort of the hovel was on option, but Elli was stirring all the while. I needed to take my leave as soon as the possibility was made available to me. I lined my boots with cloth for an extra layer of heat. I would be trudging through deep snow. That would be some feat for a barely able person like myself. It would be better to risk such endangerment than to brave the other, more fearful peril of facing Lizbeth. Her name had become a bad omen to me despite its previous meaning of comfort and kinship. What a cruel joke.

I vanished just as mumbles began to escape Elli's chapped lips. He was still unconscious, but the fear was immense and I struggled over my own feet to get out the door. The apprehension remained with me as I shoved my gloved-hands into the warm pockets of the overcoat as I shoved my way through the snow-obstructed doorway. The coldness was lesser than previous and I was quite thankful for that fact. There was nothing but fields and fields of medleys of blue and white ice all around me. My legs stopped moving for a second as I spun around in awe. I had never observed such a lack of buildings and trees ever in my life. I'd only resided in the palace or gone to places in which snow-crested trees lived. I was breathless and blinded with the brilliance of the sun's reflection, but my fear was far worse than all of those aspects. I couldn't stand there oblivious to the monster within the hovel any longer.

The fierce Andrian wind had siphoned off the top layer of snow. The decrease was just enough for me to trudge through with the security of my worn snow boots. The tides had turned in my favor. My breath came in great clouds of steam as I began my trek. I spun around blindly and chose a random direction to travel. It didn't seem to matter anyways. I couldn't find any other, more logical manner of choice. No visible landmarks popped up on the horizon. The sun was behind me and it was slightly easier to make sense of the bright mural planted before my eyes. There was a contour of an edge of a forest a vast distance from me, so I plotted it as a point and moved towards it. I looked behind me every so often in order to check whether or not Elli was on my tail as I expected him to be. In truth, he was still unconscious in the rapidly diminishing hovel.

I counted my blessings all the way. *I'm not dead. I'm not a hostage. I've only gained two scars. I'm in love, I'm in love, I'm in love.* Or was I in love? I latched onto the silver lining of my blessing as a coping technique, but in truth it had revealed plaguing questions I could not answer with the meager amount of sanity I had remaining.

Lizbeth's Perspective

The hour has grown closer to that of the assemblage I had called for. I still hold the teacup in my hand, only now the liquid contained within the vessel has gone cold and my grip on the dainty handle has become clenched and possessive. I haven't moved from the overstuffed armchair and I fear that I won't be able to force myself up until the action is absolutely imperative. I'm worried. Worried for Alexander. It's been a week since he was reported missing from Elli's tiny barley farmstead. My eyes have become glassy from fixating on the same object for far too long. A slender vase atop a mahogany stand. No fronds are contained within the ceramic holding as they usually are. Just a vase with no purpose. A servant without a master. My eyebrow twitches as hot anger enraptures me. A tentative longing to smash the useless piece fills me and I'm appalled by the emotion. Still, I oblige.

With one, furious sweep, I knock the vase off of its table. It shatters and the priceless pieces fall to the ground. A dusty circle reveals itself around the spot where the vase used to sit. I blow and watch dust particles fill the air and become illuminated by the half-light of midafternoon. Only a few hours before we enter the final stages. Only a few more hours.

Peter enters the room, a begrudging expression splayed across his noticeably admirable feature. A rage other than the petty twinge that influenced me to smash the vase fills me and the teacup drops from my gripping fingers. Now two priceless pieces lay shattered upon the unkempt floors. I stand on my feet with a spasm of fury. I look Peter dead in his clouded eyes. His faraway expression peeves me even more.

"And what do you believe you're doing by entering my presence in this manner?" I whisper, gesturing towards him boorishly. I smooth the wrinkles in my ivy green dress with a hint of regret. I should always act like a lady, even if Alexander is absent from the scene. I see the evidence of fear crowning Peter's face as he takes a step back. I reach into my top and grasp a knife gingerly. I always keep weapons around for occasions such as this one. I pull the long, sharp knife out deliberately. I want to see more of that gorgeous fear in him. He takes another step back, this time raising his arms into the air. "Explain yourself before I force you to with this knife I've suddenly acquired," I demand blatantly. I allow a rough smile to form on my face.

"Calm yourself, woman. I'm only accepting your request and joining you for tea."

I frown thoughtfully. I did ask him for tea, did I not? I slowly veil the weapon in its previous hiding place. I take a deep breath and remember myself.

"Well then, sit. I insist," I reply, my manner changing in an instant. My smile becomes easy. The very sight of his face vexes me though, so it's quite difficult to restrain myself from pulling the knife again and stabbing his stupidly handsome face. I lick my lips and pull myself back to reality yet again.

"What do you *so desperately* wish to discuss with me?" Peter asks in a disgruntled tone.

I turn up my nose. Every single action he facilitates makes me increasingly angry. Oh goodness, I just want him away from me. I clear my throat roughly and take a staggered seat.

Peter sits in the armchair opposing mine. He brushes the various shards away with distaste and I sneer at him.

"Many things will change as of tonight. Your face will

become public and your challenge will be extended to the king, your brother Edward."

A grimace forms on his face as those words leave my lips.

"Based on sovereignty and birthing order, you're the only true candidate that can challenge. Trust me, I dislike this agreement just as much as you do. I dislike you just as much as you dislike me."

He looks up from his knees, a ghost of a smile forming on his features. "Madam, I don't merely dislike you or our agreement," he reminds me in an idle tone. His smile only grows.

I grit my teeth scornfully and look away. "I know that. I am the cause of your children's deaths and I—"

"You won't hesitate to end the rest of my family. I know that," he finishes in a mournful tone. A half-shadow falls over his face as loneliness creeps over his chiseled form. I feel like laughing.

"Just reminding you of your place," I add hesitantly, a small smile finding its way onto my face. He practically growls at my enraging words. I meant the lash to rouse his emotions. He takes a deep, slow breath in order to calm himself and straightens his necktie. My eyes pierce his ice-filled eyes.

"There are parts of you that resemble Alexander. Your facial features are quite similar and you both share the same sort of jawline," I note with a hint of awe. His eyes flicker back and forth uncomfortably.

"Yes. Well, we do share half of the same genetics after all," he responds despondently. His sadness satiates my need for dominance. I reminded him of his place. I hope I won't have to do that again any time soon, for the ramifications he would owe me would be far more harsh than just the ending of his remaining family. Yes, I could make him sob.

"I would like to review the plan one last time before it comes to pass," I state in a low tone. I have his attention fully ensnared. Now is the best time to speak. A beam of warm, afternoon light hits his face and he squints in order to see. "All of our associates will be assembled in the rotunda room. We will have a runner boy, someone of little value, deliver a formal request for challenge. We will set a time and place. Other, less valuable agents will place flyers for such an event in different places so that Alexander is made aware of such an exploit. Alexander is a smart man and is prudent enough to follow the obvious hint to the location of Cordella. He'll arrive before the duel has commenced and will get to observe the action firsthand." I pause to smile in a somewhat malicious manner before speaking again. "I'll allow him to speak to Cordella one final time before she is brought to the Palace Andria. Then he shall share company with me as we watch the makings of the destruction of Andria play out before our very eyes. He'll be pleased, yes indeed."

Peter gawks at me with a fearful sort of fascination. It's as if I'm the mythical creature he's been hunting all his life. The only exception is the fact that I'm hunting him, so I've therefore found my prey. I'll stab him with one of my magic-filled horns or something of that sort.

"And so you're just planning to let those agents and that runner boy be tortured and killed? You're going to break Alexander's heart haltingly when you could just send her away in the beforetime? You really are as cruel as they say."

A self-righteous sort of shock fills me at his words. "Whatever do you mean? It isn't *my* fault if those mere servants aren't fast enough to escape. I'm giving Alexander the chance to tell Cordella that he doesn't love her as she so presumes," I reply with all my pondered logic intact.

Peter still appears miffed by the masterful plot. What a simpleton. "You judge people by their value, not their souls," he states wearily, a frightened expression plastered on his face. My eyebrows turn downwards as I stare at him. He's quite foolish really. I strongly dislike foolish people and I'll kill him myself once he is no longer needed. But, I will keep my end of the bargain and spare the rest of his family if he complies. I'm many things but I'm not one to break contracts and promises.

"Well of course! I'm not God, am I? I don't judge souls. I don't know the souls of those who die and I wish to keep it that way," I retort as if my reply is the most evident out of all the many things I could say. He nods, a flicker of inspiration in his eyes.

"Well then," Peter says, folding his hands in his lap idly, "consider God in this situation then. Do you believe he would forgive you after all of these actions? Do you believe you'll make it to heaven? It's not too late to repent and give up this ridiculousness."

I scoff at his words. I have my own opinions on where I'm going and I'll be happy to make him aware of them.

"Alexander has told me many times that he's certain he'll go to hell. He told me that his very existence has caused so many deaths. Now, Alexander has never killed anyone intentionally. He's never ordered the death of someone despite him flaunting the ability on many occasions. But, he still believes he'll go to hell because people have died on his account. I'll follow Alexander anywhere. Anywhere means anywhere, Peter." My voice drops to a whisper at the end of my rueful statement.

Peter looks even more terrified than he was previously. He leans as far from me as he possibly can while still remaining seated. "That poor, poor boy. You're quite insane, madam," he says almost inaudibly. His armchair groans as he leans back even farther if possible. His pupils waver within their sockets, almost as if he's about to cry. Another bout of laughter hits me.

"I know of my own insanity, Peter. You're going to go mad as well. I see the twitching of your eyebrow and your lip. You have a gene. In fact, many people in positions of power aren't in their right minds. Only Alexander is not doomed to a fate of losing touch with reality. Whatever eccentricity he's attained will fade with time," I explain to the increasingly daunted man.

His clasped hands fall limply to his sides.

Alexander's Perspective

It had been three days since I left the hovel when I found a village. My extra layers of warmth supplemented my own clothing nicely and I was faring quite well out in the wilderness. I made it to the edge of that forest I had seen in a few hours' time and I decided it was best to travel through it. It was more than likely that there would be a worker's village that I could stay in for a night or two. I was correct. Just when the third night was beginning to grow black as pitch, I found a village.

Villages such as these on Royal Andrian property house craftsmen, artisans, and farmers that supply food and materials to those of the highest upper class. In return, these people are allowed to keep some of their masterful works and live in the splendors of money and other valuables sent to them by other working villages. This place in particular crafted furniture orders for nobles. A separate village created pieces for the royal family.

I pulled a rag over my head and traded my silver wristwatch for a few nights at the local inn. The lights went out early in the night and I was left only with the company of myself. The room was spare. A plain, wooden desk sat in the corner of the tiny room along with a hard, twin-sized bed. The sheets were prickly and stiff. The entire room was immensely incommodious to say the least. I opened the blinds and I gasped as a full moon revealed itself. I had been watching the moon wax for all three days I spent in the forest, but never had it swollen to this size. I marveled at the sight of the glowing, white orb in the sky. I felt like a wolf, lamenting at the sight of it.

I took off the coat for the first time in a few days and washed my body with the help of a small water basin left by the staff. I checked my wound in the mirror the vessel provided. It was healing unevenly, but at least the purple infection had disappeared with daily applications of the stinging alcohol. I sighed and re-dressed the gash with another one of the rags I had brought with me on my voyage. As I worked, I contemplated my time in the forest.

Every night I had crawled under the roots of a gnarled tree, hoping that nothing would try and attack me. I was blessed in that manner, for all the creatures of the night had left me to myself. I lit a small fire and gazed at my creation until I nodded off. That was a miniscule comfort.

After that night, I couldn't uncover any dry wood and was unable to provide myself with that security again. I was just so afraid, afraid of all that lay out before me and all the many things that could befall me in the darkness. Nobody would ever even know. The only one who would even worry slightly would be Lizbeth, a crazed admirer. Thoughts of Cordella and all her many nuances were the only ideas that drove me onwards through the darkness of night. In the forest, the whispers in my mind grew louder to balance out the deafening silence. My own heartbeat was a chorus with those words. Snow-covered logs again turned into my mother's uninhabited body and a branch behind me was the former king and all his torturous glory. I again felt the burning sensation in my side and again heard him speak those agonizing words of blame. Needless to say, I was immensely reliant on my little leather notebook and the counting of my own, meager blessings. No storms took hold of the land in my time of travel. God had cleared a path for me and I was following it as best I could.

Help me!
Save me!
Why does death always seem to crave me?
Is my soul that great a desire,
That my chances of perishing seem to be much higher?

I noticed a peculiar thing as I scrawled verse upon verse onto new, blank pages. The remaining pages in my notebook were beginning to grow fewer. I had only a quarter remaining of the thick volume. Now, this usually wouldn't be of such great importance. I could pull another from my stash and place this one in my collection of deceased notebooks. But I had no money or anything left of monetary value. I couldn't even enter a shop without being caught. My most prominent source of coping would be ripped from my grasp soon. The volume was filled with my most melancholy thoughts. All the agonies I had endured in the past months were recorded in this notebook. Hope flickered through me for a hilarious second. Could the ending of my little leather notebook be the ending of these greatly ruinous trials? No, not in slightest. I thought the same thing about my fifteenth birthday and nothing good had come of that. Hope is a devious thing, yes indeed. All I gained from my fifteenth birthday was a love that was irrevocably torn from me.

Lizbeth's Perspective

The assemblage in the rotunda room begins in a half hour and I'm certain that Alexander will arrive promptly. I demanded that our agents and the runner boy be sent out a day before I spoke to Peter about the prospect and Alexander's a quick study. He knows much of Royal Andria's grounds and the Sun River that spreads throughout it. He'll find his way to the river and a vessel will be awaiting him at every lamp-lit point. I've had various servants of mine guard the halls. If even the inkling of our whereabouts was leaked in the letter Jakob and I collectively penned, then we best prepare for an all-out ambush. I'm sure Edward, Andria's sovereign, has the best detectives in the nation working out the most miniscule details of the note at this very moment. I should be distressed by this development, but all I am is expectant and filled with the anticipation of Alexander's dulcet arrival. I long to dive into his bejeweled eyes and feel the warmth of his pliable skin against mine. Hell, I want to feel anything at all. Whatever pleasant emotion he invokes in me, I'll accept willingly. Oh Lord, I want to feel again. I want to feel something other than inferno-blackened rage.

I stare into the rickety vanity's mirror at my painted lips and long eyelashes. My green eyes stare back at me, cold and indifferent. I tuck my hair into a delicate bun balanced precariously atop my fire-adorned head. I let a few gentle tendrils curl down the sides of my face to deter from my severe expression of longing. I try to relax my face, but my skin feels oddly tight and strained against my bones. I jest the oddity off and ignore it as I apply more of the red lip paint. I enjoy the way it contrasts against my alabaster skin. I look absolutely immaculate. Not an unintentional hair out of place. He loves me. He loves me. He loves me.

Dear Miserable Monarchy,

This is a formal letter of challenge. Challenge for royal sovereignty in the great nation of Andria. Addition no. 8 states that anyone with royal blood can challenge for the throne, no matter who they are and what their previous occupation was.

My associate Peter of Nowhere was cast out at a young age due to fear of illegitimacy. It has been proven that he is of pure, royal descent. He is challenging for the throne because it should have been his, it's his birthright after all. The sovereignty was ripped so easily from his hands and now he will take it back in a duel.

Peter of Nowhere and his associates will meet you in the Stone Chapel at sundown on the 17th of October (16th). The rules of Addition no. 8 state that a singular weapon is allowed to each participant. No outside help is granted to each participant. The prize is the crown. The fight is to the death. The victor gains all the dead man's belongings and the dead man is to be either buried behind the church, or buried at the Palace Andria. He will be given an unmarked grave. This will also be the point in which the queen is returned safely.

If Sovereign Edward Aerabella Angel Paul does not arrive at sundown on October 17th, the crown will be taken in a less controlled manner by our forces. Thank you for your compliance and may the most prominent man win.

Coldest Regards,

Verdigris

Alexander's Perspective

I stayed three days in the village. A forlorn sort of fear had enraptured me. I didn't want to leave the restful asylum I had found. I was able to consume ample food and drink. I was clean and warm. I was allowed to come and go as I pleased and most importantly, I didn't have the need to act and paint a humorous smile onto my preferably sullen features. It hurt my face anyways due to the slice. It just seemed so miraculous because of the fact that I had been ensnared in such stubborn confines before. I was forced out of this warm stagnancy once a couple hundred flyers were posted on the village's board. Every worker's village had a board such as this on which instructions and demands for work orders were displayed. But when I awoke late afternoon from a pleasant nap, I saw a scuffle out the small, dingy window of my room.

The wooden board, instead of being consumed by orders, was consumed with pieces of parchment with loopy, red scrawl all over them. I clothed myself as hastily as I could and gathered my belongings, knowing the note probably involved me and my many issues. I would have to sprint out of the village as fast as I could on my afflicted legs. I nearly fell through the weak, wooden door of my room in an attempt to leave.

I left it ajar, not caring who came and went. When I finally reached the crowd of what appeared to be the meager village's entire population, I had to shove and knock over countless men and women to get a look at the parchment. I recognized the penmanship almost the second I read the first letter. Recollection took over my consciousness. Lizbeth had left me countless notes during the golden days in which we were best of friends and my life wasn't nearly as convoluted as it's now. I would admire her curved scrawl and neat letters. I was always quite envious, for my penmanship was quite stark and wanes with time.

Before I knew what was happening, I snatched a copy of the parchment from the board and shoved my way out of the suffocating mob. Dark clouds were forming on the green-tinged horizon. I observed this fact as I took my leave. I ran, for I knew this letter involved me somehow and the villagers would put two and two together feasibly. These people weren't only kind, they were smart. I would have to outrun the brewing storm.

Once I was safely outside of the village limits, I stole away underneath a grand spruce and read over the notice thoroughly.

Dear Andrian Wraiths,

A challenge has been extended to the Andrian monarchy. A challenge for the throne.

The claiming of sovereignty is completely Lawful. Everyone involved in the claim is exultant to declare themselves a part of the revolution and we wish that all of Andria would join us in that view. We only wished to make you aware of such a prospect so that you could prepare yourselves for the possibility that many aspects of your life will change. Do not be afraid. Expect your own safety. Redeem yourselves and submit easily.

Some will protest, but others will join easily. We hope you chose correctly and join peacefully. Under our guidance, Andria will be the most golden it has ever been in all its days and you will all be a part of such glory. Nothing you've ever experienced compares to half of what we can give you.

Ride into a new generation and forget the past. Ill intentions are something we do not possess. The venerable new king is far superior to the current wretch who sits upon the gilded Andrian throne. Risk everything and reap great rewards.

Warmest regards,

Verdigris

The promises contained within the letter became repetitive and empty to me after only moments. Many times was current Andria besmirched and many times future Andria was told of. No tangible benefits were mentioned in the note. Confusion flooded my mind until a fateful beam of strangled sunlight fell upon an emboldened letter in the middle of a stark phrase. Soon I realized there were many more emboldened letters in each of the three paragraphs. A-L-E-X-A-N-D-E-R - S-U-N - R-I-V-E-R. I took out my pen and connected the letters on the page. My heart stopped and dropped to my feet. I'm currently staring at those very same words now, a few moments later.

This is obviously a copy of an original letter Lizbeth penned with her very fingers. She emboldened letters to spell out a clue as to where she and Cordella are located. She's calling me to the Sun River, an eternally heated river those who reside in Royal Andria use for travel. I must uncover the location of the Sun River in relation to my own location. There are branches of it everywhere, some not even charted on a map. There must be one near me. I could follow it until I find Cordella. Madness shrouds my logic and I feel as if I'm about to collapse in on myself.

I close my eyes for a moment. Strenuous pain captures my wellbeing. I'm frightened senseless. How did I ever become involved in such a grievous gambit? How did I ever come to deserve such torture? My breathing slows and I feel as if I'm being suffocated by the sheer weight of the bolder that's been planted on my shoulders. I never noticed the sword over my head as fully as I am now. I'm struggling to force air into my lungs. The counting of my own blessings seems impossible at this moment, but I force myself to. I need to. The only prospect I can push into my mind is the fact that I'm not dead. *I'm not dead, I'm not dead, I'm not dead.* It's as if everything else has fallen away. The rest of my memory is sealed off and I can only contemplate the remarkableness of the fact that I'm alive.

After more time spent in this state of wonderment, my breathing becomes slightly steadier and my heart rate returns to what is perceived as normal. I check the throbbing pulse in my neck with two of my pale fingers. I have to find the Sun River. It's all I can do. All I can do is turn to the next chapter in my story. The invisible hand that guides me is pushing me in that direction. All I have to do is submit and follow.

CHAPTER 16

Despair clings to me as I compel myself to focus on the task ahead. I once saw a map on which all the worker's villages were marked and labeled by name and trade, but I can't seem to remember the exact positions in relation to each branch of the Sun River. I don't have the best memory. The reason for that is probably the fact that most of my recollection is filled with unpleasant memories. Stubborn thoughts that become clearer the more earnestly I strive to forget them. I glance towards the skyline and view the mass of clouds pressing closer and the horizon. The blue outlining them begins to fade into the deep green of sunset. Twilight is approaching and I should most definitely pinpoint at least one branch of the Sun River by dusk. It will take me all night to find Cordella, for Lizbeth wasn't exact in her clandestine message.

A saddened outrage claims me. What if Lizbeth expects my arrival this very evening? She'll slaughter Cordella if I don't arrive on time. I don't know what Lizbeth is capable of. My view of her has changed broadly as of late. An idea hits me and I reach for the little leather notebook in my right pocket. The worn leather feels consoling and reassuring under my cold fingertips. Before the wedding, the event that I associate with the commencing of my misfortune, I wrote ordinary drabbles about ordinary things, even drabbles so fiercely ordinary that they would tell about amply monotonous prospects such as rivers. Rivers are so very boring. Their course only even slightly differs after many years have passed. In my lifetime, all the rivers I've ever observed will flow their same, plotted course. My style isn't steady, I suppose.

I claw through the ink-filled pages, probing for something even slightly informative. I faintly recall penning a poem that inhered the direction one would follow to assuredly find a branch of the Sun River. I thought one direction always leading back to the same spot was somehow poetic. I was in desperate need of something to scribble about. I cannot remember the contents in full and I hope to find the poem. After only a few, agonizing moments of wrestling with the unruly pages, I cry out and slam the book down against the moist dirt below me. A puff of water vapor floats through the air in its wake. I'll never find it with so little time provisioned. I release a breath that I didn't know was in me and re-adjust the misshapen rag around my face. There the poem sits, bathed in a tranquil penumbra cast by the dying sun. This must be an act of God himself, a miracle. My heart flutters as I grab at the page. I feel like a small child roaming a candy shop. I have finally found the peppermint chocolate.

> River of Sun.
> Facing the sun,
> All will be sure,
> To find a thread,
> If one walks without dread,
> Walk towards the sunset
> And all will see what has begun as of yet.

I eyeball the words and consider how remarkable and arbitrary it is that one of my poems could be useful. My artistry has certainly improved since then, but it's useful and that is very prominent in my eyes. An odd sense of pride captures me. The sense of foreboding allotted within the words is also quite impressive if I do say so myself. It makes me ponder whether or not I previously knew that something awful was to befall me. A crazed smile leaps onto my face. *Walk without dread, walk towards the sunset*, it said. If I regain my composure for the hundredth time today and walk in the direction of the rapidly sinking sun, I'll most certainly find a discernable thread. The sight of the horizon makes me feel panic-stricken, so I'll refrain from looking up as much as I am able while conforming to the contents of my own poem.

I turn west towards the sun and begin creeping through the shadowed trees as steadily as I can. Every inch of my being wants to fall into pace with my rapidly beating heart, but if I miss even the slightest trickle of water, Cordella could die and it would be my fault and my fault alone. I cringe at the thought.

Time passes at a crawl. It feels as if my feet are dragging against the coarse soil when in reality I'm walking as fast as I can allow myself. My heart thuds deafeningly and I feel as if every creature that resides within the forest can hear it. I could bet that the villagers hear it faintly as well. I clutch my notebook between my pulse-throbbing fingers. The acute awareness of my heart is making this increasingly difficult.

I fret over many things. What if Cordella is already dead and I'm suffering for nothing? What if I don't hear the water over my pounding heartbeat? What if some sinister force hurts me out here and I die alone, knowing if I had only been a bit faster that I could have saved myself and Cordella and Andria in general? So many what-ifs. What if I too consumed in the catacombs of my own what-ifs to notice the Sun River? I slap myself across the better side of my face.

"No, you aren't like this. You are Alexander Aerabella Aaron Mattias, but you loathe it when anyone deigns to address you that way. You flaunt your power like you gained it yourself. You craft worlds with your words and you are so very attractive that you could influence anyone of your choice to fall treacherously in love with you, so much so that you could ruin their lives at any moment with your frigid rejection. You are a little pompous maybe, but that adds to your allure. You are resilient and self-righteous and don't attend anything that isn't mandatory because you are far too good for such affairs! You are smart and prudent! You are savvy and deft! And you will follow the path God has set out for you without worry!" My speech begins in a whisper, but in the end I find myself yelling at the top of my lungs in the most strangled tone I can. I have not changed. I am simply myself. I am Alexander.

My breathing slows as the quietest of sounds reaches my trained ears. The slapping of water against a rusted river rock. I hold my breath and listen to the waves of sound circulating the forest, but I cannot pinpoint a direction to walk. I close my eyes and block all other senses until hearing is the only remaining. My feet carry me in an unknown direction and the sound grows louder. Louder, louder, louder until the roar of water crests my ears.

I blink and pull my eyes open. A thickset stream of unfrozen water gurgles right before me. Lord, I've found it! A wrought iron lamp post lies on the other side of the miraculously rushing water. The lantern it carries illuminates a vessel floating slowly down the steaming stream. Royal Andrians planted these lamps for light during aphotic storms, but nobody has authorization to travel at night. My breath catches in my throat for a second time. The boat is still a while away, I could run now. I am Alexander. I do not run from a petty challenge. I stand my ground until the boat is right before me.

"Alexander Aerabella Aaron Mattias, you have been summoned by Lizbeth, dealer of secrets and other less innocuous ideas. Come with me quietly and you will not be subjected to any form of pain," a high voice states as robustly as it can.

I let out a long sigh. A grim smile crosses my lips. Lizbeth sent a vessel to take me to them. I should feel horror and distaste, but the only emotion I feel is relief. I won't have to travel and search all night in order to save Cordella. I'm being taken right to her. I can take her from whatever cramped cage Lizbeth has trapped her in and we can leave here, once and for all. I want to hold her in my arms again and tell her she'll be all right. I want her to promise me she'll be alright. I want to see her rounded macrocosmic eyes and feel her smooth skin against my own. I want to kiss her reddened lips and smell her blood rose scent. I run my hand along the top of the heated water before walking through it. I don't want to boil off my own legs. I need those for the inevitable bout of running I'll have to endure soon. Once I determine the temperature is safe, I stroll easily through the warm darkness. My legs tingle pleasantly beneath me and I let out another exuberant sigh.

"I would substantially prefer it if you only called me Alexander. Substantially," I reply idly. A small, bleak smile graces my lips as I saunter close enough to see in the meager lamplight. The figure clears her throat in an obviously paranoid manner.

"Yes, madam did mention your odd preference." *Madam.* Lizbeth must revel in her newfound power quite a bit. When I was first bequeathed power in the court, I had all who served me call me *M'Lord* or something of that sort. My smile drops and my customary sullen expression comes over my face. The girl with the soprano voice sits in the front of the tar-laden vessel. I suppose the tar will keep the heat out. I pull myself from the shallow depths, being careful not to trip on one of the many river rocks.

The girl has wispy blonde hair pulled back into a neat tail at the collar of her neck. Her pale eyes dart left and right agitatedly, almost as if she's looking at invisible phantoms. She's very comely. Her delicate features are twisted into a deep-set frown. Her long, blue gown is wrapped tightly around her slight form.

I nod despondently at her. She makes a sound in the bottom of her throat, almost like the sound a frog makes before it chirps.

"We shall depart now and arrive in a half hour," the girl adds in the same, mechanical tone.

"Alright," I reply in the most monotone voice I can muster. The sound of my voice makes her jump. Is it the rag tied across my face or my many layers of ill-fitted clothing that makes her frightened? I shift uncomfortably as the journey progresses and the tiny vessel jerks through the water. The girl huffs and tugs on two oars. Her arms appear to be quite strained. Every time the oars turn over, she snorts involuntarily. "Could I offer you some help, miss?" I endeavor cordially.

Her body stiffens yet again. "Madam also spoke of your kindness. I'm afraid I'm not allowed to accept it." The mood becomes hushed and dismal. My heart races again and my fear relating to Lizbeth leaps a great feat higher. Still, this girl looks as if she's experiencing a lot of pain. I should try again.

"I won't tell her, I can promise you that, miss," I reply in the same, amicable tone. I try to implement as much smile into my voice as I can.

"N-no!" she cries fiercely after a moment of quiet consideration. I return to my seat on the small vessel and remain a silent observer. The trees crumble into the immense twilight and the light of the lantern fades away completely. The clouds from before circle above us, threatening to drop frigid bits of frozen water. The only light that penetrates our path is the meager light of the stars and the moon. Each swirling beam of light seems to fade in and out of existence, almost as if the life force of each separate solar system is waxing and waning.

I am worry-stricken. I can only hope, only pray that Cordella is alright. It feels so enraging just to have to sit placidly. I can't do a single thing to help her and I'm so very close to the point where I can. I reach a hand towards my right pocket, but I stop before I fully pull the little leather notebook out. I don't want to waste the precious pages I have remaining on something as useless and as petty anticipation. I most definitely have a realm of pain and sorrow ahead of me. Those few remaining pages will bring me solace when I most require it.

I look up at the girl again. We pass another wrought iron lamp and light sheds itself briefly over her hands. Red marks spread up and down her fingertips from the friction of the oars. I cringe in disbelief. How cruel this is. I feel as if I should offer my aid to her again, but she seemed so very distressed when I last attempted to help. I bite my lip and lean back into the seat again. The gentle swaying of the heated water below us puts me in a depressing lull. I feel so desperately hot. I don't think I've ever been even the slightest bit warm outdoors before. This feeling is quite strange, even compared to the series of incredibly strange events that have befallen me and I did have part of a door floating around in its own, personal cavity.

"How did you find me?" I ask abruptly. I don't really wish to know the answer to that question. The only reason I'm beginning a conversation is to keep myself from passing out from heat fatigue. My mind is clouded by the rising steam. I can only wonder how she stays conscious. It may be due to her conspicuous fear. The girl's figure stiffens every time I shift or make a sound.

"Madam told us you would ask about that. She and her colleagues deployed vessels to travel down the branches of the Sun River at sunset. I was first to find you."

It's my turn to stiffen uncomfortably. Lizbeth and her "colleagues" sent out *multiple* river boats to seek me out and deliver me into her now appalling hands. I swallow the lump in my throat and straighten my posture. I must be as brave as can be. I must have courage. Lizbeth is diabolical. She has amassed a following of servants and colleagues for the sole purpose of gaining my love. Flattery is only an inkling of what this emotion could be called. In fact, I'm not even flattered. I'm completely and utterly terrified. Of course many people wish to see golden Andria be crushed beneath their feet, so I can see how she gained so many comrades. But still, how could anyone partake in such fantasies?

Lizbeth's Perspective

Alexander did not wind up before the assemblage. The mood was dim and dreary because of that. My stance was poised and ready despite my personal feelings though. I compelled Jakob's and my collective followers deftly. I held the right balance of power and beauty in the palm of my hand and I used it for my own good. I also implemented a hint of animosity, animosity I had gained because of Alexander's belatedness because I was beginning to feel worried for his safety.

I stood atop a large notch in the center of the rotunda room finishing my manipulative speech about future plans. I sugarcoated all the evils contained within them. A small boy, probably only ten years of age, came to me with a note. Jakob's handwriting was scrawled swiftly over the small piece of parchment, making me aware of Alexander's safe arrival. I couldn't help but let my jaw drop and my pupils round substantially. I let my notes fall to the ground and uttered a loud apology and dismissal to all who had come.

I rushed through one of the ample sets of oval-shaped doors leading out into the vast halls. The gilded handles were difficult to pull open. That simple fact peeved me greatly and if it weren't for my audience, I would have yelled boorish curses in Hyvernian. My cheeks were flushed and my precarious bun sunk as I took my leave. I met with Jakob in the second corridor to the left. He ran a tanned hand through his salt and pepper hair, a grim look of amusement spread over his deceivingly kind features. Behind him, two guards held a chained Cordella roughly between them. I stopped to catch my breath, licking my lips and nodding slowly at Cordella. That all happened rather swiftly in my perception. I'm now observing Cordella nod back at me almost as if in slow motion.

"You're man has come," Jakob states boldly. His eyes twinkle with a sort of fascination. Jakob has the strongest Walsian accent of anyone I've ever met. He came to Andria on a whim of course, so he had little time to learn the language. I don't mind this defect much. My Hyvernian jargon still slips out when I'm angered by something. None of us our perfect, nor will we ever be, so I will not waste my time by striving for perfection. At least when I'm not in the presence of Alexander.

"Yes, he most certainly has," I reply in a faraway tone. I turn to Cordella. Her lower lip is trembling as it has been for the past week. Her fear never ceases. She's just so very cumbersome to me. "As for you, you'll get a final hour with him after he freshens up."

She parts her heart-shaped lips as if to speak, but cannot find the words to do so. Her eyes waver and twinkle in the half-light. Her beauty is another factor that adds to my hatred of her. How can she ever be so sad with her looks and amorous allure?

"Let's go then," Jakob whispers tersely. His unchaste eyes scrape Cordella's sensual form. Her lip twitches slightly as she observes him doing so. I turn away from the vile display and walk briskly in the direction of the main entryway. I hear the footsteps of the four behind me. My elation grows with every fateful footfall. Elation is defined as pure joy, euphoria, and many other meaningless words. I can't ever hope to describe what I feel in this moment accurately, but I will most certainly try my hardest. My vision is stained yellow by an invisible sun. Every image captured within my recollection is brighter and more vivid. The air smells of wet forests and snow. The air smells of Alexander. I breathe in deeply with pleasure. My skin is tingling exuberantly and my heartbeat seems to speak his name. My legs walk without my control and my eyes dart to their own accord. The air tastes of honey and white chocolate. I'm elated.

"This is what you were waiting for, correct me if I'm wrong," Jakob calls after me animatedly. His excitedness amuses me. I understand his reasons for being in league with me are massive. He wishes to claim Andria's land for himself and inherit my tradeship once I'm finished with my plan. Still, he has become somewhat of a friend to me. We have both committed unspeakable deeds and we both don't care in the slightest about them. We don't feel guilt or anything similar to remorse. We are both creatures that children have nightmares about. In a way, a cold sort of empathy has formed between us. A symbiotic reliance for assurance in the other's plans has formed. I would call this small growth beautiful.

Jakob knows what it feels like to be hopelessly, desperately, awfully in love with another human being. Jakob once felt that rare flicker of emotion I feel in the presence of Alexander. The woman he loved didn't love him back. So he killed her. He then made a career in similar crimes and built a secret and contraband trading empire in Walsia in which he could live comfortably from and entertain himself by ridding people of their lives.

"You're correct Jakob, Alexander is here. The love of my life has arrived on the premises." I confirm in a whimsical tone. My voice sounds like someone entirely different from myself, but I feel far too different to care much about that. I hear a low chuckle from behind me.

"Yes, I recall that feeling. Everything weighing on his half of the scale, none on your own. I wish the best of luck, Lizbeth," Jakob replies in an enigmatic tone. I let out a laugh of my own, but this time mine is uproariously loud. I rip out the already weakened bun and let my red hair cascade down my back like a flaming wall of inferno.

"Do I look beautiful enough for him?" I inquire. Jakob lets out a soft sigh.

"Yes, indeed you do," Jakob replies in a more somber manner

than customary for him. Suddenly, another voice speaks. I want to rip her vocal cords out of her rounded chest so that she'll never speak to me or anyone ever again. Intrusive thoughts such as these plague me when even the slightest hint of a word leaves her lips.

"You're the red-haired girl that he writes about in his notebooks. I always thought he was referring to his mother, but I suppose I'm wrong." Her voice is strong, not feeble and shaky as it usually is. My heart flutters and bounces as her words continue. He writes about me in his notebooks. Of course I know that, but it's so very satiating to hear it from another's lips. Her vocal cords can stay where they are for now. I'll let the king do what he pleases with her vocal cords.

"I do believe that is a sign of his love," I reply in an amicable tone. The girl huffs in a miserable tone and the guards clink around as if she's trying to break free from their hold.

"He never spoke of love with me. He spoke of how you abandoned him. I picked up the shattered Alexander you left behind and put him together again." I bite my lip, fighting the urge to stab her right here and right now. She deserves to die. I was actually managing to be friendly with her, but she wrecked that feasibly.

"Well, bones have to be broken again sometimes to heal properly," Jakob says in my defense. A small smile graces my lips. I turn around and stare directly into Cordella's opalescent eyes. I wait for a hushed silence to fall over the dismal corridor before speaking again. It adds more fear to the situation I suppose.

"Cross me again and I'll snap your neck before you have a chance to speak to Alexander or anyone else ever again," I threaten in a low tone. A look of awe crosses Jakob's smiling features. Cordella fixes her gaze on the floor and continues to walk.

The rest of the time passes in silence. Our footsteps echo off the grimy roof and a cobweb or two falls in our path from all the commotion. This old wing hasn't been cleaned in a long while. It doesn't matter much though. This won't be my residence for much longer. We arrive at the main entryway. The gold-threaded wallpaper seems to close in on me as we approach. I'm so very fearful that he's hurt in some way. My elation overpowers my worries easily as I grapple with the frozen door handle. The ice that fills the keyhole breaks as Jakob pushes me aside and gives it one last firm nudge. Jakob gives me a reassuring look and we plunge into the frigid darkness of the night.

Alexander stands in the center of the overgrown cobbled path. His hands are tied tightly behind his back and a blonde-haired girl with a frightening expression holds him steady. She has a small pistol in her hand. Alexander himself looks to be in a terrible shape. He wears three muddied shirts of different colors and a large, brown jacket. A blue rag is wrapped around half of his gorgeous face and his hair hangs limply around his eyes. His lips are turned downwards in a bitter frown and his singular blue eye stares up at me with a mutilated sort of awe and disbelief. The elation overcomes me completely. The giddiness clouds my vision and I rush down the uneven steps of the great entrance, a massive smile plastered across my powder-smoothened features. My painted lips turn upward as I come closer to him.

Alexander's Perspective

Lizbeth wraps me in a strangling, invasive embrace. My side burns agonizingly as one of her small hands grips the exact spot in which the injury occurred. I let out a small gasp as we topple over. The dim light from the entrance illuminates her pale face slightly. She smells of buttercream and lemon, but I can't enjoy her tantalizing scent. My senses are clouded with adrenaline. I try to free my hands from their bindings to push myself away from her sobbing form, but I can't. I sit in the half-light, an expression of complete bewilderment on my face as she touches me.

"Oh Alexander!" She sobs maniacally into my shoulder and her arms threaten to squeeze the life out of me.

I lay motionless in her wake. I suppose she's wished for me for a long time, hasn't she? All I can recall as she clutches my body tightly is how abashed and hesitant I was to join her on a modest, wooden bench in a church on an Easter Sunday. It was one of the astonishingly warm days in Andria, the kind that only occur once every few years. The sky was a mix of cerulean and verdigris, like the color she uses as her nom de plume.

I had strolled into one of the many small churches behind the palace walls that day to attend a service all by myself. A pocket bible joined my little leather notebook that day. I saw Lizbeth, her hair tied in a knot at the nape of her neck. Wisps hung down around her heart-shaped face and a small, delicate smile graced her rosy features. Her eyes flickered back and forth from the priest to the brightly-colored murals on the walls. I sat next to her with great effort and asked her how she felt. She answered me, looking directly into my eyes as if my vanilla words resonated deeply with her. She told me how she felt. She told me she felt yellow now that I had joined her. Yellow seems to mean pleasant in her mind. I laughed amiably and told her I felt alabaster, bleak. Then, I told her how the sky on that day reminded me of her eyes and she blushed, a perfect, strawberry hue painting her cheeks.

"Lizbeth! What on Earth?" I call in a tone that even I find somewhat surprising. My voice breaks and cracks all throughout the phrase. Hurt, pain, angst. They all show in my voice. *What on Earth?* An elementary phrase that anyone could use to display their surprise. It means something far different between us. The words I'm trying to release from my throat are *Lizbeth! What on*

Earth have you done to our lives? You've drenched me in fire and turmoil! You've tied a noose around your own neck! And for what? A love that was never meant to exist in the first place? What. On. Earth? Lizbeth pulls herself from my ragged form for only a second so that she can get a look at my face.

"Oh dear, whatever happened to your face?" she inquires in a tremulous tone as she gingerly unwraps the cloth from my head.

My raven locks fall loosely around my face. Her eyes narrow as she observes the growing scar. It's not a sight for the faint of heart, that's for certain, but she's murdered countless I'm sure. A pale, translucent line of weak, pink flesh runs up my right cheek. It no longer hurts as much, but it certainly does look rather disfigured. I grimace in distress and wrestle against the binds. Lizbeth is too caught up in her own excitement that she doesn't realize how embarrassing and unseemly this position appears. She's straddling me as I lay here helplessly beneath her.

"I—" I try in response. I struggle, but she doesn't seem to take note of it. It's as if she's transfixed with my eyes. A sense of serendipity hits me as I catch sight of Cordella out of the corner of my eye. I was looking at Lizbeth's graceful features, but I saw her form. She stands only a few feet from us, an expression of reserved pain plastered across her lovely features.

My eyes round and my mouth falls. "Cordella!" I shout emphatically. My cry echoes off the tall trees and dilapidated buildings. A sprinkle of rain falls over the scene as if I triggered it with my tone. Pleasant bewilderment fills me as I appraise her form. She's not hurt, is she? "Cordella! Good lord, Cordella! My love! Are you alright? You're not dead, are you?" Cordella's eyes were turned away from the shameful display, but her vision latched onto me as soon as I began to speak again.

"Alexander! I'm alright. They didn't hurt me," she calls. She tries to move towards me, but two gruff men behind her tighten their grip on her arms. A sick fury fills me as I glare at the men.

"All in due time, Cordella. You'll get your time with the man. All in due time." A man with a kind face steps out of the shadows with a sincere smile. Cordella lurches again, an expression of rage finding its way onto her face.

I turn my attention back to Lizbeth. My display of affection towards Cordella hasn't perturbed her in the slightest. The same deranged smile remains on her fair features. Fear. I feel it coursing through my veins. After one last suffocating embrace, Lizbeth leaves her perch atop my torso and pulls herself to her feet.

"You!" Lizbeth growls at the blonde girl who brought me here. I hear the girl whimper in a saddened tone. I crane my neck to get a look at her. Tears are beginning to fall down her porcelain features. Lizbeth's frightening her. "Free him this instant," Lizbeth demands in a harsh tone.

"Y-yes madam," The girl answers. I feel the leather cords being removed from my wrists and I let out a sigh of abatement as the pressure wanes. Blood begins to flow into my hands again.

"I'm so very apologetic, Alexander. That was rather boorish of her," Lizbeth gushes quietly. I've never known Lizbeth to gush or display even the slightest bit of unfiltered emotion before. Always a small smile, never a constant flow of nonsensical words.

I rub my wrists and leap to my feet before she can pounce on me again. My heart thuds against my eardrums. I should go to Cordella while I still have the chance. I can protect her. I can save her. I swallow my fears, a foreboding echo in my ears. My side stings incessantly as if the wound has been reopened. In the end, I'm too much of a coward to go to her.

"Alright, alright, alright, alright. Alright!" Lizbeth laughs. I stare at her. Is she possessed by some hilarious fiend? "Jakob, I'm a bit too quivery to explain this understandably, c-can you do that for me, pretty please?" The man with the gentle face nods and chuckles garishly. The skin on his face tightens as an unnatural smile forms on his features. I take a step back and Cordella inches away. I feel as if I should run. Lizbeth hooks herself onto my arm, squeezing tightly as if she's a child.

"The sovereign Alexander will be shown to his chambers soon and will be provided with a bath and clean garments. He will be given ample time to freshen up and will then have an audience with the queen. They will be given an hour to speak before she is sent back to the Palace Andria."

I haven't heard myself addressed as "second prince" or "sovereign" in some time. It feels almost surreal that it would come about in this manner. I gulp and look at Cordella, longing evident in my sapphire blue eyes. Her eyes flicker back at mine, a look of aversion on her face. "If everyone complies, those who aren't useful will be spared. If compliance is not given, then those who aren't useful will be killed. Particularly in front of those who are useful," Jakob says, eyeing my form with distaste.

I attempt to speak a word, but my voice breaks off halfway through. My hands feel numb. Cordella has gone white. Her lips have become pale and her pupils have dilated substantially.

We stroll down the musty halls of Old Palace Andria. I've read many volumes about this sunken hideaway. Palace Andria is only a mile through a fen to our left. This place is consumed with filth, for it hasn't been occupied for so very long. I walk in rhythm with my heart beat. Cordella and I sneak glances at one another in times where Lizbeth isn't obsessively gazing at me as if I'm some sort of angel. We tried talking again once, but Lizbeth threatened to cut Cordella's tongue out in front of me. Jakob and Lizbeth chat idly in Hyvernian. The man speaks Andrian with a terrible Walsian accent, but he seems rather deft in the other language. I twitch and jump every time their phrases end, for they have harsh snaps to signal the end of their words. I know conversational Hyvernian, but they speak so quickly that I can barely decipher a single word. Still, I have been paying close attention to see if I can understand their meaning.

Something about money and Cordella. They address her with something quite vulgar, though. My hands curl into fists at my sides.

Jakob has a small handgun locked into a leather holster at his waist. It reminds me of the one I stole from Peter. I should have overturned Elli's room more thoroughly for it. The weapon would be quite practical as of now. I wouldn't be as daunted. I could really use some leverage to leave here. The only person of great value to Lizbeth is me though, so I would have to act as if I had a death wish in order to escape this wretched place. Cordella would also be lost.

Fresh candles look out of place in the rusty wall fixtures meant to brighten rooms. At least I can see. It seems as if the corridor gets more and more narrow every time we round a corner. I have proof it isn't just a delusion as well. We once walked in two parallel rows, but now we walk in three. The group behind us stop abruptly at a set of cracked double doors. The golden handles appear dingy and flimsy as if they could break off with ease.

"We're taking our leave now. We expect you back here in an hour to converse with the queen," Jakob states in a monotone voice. His calming smile never wanes. In the dim light, all of his deep-set wrinkles are shadowed and prominent. He looks like a creature from the blackest part of a fen.

I shiver. The presence of more people was almost comforting to me. Now I'm all alone with my worst dream. I close my eyes and take the deepest of breaths. I ready myself as best I can.

"I'll show you to your quarters," Lizbeth says in a soft tone. I can hear the smile in her voice. I snap around and turn to her. I can't hide my look of distress, but I certainly can hide my words. I seal my lips shut and follow her as she begins the journey down the hall. The silence is imminent and impending, unlike any other silence I've felt before. It's foreboding and heavy. I could drown right here and right now. Not a soul would hear my desperate cries over the sound of the silence. Nobody accept a person who I believe is soulless.

"I'm sorry for my, er, embarrassing display earlier," Lizbeth says. My foot wavers before it falls in step with her stride again. I try to conjure up the appropriate words in response, but my emotions are so random and vivid in this moment that I'm sure all explode into anger or tears if I make one more effort. I bite my lip. "Do you remember the night you became acquainted with Peter for the first time?" Lizbeth inquires. I have an answer for this question, I most definitely do.

"How could I forget? I have a long, jagged scar as a reminder and phantoms of my imagination that do the same," I reply stoically, so as to not show my true feelings.

"Before we opened that godforsaken door, you held my hands and told me you could never hate me. You blushed as if you were twelve years old and your face was turned in the sweetest of smiles. I—"

I cut her off before she can continue. "I apologize for interjecting," I reply in my most formal of tones. "But that was before I discovered what the true meaning of meeting Peter was and how you were killing people on my behalf and watching me while I slept," I finish solemnly. I did promise I could never hate her and I don't. In fact, I love her so much that I'm disappointed in this path of insanity she's followed. I didn't want her to be caught up in the brambles and branches of life's darkest route. I wanted her to rise above it all and use those angel wings she was given so that someday, some way I could make her my queen. That was before I learned what it felt like to love in a manner that was beneficial for both members of the relationship. I learned what passion and intrigue minus the tinge of sorrow felt like. My love for Lizbeth fades completely when I gaze into Cordella's eyes.

"So you do hate me, then. I will convince you otherwise, for I love you and need you far too much. In fact, I don't care if you love me back. You give me feeling, sensation, emotion, whatever you wish to call it. I will keep you whether you want it or not, for I want to feel."

I choke and stop mid-stride. She's treating me like an object, which I am most certainly not. I'm not a piece is a game of chess that she can move about however she pleases.

"Lizbeth! I don't hate you! I'm scared for you and I'm scared of you, that's all," I reply softly. I turn to her and grasp her hands firmly as I did before I sustained that life-threatening injury to my side. I look into her eyes, deep, deep, deeper still. "Give up this gambit and leave Andria out of this. There are better ways to go about loving someone. You did it entirely wrong, for I love Cordella now. To keep me from her is cruel," I explain with angst. My eyebrows furrow as I look into her eyes.

"I don't care if I'm cruel. I'm doing this for your own good. Cordella was a fling, you are her paramour. You loathe the monarchy and so do I, for they will never let us be together. I am breaking those walls for you! I don't care if I scare you or if I lose myself in this process. I love you more than anyone, anything, or even myself!" she yells. "You want to know something, Alexander? I cried for the first time ever today because of you. I've never cried before. You gave me that, whether I wanted it or not. Now I will give you something, whether you want it or not," she finishes.

I feel just as woebegone as how her words sounded. She grasps my shoulders and presses me against one of the dust-encrusted walls. "You are mine. It's irrevocable. You're lucky I'm letting you see Cordella one last time before I send her off to die at the hands of your brother. To say goodbye, I suppose."

My heart presses against my ribcage as if trying to escape the earthly bounds of my body. I let out a strangled moan as she presses her lips against mine in a possessive, deranged manner. I don't move my lips against hers. I'm far too astonished and horrified. My legs slacken and I sink down against the musty wall, inevitably taking mounds of grime with me. She pulls away and looks me dead in the eyes. "Never forget it." She opens the door to a chamber down the hall and motions for me to enter before stalking off in the other direction.

CHAPTER 17

Edward's Perspective

My hand is clenched furiously around this hateful piece of yellowed parchment, as it has been almost all hours of the day for the past week. This letter contains the most enraging information. The joints within my fingers are beginning to ache, but I've dealt with far worse. In fact, there's been an ache within me for many, many painstaking years. It became so common for me that I just began to think it was nonexistent. An ache, a suffering in my head. The remnants of a ghastly memory. The memory of my brother promising he'd come back to me. Now he has, just as he promised he would, as if he didn't already take enough of my soul when he left without me. He has to come back and take the rest now, finish the job like a man. I know for a fact that he is more gallant and more of a man than myself, although I also have fragmented memories of my father lobbing many insults at him related to his masculinity. Ah yes, my father always did have a rather fragile masculinity himself. His carriage was too big and his nose too small.

There's one truth and one truth alone regarding the situation I've found myself in. I have to end him. My past either consumes me or I consume my past. I will most certainly choose the latter if it means that my life will gain continuance for many years to come. My story isn't finished, that's the truth. I need to find true happiness before I pass on. I was beginning to fix it all, myself and my ruinous life. I was about to end Alexander, a reminder

of past sins. That was when it all went to hell. Cordella ruined
that aspect of my revival and I can understand why now. She
has a paramour and I know who this enigmatic man is. She
followed in my mother's footsteps and I'm glad she didn't carry
to full-term. That child would've been cast out due to this
newfound knowledge. My half-brother Alexander could have
been its father for all I know. That's why she saved him. That
little son of a harlot. It's all coming back to me now. All of it. All
of the ghosts and apparitions anew. The wind is more daunting
than it ever was and I can't dress myself in the color white
without traveling back to the day of that forsaken man's funeral.
Alexander was a small boy then and he was all I had to hold
onto. I've had the epiphany of how shattered and broken I am.
I'm just as impaired and damaged as the period of time when
they all left me. All my endeavors to fix it all have been
blundered. I need to try with more intent. I need to. I need to, I
need to, I desperately need to. I have to for my own good and
the good of the great nation Andria. It has to be perfect, not
another blot of ink in the wrong place.

When I stare at my immaculate reflection in one of the silver-
rimmed mirrors of my study, I notice the imperfections that
appear alongside worsening thoughts. A hair bent at the wrong
angle or one pupil dilated slightly less than the other. One of my
eyes is slightly more diversely colored than the other. My nose,
instead of appearing straight, seems to be lopsided and
dilapidated as if punched in. That button on my suit jacket has
a slight scar on it. One of my sideburns falls slightly lower than
the other. I have the desire to hold a mirror up to half of my face
to see if the other half is symmetrical. I'll correct it if it isn't. These
intrusive thoughts will surely die away if I kill him. If I kill Peter
and Alexander. If I kill Peter, Alexander, and Cordella for their
sins. Oh Lord, please help me.

I float through my own mind, thoughts of ridicule battering
the feeble boat on which I sail. My raft will capsize soon enough

if I don't make it to dry land, I'm sure of that. I need to make it
to a place of stability. Solid, intact ground to stand on, not some
floating mirage. The sun will set on my life soon and I will most
certainly not find a proper place to support me in the complete
blackness of the night. A knock brings me back from the inner
depths of my recollection.

"I'm so deeply sorry to interrupt you, your highness, but you
haven't eaten anything in three days. That famed duel you were
told about last night is on our heels. You must gain strength."
His words sound suffocated and far-flung as if from under
water. Damnit. My eyes flicker up to his tall form, blurred and
unsteady.

"How dare—" I find my lips moving against one another
without my command. The vibration is unnerving. My hands
rub against one another until the skin is raw and a small rivulet
of blood forms in the cavity. My words are so low and throaty
that I'm sure he can't decipher their meaning. I hear him
articulate some other phrases in a formal manner and my eyes
go dark. His petulant voice melds with my other thoughts as if
added to a pernicious cocktail. I just want him to shut his mouth
and cease his rambling speeches.

I've known this man for years. Butler to the highest
monarchy, the queen and king. I didn't know his voice could
cause me to be this agitated and panic-stricken. Maybe it's the
thought that a mere servant is commanding the king to do or not
to do something. That isn't how the monarchy was crafted. Life
doesn't function in that manner. The king commands his
subjects to do or not to do something. That isn't the order of
power. The man chatters on amiably. His crow-like coattails flap
in the draft. They fold in on one another in a deceiving manner.

"Shut your mouth this instant or I'll do it for you," I murmur
in a tone so low it's inaudible. He can't hear it over his own
voice. This slicked-back dimwit can't focus on the words of his
own king. My jaw tightens painfully. A look of consternation

spreads across his bleak features and he moves closer to me, more words piling out of his lips at a faster rate. He lifts his hands in front of him for some reason. It's as if he's deflecting a blow. I'm not striking him, however. I'm not moving at all. Suddenly, a lanky figure stands up out of my body. He's quite tall, humorously so. A defect, I would say. His dark blue suit is quite drab as well. It's far too short for the length of his sprawling form. His hand twitches uncontrollably as if possessed by some sort of tactile demon. He's blocking my view of the fool, so I crane my neck around the figure. He seems oddly familiar, but a daze has fallen over me. The daze feels favorable and warm, as if someone's wrapped a fur around my shoulders. I miss my mother.

An addled fear fills me as I recognize the face of the figure who stepped out of my body. My body is far too heated now, almost as if I'm sinking into hell. His face matches my own down to every devastating detail. Crooked nose, mismatched pupils, a single hair turned to the wrong angle. His eyebrows dip far too deeply into his face and he looks rather maniacal. I stand up and rub my eyes. This is a hallucination, it must be, another ghost I'm sure. To my horror, I'm this man's monstrous height. I'm just so horribly ugly. I should be of lesser stature! The man steps eloquently around my massive mahogany desk. At least he has proper form. He buttoned his suit jacket as he stood and folded his arms behind his back. His lips are moving and I can hardly hear the words. He's speaking oh so quickly and I'm far too warm to concentrate on such trivial things.

"I'll kill you, I swear I'll kill you if you keep speaking to me. You must learn your place you inane fool! I'll add you to the collection of graves I keep on my grounds. Your family would never know it was me either. I would buy their affection if they did or simply end them as I did you. Take heed of my gracious warning and take your leave. Take it, I'm begging you." His voice sounds tearful and wretched at the end of his phrase, almost as if he's crying. Crying? How flaccid would that be in such a situation? He's the inane fool. I hate this man.

Suddenly, my perspective switches to that of the man. I cower over the butler. His-my hands are curled in fists. His back is pressed against the door and his hands claw for the handle. Countless apologies fall from his lips, but he's still speaking and I demanded for him to refrain from doing that. The warmth has left me. I wish to be back in the warmth, the lull. I'm aware of all my imperfections here. All the imperfections everywhere. All the blemishes and smudges on the face of this realm. This man is one of them. I'm abruptly pushed back in the corner of the room, the warmth enveloping me. The lull returns to me and my mind becomes muddled.

To my horror, the man standing over the butler takes a cutlass from his belt. I have that very same blade hooked in my belt. Bejeweled handle, bronze tip, even the same inscription. *The one who owns this does not wish to use it, but he or she will.* My father owned this knife. There's an edge of blood stained on the tip. I'll never know who's blood that belongs to. A servant, my mother, even his own maybe. I felt like brandishing it when I lost the case for Alexander's death. It gleams in the sharp light from the large aperture behind my desk. I cry out against the pressing fatigue and reach my hand towards the scene. An awful pain spreads through my throat and no sound comes.

I can't move any longer. I'm an empty husk with shining eyes. I look at the display with a blank expression as my insides scream. The tall man takes the cutlass and... My vision fails me and the darkness replaces the warmth. Now I'm so very cold. Far too cold for my own good. All the ice in the vast reaches of the universe has surrounded me and sheets of frigidity fall over my form. So very cold and so, so dark.

I wake. My eyes flutter open. I'm lying on the carpeted floor of my study staring at the ceiling. I know where I am because of the surreal clouds painted masterfully on the ceiling in wonderous powder blues and spring yellows. This used to be my nursery when I was younger. So many memories were made within this very room. This is the place I feel safest, but it isn't impenetrable and the darkness sometimes finds its way through the cracks in the walls that I let nobody touch. My arms are stretched out at my sides. I clutch my cutlass in my right hand. The tip digs into the fragile flesh of my exposed wrist. I squint my eyes and pull it out with my left hand. The pain that I expected to be agonizing isn't as painful as I expected it to be. It feels dull and far off, almost as if I'm feeling another's suffering. Did I drink too much again? I let out a mournful groan. As I sit up, the room around me begins to spin. I can't recall what occurred today. I scan my recollection, but nothing of any interest remains. Whatever happened?

The room slowly stops its nauseating spiral. My vision clears fully and I push myself to my feet. The spiral returns fleetingly, but it dissipates just as the first bout did. My hands still appear a bit aloof in my vision, but I've experienced worse. I turn around and the sight I'm met with perturbs me greatly. The nausea I felt before is nothing compared to what I endure now. A man with long, black coattails lays splayed across the floor before me on his stomach. Blood dribbles slowly from his hushed form. The sickly sight makes my eyes bulge. I retch loudly and stuff my fist in my mouth to keep the hurl down. It's to no avail. I still end up vomiting all over the corpse. The dead man's eyes still lay open, but he's surely passed. What happened to him? Who committed this despicable deed? I wipe the knife on my suit absentmindedly. The blood on the blade originated from my own wrist. Did the murderer stab me in the wrist with my own knife? When I fell, I must've hit my head. I can't remember him or her or the reason for such a crime.

A sudden, awful epiphany hits me like a bullet to the brain. A numb feeling washes over me. I'm the one who was holding the knife. It's his blood that now stains the knife, not mine nor my mother's. The cutlass drops from my hand and clatters deafeningly to the ground. I focus on the reverberation of the weapon against the floor as I attempt to ground myself. The door to the study is ajar. Anyone could look through at this moment and see an incriminating scene. I slam the door shut with my good hand. It was I who killed this man. It was I. I lift a wavering hand to my lips, ready to cover the reproachful cry that will inevitably escape my lips. My eyes widen and a splitting headache hits me. Memories of the event course through my mind and I nearly double over again. I watched myself kill him from the corner of this very room. It wasn't me, it was some demon that possessed my body. I stood motionless in the corner and watched as he took my cutlass and... I close my eyes, but the searing memory's remnants remain even in the darkness of my own mind. My hands become useful as a raucous sob leaves my lips. I stood in a warm abyss and watched what I believed to be a phantom but now know was myself kill that man with no reason to, save a bothersome interruption.

"Oh no... Oh no, this can't be!" I smother my words with my fist again. The red blotches staining my family's heritage have spread to my own life, just as I feared they would. The stain has spread and it's still spreading despite my best efforts. I should have seared off the source while I still was able. I don't need the court's approval to take my cutlass to Alexander's throat. It's far too late now. I have to end Peter, Cordella, Alexander, and myself for it to be gone. It has to be gone. I need it to be gone. At least my heir died while in the womb. At least I don't have to kill it with its mother. The shining image is tarnished and I must make it pure, I must rid it of such iniquity, such dreadful sin. A sorrowful burden has been placed on my shoulders, sorrowful indeed. The words of the holy book won't help me now, for God won't help murderers without a plausible reason, such as the fact that they were sinners. This man was not. Nobody can help me now. I am my father's son. The world has gone dark.

Alexander's Perspective

I've pressed my back against this wall for so long, as if I'm trying to press myself through it in order to disappear. Lizbeth left me a quarter hour ago, but I haven't moved. I feel so disgraced and used. The very hands at which I have been suffering touched my body and kissed me with deathly passion. No, she *is* death, she doesn't possess the warped power of death. Death has kissed me and held me and pressed me against a wall. Death has claimed me for herself. She will rid me of the world I've come to know and pull me into her own realm.

A stunned silence consumes me as I gradually move to my feet. I have to cling to the wall for support as I stumble in the direction of the chamber death showed me before she left. My vision flickers without the help of the dim candles and my mind is muddled with such worrisome thoughts. I can't permit my mind to get in the way of seeing Cordella before she is inevitably taken from me as well. I have one piece of reassurance and guidance I can bequeath her before she faces my brother. I only wish for her to live on, do everything she ever wished to do before her life comes to a close. She is the only reason that I decided to face death herself. I knew when she stood over me in the infirmary that she was the angel of death. I should have recalled that imminent fact.

I careen and fall as I amble through the door. I'm met with a plume of dust which makes me cough emphatically. My side aches with each puff and I sense the scar contracting.

Dear Lord, I don't speak to you very much. I apologize greatly for that misdemeanor. I have been your faithful servant for some time now though. I need to ask, implore something of you. If it's in your will to take Cordella from this world, refrain from doing so until she is old and grey. Instead of her, take me instead. Send me wherever you wish, just bless her. I love her so. She gave a bright patch in this life I was meant to live and I am forever in debt. I know you are good and that you love every one of your creations no matter what, so save her and allow her happiness, the truest of sorts. I understand that you created us to love you and nobody loves you more than Cordella. Please, don't let another angel enter your gates today. Let her enter your realm many years from now. In the name of the kingdom, the power, the glory forever and ever, amen.

I open my eyes and pull myself from the threshold of the doorway. I haven't prayed since I was a young child. I attend services and read the word, but never have I prayed since my mother taught me to. The chamber is lavish and far more well-kept than any other part of the miserable Old Palace Andria. A candle lit chandelier dangles from the ceiling in the center of the room. A hearth sits opposing a bed with blue silken covers adorning a feather-filled mattress. Red carpet lines half of the room and paneled wood the other, just as my chamber does. In fact, this entire room has similar decor to my own. An aghast feeling consumes me, almost as if my spine is attempting to leave my body. What morose measures, such disturbing love.

All the doors are painted a bright, alabaster white. That is the only difference between this chamber and my own. This factor calms me in a peculiar manner. That dark colored wood frightens me for delusional determinants such as the color the door was when it decided to attack me. Lizbeth most likely knows and appreciates much more about me than I know and appreciate about myself. An entryway to a bathing room calls to me and I hear the soft gurgle of heated water. I haven't had a proper bath since before Cordella and I professed our love to one another. I grimace and clash with the smothering emotions. The one remaining physical dignity I possess is the fact that I have not shed a tear and never will. I hastily claw at the pocket of Elli's coat for my notebook. I will use one of the precious pages remaining to write my disturbing recollections.

I am the one I blame,
it's me who has shame,
She is the bane,
Of life itself,
My head on her chamber shelf

I tuck the notebook into my pocket again and leak out a tortured sigh. My feet move towards the washroom idly. It's as I suspected. Almost exactly the same as my own, save the shape and the darkened wood. A large, steaming bath sits in the corner of the room. I strip and wash my skin thoroughly, making sure to remove every bit of grime from between my blistered toes. I've never traveled so far on foot in my entire life. Lizbeth even procured a tub of lavender foam, a soap that I prefer to use when bathing and washing. It reminds me of Andria's pleasurable spring months. Another shiver runs through me as more horrifying thoughts enter my mind. How did she gain the knowledge of what soap I prefer to bathe with? The warm water is gratifying, but I cannot fully enjoy the luxury of it in this state of anxiety and confusion. I wash the slowly healing scar on my face and the distorted scar on my side with docile care, for applying pressure to each spot influences me to feel justly stricken.

When I'm finished, I grab a silken towel from a white rack in the corner of the spacious area. It's exactly the same piece of furniture, save the color. For a reason unknown to me, I can't get over this fact. I dry the mess of thick, stygian curls atop my head. The bangs are growing back gradually. My hair will be back to its usual state of disorganization soon enough. The thought is somehow consoling to me in this time of great strife. At least my hair is a constant. The only constant in the universe is change and my hair. I'll allow myself to believe that as of now. I have nothing else to believe in.

Clothing was also laid out for me. A cerulean collared shirt with long sleeves and tight, dark blue trousers. No cravat. A note that says "no cravat" in its place, though. The next article of clothing horrifies me the most. It's the suit jacket I wore the night of that drunkard's engagement party, the night I met Peter, the night I gained this long, jagged scar. Another note: "I only left it with you when I was finished wearing it. I never returned it properly."

Vomit fills my throat and I turn away. I grab the suit jacket as memories attempt to drown my mind. I squeeze my eyes shut and command myself not to allow panic to overtake me yet again. What was the point of coloring the wood if she decided to leave the very article of clothing that would bring me the most distress? Some sick part of my mind considers that fact that she may have thought it romantic. I wrapped it around her shoulders and later that week, she carried my unconscious body in the jacket. I restrain another round of vomit. I toss the sinful piece across the room and focus on dressing myself in the other clothing she provided. I marvel at how she managed to get the blood out of the coat. I suppose she would have a lot of expertise removing blood.

I shudder again and revoke these thoughts. I pull on a pair of uniform dark blue boots. All the clothing she left me is tailored to my form and the boots fit me just as evenly, no astonishment there. Even a leather wristwatch she left me fits correctly on my slender wrist. I examine the scraps of paper on which she wrote her cursed notes. These are rather eerie. Another piece contains a poem I wrote about her in earlier times. My mind wanders as I try to make sense of it all. I have but a few minutes to the room in which we were instructed to meet in, but I'm far too tired to run and it's only a few doors down the quiet corridor.

I saunter through the uncannily familiar room and out into the generally uncanny hall. The candles flicker in turn with my slow movements. I feel as if I'm a prisoner walking to his own demise, a rather cruel thing if I were inquired on the subject. One of the flimsy light fixtures clatters to the ground before me. I step on the flame of the candle to save the building from a scorched disaster. If I were to take anything as a sign of forewarning, this would most definitely be it. I've had an awful feeling for the past few days. I sense a climax. Cordella will be sent away soon.

The door is ajar. Golden light seeps out of the room from within. A false sense of welcoming. I plant a foot in front of the doorway and relax my jaw. I could leave and run now. They're all occupied and they would only believe me late as I always am. My punctuality is rather questionable. I could steal away now and never look back. I'd be out the gates in no time at all. I would be all alone again in the fen between Palace Andria and Old Palace Andria. I cast these thoughts out of my mind. I've come too far to end it all now. I have to finish my pursuit. My hand finds its way to the door. I push it open and step within the reaches of the room.

I feel a rich golden carpet beneath my boots. A pleasant fire crackles in a small hearth. The orange flames match with the brilliant vermillion of the furnishings. My heart stops. Cordella's favorite color. This was purposeful. A vermillion sofa threaded with gold sits across from another of its kind in the center of the room. The dimness of the golden light gives the room an amorous ambience. A singular red candle sits in the middle of a wooden table between the two furniture pieces. Cordella sits atop the left of the two. Her eyes roll towards me as she hears my muffled footsteps against the soft carpet. Instead of the dull purple gown that she wore before, now she wears a marvelous vermillion gown that accentuates her figure beautifully. Her eyes are the single most splendid thing I've ever seen. The gown is aught compared to the jewels embedded in her face. In the light, her eyes display more than just the cosmos and all its splendors, they display her soul, pure and bright. I open my mouth, but close it immediately, for another person than just us two resides in the room.

"Alexander, you've joined us," Jakob says quietly from the corner. He has a slow sort of smile playing about his deceiving face.

I look up at him and then back at Cordella. Her features look labored and forlorn. She pushes herself to her feet with deliberate movements.

"You have a single hour," Jakob informs in an even more hushed tone before leaving through another door than the door I entered through. As soon as the exit closes, I rush towards her. She stands only a few feet from my previously stagnant form. I don't notice this fact until it's far too late. My arms wrap around her slight form and we collapse upon the vermillion furnishings. Her warm body against mine brings about a deeply heartfelt emotion that I can't name. I suppose I can name it. I only don't expect the emotion to be displayed as such a short word. I am sad.

"Cordella," I murmur into her ebony curls. I feel her soft lips kiss my ear.

"Alexander," she replies as her lips move to my own. We share a kiss of passion before reluctantly pulling away from each other. "So many colors," she whispers to me, immense unease finding its way onto her lovely features. "There are far too many colors, Alexander."

I stare into her eyes, the meaning of her words revealing themselves. I wrap her in another embrace, my heart melting in our shared agony.

"I know there are. There are far too many colors here," I reply in a wild tone of discomposure. She breaks the embrace and holds my face in her hands.

"I despise it. That demoness knows far too much about color," she whispers hollowly, an expression of remembrance forced upon her features.

"I know. I know you're frightened. It'll be alright. I'll save you if it's the last action I commit," I swear desperately. She nods and swallows more tears. For long moments, we only hold each other and assuage the other's pain. A heavenly peace fills me. Nobody can take her from me at this moment. I have her. I have her. "I have you," I promise quietly.

"Oh no, but I'm saving you as well. The colors of death are far too many to bear together. When my baby passed, the world was stained plum purple. When my light died, the world was stained blood red. When my hope died, the world was an awful shade of summer's yellow. When you were taken, the world was stained spring green, verdigris." She utters those last words with enough rage to move mountains. She knows Lizbeth's nom de plume. "And now, I will die and the only color I see is loathsome vermillion, the one color I allowed myself to avoid associating with death. The color vermillion is far too vibrant to be in relation with death. That and the sapphire blue of your eyes."

A stricken melding of all the unpleasant emotions fills me. "You aren't with child any longer?" I inquire in my most soothing of tones.

She grabs my collar for support and stares into my eyes. "It happened a week before we were together. Edward, may he burn in hell, sauntered in on my miscarriage and left me there to witness the death of our child alone."

An uproarious rage fills me. The most prominent of the melding is anger now. I hold her hand and stare into the flaming hearth.

"There are far too many colors," I agree in a somber tone. "Now you see why I prefer the absence. My world is far too colorful." I kiss her forehead and sigh. Her quivering form wraps itself around my waist.

"How much time do we have left?" Cordella queries in a hopeless tone. I don't wish to look at the watch. I wish time itself would disappear and I could hold her forever, let her protect me from the colors of the world. We still haven't discussed so many topics. The seven seas haven't been filled absolutely with the words we wish to speak to each other. We were about to discuss serendipity. I only wish that we could. I take a shaky breath and glance at the watch.

"We have a half hour," I reply in a low tone of quiescence. We sit in silence for a few more moments. The poundings of another blizzard beyond the heavily curtained windows create a rhythm with our joined heartbeats. "I wish love was perfect and angels would sing whenever our eyes met. I wish I could have more time with you, more than two months. The significance of this time in my life is great, even if it's so brief. I've never ever been this happy before, even if blue sorrow tinges my vision. You gave me that. You are my first love," I proclaim quietly.

"I never did say I love you," Cordella whispers into my hair. The silence continues as I register her words. She doesn't love me? I love her and that's all I care for.

"I love you," I reply in a reserved manner.

"I love you, too." My heart flutters in my chest. She loves me. A consoling warmth envelopes us as our time wanes. I catch small glances at the watch. A quarter hour left. I have to tell her something, I have to tell her how to live through the wrath of my brother.

"Cordella, listen to me, listen earnestly," I implore in an ardent tone. I plaster a desperate guise onto my face.

"Alright." She replies in a stifled tone as she notices my urgency. She pulls away from my form and a frigidity falls over me. I shiver and prepare to speak.

"Above all things, my brother hates most of all being reminded of his past. Tell him he's like his father in ending your life. If that doesn't work, scrutinize all his imperfections and tell him of the searing Andrian winds. He hates the wind," I say softly. She gazes into my eyes with a look of bewilderment. My words are rather cryptic, but I know they'll save her from a seemingly inevitable demise.

"I will do as you command," she promises in a strange tone. We spend the penultimate moments kissing each other's lips and making more empty promises. *I will see you again. We will be together. My love will never die.* I feel as if I'm in a character within a book, perhaps a large volume about the joys and sorrows of a summer romance. After only two months, the love disappears. It's customary for a leading figure in novels of that type to give the other leading figure something to remember them by. I gingerly pull the little leather notebook from my pocket, a regretful air falling over us.

"This is for you. It's yours now." I hand her my pain and the pen that etches it into the pages, a melancholy twitch in my fingers as I do so. Her mouth falls open as she stares at the volume. She knows the meaning of a gift such as this. "I hope you will fill the remaining pages with dulcet thoughts from your fantastical mind. This recollection certainly needs more, a hint of intrigue. Read my poems. Someone other than I must."

Her hands still lay limp at her side as she gazes at me in complete and utter awe. Her lower lip trembles as she closes her mouth. I try to memorize her face, for I may never see it again. There is a chance that either one of us could die in the next few weeks. I will miss her eyes and the heavens within them most of all. I take her hands and press the notebook and the pen into one of them. Another long silence fills the room. The storm outside is beginning to grow just as raucous as the one I endured a few days ago. I was not given gentle zephyrs as I wished for, but instead another blizzard. I glance at my watch, two minutes before the hour is complete. My eyebrows turn downwards with fury. How dare I be given so little time with her?

Just as the thought leaves my mind, the grandfather clock in the corner of the room strikes the end of the hour, a drawn-out chime echoing through the bones of the musty old building. Damnit! The watch must have been off! I throw my lips against Cordella's as the clock rings out. We pull close to each other in the final seconds, trying to learn every nuance of the other's lips. The red candle atop the table flickers out as the door swings open. Lizbeth stands stiffly at the doorway, a look of immense repulsion circling her brow. I let an agonizing smile slip onto my features as I look at Cordella one last time.

"May God save you," I whisper. She doesn't cry and grasp at me as I assumed she would. She only turns away and looks blankly in Lizbeth's direction. Her fingertips trail off mine as she ascends from the sofa. I savor the remnants of her touch.

"May God end this all, Alexander," Cordella breathes in a wistful tone. Dreams fill her eyes as she looks back at me one last time. The ghost of the most heartsick smile I've ever seen fades off of her face and into the abyss and she turns away as she's pulled to her likely demise.

CHAPTER 18

J ust as the hereafter of Lizbeth's non-consensual kiss was lengthy, the hereafter of Cordella's leave is drawn out as well. I watch the door to my better dreams seal shut as the door to the vermillion chamber closes. I don't attempt to move after the pair. The only thing Lizbeth and Cordella have in common is the fact that I once loved both of them. The invisible force keeps me rooted to my spot on the gold-threaded sofa. I feel far too lethargic to move. I reach my arm towards them as the door closes in a forlorn manner, a small croak leaving my throat. My heart grows heavy in my chest. It feels as if the beating organ is about to rip through my chest cavity. I release a sigh. Philosophers say that an individual loses a drop of that golden happiness every time they sigh. This poetic statement becomes more and more tangible the longer I sit on this sofa. I have the urge to pull the leather volume from my pocket, but it's no longer in my possession.

I've given my heart to my first lover along with it. The notebook has a single blank page remaining within its seemingly vast bearings. If my prayers are answered and I'm given the chance to see Cordella once again, I would love to gaze upon the final page. I cover my mouth with my hand to keep back a wave of dry coughs. I'm holding back forbidden tears and the sadness flows down into the depths of my throat.

I stumble to my feet in deep restitution. She's departed and I may never be able to memorize her handwriting or brush a lock of that ebony hair from her soft skin. I seal my eyes shut and attempt to make the world disappear. It would be oh so consoling just to not exist for a short time. Lord, I wish I didn't exist. My efforts are not met with the profit I long for. The world around me hasn't hidden itself. The ground is still solid and I could still fall through clouds if I so desired. I swallow the sadness in my throat to prepare for the next bout. With that act, I've made myself numb. A typewriter focused on printing the next word correctly. All I'm required to do is print the next word. All I have to do is make it back to the odd chamber Lizbeth prepared for me.

I happen on Jakob outside the spacious room. His eyes are a profound contrast to the dingy corridor. They have a malicious glint within them that one would not descry on first appraisal. He has one of the kindest faces I've ever seen from far away. He gestures down the hall, his dimples dredging. I nod at him and my eyes cloud over. It's as if a thick mist has overtaken me. My vision is blurry. It's my body's feeble attempt to block out this malefic world when my mind failed so miserably. Each step feels like a herculean effort. Stupefied sadness. The ironic thing about numbed pain is the fact that the numb sensation is equally as uncomfortable as the pain. Jakob follows close behind like a predator waiting for its prey to drop dead from a mortal injury. I feel as if I'm already dead, though. Why isn't he attacking me as all others do? My side aches acutely as I recall such persons.

I glance up at a piece of peeled red wallpaper. It sticks out like a branch and a spider has made its nest between the peeled fragment and the wooden wall behind it. The gossamer thread glimmers sinisterly in the half-light. The spider climbs methodically around its web as if dancing a waltz. A fresh layer of string falls in its wake. I turn my eyes away. Spiders are slightly disturbing to me, especially one in a place such as this. The spider fits with the dilapidated decor.

"Did you relish your romantic rendezvous as much as I believe you did? The silence was quite impressive. How did you manage to get her pretty lips to stop moving?" the man inquires boorishly. A jolt of rage shoots through me like an arrow. I'm tired and dejected. This fool's constant blabber doesn't help me, especially when it concerns the one I love. My hands curl into fists and my feet stop moving. I cock my head slightly and prepare to speak.

"What do you imply with that crude statement?" I reply in the most polite tone I can muster with the amount of fire coursing through my veins. My eyes are alight with that same fire. A rude chuckle echoes off the walls and I grit my teeth so tightly that I can hear the scaping echo around my head. My chest tightens and I can hardly breathe.

"You know what I implied. After all, you were the one in that secluded room with an angel."

I cough into my hand to keep it from slapping this vermin across his kind face. He releases another chuckle at my lack of movement and stagnant speech. I trip over my next words. "The lady's chastity of none of your business," I utter through a clenched jaw. I find myself spinning to look this sinful man in the eyes.

An amused grin plasters itself on his face. "I would call her many things, but chaste is not one of them. I can assure you of that," he finishes. He finally picks up on the obvious threat displayed in my icy eyes, but it only perpetuates his cruelty. Another tasteless remark leaves his lips and I realize just how drenched in filth this man is, even more so than the building we stand in.

"Lizbeth wouldn't want you speaking to me in this manner," I chide in a last attempt to close the vault of fury within me.

"Lizbeth only wants to—" Jakob starts, another unchaste articulation threatening to materialize. My grimace drops and my expression becomes icy. I cut him off mid-phrase.

"I don't believe you should finish that uproarious phrase," I warn. My pupils narrow as I stare into his slowly darkening eyes. I swear, he's begging to get himself killed. He's on his knees begging to die with these words of his.

"And why is that? The so-called great kingdom of Andria promotes the freedom of speech, does it not?" He asks. He stretches his arms out and spins in false awe of Andria's glory. So now he's disrespecting my country?

"Because I'll put my fist through your nose," I utter in the ghost of a whisper. It would be rather relieving to hear the sickening crunch of his nose against the floorboards. I have the opportunity to pay the universe back for smashing my nose against the floor of the infirmary a month or so ago. Lizbeth set the broken bone while I was unconscious. That's the only reason why my nose isn't crooked. I would rather prefer if it his nose became crooked. The defect would display some of his inward vileness to the unknowing onlooker. I find my fingers snaking up to my wrists to unhook my cerulean shirt sleeves.

"Ah, with your puny arms? You couldn't even but make a single scratch." He replies in a manner that shows how hilarious he believes himself to be. He continues raving about my lack of masculinity and it becomes more and more difficult to retain my composure.

"I honestly don't recall asking you to continue speaking," I retort in a slightly louder voice. More of that horrible chuckle escapes his lips. That's it. I haven't even dealt with a drunken noble this ridiculously repulsive. I shape my hands into fists as if I'm molding them from clay. Now, it should be noted that I've only ever hit anyone once before. My brother was that man. He once threw me outside the warmth of the palace in my underclothes for a full minute to entertain his high-standing friends. I genuinely believed death would take me. But then, he miraculously allowed me back from the balcony I was out upon. I thanked him profusely before having the grand epiphany that it wasn't my fault. That's when I slapped him across the face, making sure that my nails dug into his flesh. This is my second time. I wish for the blow to be far more impactful than a mere scratch. I swing my fist with rage-fed strength. I let out a cry of defiance as I do so. To my horror, my fist misses him completely. I didn't even make contact with the meaty mass of his body! He stepped deftly out of harm's way.

"I don't recall asking you to throw a fist at my face," he replies in a deadly tone of mocking. His features become cross for a brief second before returning back to their customary sickening jovialness. "Now, now, be a good boy and return to your chamber just as Lizbeth wished for you to do. She sure chose a fiery one."

I swallow my rage along with my sadness and my pride. I nod slowly and blink a few times. I traipse more quickly down the uneven corridor. I don't want to be near him. I may act carelessly again and get hurt. The last thing I need in a time such as this one is to get hurt. He's most likely armed with a weapon other than his menacing fists. I don't want to gain another scar. I want to keep living. I remind myself of these perilous prospects as he continues speaking.

He leaves me with a final comment about something so awful and disgusting that I have to slam the door in his face to keep myself from attacking again. His words ring through the silence of the deserted room. Silence, a state I know very well yet have come to dislike in the past months. Odd things happen in silence. I breathe in and out to calm myself before reaching towards the top button of my shirt. This day has exhausted me more than any other. I only want for one thing at this moment. I want to sleep peacefully, although I know that isn't an option tonight. Far too many climactic events have occurred today for me to sleep without dreams.

The buttons of my shirt pop out of their respective holes. Only when I'm finished unbuttoning my shirt do I realize how dangerous it would be to slumber in the cavern of a dragon. Very dangerous indeed. I could be eaten or scorched in my sleep. In other words, it's quite foolhardy to rest with a killer on the other

side of the door, even if she does love me more than herself. I
slink towards the door as quietly as I possibly can to check the
door for a lock. Of course there isn't one. What kind of person
who reads my poetry would allow a lock on my door? A careless
smile creeps onto my face followed by a laugh at the hilarity of
my act of smiling at a time such as this one.

The edge of fear is sobering enough to keep my eyelids from
drooping. A pot of tea would assuage my fatigue as well. A
roaring flame was lit in the hearth across from my bed in the
time I was away. I make do with a kettle found on one of the
unnaturally painted shelves and breakfast tea from another
cabinet. The water was drawn from a basin left in the washroom.
I make myself comfortable on a large crimson armchair before
the fire and watch the water boil absentmindedly. If I'm not able
to sleep, what can I do to pass the time? The water begins to boil
in the black pot and I pull it off the fire. Tea is a nasty concoction
without milk and sugar in my humbled opinion. I sip the dank
liquid anyways, my nose turned up at the putrid scent. This will
keep me alert for longer.

The real truth is that I'm not afraid to sleep. I'm afraid that
she'll watch me when I sleep as she did for the months we didn't
speak to one another. The thought of her staring at my dormant
form is unnerving and I don't want it to ever happen again. Time
passes and the wandering of my mind grows morose. I feel as if
spiders are crawling from my ears. I instead focus on the small
details of things such as the teacup I hold to distract myself from
constant angst contained within my chest.

The vessel is black just as its counterpart is. It looks to be of
Walsian descent. Andrian tea sets always have a smidge of color,
even if it's just a flower or a bird bold against a darkened set.
Ceramics are a specialty in Walsia. This ceramic piece is
masterfully crafted. I do wonder how Lizbeth or Jakob procured
something of such great value on this short notice? The man who
I believed to be my father waited four years for a set similar to

this one. He smashed it all to bits the day after it arrived. Edward
told me that story. I admire the way my face distorts itself in the
dim reflection the cup casts. My jawline appears more square
and my eyes larger and more eager. The vessel may be plain and
seemingly ordinary, but it's quite rare and priceless. That alone
contains more beauty than the piece. If one put a lengthy price
marker on an old boot, the rich would swarm it to prove their
monetary blessings. This is rather boring, staring at my own
dim, silvery reflection in a teacup.

The rousing effects of the dour liquid wanes as the hour ends.
An hour since she left me. I lean further into the upholstery of
the armchair. The candles that sit on the nightstands died
moments ago and the dispirited light has become even more
languid. The only light that remains is that of the fire. I begin to
ponder the fact that Lizbeth may actually come. She doesn't
know whether I sleep or lay awake. She may just assume my
unconsciousness because of my customary sleeping patterns.
She'd be rather daft if she did though. I'm in a terrifyingly odd
place and she should not assume me to be comfortable enough
to sleep. Of course, I could sleep anywhere because of my
natural strength for falling asleep. That doesn't mean I'd choose
to.

Speak of the devil—in this case, ponder the devil—and the
devil appears. My body tenses as the door to the chamber creaks
open in a weary manner. At least she's taking the precaution of
being silent. I wait until she realizes her dire mistake before
standing to my feet abruptly and turning to face her. Lizbeth's
eyes widen as she notices my figure lurking in the brighter half
of the room. I let a dismal frown seep onto my face.

"Well then, I suppose this night will be longer than I
expected," I gripe quietly. She giggles mindlessly in a perturbing
manner.

"I didn't expect you to be awake at such a late hour," she
notes as her composure returns to her. A grim smile sinks onto

her face as she takes a step in my direction. Her form radiates intimidation. The very sight of her strikes fear in my heart after the earlier occurrence. I quiver at the thought of it. I take a step back from her as she moves closer and an expression of hurt plays at her face. It's gone too soon to dissect. She sighs and reclines on the armchair opposing mine, resting her head delicately on her fist. Her emerald green eyes glimmer perniciously as she stares at my ever-wavering form. Half her face is concealed in the midnight purple of a shadow.

"Have a seat, I insist," I whisper in a witty manner. I try to plaster an assured smile on my face, but all I want to do is hide in the wardrobe like a child does from an imaginary monster. I haven't had this strong an urge to run away in quite some time. I believe I did after my mother passed, but someone caught me before I went too far.

"You're in my house Alexander. You're a guest. Now, have a seat. I *insist*." She smiles into her words. She's staying strong in her earlier promises. I let out a stifled sound and hesitantly push myself back down again. I clasp my hands together as tightly as I possibly can to refrain from moving. I'm a man. I shouldn't be so frightened of her. There's just something so... So malevolent in those eyes though. Or perhaps, the absence of something that makes all eyes less malevolent. She appears inhuman in this light. Truly a bronze statue. Verdigris.

"I am an object to you, but I have the right to information and I wish to inquire but three questions." I collect my most burning queries into three definable questions and prepare to ask.

"Alexander, you are so much more than an object. Object is an androgynous word, many things fit into the category of object. No, you're more of a conduit. A conduit I wish I could keep happy, but could do without happiness." She moistens her lips and continues speaking. "I will grant you three questions if it will bring you joy," she responds, her voice peeling off at the end in a morose manner.

"What you mentioned earlier, the part in which you told me that I make you feel, feel what exactly? You didn't finish your phrase properly," I begin. This inquiry is only to confirm my worst beliefs.

"Alexander, I'm an empty person. Broken, not from any pain or suffering I've endured, although I have had my fair share in that respect. You allow me to experience the emotion that you feel every waking hour," she clarifies in a peculiar tone. I'm taken aback despite my previous knowledge. Lizbeth is unfeeling, void of emotion. "I glean emotion from you." She simplifies as if I'm a small child. A deeper frown flickers onto my features. The fire begins to die and Lizbeth takes a long stoker with a darkened tip from a container next to the hearth and pokes at the embers mindlessly, a look of tranquility on her face.

I sit back, dumbfounded at her placidness. "Why didn't you murder Cordella as you do all the others who cause you problems?" I inquire, biting into the last few words with some leftover rage. Now this is an inquiry I genuinely wish to be answered. I let my hands claw against the arms of the armchair.

"As I told you before, I wish to keep you happy. You seem to have a rather firm connection with this particular issue, so I decided to allow your brother to be responsible for taking her life," she finishes, a jubilant smile on her face at the prospect of Cordella's life ending.

I nod hesitantly and prepare for the final question. My heart thuds. "What would you do if I suddenly perished?"

Her features darken for a moment before the amiable smile returns to her face. If I disappeared, perhaps Andria's future would be better for it. The sovereignty could continue without challenge.

"That's a good attempt. I would still take Andria for myself if you suddenly perished. Your death would do nothing to benefit anyone." Her phrase ends with a precise laugh. A rather bewildering way to end such a grim response. If I passed on, it would do nothing. Now I know that isn't a feasible solvent. We sit in a heavy silence until the embers become unrevivable and Lizbeth has to acquire another log. She lights it with a match she pulls from an ornate ebony match case. I wait and wait for her to leave, but she doesn't move. She stays rooted to the armchair. Lord, she's not even blinking. I scarcely believe she's breathing.

"Lizbeth?" My heartbeat deadens my own words. I only feel the vibrations against my heart strings. How long will it take her to reply? Was she replaced with a statue in a less attentive moment?

"Yes, Alexander?"

"Do you just intend to sit here all night?" My lips curl upwards restlessly with the unnerving prospect.

"I only granted you three questions." She repositions herself so that her head rests on her other arm. I imagine it's gone numb by now.

I clear my throat and shift about as the skeletons on gallows do in the wind. "Pray, could I have another?" I ask wearily, hoping she'll answer positively. She cocks her head to one side stiffly as if an idea has come to her during the moments of silence.

"That's another question, Alexander," she responds matter-of-factly as if it's the most apparent response. I nod my head gradually and cast my eyes downwards. She doesn't wish for me to die. She only wishes for my love. I'm suddenly acutely aware of my shirt being unbuttoned. I've never exposed myself to a woman other than Cordella and I pull it closed, a blush settling on my face. My rapid movement captures her attention.

Lizbeth admits a slight laugh at my misfortune. "I was waiting to see when you'd notice," she states in a humoring tone. Her teeth appear to be fangs in the deceiving light. I'm tired of her childish antics. The rage attacks me again and I pull my shirt off entirely, flinging it into the fire swiftly. My eyes burn with fury and her mouth opens slightly. The audacity! She doesn't even try to avert her eyes!

"Now I'm playing the game. How does it feel?" I reply in a dangerously low tone. I attempt to mimic my brother's intensity in my expression. My eyebrows furrow and I blink back tears as I watch my shirt become scorched in the blue-tinged inferno. I turn my back from her and gently massage my own temples. I feel as if a band of tension has been wrapped around my head.

"That's another question, Alexander. I always win the game." Now she really appears to be a demoness. My pounding heart rages with angst and I back away from her. My footsteps lead me back to the door in which I entered through. She stays seated, an expectant smile on her face as I rattle the handle. Apparently the door does have a lock. I curse her blusteringly.

"I won't ask you, then. I'm demanding this of you. Leave at once and don't come back tonight!" Her eyes travel down my toned chest as she nods. I run a hysterical hand through my hair and my blush becomes more prominently furious. I feel far too soft at this time. Far too soft for this rough world.

"It's delicious how hastily your emotions can waver out of control. Delicious. For that reason, I'll leave you as of tonight. You know, I never ever believed the day would come in which I would show you, of all persons, an edge of anger. I apologize for that, but it's the only way I can get through your stiff skull. I love you, Alexander." She pulls herself to her full height and strides past me. "You've grown taller," she mentions as a parting gift.

I hover behind her to see how she fastens the door, but it opens effortlessly with a mechanical click. I wait for the sound of her footsteps to dissipate before sinking down to my knees. I no longer have the stamina to remain on my feet

"Control yourself. Control yourself. Control yourself," I whisper in an erratic rhythm. I'm on the verge of tossing my final piece of dignity to ruins. My face will not become wet with the trivial tears all individuals wear at least once in their lives. "I refuse it. I will not let her take both my love and my dignity from me in one fell swoop. I refuse it," I mutter to myself.

My knees waver and collapse beneath me. I feel a triangle of angst sear itself into my chest. A deep-set feeling of utter loss of control erupts within me. The world around me spirals in and out of existence, the only sound being the chorus of my own voice. "I won't, I won't, I won't." Over and over again. As I sink deeper and deeper into the crepuscular pool I've found myself in, the more difficult it becomes to breathe. What in all creation is happening to me? It's as if I'm stepping in and out of a separate realm. I let out a dry sob, thank the Lord. Why is everyone being taken from me, why can't I keep one person safe and well within my grasp? Why am I so utterly alone? My chest burns and constricts as if it's about to burst. Then it's all gone.

I stand on a precipice all alone. I'm astonished to find myself here, for I was on the floor of an eerie room only seconds ago. Mist encircles every aspect of the world around me, save the massive cliff laying out before me. The air is frigid and stagnant and I'm without a coat or even a shirt. The panic and turmoil has left my body and I feel oh so serene, almost frighteningly so. I blink in disorientation. I turn in a circle once to observe my surroundings. Something within the mist behind me catches my eye. It's another set of human eyes. Icy and pale. Soulless and impenetrable. Deadly calm. The eyes of the former king of Andria, the man I believed to be my father. A sense of acute understanding courses through my veins as I stare at him. The mist curls into the shape of a man, the shape of him. The rest curls into the shape of my brother's crown atop his head. He strides towards me. I'm not a small child as I was the last time I saw him in a dream. I'm still about three quarters of his height. A customary blue suit wraps around his form as he saunters nearer.

"Hello, Alexander," he greets me in a gravelly voice. I still remember the sound down to the very detail. His voice always drops to a bass tone at the end of his phrases. It isn't graceful like my mother's voice or brash like my brother's voice. In total, it's more frightening than any sound I've ever heard.

"I've had dreams like this before," I state robustly. He nods contemplatively and folds his arms behind his back in the manner Edward does. A rule of conduct.

"Good observation," he notes, a hesitant smile playing at his lips. His tone tickles my senses unpleasantly.

"What makes it good? Or are you playing that game as well."

His eyebrows furrow at my cryptic phrase as if he doesn't understand my meaning. Of course he understands my meaning. He's a figment of my own imagination! "Game? What makes the observation good, is the fact that it's half true?" The mist curls around his fingertips.

"Half?" I inquire quietly. He moves ever closer to me, so close I can smell the remnants of red wine in his teeth. That was the former sovereign's poison of choice. He always smelled of it. My phantoms are growing more and more realistic. I hope they don't cross through my mind and into the tangible world. I wouldn't be able to tell phantoms and people apart.

"I'm not a dream, I'm a figment of your imagination, just as you believe. Think of a color," he commands. Why should I follow his orders? I grit my teeth and shake my head. I try to clear thoughts of Cordella from my mind.

"I prefer no color." I reply in the most cordial tone I can muster. The world around us slowly fades from grey to black. Only the cliff remains in color. He stretches his arms out as if displaying a creation, a smile splitting his features apart. Cordella still plagues my mind and I close my eyes. When I open them again, stars and colorful planets twinkle in the sky, some close, some farther off. My mouth parts hastily and my eyes widen as I marvel at the celestial lights before our very eyes.

"Your mind is a beautiful thing, Alexander," he notes as he admires the masterpiece above us. "Love is an incredible thing." He speaks deliberately, a trying look in his eyes.

"So you aren't Angel, the former king of Andria?" I inquire.

"No, I'm not. I'm you. Your mind created me in this image so that you could blame an evil figure for what happens to you next. I'm here to help you cry." His words daunt me greatly. I don't want to cry, I don't need to cry. It's irrational. I plant an expression of fury on my face and he chuckles miserably.

"I refuse it!" I yell as he grows an inch nearer. An epiphany strikes me. The precipice symbols my tears. If I fall, then I cry. I begin to start, but an invisible hand holds me firm as he approaches, an apologetic expression plastered across his stone features. I see my own frightened reflection in his eyes. "Stop! As the second prince, I command you to leave!" I yell as a last resort. I feel as if I'm being drowned. I back away farther. Each footstep echoes across the vast confines of my mind. I look upwards in despair, a look of distress complimenting my features. My heart pounds against my ribcage. Cordella's cosmos glimmer above me. I wish I could soar up to them and reside on one of the many paradisiacal planets within its reaches.

"Listen Alexander, please, I beg of you, don't do this. We have to survive, live on, be strong. I have to be strong so that one day I can go up there. I'll crumble and fall apart if I cry. I'm similar to a piece of parchment. If I get wet, I'll dissipate. I'll die! Oh Lord, I'll die!" I plead. It's as if my voice consumes the entire realm of my imagination. My words echo back through me deafeningly. "I'll die!" I repeat.

The part of me in the body of Angel of Andria is far too close to now. He grasps my wrists roughly and grits his teeth. His eyes bore into my own, a shattered look filling his eyes in the final moments. I yell out more hopeless pleas. I even call to the celestial lights above me. He lowers me backwards and I feel a wetness accumulate around my sullen eyes.

"Life is good. Someday it will be as it should. I love the stars up in the sky. Someday we will see them up close with our naked eyes," he promises firmly. He gives me a resolute nod. His icy fingers loosen around my wrists, but I no longer protest. I understand the inevitable. A single tear falls from my right eye. He smiles nostalgically, a wistfulness in his eyes as he watches it roll down my face. An overwhelming dejection overtakes me as the tear drops from my skin. I watch the glistening tear drop hit the ground below us. The world around us explodes with color. Every color imaginable, sharp blues and alluring purples flood my vision along with brilliant greens and potent yellows. He releases my arms and I fall, tears falling freely. I let out a sob as I fall and reach my hand towards the place on which I stood. Angel of Andria cries too, but a grateful smile curls his lips upwards. I fall until all the colors disappear, and the rock around me, as well. I fall until darkness has returned to the realm of my mind again.

I'm back in the eerie room, curled in the same spot on the floor. I push myself lithely into a sitting position and grab at my face hurriedly. A single tear rolls down my cheek.

CHAPTER 19

Third Person Perspective

Peter of Nowhere sat alert, a morose simper on his features. He felt like laughing more than anything, even more than he felt like dying. The situation he'd found himself in had far too much irony and all he could do was laugh. He had been exiled from Andria only to be brought back by a ruthless maiden. He was surrounded by so many other people, yet he felt alone and forsaken by both his family, his friends and even God at times. Peter was astonishingly religious, even with his misfortune in mind. His faith led him through many of his lesser days. He couldn't recall a single night in Hyvern where he hadn't prayed for his life.

His chamber was the smallest Lizbeth, dealer of secrets and less innocuous ideas, could procure for him. She searched tirelessly to make him the least comfortable she could. He had disobeyed her instructions when first given, so she revoked him most rights, such as the right to freedom. Lizbeth was neither a hard worker nor a slacker. Her mediocre values would not change for a man who had wandered the ends of the continent for half his life, even if he was a blood sovereign. Her values instructed her to punish him for his disobedience, for all things were under Lizbeth.

The chamber was spacious, yet sparsely decorated. The wallpaper was musty and peeling under the weight of many years and the floorboards creaked wherever one would step. The windows were boarded up with splintering strips of wood so that Peter would have to dwell in the empty light of a few waxy candles. After a while, the old stubs gave off the scent of death. Peter could not escape the room, nor could he escape the stench. Peter had forgotten his place in the last few days and Lizbeth decided it was fitting to teach her subordinate another lesson. Peter was locked in the chamber, only to be released when departure was in order. They would leave the next morning for the Stone Chapel, the dueling grounds on which he would end his brother. There was still a place in his heart where young Edward resided, but his family was worth losing him. He would do all things for them, even if it meant driving the blade of a sword through his younger brother's skull. He winced at the thought of it, his thumbs sinking deeper into his starched pockets.

Peter collapsed atop a decayed twin bed that rested in the corner of the room. The furnishing looked odd and out of place amongst the nothingness of the vast space. The moldy sheets crinkled under his weighty form. Peter was taller than his younger brother Edward, but only by an inch. He closed his eyes and pulled the pillowcase off the singular pillow. He put the covering over his eyes, for he didn't have the will to keep his eyes sealed in such a hostile place. Old habits die hard and this was another one he picked up in Hyvern. He rustled and shifted, but the mattress was sunken and more rigid than the ground. He considered sleeping on the ground, but he'd seen a suspicious looking bout of spiders swarming about the floor and he believed them to be poisonous. The silence was deafening and Peter had nothing to solace himself with. Alexander had his notebooks and Edward had himself, but all Peter had was his own, disturbed memories. Peter always prayed when times such as these came, but he felt too lost for that. It was easier to turn over and whine into the thin mattress. With time, anything is possible. After an hour or so alone with his hateful self, Peter began to pray.

Dear Lord, hallowed be your name. Your kingdom come, your will be done, on Earth as it is in heaven. Give us each day our daily bread and forgive us our sins as we forgive those who've sinned against us. Lead us not into temptation, but deliver us from evil. For thine is the kingdom, the power, the glory forever and ever, amen.

All Peter could pull off first was the Lord's prayer. It was mechanical and committed to his memory. It seemed as if the rest of his mindscape was drained and sequestered. He laid in silence with the pillowcase over his head. He felt absolutely ridiculous, but it was all he could do.

Dear Lord, please grant me your mercy. There is a moral choice in this matter and my simple mind can't comprehend it. Either I end my brother, or my remaining family perishes on my account. Either one dies, or three. Either I murder someone, or two people die on my account and I die. Which is best? You've helped me through many times, even if I've turned my back on you and lost track of my faith in the past. I ask you forgiveness for all my transgressions and I know, I've always known you've forgiven me. But even you dislike murderers, although if they give you their hearts, they're saved as everyone else is. I only wish I didn't have to be begrudgingly saved. Don't let me stain my hands with the blood of others. Please, that is what I ask of you. Thine is the kingdom, the power, the glory forever and ever, amen.

Peter finished his second prayer. A cold sweat slid down his plain shirt as he pulled the pillow case from his head. Lizbeth stood before him, a scowl splayed across her features.

"Peter, whatever do you mean by wearing a pillowcase as a crown should be worn? I suppose that's good spirit, seeing you'll claim sovereignty in a matter of hours, but why?" Lizbeth inquired humorously. She appeared to be in a pleasant mood, but Peter didn't know the reason for that. How could anyone ever be happy in a world as dismal as this one?

Peter had just renewed his faith in the Lord, but he still felt stiff and numb. "I was attempting to get some rest. I need to conquer Andria in a matter of hours, just as you said," Peter retorted scornfully, a scowl settling upon his comely features.

Lizbeth only smiled, a true joyfulness marking her gaze. She was blind to the anger in his words. "You were speaking in a hushed tone. You weren't trying to sleep," she stated, taking a step closer to the man. Her eyes flickered around the bare room in disgust before turning back to Peter's strong stature again.

"I was praying. I'm about to commit the murder of my younger brother," He disclosed thoughtlessly. "I'm praying for his soul and my own. And Alexander's," he finished heartlessly.

Lizbeth grimaced. A reprimand lay waiting in her throat, but she wanted to encourage her figurehead as much as she could before he fought to the death for her. Even Lizbeth had a sense for wrong and right, even if it was faint. The least she could do for the man she shattered was encourage him in these penultimate hours.

A long, silver sword rested within a scabbard at her side. She'd brought it for Peter to appraise. It was of the finest craftsmanship and the weapon he'd use to do the deed. With that said, the sword had a sense of foreboding about it. The sword was unburdened, yet potent. It could slice through bone in one fell swoop. Lizbeth had tested that bearing before presenting it to him. She'd taken considerable care in removing the blood from the blade. She wanted Peter to feel as readied as possible in these final hours, even if it meant scrubbing. A candle stub sputtered out on a rickety nightstand and Peter stopped the meager flame with his bare finger. It appeared he didn't fear pain and Lizbeth was pleased with that. She drew out the blade and held the weighty piece with both of her freckled hands as she stood before Peter. He seemed repulsed by it and for a second, Lizbeth worried that she hadn't removed all the blood from the weapon. There was no need to fear, though. All the blood had been removed. It was only Peter's genuine repulsion towards swords. His father had a cutlass. His own sword had been used against him. These memories were enough to at least deter him from the prospect of sword fighting.

"Take it. Let me know if the proportions are enough for you. I wish for it to be perfectly balanced if it'll aid you in battle." She nodded, a malevolent giddiness in her eyes.

Peter was frightened for the girl's soul. She appeared to be possessed. He took the silver piece from her and turned it over in his hands as if he was getting a sense for it. Lizbeth retrieved a gun from her pocket. It was a small, black pistol. She pointed it at Peter as he held the weapon. It was only a forethought and Lizbeth was not a fool. She knew her death would cause the end of this gambit and many wanted only for her to die.

Peter didn't care for the blade. He didn't care about its weight, beauty, or cleanliness. It was only as good as any other weapon would be in the end. Dueling is a game of odds. Peter knew that. Whoever got the first swing would be in line for victory. If you were caught from behind, you're dead. If you get lanced in the abdomen or the head by blades of this caliber, you're dead. Many other layers of chance such as these are a part of dueling.

"It's fine," he answered listlessly.

Lizbeth nodded, her smile shrinking only a bit. She took the blade from him for safe keeping. She didn't want him to harm himself in the beforetime. If he really wished to, he could find a way, but Lizbeth didn't want to make it plausible for him. He would really have to struggle if he wanted to harm himself. She left him with a parting gift before she reached the door as she did after nearly every less than pleasant conversation.

"If you don't win, your family dies. If you don't win and survive, you and your family dies. If you win, only Edward dies. Don't let him live, even if he pleads with you or you'll all die," she threatened, the soulless smile still etched in her eyes. The door pivoted shut. With a metallic click, Peter was locked in again with the shadow of a sword on his hands. What decision would he make?

Meanwhile, in Palace Andria, Edward was in a similar position to Peter, the only difference being the absence of Lizbeth. In this case, Edward was his own ruthless maiden. His own mind hurled insult after insult at himself as Lizbeth would do to Peter when he misbehaved. Edward had done well with correcting the tragedy he'd endured a few days previous. He cleaned up his mess, dotted all his I's and crossed all his T's. Not a single whiff of evidence pointed to him, in fact, technically he hadn't even seen the corpse. He was skilled in the regard of feigning sadness. He'd done it many, many times before. He would've made a good actor. The only loose knot was the sound of his own mind, the words he told himself and all. His mind sounded like a petulant child that didn't get their way. He couldn't sleep.

"Oh, so now you've somehow begotten a conscience? That's absolutely marvelous, well it would be if it were true!" Other Edward retorted deafeningly as real Edward lay stiff atop his neatly-made sheets. "You deserve whatever death you're met with. You deserve Cordella's infidelity. You deserve every ounce of poison you've been fed throughout this life you've been given, which is too long a time. You're a waste of breath."

Other Edward had been silent for a time before Edward's thoughts had happened upon the murder for the hundredth time that night. The sovereign even had an inkling of hope that he'd get some sleep before the duel. He hadn't slept since the death of that man. The shadow traversed across the room until he was only feet from tangible Edward. Edward stared into his own eyes with unease. It was rather unnerving to look into his own eyes without the assistance of a mirror. He wondered how his mind could conjure up an image such as this. It only looked so real.

"Could you please leave me alone for only but a moment? That's all I require, only that. A moment. If I could only sleep one last time? My death may very well be tomorrow," he implored the other. A scornful facade appeared on phantom Edward's face. The shadow crossed his arms and turned his back, his shoulder blades bulging through his royal blue suit. The sound of the blizzard battering at the confines of the chamber was the only sound heard for the next few seconds.

"No. I refuse, just as you refused to end the one who was unfaithful to you. You gave in after only a *moment* of listening to her pleas. They were most definitely given to her by Alexander, yet you still gave in. See, I would be doing the exact same as you did if I gave you a moment, Edward. I don't want to be like you, nobody does. If you'd met your son, I bet he wouldn't have even wanted to be remotely similar to you," the ghost said, rage adorning his features. Edward shifted unpleasantly as he gazed upon himself. He needed another in the room with him to disprove this ghost. He would have Cordella brought to him. Yes, he could ask her to explain her reasons for betraying him. He already knew a few, but he thought her better than to use his own brother.

"No! That's an awful idea! You'd just end her as you did that poor man. You aren't in your right mind. You're far too fragile to—"

"I don't care!" Edward yelled, pulling himself into a crude sitting position. He felt like a child whining to his father. As a matter-of-fact, he does appear similar to his father. So does Peter, although his hair is much darker and his eyes rounder. His nose is crooked, most likely from a broken nose he endured during his many years of travel. A slick smile crowned the shadow's face. Edward sealed his eyes and rolled back on his side.

"If you don't care, then why aren't you calling for her now, you thick-wit? I'm correct, it would be an awful idea," Ghost Edward stated, a grim joy lining his voice like a silken suit. Edward pulled a pillowcase from one of his many pillows and shoved it over his head in the same manner Peter had. It only muffled the scolding, but it lessened the oddity of the situation.

He could no longer see a perfect copy of himself, only hear its shrill voice. It felt oh so sadistic, the sound of the smile and the scorn in the other's eyes. It was ridiculous, so Edward laughed. He laughed until his own voice drowned out the sound of the ghost. When he finally ceased, all sound had stopped. It was utterly silent. Edward didn't dare to move, even an inch to make himself comfortable. It was finally silent. He'd lived with the sound of the shadow's voice for a few days and it wasn't a pleasant recollection.

Edward began to ponder details of things, such the fact that duels always took place the day before they were scheduled. This tradition had begun many years before when commoners began to observe the duels that took place between members of the court and the monarchy. They took it to be some form of costless revelry, something to bet on. It was appalling to the monarchy; duels are grave matters in which one or both participants perish. The death of another is not entertainment for the people. The day prior act was meant to mislead the commoners as to when the duel would commence. Now it was an act of solidarity towards the sin of making an honorable death public. Edward had observed plenty of dishonorable deaths, one of which being the death of his father. They had cast him out in the dead of winter to fend against the searing Andrian winds. Of course, Edward's father hadn't lasted long. He'd died as the rest had. They found his corpse bent over a tree branch. The wind had been so intense that day that it had knocked the man's lifeless body into the tall spruce. Edward didn't enjoy pondering the gruesome thought, but at least it was silent.

"Lord Edward, even without my help your thoughts turn to morose subjects. What are you, a maniac?" Phantom Edward inquired. Edward could hear the other's hands whirring through the dense air. Tangible Edward groaned sorrowfully and rolled over yet again. Yes, he was indeed a maniac. His mind wouldn't relent.

"Yes, I am a maniac," he whispered, voicing his thoughts disgracefully. It was a last attempt.

"Well then maniac, this should be enough incentive to help you gain victory tomorrow. You've finally discovered your true self and you can do much with this. You have many more years remaining. You can escape the bindings you've been ensnared in for your entire life and be the continuance of your father's legacy. It would be so very easy," the voice whispered back. At the curling lilt of the other's words, Edward snagged the pillowcase from his head and tossed it across the room. The proposition was seductive and enticing. The tone of the conversation had changed so quickly that he'd been given whiplash. Edward felt an inexplicable gravity pulsating through the room, tugging him towards the ghost.

Tangible Edward's eyes became darker as he rose to his feet, the flicker of a dim candle illuminating his face. Edward felt an aspect of himself leave him in that moment, something rather imperative although he couldn't tell what. He did, however, feel power. Power that replaced the sudden emptiness in full. He felt it in his teeth and in his fingertips. He felt it in his feet and torso. Lord, he even felt it tingling at the tips of his immaculately-coiffed hair.

"Take my hand," the shadow whispered in a demented, fathomless tone. His very words wavered on the stream of tangible Edward's understanding. They echoed through the souls of those in the building. They echoed through Edward himself. These words were so very compelling that all he wished to do was grab onto the hand of the figure who stood before him. But, he hesitated right before their fingers made contact.

"I—" he said wearily, an expression of fear upon his features. It was as if a match had been lit and was being held to the carpet. Tangible Edward's eyebrows furrowed as he stared into the eyes of the decided spirit before him. There was something so very empty about his face. No life, no memories. Something was missing. But then, he spoke again and Edward's consternation vanished, never to be seen again.

"Take my hand Edward. We are one in the same. We can truly be one if you would only take my hand," he crooned. Yes, this figure certainly possessed a silver tongue as Edward himself did and Edward could never resist himself. He was as narcissistic as he'd always been. That was his downfall. If only he cared a little less. He grasped the man's frigid fingers firmly, an assured look in his eyes. And there it was, the warmth that had enveloped him a day or so previous. He was trapped in the lulling warmth of the abyss. And then it was only darkness. And then there was somewhere far different from this Earthly realm. Somewhere with white fire and deafening, roaring screams. From the ashes rose Edward without himself.

The third and final brother lay awake as the others did. The only aspect of his sorrow that was set apart from the others was the fact that his face was wet and he hadn't bothered to dry it. It had been hours since that first teardrop had tarnished the floor. It had been hours since the world had been distorted with color. It had been hours since the one shred of dignity that remained with him had been pried from his rigid fingers. And as if that one tear wasn't enough, others fell along with it.

The second tear was more difficult to bear than the first. The shame of the first pressed in on Alexander as the depths of the ocean do a submarine. The passengers within the vessel have nothing other than the metal confines to defend them from the perilous expanse beyond. Alexander felt that way, only he felt as if his fellow crew members had forced him from the submarine. He still had to hold on though, he still had to hold his breath until the very last moment, until his lungs caved in from the thousands of tons of pressure. The third was easier, but only slightly. It felt so very peculiar as it rolled down his pale cheek. He wasn't accustomed to the sensation yet. He soon would be.

As the fourth and fifth fell from his face, another new feeling settled around him. The fire had died away and he was shrouded in complete darkness, deprived of his most prominent sense. He was very grateful for the lack of light; he didn't want anyone to see him in this shameful state. Lord, he didn't want to see himself in this state. The blackness enveloped him and the sixth tear fell from his right eye. It trickled down over his newly-formed scar and Alexander let out a stifled cry. So many wounds, both physical and emotional. He felt as if he were a character in an epic. He was about to meet his end in a tragic manner to display some form of heed-worthy tale. Alexander didn't want to be a heed-worthy tale. He wanted to be a victor, one loved by all. Yet he still found himself wrapped up in the spiral of sadness that heed-worthy tales contain.

With the seventh tear, Alexander found himself disgusted by himself for another reason. He was displeased with the fact that he was beginning to revel in tears. He loved the kind embrace they gave his face before falling to the ground. At least they said goodbye before leaving him. Alexander shifted to a sitting position. He let out a long, quivering sigh. After he accepted the warmness of his own tears, each droplet was unable to count. Well, if he really desired to, he could have counted them as they seeped from his eyes. But Alexander didn't want to count them any longer, at least not as bouts of shame or drops of embarrassment.

Alexander grasped a leg of the large bed on which his back rested. He hoisted himself to his feet using the support from that leg, for Alexander's own legs wouldn't support him. This agony in his body felt painfully good. He hadn't felt this way in so very long. It was almost mythical to him. He hardly made it onto the bed with such thoughts spiraling through the catacombs of his mind. It was a relief when he did. He didn't have to aid himself any longer and could let something else deal with it for once. The floor was before, but it was oh so cold and rough. Alexander stared towards the ceiling fervently, his lips trembling. The tears seeped onto the pillow behind his head. He folded his hands neatly across his bare chest in resolution. He was too weak to stop the flow. He would not concern himself with his own dignity any longer.

Alexander stared harder at the ceiling, deciphering a few mystical shapes from his rigid position. He hadn't noticed the artistry before. A mural was painted on the expanse of the ceiling. Angels and demons. What an odd creation. A cherub and a few more of his kind rested on the right half of the ceiling, immaculate faces of horror blushing at the sight of the differing being. The smallest of the group pointed across the display at the single demon, which looked to be a hairy, shrunken creature with undergrown wings and red-tipped horns. The hell beast didn't look back at the other group. The demon shattered the fourth wall by staring into Alexander's world. In fact, their eyes met as Alexander appraised the scene.

"A demon in the heavens," Alexander murmured softly as he looked upwards. A chilling draft swept through the room and Alexander quivered, daunted by the painting. "What a peculiar display," he ventured, his eyebrows sinking along with a fresh bout of tears.

He licked his parched lips. He felt judgment searing through him. The demon was looking at him, in fact it was glaring at him. What did a demon have to judge him about? Still, the judgement was present. Yes, the tears felt gentle and pleasant upon his skin, but it was mortifying to be caught crying, even by a painted figure.

Another sob caught Alexander by surprise and he ripped the pillowcase off of the pillow his head rested upon. He instead pulled it over his own head as both his brothers had done. Now, all three brothers were wrapped in the warm embrace of a pillowcase. Many had sought comfort in the trappings of pillowcases, but nobody had ever needed comfort more than these three.

Alexander felt a childish sense of security as he hid himself. *If I can't see it, it can't see me, at least not my tear-ruined face.* Alexander quoted to himself. Now safe in the stygian realm of a pillowcase, Alexander was entirely alone with his tears and his thoughts. He didn't mind the tears as much as he did the thoughts. The thoughts were burdensome, but Alexander had dealt with such thoughts before and he would deal with them again, this time with the comfort of tears. He decided to dwell on other things, such as what his life would've been if Peter had never been cast out, if the former sovereign hadn't gone insane, and if his parentage was never revealed. Life would be a fair thing, yes it would. One thing that wouldn't have been different would be his affair with Cordella. She would still marry Edward and Alexander would've still fallen deeply in love with her. It only would take longer for them to find each other. Edward would be a kinder man if the past hadn't occurred in the manner that it did. He would love Cordella and they would be happy. Only not happy enough. Someday, somehow, Alexander would have found a way to love her.

Alexander cursed himself under his breath as if the hairy demon was listening. His thoughts had wandered back to the subject of Cordella. He always found a way back to her. He hoped he would again, at least to read what she'd written in the little leather notebook. An underlying truth surfaced again as he pondered her further. He remembered the exact moment the harrowing feeling settled in his chest, the feeling that had remained with him since that day. It was a moment when he sat in his study before the wedding. He was pondering the fact that hope is merely a distraction. He hoped he would find Cordella again, but hope is a distraction. He would forever be reminded of that.

Lizbeth would bring him to witness the death of one of his brothers as of the next day. One of them would die and that was a fact. Either the brother who he'd known all his life, or the brother who he'd known for two months. He didn't care for either of them. They had both been horrible to him. They both deserved whatever fate they were granted. It would be a dreadful comeuppance. Dreadful indeed.

Perhaps death would meet him tomorrow instead of the others. Perhaps it would. The tears ceased and Alexander was alone again. With the tears, the good, painful feeling left his chest and he was empty. He knew what he needed to do. The thought came from the depths of his mind, an echo across a precipice. The echo became a rumble. A stampede approaching. After that, a roar. It burned through his mind, leaving nothing but itself, greedy like a flame. He knew what he had to do indeed. He wouldn't realize the half of his obligation until the day after.

The three brothers were left with three different callings. The first wondered which route he should follow. The second, gone forever. The third, decided and bathed in truth.

CHAPTER 20

I didn't sleep last night, even with the pillowcase. I never had the opportunity. There were far too many subjects to ponder and far too many fears to mitigate. In fact, some of my fears weren't even mitigated in those restless hours. Those fears remain with me even at this time. It's four hours before noontime, all in Palace Andria are awakening and all in the Old Palace are doing the same. I would be incredulous if someone told me any one of my regnant brothers had slept last night. I still lay atop the large bed in the chambers Lizbeth provided. I still have the pillowcase over my head. It's light now, but only barely. I can see the sun beams filtering through my covering. The blizzard must have broken. Andrian weather is erratic at times. Still, this will be detrimental towards the chances of victory for each of the chosen parties. The ever-strident wind will have blown away most of the snow by sundown, but each combatant will have to make do in the ankle-deep frost.

I'm also quite bothered by the chosen bearings of the duel. The Stone Chapel. That name would stoke fear in the heart of any Andrian. That place is far less honorable than a church. No, it's not a church at all. That place is an execution ground. The very same the former sovereign died within. I've been there once before, needless to say. The family of the criminal are made to watch the macabre murder. There is an actual building in the center of the land that presents as a church. The building is only used to attend funeral services though. It's a tradition to attend the funeral of the one who was executed soon after their execution as to banish their nefarious soul. The body would be buried in a shallow grave behind the funeral church. That would've been the case with the man I believed to be my father, but he was royalty. He instead was buried in a similarly shallow grave on Palace Andria grounds. If Peter perished, then he would be buried behind the church. If Edward perished, then he would be buried as the former king was. It's rather biased if I was asked. I'm formally not allowed to have an opinion though. I am the least legitimate of the brothers.

I sigh. I wish life was transparent and simple as it was but a couple months ago. I pull the nullifying pillowcase from my head and toss it to the ground beneath me. My most prominent sense returns to me and I glance around the room for any intruders, Lizbeth to be faultless. It's highly possible she entered again after her previous grievance. I wouldn't put it past her any longer. I used to think so highly of her. She was righteous, without fault. She was never wrong. I feel the cold pressing against the constructs of the chamber. I scarcely know how I didn't die of cold last night. It was most definitely the warmth of the tears on my face and then the numbness that followed. Yes, indeed it was that.

I've had a feeling of foreboding since the day this all began, the day of the wedding. There were times in which it waned and there were times in which I felt it as much as I felt the beat of my heart against the curling upper end of my scar. There were times when I believed the feeling would disappear completely, days I expected to be the end of all this peril, but it hasn't ended. Today I feel the foreboding as if it's gravity, a constant, fundamental force in the universe. I've become accustomed to it. It's a constant whisper within me, warning me of future prospects and ending spontaneity. Instead of *carpe diem, seize the day,* it tells me to *stay inside. Stay in the wardrobe and hide. Leave through that window. Now's the perfect time to run. Nobody's looking for you. Nobody cares, nobody'll find you. Just in case, look behind you because of the lunatic you've attracted.* I glance behind me and sigh hatefully. I should hate this whisper, I absolutely should, but I would most definitely be dead without it, and, as of now, I value my life. One of my best qualities is the fact that I'm alive. It's more than my mother could say.

I hear a resounding knock on the strangely sealed door. It's less of a knock and more of a strident pounding. I still myself and turn towards the door deliberately. The knocking ceases for a moment before beginning again, this time louder. The echo traverses throughout the whole of the structure. I hurriedly pick up the pillowcase from the floor and cover my exposed chest. My scar is to remain veiled.

"Come in," I call in the most passive of tones. I don't want anyone to get the notion that I broke a promise to myself last night. For all anyone knows, that never happened. I would like it to remain that way, clandestine like my scar. I hear a muffled sigh through the door before the metallic click of the seemingly invisible lock. The door swings open lightly and, no surprise, Lizbeth barges through. She stops as soon as she enters, for a gasp overtakes her. She's transfixed by the window behind me.

"Oh! It's beautiful. And it's so much like me!" Lizbeth gushes heartily. The thought of Lizbeth gushing is still off-putting. She never so much as smiled in the past years. The landscape is quite beautiful. Cold as well. It's just as it was the morning of my birthday. The entire terrain, both forest and rock, petrified in ice for all the world to see. A crystalline realm has overcome my own and I'm enraptured in the clutches of the echo of a swirling ice storm as I gaze upon what it left behind. The Stone Chapel is in the center of the fen that separates the Old Palace and Palace Andria. It'll be just as shrouded in crystal glaze as these parts. I wasn't expecting the ice to remain in the gentle heat of the sun. My heart misses a beat as I observe the blueish color of the ice. That's a temperament of hardy ice. The freeze will remain until sundown, but be gone tomorrow. That's rotten luck. It seems as if the entire nation's luck has been rotten as of late.

"How do you mean?" I inquire quietly, still gazing at the frigid expanse beyond the glassy frame. Lizbeth whirls around, her red hair flowing down her back in the same manner summer does a mountain. She has two strips of hair pulled from her face and tied behind her head. It's a beautiful style, but I've never seen her wear her hair that way before. In fact, she looks comely in every sense. Her clothing shines and is the most brilliant shade of vermillion. What an evil being. How dare she do such a thing? She looks fair in it, but still, that color belongs to Cordella. First with the room, but now with her clothes? I shiver and grit my teeth, not wanting to make my sullenness apparent to my adversary.

"I mean that it's unfeeling, yet beautiful," Lizbeth discloses, pushing her lips into a hesitant smile. Humor flickers in her eyes. Her sense of humor is warped. I never knew she had one though. I'll have to get a better sense for it.

"Oh," I reply in a small voice. What else am I supposed to reply with? She left me nothing else. I feel something cloth hit me as I look back upon the steppe. A crisp roll of purple clouds lies stagnant on the edge of the horizon. I curse under my breath. More clouds? Another indication of a brewing storm. The elements have been relentless as of late. I turn to where I felt the cloth.

"I brought you a replacement. We all feel like burning our things sometimes, Alexander, but I never believed you would burn your shirt of all things!" Lizbeth finishes gaily. A smile encircles her eyes. My frown deepens. This newfound humor is rather bothersome.

"How could you ever find it necessary to joke and jest on a day such as this one? Today, you'll either be responsible for the death of one person or the death of two," I spit.

Lizbeth appears amused, at ease. Her stance is loose and lithe. She's not threatened by my words. Her eyes turn brighter and her dimples deepen. "Today is the beforetime of the best day of my life, Alexander. I would be absolutely dismal if it weren't for this humor. I'm very impatient and I wish for this to be over with so I can take you away from here with me," she admits evenly. "Yes, I know, 'the demoness,' impatient. Ridiculous. I know what you call me," she adds animatedly, her hands flying to the top of her head in the shape of horns. That action was overzealous and unnecessary. I'm astounded with this new side of her. I suppose the lore regarding Geminis is true. Two-faced and unpredictable.

"That's hilarious," I respond despondently. A bitter frown takes shape on my face as I pick up the lavender collared shirt from the floor beneath me. I drop the pillowcase. Lizbeth again eyes my bare chest and to her astonishment, I curse her loudly for it. All I get in response is a melodious laugh. It echoes around the chamber as if the first wasn't enough. I pull the lavender shirt into place and wince as I always do when I place my left arm into a starched sleeve. Lizbeth eyes me wearily as my hands tug at the buttons. Silence falls over the room. I'm perfectly happy to remain this way. I, in no way, enjoy speaking to this half of her.

"So, conduit, how does it feel to attend the funeral of one of your brothers? I don't know yet, but my money's on Edward's death." Her crude words tickle at the base of my spine. I feel my jaw quaking. The world around me suddenly feels so very wrong. Everything is flawed.

"Oh, it's a hateful feeling. I can't do anything to stop it and it's all my fault. My fault for existing," I reply truthfully, a bright look falling onto my features. I feel oddly strong. I can resist a lot more of my emotional urges as of today. The tears strengthened my stamina. A faded smile appears on my face as I realize this.

"Yes, it is your fault, but why do you believe that? I'm the one who arranged the duel. I'm the one who brought Peter from Walsia," Lizbeth articulates unerringly.

I turn away from her to tuck the last button into place. I have a matching reply. Maybe if I flirt, she'll leave me. I've done everything I can to push her from me, but none of that's worked. "I'm far too irresistible. I don't blame you, taking over the kingdom on my account and all. I still can't understand how you believe you're in control. I don't wish to see the monarchy fall, but I'm compelling you to do these things. So, therefore, I've come to the conclusion that I'm irresistible, a second pastry off a tray." I turn back to her, a fiery smirk setting my features ablaze. I feel the ghost of past arrogance stir within me. This is the man I used to be.

"I am in control! God, Alexander, you really make me angry at times. Angry. It's a delicate word, a maiden with an umbra over her face, a look in her eyes that tells the onlooker how prematurely she aged." Lizbeth whirls over topic after topic in her phrases. Her eyes roll down my form once or twice. I'm beginning to feel angry as well. Her ramblings and oddities are strange to say the least.

"Oh, is that an emotion you didn't *want* to feel? See, it isn't your choice. It isn't mine either," I respond, a deep simper prowling across my face. Now I'm making strides. I hope she'll hate me enough to let me go. The hope is a faint light in the ever-present darkness, but it's not nothing.

"I *want* to feel everything, Alexander! I love you, inescapably, irrevocably, forever and ever. I *want* to feel you!" she cries, her eyes darkening. Her disposition turns from one of humor to one of hostility rapidly.

"Yes, but that's not your choice, now is it?" I challenge, biting into each of my own, savory words. "I made myself very clear before. You're not in control." I nod my head along with each of my words, my smile deepening with every flare of rage in her eyes. But there's something else as well in those vast green plains. What is it? Longing? Sadness? No, it's yearning. She wants more.

"That's where you're wrong," she whispers in a low tone, taking even steps in my direction. My foreboding whisper commands me to back away from her and I oblige. I oblige until my back is pressed evenly against the window. Only now do I realize that flirting only attracts her more.

"Why kiss me when I won't reciprocate?" I ask her in a last attempt to separate myself. I've spoken too much. I shouldn't follow every dim glimmer of hope, for hope is a distraction as I keep forgetting.

"That's another question, Alexander. I *only* granted you three," she whispers in my ear, now only inches from me. I feel her frigid breathe on my neck and Cordella echoes throughout my mind. I love Cordella. I can't let this happen. And then, Lizbeth kisses me. "Yes Alexander, that's the passion I wish to feel," Lizbeth murmurs into my lips as the world around us dissolves into darkness.

That's an odd statement. I'm not reciprocating her kisses, just as I said I wouldn't. She continues to kiss me though, harder, faster, more potently. My lips are stone against hers, but she continues to urge, urge until I feel as if my lips are about to burst. She doesn't give in as she did the first time she kissed me. She keeps urging. I feel the force of a thousand tides beat against my lips. The burden only grows, the intensity gradually spiraling higher. I feel my knees weaken beneath me. I feel the impact all the way down to my feet. My mind fades away and my lips press back into hers, but only in retaliation. I need to breathe, I need to find a way, even at the bottom of a ripping tide. After a moment or two of the subdued kiss, she pulls away, her teeth scraping against mine as I open my mouth for air.

"Why do you insist on such barbaric ways of getting what you want?" I inquire as she pushes herself from my bearings. Her eyes are still closed as she stands before me. A smile traces her lips. A bit of blood trickles from her upper lip. I realize it isn't hers, it's mine. I lick my lips and taste blood congregating around my mouth.

"You kissed me," she whispers in a low tone, almost as if she's speaking to herself.   I shake my head deliberately, words forming and crumbling in my mind like great civilizations. She can't see me. Her eyes still remain closed. She's holding onto the moment with everything she's got.

"No," I respond in a quivering tone. I'm surprised by the amount of hurt in my own tone. My voice broke around the end of the word. A simple word. No. Despite its simplicity, it should be taken seriously no matter what the circumstance. No.

"You taste like licorice," she utters as her eyes open. "I didn't get a chance to memorize your flavor the first time we kissed. I always wondered what your lips taste like. Lips of a forgotten sovereign," she whispers her irises rolling upwards towards me with every word. I close my eyes and shake my head again, muttering consoling phrases to myself. Lizbeth breathes in deeply.

"Lizbeth?" I ask waveringly. I hear my phrase shaking through the uneven air. Weakness.

"Yes, Alexander?" Lizbeth replies, her eyes cutting into mine.

I hold her gaze, making myself look her in the eyes as I speak to her, just as I was taught. "I haven't cried in nine years," I admit in monotone. A draft swirls through the upper half of the room, tousling my hair into knots.

Lizbeth's eyebrows fall downwards as she processes my phrases. "Whatever do you mean?" She replies garishly. She takes a step back from me, her eyes traversing my face.

"Well, that was the truth until last night. You weren't the only one who cried for the first time in this period. *You made me cry*," I affirm, my voice singed with rage. I stare into the eyes of the girl I used to love. I had even loved her last night as I cried on her account. I had loved her every second those burning tears ruined my face. I loved her as I hated her. And now, I neither love nor hate her. I *despise* her. I despise her silken skin and her bewitching eyes with all their facets. I despise her rosy lips and her graceful figure, alluring as it is. I despise her hair, the color scorched by the inferno. I despise every nuance of her words and despise every expression that forms that face of hers. And, most of all, I despise *her*. "It's not my fault, is it?" I utter, trapped in the caverns of my own mind.

"What?" she asks, her accent cutting into the roughest edge of her word.

"I never asked to exist, so it isn't my fault. None of this is my fault." A bitter laugh comes from her throat as she stares at me. Her laugh sounds cruel, incredulous, empty. I'm a hypocrite. Only moments ago I contradicted my present statement. No, I'm not a hypocrite. I didn't know the truth.

"Of course this is *your* fault, Alexander. I am only fulfilling my dreams. You—well, you're the reason I am," Lizbeth mutters heartlessly, a smile resounding through her voice. I take a step towards her, confidence in my stride.

"No. This isn't my fault. It isn't my fault I was born. It's my mother's fault for dying. It's your fault for loving me. It's my brother's fault for hating me. The only thing I'm at fault for is loving Cordella," I explain, my own voice echoing the astonishment I feel. A burden leaves my battered shoulders. I sense the presence of a God I never knew existed, more than I did my birthday, more than I did ever, even before my mother's death.

"Silly conduit. Your realizations are meaningless. You only ever feel a certain way for moments at a time. All the more useful to me. That's why I love you."

I brace myself for the impact of her words, but they don't strike me as they usually do. I'm out of her influence. "Leave. You'll get more of these *fleeting moments* later at the duel. I'm sure they'll give you a good high, Lizbeth. I'll even cry for you. I'll laugh, maybe I'll sing in my broken, wood chip-filled voice. I could smile, I could frown. You utter the command and I'll oblige," I proclaim in the loudest voice I can muster. I hear the light music in my voice and I allow myself a quiet chuckle.

Lizbeth smiles back, her eyes clouded with ecstasy. "I'm looking forward to it." She leans into her phrase. She forgets her trained poise and allows her words to fall from her tongue with the harshest accent I've ever heard. I can barely decipher her meaning over the intense, halting breaks. She twirls around once, no grace in her step, before skipping across the dusty wood. I watch her leave as I tuck the new lavender shirt into my pants. I've gotten her to leave twice now. Once from anger, another from promise. I am in control, for I know how I feel.

I saunter disdainfully onto the carpeted half of the room to the shelves. I recall a set of Andrian gold-tipped quills and a vessel filled with blue ink amongst the ornate display. I have a set of the very same in my chambers. I believe Lizbeth brought them from the New Palace in order to provide me with more comfort. That act did the exact opposite though. I have the perfect use for them as of now, hatred coursing through my veins. I grasp onto the fragile penning set with vindication. This ought to leave the proper message, if she ever does see this place again, that is.

I take more smooth strides across the room, now equipped with a set of harmful pens. One last poem before the duel. A blank space lays waiting for me to sully it with my words. The bones of the building wait to be infused with my words of truth, for all Andria could do with a little truth. I hold my breath as my hand works against the coarse barrier. The ink dribbles down the wallpaper in the same manner blood does.

What is the purpose of a shining image, protected by lies,
If you never see it with your eyes?
What's the purpose of being to blame?
Aren't we all only one and the same?
Heed my warning,

Heed it well,
I'll tell you no,
Respect that or go to hell.

The work satisfies my need to scream these very words at the top of my lungs for all of Andria to hear. If only one person enters this room, then my message will have been delivered, my morals accepted. Well, at least displayed. There are evil people in this realm who do not respect others and will deceive through their shining images, defending themselves with lies.

I recount my own life for a moment. *He's finally broken the surface of the ice, his head clear, his mind on God and nothing other. Someday, he will see the journal and the celestial lights. Someday, some way, the colors will cease and he will be at rest.*

CHAPTER 21

When staring adversity in the eyes, the most important thing to remember is not to look away, even when your eyes begin to sting and tears rush down your face. Adversity should break its gaze first, for deep in your heart of hearts, you know you're stronger, you know you can persevere. This most important rule is becoming difficult for me to uphold though, for I have two adversaries instead of one. Is it even possible to stare into the eyes of two people at once? I mean, perhaps if their heads are melded together, but other than that, it's highly implausible.

The gold-tipped quill from the Old Palace is slick against my greased fingers despite the cold. If I drop it, my single tool for survival is thrown to ruin. This sharp-ended quill is my only weapon in a grave battle, a battle I wasn't meant to fight in the first place. Despite this fact, this is my battle to fight and mine to win. I'm not at fault for this, but I believe this is the reason for all the trials and turmoil I've faced in the past months. I've felt the tension building and building to today. This is it. Here I am, staring adversity in the eyes.

Edward grasps his and Peter's father's cutlass with a firm, unwavering hand. The stillness is out of character for him. One part of him or another always twitches, moving as if he's only half of a statue. He's clad in the appropriate duel garments. Pure, bleak white, the color of death. Even his coat, a prohibited article of clothing, is the same, alabaster white. His jaw is slack instead of set. He appears loose and at ease. His eyes, his eyes are the most curious part of him. Terrifying, not curious, forgive me. His eyes have lost their pale color. They seem to be the same color as the bleak ice and snow around us. Lines lay surrounding his invisible irises and his pupils are as dark as ever, but no other color resides within his eyes. One thing remains constant in this new appearance, though. His temperament is still as animalistic as ever. Even bathed in the color of death, he still seems to be filled with life, but not human life. He's a wolf, hungry for the suffering of those around him. Hungry for his adversaries' demises. A fear-worthy foe he is.

Peter, on the other hand, looks to be just as woebegone as me. His figure is haggard and trembling, cold and tired. He's frightened half to death. I'm certain Edward will make sure the other half is gone soon enough though. He wears the deathly color as well. Despite the frigid temperature, he has no coat. He's practically invisible, naked in the snow. He needs a shave and a haircut. He needs sustenance and rest. He lacks many things, but he does not lack animosity. I see it in his eyes. His eyes are darker than either of ours. His eyes are a deep, electric blue. He could smite me with one gaze. Lucky for me, his eyes are trained on Edward. His long, silver sword is also pointed towards Edward. The blade fits perfectly in his hands as if he's used a sword of such status before. I'm certain he has long ago, but he doesn't seem the least bit out of practice as I assumed he would be. He's also a fear-worthy foe.

I'm not anything like either of them. I'm weak, helpless, futile. Any synonym for weakness would describe me. The very look in Edward's eyes makes me want to roll over and die. I don't have a proper weapon, only a keen quill that could be used as a knife in close combat. Lord, I don't even have the proper dueling garments. I only have Elli's worn coat and my own fear. Fear can be a most potent motivator, however. I'm leaning heavily on it for support. Fear is an instinct. Life or death. Survive or don't. I choose to survive. I choose to live. I choose to claim the kingdom of Andria for myself. I will strive to restore peace to this hallowed land once again. I will instigate it. Lizbeth's gambit will fall along with both of my brothers. I'm determined, relentless as well as weak. They won't be able to pick me off easily. Even now I wonder how I got to this point. How did I conquer fear only to harness it?

A Half Hour Earlier...

"You have to leave the carriage, Peter! Lord, I knew I should've made him walk," Lizbeth muttered under her breath, exasperation prominent on her face. Her actions triggered a laugh in my throat. I didn't even try to conceal it. My face split into a twisted smile as I watched the grim display. The full-grown man was hiding away on the seat of a carriage, refusing to so much as blink. His knuckles were white against the window ledge. Lizbeth's scowl was priceless. For some reason, Lizbeth thought it best that the illegitimate prince, the lamb for slaughter, and the demoness all travel together in one carriage. It made for good conversation. I laughed aloud sporadically only to perturb Lizbeth and her lamb. Once, I even managed to scrape a few tears from my eyes. What did I care if it scared them? I wanted them to know how I feel every single moment.

"I don't want to die. I don't deserve it," the stricken man whispered to her, his voice imploring. He couldn't possibly be looking for an out, could he? Despite my prior knowledge, I made myself look at the man before me as a coward. I had to, for I knew what I was to do. He was a coward, a coward for attempting to abandon the wellbeing of his only remaining family in the final moments. He would die either way. A thick-witted coward at that. Yes, dumb and fearful. That's what I decided. It would be easier to face a coward, for I was a coward myself.

"And Alexander, why aren't you wearing the coat I provided for you? Instead you're wearing that filthy man's coat," Lizbeth inquired, one of her sharp eyebrows soaring up her face. I smiled gravely, my eyes squinting against the long shards of ice carried by the wind.

"I preferred it," I justified haughtily. Peter's pleas had stopped as he noticed my jacket. I didn't prefer it. No, not at all. It was too large on me and not tailored to my slim form like the one Lizbeth provided, but it was the warmest garment in my possession. It had gotten me through the barren tundra of Andria. That accounted for a lot. I knew my plan, so I chose to wear it because of that. It would allow me to become less of an icicle and more of a victor. Lizbeth sighed insolently and turned back to Peter. He appeared stricken as before, but motionless, staring at me.

"What d-did you do with Elli? He w-was my friend, m-my only one at t-that." Peter shivered, his teeth clacking together unevenly as the cold swept in. It was my turn to sigh. The release hid my feelings.

"He's all right. He slashed my face open and got drunk on a bottle of something. I left him passed out on his cot. I checked his pulse and he'll be just fine," I said helpfully. I didn't want him to be frightened in what could be his final hours. I should have hated him, he was a coward. He took Cordella from me and offered to end my life for my own good. I don't. Taking Cordella was an order from Lizbeth, but offering to end my life was not. He was doing it out of the kindness of his heart, for he genuinely believed it would end my suffering. He was offering to shoot me dead as a soldier does a suffering comrade. I'm begrudgingly grateful for that.

"No he isn't," Lizbeth admitted in the ghost of a whisper, a cruel smile finding its way onto her face. A flicker of fury illuminated Peter's eyes, but he remained silent, his shaking continued. His face melted into a medley of despair and hurt.

"Alright then, let's go," I offered in an enthusiastic tone in order to irritate Lizbeth. I turned deliberately and stepped towards the wind-shrouded building in the center of the frozen fen. A small gathering had amassed before it. Further beyond the building, I could see other structures. A clump of small, abandoned houses lay beyond the church. Any land on dueling ground is free range, so this would make for an impressive fight. There were so many nooks and crannies to hide oneself in. I realized how long the duel might last for that reason.

I felt a hand grip my collar. It was Peter's. He and I lagged behind for a brief moment as Lizbeth started towards the gathering. I glanced up at him. Lizbeth was correct, I was growing taller. I could look Peter in the eyes without so much strain on my neck.

"Hello, Alexander," Peter mumbled quietly.

"Hello, Peter," I replied.

"I would like to apologize for—"

"There's no need. You have many reasons to be sorry, but I forgive you. I've recently become more affirmed in my faith," I said with a hint of doubt-instilled embarrassment.

That was the first time I voiced my recent promise. I'd sensed God with me multiple times, in my heart as they all promised he would be. His love pulsates through me in the same manner my blood does. His presence had become only as essential as my heart beat and I felt him now as I did then, commanding me forth towards the light. He'd saved me for this, to rescue Andria. He had his reasons, I was sure of it.

"Yes? That's wonderful news. I am also dedicated to the Lord. I reaffirmed my faith just last night. I did so just as the death-bound prisoners do." He chuckled. I looked towards my feet and smiled grimly. He would go to heaven when he perished, not hell. At least that was one of my brothers accounted for.

I looked up towards the sky in wordless prayer for Edward's soul. The thought of having faith or believing in anything less than a God who despised me was off-putting. Praying still seemed foreign and peculiar. I'd been attending church and worship studies all these years, but after my mother's death, I stopped believing in full. Now he'd returned and I was still becoming accustomed to the outlandishness of his presence.

"I wish you the best of luck, Peter." I placed a firm hand on his broad shoulder and looked into his eyes. He nodded back to me, an indescribable emotion in his eyes. He sighed and spoke again. The moment of kinship felt dire, all the demureness of our previous exchanges tossed away. In that moment, he truly felt like a brother.

"You and I don't need luck. Matthew chapter seven verse seven. *Ask and it will be given to you; seek and you will find; knock and the door will be opened to you.*" Peter folded his hands behind his back and straightened his posture.

"All we need to do is ask," I confirmed to myself. Peter nodded again and began towards Lizbeth. I followed him soon after, but not before I prayed for him. The third prayer I had spoken in nine years. My fear became my servant just as I became God's servant.

Present Time...

A stoic priest stands erect in the center of the triad of brothers. In the rules, it states that a priest must oversee duel activities, for by the end of the day, someone will be dead and the bodies will need to be blessed. His face is clad with a look of bewilderment as he appraises my peculiar stance. Only moments ago, I broke away from the meager gathering. Not only Lizbeth knows how to bend the rules. I know how to as well. Peter can gain sovereignty based on his parentage, but I can also. I still have royal blood within me, enough of it to continue the purity of the Andrian monarchy.

"Alexander! Hell on Earth! What do you believe you're doing?" Lizbeth calls from the sea of faces furiously. Her teeth are gritted against the cold and her braid becomes looser at the nape of her neck as a gust of northern wind strikes her, ushering the purple clouds from earlier closer to us. She sighs and takes a step into the empty area, but Jakob pulls her back, clutching one of her coat-clad arms tightly. I grimace and turn my eyes back to my brothers. Lizbeth wrestles against Jakob's rigid grip, but he remains motionless, unaffected by her struggles. A smile peels onto my face. He's keeping her from me for his own good. He won't inherit the remnants of Andria if Lizbeth joins the fight and perishes.

"Calm yourself. Your death in place of his wouldn't benefit anyone, Lizbeth. I've been there. I know the feeling. I killed it," Jakob whispers to her, a hidden smile lingering on his face, one she cannot see. Too many deceivers.

I shake my head to decipher my own thoughts. My grip becomes more strident on the sharp, gold-tipped quill. A patch of odd green sky remains uncovered above our heads. I recognize that I may never see the color of twilight again, nor the northern lights or the blinding glimmer of spring grass. This may very well be my final day. I imagined it a lot differently. I look up towards the sky. *Don't let me die.*

"Are all parties of royal descent?" the priest inquires, shivering and burrowing further into his white robes. Edward's glare sears my eyes and I blink away.

"Yes," Edward replies with a nerve-bending calm. Even the priest flinches away from his austere gaze.

"I-I am," Peter murmurs, his eyes flickering like the dying flames of a subdued wildfire. His stance wavers whereas Edward's is poised and reverent. I can't even remember the proper stance. I stand stiffly, holding the quill as I would a sword. I'm a mere shadow in their collective wake.

"I am as well," I confirm, rage soaking my voice. I stare into Edward's deadened eyes. He knows the rules, yet he chooses to ridicule me as he has my entire life. Life just isn't good enough for him. Perhaps death will be fairer.

"Do you swear to protect your kingdom to the best of your abilities if you happen to be victorious?" the priest queries. I know Peter couldn't swear by that without untruth, neither could Edward. They're both too far gone to promise anything of the sort, yet they will, for winning accounts for both of their livelihoods.

"Yes," Edward replies, his voice just as inhuman as previously. His lip twitches erratically. The patch of green light above our heads has closed over. The grounds are shrouded in the darkness of pre-snowfall.

"Alr-right," Peter pledges in a tone of dismay. He's far too frightened to be the victor. I want him to die less than I do Edward. He's been more kind to me than Edward ever has been.

"I swear it," I claim assuredly. I feel zeal rising in my voice. I would protect Andria with my own life, the kingdom that has made me what I am. I hate it, I love it, but I don't despise it.

"Wait!" I hear a cry from the crowd, strangled and desperate. I turn my neck sharply to see Lizbeth breaking away from Jakob's grip. She weaves through the gathering of relatives and friends, most of them for Edward, the rest Lizbeth's entourage for Peter. I glance at her hands. She grips two blades tightly, her eyes darting back and forth. Even as she reaches the triad, her stride doesn't cease. She saunters directly to the priest, a choked fury in her eyes. I see readiness in her stance. She stops before the holy man.

"I apologize, but you have heaven waiting for you and I only have this life," she discloses to the man. His white-tinged eyebrows furrow, then, with an awful slice, become spattered with his own blood. Lizbeth tucks her left knife back into its sheath on her arm as the man's body falls to the ground with a crunch of the ice. She turns away from the triad and to the gathering of horrified observers. A smile forms on her face as she stares at them, basking in their panicked fear.

A few of her agents emerge from the group and position themselves surrounding the horde of frightened people. Some attempt to escape, but in the end, they're all trapped. "Listen! All of you!" Lizbeth cries against the wind, her hair soaring freely from her head. "I'm in control as of now. The rules have changed. Anyone can join the fight for sovereignty. Respect these rules, or die. Alright? With that said, I'm enlisting." Lizbeth turns back to the brothers and takes a step towards us. Peter begins to shake violently from rage.

"Lizbeth, you demoness!" Peter cries, fury scattering throughout his voice. I stand motionless, staring into her eyes. She stares right back, her gaze more formidable than Edward's, for she looks pleased. Edward seems to have not noticed.

"I say we kill her first," I bluff in order to conceal my fright, throwing a quill lash through the air. Lizbeth chuckles and casts her gaze on the others.

"As if," she responds confidently. I bite my chapped lips, the dry skin easily giving way to blood. "You're going to beg, Alexander, beg to live once I'm done with them. Then, I'll take you as my own," she declares. Peter and Edward are my adversaries, but she is my nemesis. A flurry of snow drifts down from the swirling air above. Peter sticks out his tongue like a child, a crazed smile covering his animosity. My eyes travel up and down his body. He's going to be first to die. Lizbeth doesn't need him any longer. He's the most vulnerable target. I wish I could've gotten to know him better.

"My children never got to see snow," Peter admits in a stricken tone. He'll see them again soon. He'll go to heaven, I'm sure of it. I feel sadness in my throat, but swallow it. I permitted myself enough tears last night. Now is not the time for that. I've grown enough in the past months to suppress it, at least for a few hours.

"I will enjoy seeing tears in your eyes," Lizbeth says to me, her tone threateningly gleeful. I glare and turn away from her.

Jakob approaches, his eyes gilded and shimmering. He trusts Lizbeth. He has confidence that she'll be victorious. I don't believe it! I mean, what would happen if she wasn't? He would still take Andria for his own by killing me. Another life I have to end. I frown.

Suddenly, I hear footsteps beating against the crushed snow. I turn to where Peter was, but he isn't there any longer. I instead see his shadow growing ever smaller amongst the dilapidated buildings of the Stone Chapel.

"Well then," Lizbeth says, her chagrin becoming apparent as she slashes her knives against each other. "The duel has commenced." She gives me a knowing look, promise in her eyes as she bolts after Peter, a shrill battle cry echoing across the empty plain. I hear a high laugh as I watch her leave.

I turn back to Edward. "Edward—" Lizbeth's really quite stupid, leaving me with this man. I only have a quill. I suppose it's my turn to run. Edward advances, pulling his cutlass out and moving into a fighting stance. A smile flickers into existence on his face. His eyes are rimmed with pleasure. He's been waiting for this moment for a while.

"Easy now, Alexander. If you submit now, I'll make it painless. One slash across your throat and then, you're gone." His eyes round further at the appeal of my death. Our breath comes from our throats in great clouds. I've had someone offer something similar before, our other brother. I wanted to accept that offer then, but not now. Now, the end's in sight. I could just reach out and grasp it. So tangibly close.

"I know you want me dead, Edward, but you need my help to end Lizbeth and Peter. We could work together and then you could kill me," I return, attempting to make my counter offer as appealing as my own death. He chuckles quietly, no contemplation in his expression. My heel digs into the ice.

"You're a disgrace, a stain. I fight alone. I win alone," he murmurs. It doesn't sound like his voice. It sounds as if someone's speaking through him, as if he's some sort of possessed marionette. He speaks with more passion, the elation of my death more compelling to him than previous times.

"Alright," I call. We stand motionless for a moment, appraising each other. I break into a panicked run. My legs fly over the ground, my quill still clutched tightly in my hand. My footsteps give the silence some color.

"For the love of God! Alexander!" Edward roars. He's much faster than me. He's got a wider frame and longer legs. I got a head start. I have to hide now. I hear his footsteps behind me. They sound more like the hoofbeats of a horse to be quite honest. He is a horse of a man, after all. A centaur.

I hurdle around the corner of an old, forsaken barn, the blue paint patchy and chipped. Perhaps there's a pitchfork I can use or something of the sort. I breathe in harshly, forcing air into my lungs. His footsteps haven't slowed once. Oh Lord, I don't have the time to check for weapons. I dash away as I he rounds the corner. I feel hunted, frightened. I never once thought that something such as this would ever happen to me. I was alone, for it was safer that way. I was *safe*. Now I'm not, all because of Lizbeth. Blast her!

"You can run, but you can't hide!" Edward thunders after me. That's a cliché. I had thought better of him. I huff in the air as my legs burn away beneath me. My scars rage and my heart thuds against my chest.

"You're jesting, right?" I call after him. Humor in my last moments. I wasted my breath on that of all things? I deserve to have a laugh if he's to kill me. My own brother. Half-brother. I sprint to a tall spruce and bend around in. My knees buckle beneath me and I press my back into the bark of the tree. Perhaps I can climb it… No, far too weak for that. Fear pulsates through my veins. *Please God. Please, please…* I don't even know what I'm asking him for. I want my notebook. I want Cordella. I want… I want…

"Alexander! Get your ass out here! You know what? For your rudeness, I'm going to pull your fingernails out one by one. Then, I'll chop off your hands. You enjoy your little pens and scribbles don't you? Well, you'll never get to write again!" Edward howls. His voice doesn't sound human. He isn't human. He's a wolf, just as I suspected all this time. I won't be surprised when he begins to feed on my flesh. I have to endure, survive. *Cordella, poetry, God.* I force myself to my feet, gripping the tree for support. I hear his animalistic footsteps crunching closer and closer to me as the snow falls more heavily. Tears leave my eyes and freeze on my face. They collect on my eyelashes. I cover my eyes with my hands. I don't want them to congeal with the sudden moisture. I open them again in time to see Edward before me.

Peter's Perspective

The cold makes me see things. I was born here, yet I still haven't become accustomed to it. My wife stands beside me, her face smooth in placid, the flicker of a smile in her eyes. She wears the nightgown she wore that night. I'm faintly worried about the cold. Will she be alright in only that? She's always had a strong resistance to the cold, though.

"Euphemia," I whisper into the materialized nothingness. I sit hunched in the back of a small shack behind an overturned table. The girl, Lizbeth, she's evil. She got a slash across my legs. I wrapped them with a sleeve of my coat, but they're bleeding through the thick material for some reason. I feel faint, dreamy. I caress her face with a wavering hand. She smiles into the embrace of my hand and takes a seat next to me.

I rock back and forth on the creaking floorboards and she rests a hand on my knee. "I'm sorry. I'm so very s-sorry," I confess. "Liam, Gavin, Noah," I whisper. My sons appear before me, gratified facets on each of their deathly pale features.

"Father," Liam, the oldest, says in an assured tone. I reach out a quivering hand and ruffle his brown hair. His eyes are blue like my own. His teeth, gapped like Euphemia's. I miss him. I miss them all.

"Father."

"Father," both Gavin and Noah chorus. Euphemia takes their hands. We sit in a circle, staring at each other. They nod at me whenever a tear happens to fall from my eyes. My heart feels almost full. Only one thing is missing.

"Where's Faye?" I ask them. I hear a worried tone in my own voice.

"She remains alive," Noah answers me. He seems so serene in saying that. Did Euphemia perish despite my efforts? I let out a strangled sob, my hand over my mouth. I don't want Lizbeth to hear me.

"She's coming," Euphemia motions to the others. The sound of her soft voice tickles my ears. So long I've dreamed of that sound. I reach out as Liam fades. Gavin follows. Then Noah, then my dear Euphemia. I'm alone again. Suddenly, I feel a poignant stab in my abdomen. I glance down gradually, not wanting to believe the fact that there's a knife, one of Lizbeth's, sticking through my flesh. This can't be another delusion. The pain is so tangible. My stomach grows rigid as the blood fills it.

"I've got you," I hear Lizbeth's muffled voice through the wall. I press a lethargic hand against my wound as the knife disappears through the wall again. Blood bursts through my throat and I wretch onto the floorboards beside me. The pain is immense, but it was better than feeling nothing at all.

The pain disappears and I feel as if I'm only a head bobbing through the air. The door on the opposite end of the room swings open and Lizbeth ambles through, satiation in her eyes. She finds her way through the toppled furniture and cobwebs. She sheaths her knife and collapses beside me in the same manner Euphemia did. I let out a long, quivering sigh.

"Tell me t-this," I whisper, blood tinging my lips. She grasps my hand in hers. At least I'm not dying alone. I turn my head to look into her eyes, bewitching and enchanting.

"Anything," she says. I've seen her do this with others she's killed. She's kind to them in their final moments. I'll take any kindness I can at a time like this.

"Are you going to kill them, my daughter and Euphemia?" I ask, making my best effort to remain strong. "I-I saw them. My sons and Euphemia. All b-but Faye." My neck feels fragile. I feel the zeal leaving me as I lean my head against her neck for support.

"Euphemia passed from the plague. No, I won't kill Faye. She lives. I sent her to live in an orphanage. She'll get adopted easily. She's still young, Peter. She'll have a good life. I promise she won't die." Lizbeth hurries over her words, for she knows my consciousness is waning.

"Thank you," I whisper. Lizbeth opens her mouth to speak, but can't find the words. Even with her kind smile, I still sense repulsion in her frame. She's a fair actress.

"It's alright, Peter. You can go now, be with your wife and sons," Lizbeth croons. I hear false consoling in her tone, but I don't care as of now. I want to pass as tranquilly as I can. I take another wretched breath. Blood pours languidly from my lips. I close my eyes. Darkness. When I open my eyes, light.

Alexander's Perspective

His cold, wiry finger close around my throat, lifting me a ways off the ice-layered ground. I glare into his silvery eyes disobediently as I feel the air draining from me. This isn't how I die. I know it.

"Stop," I croak. "Weren't y-you planning t-to r-rip out my f-fingernails?" I ask in a last attempt. His grip loosens enough for me to take an immediate breath. He chuckles and sighs.

"You're hilarious. So hilarious that I'll make this longer," he growls, his sharpest teeth poking over the edge of his blue lips. I really hope he doesn't bite me. He takes a knife from his pocket and pulls the collar of my shirt from the coat. He lifts me off the ground again and I let out a strangled cry. I kick and scratch, but it's as if he feels none of it.

"No! S-stop." I've never been more afraid. Never. I've endured a lot of fear in my days, but never as great as this. He pins the knife deep into the wood of the tree, leaving me hanging from my collar. Damn the thick threads of Andrian clothing! Snow dusts the top of his head, blending in with his hair evenly. I claw at his face with my free hand. I hold the quill behind my back with the other. I tuck it into my belt so he won't notice it.

"You're a bastard, you know that?" he asks. I let my hand drop to my side. Tears fall from my eyes and freeze along with the others. I sob, letting my head lay limp.

"Don't kill her, C-Cordella. Don't you dare," I whisper, looking into his deadened eyes again. He throws his head back and laughs as villains do in novels. His eyes roll back in his head and for a moment, I can't distinguish the whites from the irises. He looks horrible. His skin is sallow, his eyes missing. He's a madman. He's the former sovereign's son, irrevocably so.

"I won't. She's far too appealing to kill. Now, tell me, how many times did you do her? I'll do her ten more times than you did." He steps closer to me as he says this, his words becoming frost on my ear.

"How dare y-you speak of her l-like that?"

"You're the man who's strung up right now. You should comply. It'll make me want to slit your throat less," he roars. He's so close to my face. I can smell blood on his teeth.

"Once," I murmur, another tear congealing at the tip of an eyelash. He brings the cutlass to my face, holding it by the blade. I shrink away from it. He's going to kill me. I'm going to die. I'll never read what she wrote for me! *Please God, please...*

"I honestly thought it would be a longer chase. You made it so very easy for me to catch you. Survival of the fittest, I suppose," he rambles as the cutting begins. He takes the point of the cutlass so dangerously close to my neck, but begins to cut my chin instead. "Little Alexander. I remember when you were only a child. Sullen and cynical even then, ruined and shriveled up by the death of our parents. Now here you are, crying before me." I grit my teeth and close my eyes. The *pain*. One, two, three cuts. Four, five, six cuts. Seven, eight, all over my face. Blood leaks from me like a compromised dam.

"At least I didn't cling t-to you for support at h-his funeral," I nip back, my eyebrows turning downwards. I earn a splitting punch in the mouth. Pain ruptures through my mind and I cry out, my teeth loosening at the impact. I'm a wreck, a palace torn to bits, tarnished with blood and tears and... And shame. One more cut. My hand closes around the quill as the agony continues. My heart flutters as I draw my hand from behind my back. I have it. I have the quill.

I bore into his outstretched arm until I reach his yellowed bones. He howls in agony, abandoning the cutlass. I pull the quill to my collar and slash it off, hitting the ground mid motion. I run from him, greased lightning in my step. He's collapsed behind me, nursing his arm.

"Alexander!" he roars. My name sounds wretched in his voice. I sprint until his calls are only an echo. The blood begins to solidify on my face in the same manner the tears did. My vision is blurred, but I can see the church ahead of me. If I remember properly, there's a tower at the top with a lock on its door. If only I could reach there.

Lizbeth's Perspective

There's a particular moment in which you can see the soul leave someone's eyes. In most circumstances, the soul leaves one's eyes as death takes hold. In other, rare circumstances, the physical body dwindles longer in the world and the soul goes to either heaven, or hell. In Peter's bearings, it was the earlier. I let him lean on me as he died. I held his hand so he wouldn't feel quite so alone. I learned a method for helping others through the death I brought to them. I realize how despicable a person I am, so I decided to compensate for it, even if only slightly. I went through the routine. Sit down next to the victim. Hold the victim's hand. Make an empty promise to them. Allow them to lean on me in the final moments, no matter how greatly their touch makes my skin crawl. Peter's soul is gone. All that remains is the corpse. I sigh and shove the quickly cooling body from my form. Disgusting. Corpses are one of the only things in the world that frighten me. It's a wonder how I create so many of them.

"Alexander!" A cry resonates through the abandoned abodes, ricocheting off of every edge. That means he's still alive. That's good. I knew he would live, but I wanted to put him through a bit of agony with his brother. He deserves it, joining the fight and all. His pain will teach him not to cross me ever again. I wipe my bloodied knife on the corpse's jacket and walk towards the door. Now to kill Edward. Alexander will beg on his knees to live. He'll surrender and Andria will be mine to destroy. I will get my happy ending.

Alexander's Perspective

I scramble up the steps of the church. The gathering gasps at my approach and Lizbeth's guards circle tighter around the group, shifty expressions on the visible half of their masked faces.

"I'll rip your throat out if you kill him, Edward!" a sing-song voice calls from a ways away. It's Lizbeth. She must be done with Peter. I close my eyes and murmur a silent prayer as I continue my ascent up the uneven steps. I peer behind me.

Edward's beginning the climb as well. I curse under my breath. Blood drips rhythmically against every weathered step. I can't even feel my legs beneath me any longer. They're trapped in a constant forward motion. My eyes flicker to the gathering yet again and my eyes meet hers. Of all the cosmos, of all the universe, hers are the most beautiful. My heart stops as I look her dead in her opalescent eyes. Cordella. She came? But how? But why? I would think Edward would either end her or lock her up in a cage for the rest of her life. My legs won't stop for anyone though. I fall over the penultimate step, catching myself on the hand of the door. I hear Edward's growl from behind me and a shot of adrenaline courses through my veins.

Just as I pull myself up again, I feel a cold, lifeless hand grip the heel of my boot.

"Hell!" I call in astonishment, fear in my muddled tone. Blood seeps from my burst lips. I squirm helplessly, my vision running left. His fingernails dig deeper through the flesh of my leather boots and into my own. I snarl in pain and bewilderment, drawing my foot closer to myself. I heave and knock my heel back. It strikes him square in the nose with a satisfying crunch. He lets out another roar and topples down the numerous stairs, at least half way down. It doesn't take me long to wrestle the ice-crested double doors open. I feel the customary tinge of pain from my side as I enter through the darker tone wood. My back presses against the door and I let out a heavy sigh as I stuff it with a handful of a musty purple carpet.

I reach a soiled hand to my eyes and wipe away the crystalized tears and the blood. I feel so dirty, so ruined. Nothing about me is pure any longer. A loud pounding on the door pulls me away from my spiral. *The tower.* There's a lock on that door. I know it, for I locked myself up there after my father's funeral. I don't recall much from that day, but I do recall that. It was a brief respite from the lostness. I felt below the clouds and steady for only a moment. I needed that then and I need it even more now.

Before me, decaying rows of pews stretch out as far as the eye can see, each made of scratched mahogany wood. A few bibles lay on the shelves behind the pews, dust tarnishing their faces. I grimace. I've never seen a holy book kept in such awful surroundings. Lord, I've never seen a church, chapel, or cathedral this forgotten. Even the coarse stone of the walls is cracked and dilapidated. The stained-glass windows have abandoned their luster. The only object in the grand margins that remains gleaming and polished is the large cross hung upon the back wall, overseeing the chaos. I shudder and turn my gaze to a small, arched threshold in the left corner of the room. That way leads to the tower. I hear the clang of metal on metal beyond the hastily sealed doorway.

I run down the putrid purple carpet, dust rising as my feet fall mechanically. The floorboards groan beneath me. My breathing is haggard and strained. My stature, diminished. All I have to do is make it to the tower. Nothing more, nothing less. This sick sojourn will be finished soon enough. I mangle the upholstery of the pews as I make my way past them with my fingernails. Angst ebbs through me. I'm not a child but still, I'm only but fifteen. I shouldn't have to die, not this way. It's not fair! None of this is fair! Yet my own knowledge bans me from this form of self-pity. I've known it for a long time. Life isn't fair. Parents pass and brothers abandon. Friends deceive and immunity vanishes. Pity helps no one. I grasp at the door frame as I swing around the corner of the arched way. A pile of uneven wooden stairs tower before me and my legs quiver beneath me. Can I reach the top?

I hear the wrenching of a door from the main hall. Edward found a way in. Fervor, just when I need it. My legs begin again and I drag myself up the stairs, a separate cry accompanying each of my steps.

"I have you, Alexander! I have you now!" Edward yells. His

cry sounds alarmingly close, not as distant as I suspected. My lips move rapidly in prayer. I've prayed more today than any other in my life. One calls on God when they need him most, I know that. Edward swirls around the corner as I steal a glance back. My heart spasms in my chest, panic burying my senses. I take the final landing, a grimy aperture casting light down upon my brother's toned figure. I heave in and pull at the bronze handle of the shadowed doorway. If I remember correctly, this leads to the tower room. There's only one issue. It's fastened shut and a wild animal is pursuing me as if I'm his prey.

"Don't do this to me, not now, not ever!" I implore, gazing towards the sky. My body feels void of energy, my vigor burning away. "Please, please," I sob, pressing my weight against the door in one last attempt. With a metallic ring, the door clicks open and I throw myself through, locking the small knob from inside.

"Open the door now!" Edward screams. I see the imprint of his massive body press against the rotting door. I back away, horror flooding me. This barrier won't last long under his anger-enhanced girth. I have to think. But how is that possible when there's no room in my mind for thinking?

"You have the agility of a glacier!" I call back in response, the coping humor dying beside me. I glance around the room. I'm met with the figures of seven or so armored knight statues, the kind that adorn the emptiest of halls in Palace Andria. They fill space. They have no real purpose other than to impress. I'll give them a purpose; I just have to think of one first.

"Says the one who spends hours scrawling four verses on a page!" Edward retorts, throwing himself into the wood. The door is thick, thank the Lord. I have a few moments remaining in this miraculous asylum.

"At least I have the courage to face you! You should see yourself, all wolf-like and morose! Your breath smells of rotten flesh!" I don't even know why I'm replying any longer. He's a waste of what could be my final breaths. I place my bloodied hands on my head, fear drowning me as I search for a solution. Time is straying. Edward throws himself into the door again.

"You have the sunny disposition of a dead man. I'll match your disposition to your state of being soon enough, mark my words unholy bastard!" he calls, heaving himself against the lock. Dead man my ass. He'll be the dead man. The center knight fixture holds a sword erect. A simple, dull blade worn away by the years and the dust. It'll do if the subject runs directly into it though. And indeed he will, going at this rate. I heave the manikin across the floor, the metal scraping at the floorboards incessantly. This statue will do my bidding. I position the sword forward, my legs going numb beneath me. A crack spirals through the door at impact.

"Edward, stop! We don't have to do this. *You* don't have to do this!" I call. He'll most definitely die if he enters. He'll run himself through on the sword. At this moment, past transgressions fade and I'm having trouble even recalling what he did to me. Something about death perhaps but he's my brother. My last living family. Without him, I won't even have a chance at being anything but lonely. The pounding abates and I hear a muffled thwack and a sigh.

"You don't understand, Alexander, you're a blemish, a stain. I-I have to. I have to." His words sink through me as his voice breaks. I slip behind another knight statue for protection. I learned my lesson the last time someone was attempting to break through a door. I cover my mouth with my hand, tears falling down my face. This feels like one of my dreams. This must be a dream. My dreams are never this awful though. The oils of my fingers sting against the jagged cuts on my face, but I need to remain silent. Lizbeth could come next.

The wood shatters across the room. The world moves slower than it would usually. I see fury in his empty, cold eyes. Fury, but deeper, beneath that, pain. And beneath that, a sinister sort of darkness. He has depth, but not all his layers are good. Now he will die. My brother will die. A gruesome squelch resonates through my surroundings. The sound hits me like a slap across the face. My eyes open abruptly and my mouth falls. The sound travels through my teeth and into my bones. Further still, it hits my soul. I grasp my middle as if a hole has formed in my chest.

"A-Alex," Edward moans. Through my tainted vision, I observe the tip of the uneven sword puncturing his abdomen. I empty the meager contents of my stomach on the statue beside me. My brother. Impaled. He drops his father's cutlass to the ground with a deafening clatter. He stares at the knight fixture and then at the corner where I stand. I rush to his side. He stares into my eyes with bewilderment. The pale blue color returns to his eyes as he contemplates my expression. His lower lip begins to quiver and his jaw tightens. He reaches a muscle-bound arm and uses my body to pull himself from the sword. If he feels the agony, he doesn't display it. Blood discolors the virgin white of his shirt.

"E-Edward." His hands grasp my shoulders as we careen to the center of the circular tower. It's suddenly so very cold. I help him down against a bare patch of wall.

"What's h-h-happening? Where a-are w-we?" He can barely speak through his stuttering. This must be a manifestation of blood-loss. I slide down the wall beside him and wrap him in a warm embrace. His skin feels frigid and his flesh has a deathly pallor. Remorse chills me. He's my brother. He's my brother! Why? Why is this happening? *He tried to kill me. He was… He was a beast only moments ago.* I remind myself of these things as he utters more nonsensical queries.

"It's alright n-now, Edward. You're okay. You're s-safe now. All the b-blemishes are erased and you'll be just f-fine," I promise him, tears dominating my face. He turns his head to me, poised fear in his now colored eyes.

"They a-a-are?" he asks, despair in his voice. I nod, my tears staining his shirt.

"Yes. I-I promise," I reply. I'm in a different time now, lying on my back. Lying in a pile of new spring grass. Lying with Edward in the sun. We were younger then. Him fifteen, I six. He took me to a secluded garden he used to play in a lot when he was younger. He wanted me to see it. He made me laugh that day. That act was equivalent to going to the moon. He went to the moon for me. He was a good brother. I will choose to remember him that way, a kind brother who stole me away from the troubles of the world, even if only a moment. Good.

I blink. I'm back with him now. The blood collects around our feet. Edward is shivering heavily. He grips my arm with surprising strength, mumbling random words, staring into my eyes.

"Shhhhh. You c-can go n-now. God has you," I whisper to him. He nods and his grip loosens. His eyes fade and roll forward. The life is gone from his body. He's emptier now than I've ever seen him. He's gone. It's not over yet, though. Lizbeth is still living. I have to endure, although I don't think I'm able, for I'm frozen now.

CHAPTER 22

Cordella's Perspective

I was once locked in a cage by the brother of my paramour, my husband. Fortune is my servant, though. She's served me well throughout my many years of ordeals and amorous afflictions. My prior knowledge of locks and ties helped me escape the thin leather cords Edward bound me with. I've had a few lovers who've been more antithetical to usual customs. My sweet skin and seductive temperament kept me alive. That, and the words Alexander gave to me.

I convinced him not to end my life. He did, however, vow to keep me locked in a mutt's cage for the rest of my life, however long or short that may be. He couldn't even follow through with my captivity. Thank the Lord he didn't become a father. On the contrary, I wish he had. I wish I could've kept the child healthy within me but, I failed. That event is in the past now. I must move ahead to save myself from the abysmal pit of self-pity.

As for the final page of the notebook, I filled that during the silent hours of the night when the moonbeams swung just far enough to the left to fill my enclosure. I felt the grooves his fixed fingers had left on the stately pen and felt less sequestered, almost as if he was holding my hand in some pitiful manner. Our romance was a fleeting one; a single, poignant moment to rule all else. It was a summer affair in the dead of winter. I love him so and I forever will continue to. It may fade if I lose him, but he will be in my heart evermore until my final breath.

My bastard prince,

I never learned to write properly. I didn't know how to read until I was thirteen years of age. I was separate, hidden until then, only a rumor passed from person to person in taverns. I wasn't meant to be a fragile doll, Alexander. I wasn't meant to be clay, molded to be what others want, Alexander. I wasn't even meant to be human. I was meant to be an elephant. Back in Walsia, they scatter themselves across the vast plains and wildlands, wandering until they're one with the Earth again. Nobody expects an elephant to be clean and tidy. Nobody expects an elephant to be soft. Nobody expects an elephant to be a romantic. As you know, I'm every one of those things. Because despite what I was meant to be, my experiences have molded me differently. I am what I am because of every mark, touch, and memory that clings to me.

You've added to me. Your touches, your marks, your memories have joined with mine. I became yours and you became mine. I became someone entirely different because of you. Not to please you, but because you tore away at some of the evils they guarded me with. You made me more of an elephant, if that makes even an inkling of sense. I hope it does. I hope you know I love you more than-no. Not all the stars in the sky. For the reaches of the sky are far too meager to contain the depths of what I feel for you. What I feel is beyond anything that can be viewed. Beyond this time. Yes, our romance was short, but it's a flicker. If you and I both live, then we could light a flame. Eternally ours and ours alone. If you or I pass on, maybe God will allow us another chance at life. Maybe instead of being sent to our eternal resting places, he'll give us another life in which we could hold that flame in the palm of our hands and watch it until it consumes all the darkness in the world. If we perish, I'll see you in the next life, for even God would allow a love this incredible to exist, to give us a life of bliss.

I'm running out of room. I have but a few more sentence spaces remaining. Alexander, hope is not a distraction. Hope is all we have. We have nothing else to do, so what would it distract us from? Hope for me, with me. Save me from the colors of the world. Fill my mind with vast oceans of your words and let us gaze into each other's eyes for eternity and then some. Break the shining image and cure me with truth. Let us be one again.

Your comely queen, **Cordella**

I truly believe we would be granted another life. Christianity isn't always rigid, austere as the Andrian form is. God is good. I believe that to be true. I've leveled myself again and again only to be pulled back by him. I've seen him in the faces of those around me, working in their lives as well. God is good indeed. He will give us another life, better than this one.

Now I have to be good in return. After I escaped the cage, I swindled the guards that were posted outside the door of the room where my cage sat. I'm aware of my God-given beauty and I use it to my advantage whenever I'm able. I shook off the dust of the ground and pulled my silken hair through my fingers. I traipsed through the carelessly unlocked door as if I owned it, which I do. I made the guards aware of a mistake they had made. I chewed them out on false pretenses. "You're meant to guard that door down the hall! A misdemeanor such as this could've compromised my dear husband's prisoner! This is punishable by death! I'll let you off just this once if you stand your post at that door for the rest of the evening until the night guards come." I swayed my hips with each phrase until the burly Andrian soldiers forgot their own names and became slaves to my will. They uttered hesitant apologies as their eyes traversed my form. I let a simper become present on my face. Victory.

I still wore the vermillion gown given to me by the demoness.

I still don't know why she permitted me to wear my favorite color in the presence of her "one true love." One would think she would cover me up for that reason. Still, the gown drew attention to me. The color is vivid enough to blind anyone, even those accustomed to the Walsian sun. I had to change. I rushed to my and Edward's quarters as the morning began anew. He had already taken his leave for the duel, always punctual, nothing like his brother. I knew of the duel and I planned to steal away with Alexander as the battle raged on between the ill-fated brothers. I would take him from the crowd and we'd hide away until Lizbeth lost interest in pursuing him. I didn't think much after that. I evaded the attention of nobles sauntering through the hallowed halls and hid in the shadows of the fire-fueled light when anyone of authority passed by. Being evasive is another experience-given skill I have. Many clandestine rendezvous have occurred under my command and I've always had a pension for being slippery.

Once in the safety of my private chambers, I locked the door and slid against an armchair set by a blackened fireplace. The servants lacked the motivation to clean our wing. They were far too frightened of Edward. He'd been a bit insane as of late. He deserved to lose his mind. He deserved all the worst things.

I let out a breath and placed my hands on my head to ground myself and fall from the clouds. I was sore from being cramped in such inhumane restraints for so long. Looking back on it made me loathe Edward more. I slept with his brother, but he ignored the loss of a child. He left me in my darkest hour, stared at me while I was in pain. He left me. I was forsaken again, this time by my husband. Better to appease yourself than to be left behind.

I sent those thoughts to the back of my mind as I dressed in something less noticeable and more humble. A navy blue gown with silver threaded into the seams. It blended in with the winter. I threw an overcoat on as well. Andrian storms were unforgiving and deadly, just as my father was. I hated it there.

They compensated for the drab, grey weather with blinding colors and lies. Contrasts were overwhelming to me.

I had an affair with a stable boy when I first arrived in Andria. I'm rather pleased I did. That was the first day Edward hit me. My little enthrallments are, in a sick way, reciprocation for my husband's wrongdoings. He hurts me, I hurt him. He commits an unspeakable crime against me, I fall in love with his brother. At first, my conversations with Alexander were just a comeuppance for Edward's slight misdemeanors. They became something more, though. Something far greater than a petty domestic war. My affair with the stable boy benefited me. For old time's sake, I called in a favor.

"Abram, it's been too long." In reality, it'd only been two months. I'd only once been in love before Alexander. We saw each other only twice each year for a month at a time. Our love lasted until I relocated to Andria. I stepped over the sod of the stable in disgust. I never did have a penchant for horses. I did, however, have one for their caretaker.

"Abram? Why so formal? Last time, you called me Abe. I remember it strongly." A boy with olive skin and brazen curls stepped from the corner stall, a sack of feed clutched in between his fingers. His eyes are dark and dull, nothing like Alexander's. His tone was jesting and confident. I'm attracted to confidence. How did I end up with Alexander? He leans an elbow on a wooden post, his greasy curls overlapping his vision.

"If you insist, *Abe*." I humored his delusions. I had broken things off with him, but this would benefit me and most likely save Alexander from a life in Hyvern filled with internal turmoil. He chuckled with conviction.

"So, are you here for some fun? I knew you'd be back. I thought about it and convinced myself I was better off without a monarchy-handled blade at my neck, but that's what I'm willing to risk for another night with you." He paused and began to pull off his stained collared shirt. Canary yellow. Odd choice.

I shifted uncomfortably on the balls of my boot-adorned feet. "It's cold out and the storm will soon overtake the palace. I can keep you warm in here all day," he teased suggestively as he pulled at the hem of his shirt. I considered waiting for him to undress himself entirely, but decided it was better if I didn't. I was a married woman after all.

"As lovely as that would be, *Abe*, I'm not here for that today. I'm here for a favor if you would be so kind as to *indulge me* in something other than yourself."

He sighed heavily as a flush came over his face. Adorable. He buttoned his shirt hurriedly and went back to work again, hanging the feed in one of his horse's stalls. I traipsed over to him, my body so close to his that he could smell my perfume. His ears became a shade less red than his hair. "Oh come on now, don't ignore me. For old time's sake, a favor. We did so much for each other." I let my lips trail against his hair.

"Alright. I-I'll help." I had sequestered half of his vocabulary with my seductive movements.

"I need you to abandon your horses for today and take me to the Stone Chapel." I recalled the name from the two letters Edward read aloud to me as I struggled helplessly against the iron bars of the cold cage. He raised an eyebrow as he cleaned a bridle that hung on a hook.

"The Stone Chapel. Well I'll be damned. They executed my father there for crimes against the nation."

Questions plagued my mind, but I dared not ask. He was going to aid me after all. "My condolences," I told him instead. I tried to raise genuine sorrow and empathy in my voice. I had seen him without clothes after all. I'm not heartless.

"Fine, fine. I'll take you." He grunted as he pulled himself from my gravity. He went on to prepare a black and white blotched horse for our escapade. He draped the horse in a special heating garment and a two-seated saddle. He was right to cloth the stallion. It would take us three hours to evade the prying eyes of soldier patrols and to traverse the fen. We made idle conversation during the quietest of parts. His words were bleak and dry, no clarity in his phrases. I'd become spoiled by the eloquence of Alexander's tongue, in more ways than one. At least it was something to pass the time. As I mentioned earlier, I don't particularly like horses.

"Isn't a duel for sovereignty taking place today at the Stone Chapel? I saw a notice posted on the door of my residence. We all know they happen a day before because of that odd law," he inquired as we entered the fen, the darker green of the spruces appearing before our eyes.

"Yes. That's actually why I want to go there, preferably before sunset." I glanced restlessly at the sinking sun.

"Easy, easy. We may be a bit late, but you'll be there soon enough, I promise." My grip on his woolen coat became tighter with his words. He chuckled good humoredly. "This involves your husband, does it not?" he asked after a moment of pressing silence.

"Yes... But he's not the reason I wish to attend. I wouldn't mind if he died. That would be helpful actually. Abram, he's done cruel things to me," I finished in a cryptically grave tone.

"Ha, king of Andria, cruel to his wife. That's an uproarious picture. I'm sorry he's unkind to you Cordella. I'm not legally allowed to call him a nasty name, but I wish I could." Abram had been one of my kinder lovers. He was always gentle and considered my needs. He didn't know I was the queen at first and asked me to go for a picnic with him. I laughed until I cried, but it worked out favorably for him.

"Thank you, Abram. You're a good man," I recognized. He nodded with ease, a smile making his posture straighten.

"I don't mind if you forget about me. Let's call it even, alright?" he asked willingly.

"Sure, sure." I was grateful he didn't ask more about my reasons. I hoped he found a good, loyal girl to settle with. He was good. Few people were good.

The rest of the journey was uneventful. We passed wolves once. Their mannerisms reminded me of Edward, that mutt of man. The clouds overhead gained a purple tone the farther we went. The ice would be treacherous. Abram covered the horse's eyes to keep them from congealing.

At long last, we arrived. He let me off a quarter mile from the clearing. I wished him a safe journey back and he wished me good luck. I knew I would need it, but I also prayed. I prayed to God and asked him to deliver Alexander. I couldn't bring myself to ask for my own life. My sins were becoming more and more heavy on my shoulders as the days went by. The sorrow I felt for all my losses and turmoil was too immense to consider myself worthy of.

When I made it to the large, crumbling church, I let my bag drop to the ground before me. A priest lay dead before it. I caught an inkling of Lizbeth's scorched hair out of the corner of my eye and turned to see the girl chasing Peter. What happened?

I connected the dots. The priest, dead. Lizbeth, chasing Peter, her loyal servant. Alexander nowhere to be found. Edward, out of sight. Peculiar. Lizbeth was the most murderous of them all, so she must have ended the priest's life to gain a spot in the duel. Why would she do that? Well, Alexander's absence explained that. He must've realized that he could fight in the duel because of his half-sovereignty. Damn his brilliant logic! He was in grave danger now because of it. He was matched against three roughly skilled combatants. If I had placed an impartial bet, I would have said he would be the first to die. Lizbeth would protect him at all costs though, so I had to assume he was still alive.

I waited for a grueling hour of deadened screams as the storm worsened and the wind tousled my ebony curls. My face was set in an expression of worry. I lingered a few yards behind the majority of the crowd as to not be noticed. It would be a terrible thing if one of Lizbeth's men took heed to my wintry inconspicuousness. My eyelashes soon became crusted with snow and the wind forced me to my knees once or twice. The gathering was beginning to grow antsy and I noticed Lizbeth's men form a tighter circle around the bewildered people. A quarter hour later, they led the people inside the church at stark gunpoint. I had seen a glimpse of Alexander stumbling up the steps beforehand, his eyes glistening with both blood and- were those tears? The nine-year promise he made, broken! Thank the Lord! I could tell he desperately needed to cry. I cried every day. It was a sound way of releasing plaguing emotions. Crying was never the wrong thing to do, never. What a bother shame was.

I joined the herd inconspicuously. The handlers couldn't tell the difference between the queen and her subjects. Part of me was slightly offended, seeing I'm far too distinct and recognizable in most cases. I swallowed my pride for Alexander's sake. My confidence was not needed in this particular situation. I wrapped my overcoat tighter around my shivering figure as I seated myself on a broken set of pews. To be in the house of God at a time such as this one.

As per usual, a glimmering cross adorned the far wall. It was the only pure object in the room. I was glad to be indoors at last after the saddle-rash ridden journey and the icy ordeal of waiting. It was difficult to focus on such things, though, for my mind was absolutely consumed with Alexander. I hoped he was alright, I hoped he lived. I hoped we could be together after all of this madness was over.

But even as I don't believe them, his words circulated through my mind. *Hope is a distraction* or something depressing such as that. I clasped my hands together and bowed my head against the pew in front of me. I wasn't the only one praying in the decrepit church. Many others clasped their hands and bowed their heads.

I couldn't find the words for my prayer. I didn't even have the will to recite the Lord's prayer. It had always been far too definable and verbatim for my taste. My prayers were odd, conversations instead of requests. He spoke and responded through actions.

Lord... I pour my emotions into the word, all of them, good, bad, and awful. The facet I've clothed myself in for the past hours falls for only a moment as I reveal myself in the center of a sea of frightened persons. A profound moment, something a philosopher, or Alexander, would write about. Suddenly, it comes to me. God helps those who help themselves. I lean into the thought as if it's an embrace from a lover. I must help myself. I must be the change, for nobody else will. Alexander. If he's still alive, he's had to kill his own brother and lost the other to Lizbeth. He's not fit to fight her. I will bear his burden, take his place as he's done for me. I will save him again as I did the night of the trial. I will save him until I can't any longer.

As my thought comes full circle, the wind blows the stout door wide open, a drawn-out gust of wind dressing the room with bits of ice and snow. I stand abruptly. My head turns as if pulled by some sort of dark gravity, an invisible hand. My eyes meet hers. Verdigris. Lizbeth, dealer of secrets and other less innocuous ideas. The servant girl who fell in love with the man who saved me from my own dire ways. Suddenly, I feel barren. I'm unarmed. Two glinting knives lay dormant at her wrists. They have a nasty jagged pattern about them. Each tip is marked with fresh blood, most certainly that of Peter. Her stance is one of intimidation and superiority. Dominance emanates from her. Many turn from their prayers to gaze at her, for the devil can sometimes be more enticing than the Lord.

"Where are they?" she roars, murder in her eyes. Never have I seen a monster so woeful, never have I been more frightened. Never have I been more *brave*. My heart thuds against my chest irregularly and I succumb to a cold sweat. I've only ever seen a monster half as horrid as her, that man being my father, the enigmatic king of Walsia. Those who rest comfortably in positions of power are monsters, all of them, but my father was the worst. The details are my own to keep, mine to nullify. Love does strange things to perceptions of others.

"Don't worry about them, your only threat on this holy ground is me." I find words leaving my throat. A tinge of regret strikes me as I finish the phrase. My voice sounds far-flung, detached. Panic rises in my chest. She cocks her head to one side, her eyes narrowing. Her form begins to quiver like solid ground does before it splits into a chasm.

"Cordella of Walsia. Or should I say, Cordella of the brothel. I see you've fornicated your way out of another predicament. I thought he'd kill you. I suppose I was wrong, for you're still of use to him. A dog that hasn't run out of tricks. I wanted the blood to be off my hands, but I surmise that a bit more red in a vast ocean can't do much harm." Lizbeth paces towards me. She relishes the afterthought of her meticulously crafted insult. She enjoys her words and the ways she can twist them to make someone else hurt.

I'll make her hurt, hurt for the week of torture I endured under her command. For every horrifying phrase she uttered, for the way she beat me and took me from my moment of greatest happiness, when I had finally been accepted as more than just a notch to add to one's belt. I hold great passion, but also great strength in Alexander's and my collective purpose. To save Andria from the horrors of my husband and from the horrors of this deranged girl and her partner Jakob. Yes, now I see it, we were placed here for something more, something far greater than ourselves. Andria lies in the wake of Lizbeth's evil. I must save it. *We* must save it. Hundreds of thousands of people reside in Andria's pain-etched prosperity. Hundreds of thousands of lives would be filled with trauma and torture and abuse if any of our adversaries remained in control of it. Only we could take the agony, only we could create a ripple in this vast ocean we call life. And that is something I would die for.

And that is something he would die for. And that is something every soul-laden person would die for. The suffering of one to take away the suffering of all. Humanity.

"Oh, playing at my most prominent flaw, are you? I hardly think passion and beauty is something to scoff at, Lizbeth, maddened admirer. I didn't sleep my way out of my issues *this time,* I did something far worse in your eyes. I took the words of Alexander right from his lips and used them for good. You were destined to rot in the ground. I, however, was destined for more." Again words flow from my throat. I can't find the source of this new ability.

"Your beauty and passion? I'm sure the boys *love* that. I never pegged Alexander to be the type to *pay* for his pleasure." She rambles on about my promiscuousness and all that. As long as I can keep her insults flowing, I can make progress towards the archway in the corner of the room. It most likely leads to a set of chambers of a bell tower or something of that sort. Alexander must be up there. I hear stifled sobs through the thin floorboards. He has a weapon, he must if he's not dead. If I can only reach him, then I can slay the demoness with his weapon. Every time she steps closer to me, I move a foot or so backwards, out of the pews and into the center aisle. The gathering listens with intent, their eyes ablaze with sudden interest. They cling to every word as if it will give them some remnant of knowledge.

By some act of God, I reach the arch. I've traded many insults with this sociopath. She sinks her teeth into every harmful phrase, my suffering her sustenance. She feeds on my soul as a proper demoness would. I let her, for it'll save Alexander and many others. *Sticks and stones can break my bones but words can never hurt me.* I have no idea how that phrase came into existence. I hate nursery rhymes such as that one, for they're too untrue. Words hurt, words drive others to the edge of insanity. Words can hurt so badly that they kill. If I had any self-esteem that wasn't a visage before, it's gone now, taken by her. I nearly collapse around the corner, only to be met with a lengthy bout of stairs. I'm exhausted, emotionally, physically and spiritually. A heavy part of Lizbeth's attack was on my faith and its hypocrisy. Good Christian girls aren't meant to seek what they want. They're meant to be demure and submissive, two qualities I do not have. They're meant to be chaste and to frown upon the seeking of pleasure, shame as their influencer. *God is good. He wouldn't give me more than I can handle,* I remind myself.

"Hey easy make, get back here and I won't draw out your death for too long!" Lizbeth calls. I hear her heavy footsteps pounding against the sinking floorboards. I observe long, pain-etched scratches in the clapboard of the walls. It must have been a very distressing climb for the last person who ascended the crooked stairs.

"Hey coward, might want to use your blades instead of your words!" I shout back. I've been gradually provoking her to follow me. Her footsteps pound harder. I'm halfway up the unwieldy stairway, the light disappearing from an upper aperture as the raging blizzard overtakes the building. A massive gale of wind pummels the building. A mutual groan resonates through the people and the structure of the building. I'm not bothered though, for this sanctuary must've stood strong through many a storm before. Still, the quivering of the structure is frightening. I teeter up to the top step. The door before me is slightly ajar. I peer around the corner.

A knight statue stands poised before the door, his metallic arms erect as if holding a sword. There is a blade as I suspected, but it's fallen to the floor beneath. The tip of it trickles with rich, red blood. My eyes turn from the statue and onto the wall beside it. Peeled and cracked as it is, the wall itself isn't the most interesting thing about the barrier. My husband lies dead, his prematurely rigid corpse propped up against the wall in a peculiar manner. Alexander leans back beside him, his eyes a glacial blue with glistening tears, some frozen halfway down his face.

"Alexander," I breathe. "You're crying." I forget the imminent peril behind me and instead stare into his eyes if only for a moment.

"I lack any dignity. I've killed with my own hands. I've cried. I've loved. I'm not solid anymore," he whispers with astonishing strength, his phrases thick and meaningful. His hands are in his hair, his fingers toying at separate strands nervously. He's torn up both physically and emotionally, but he's alive. I stare into the dilated eyes of my husband's corpse. I'm angry. I can't feel for him. I can't bring myself to feel in any way sad about his death. He's done... He's done awful things and he deserved what came to him. Still, it's rather odd to see the deceased with his eyes open. I cross the room hesitantly as if one of my foot falls could break Alexander. I close Edward's eyes with a cold hand. He's going to hell, for he's inflicted hell on others.

Lizbeth's clamor brings me back to myself. She's giddy with the pain and peril she causes.

"Get behind me," Alexander says in the ghost of a whisper. His eyes are bulging and his stature is meager, yet he stands. I see love circling his irises and my heart glows faintly, a warm light in a gale of wind.

"No, I've come here to help you, save you." My words are hurried and slurred. He eyes me wearily, his facet telling me many things wordlessly. I crouch to my knees and my hand closes around the bloodied sword. To my surprise, Alexander reaches for his brother's cutlass, the one that was used to hurt him and to kill his mother. I would never think that he could bear a burden such as that one. Alexander has changed. I see it in his face. His eyes are more deep-set, his frown less permanent, his tears woeful. He was the stoic prince who comforted me when nobody else, let alone my husband, would. Now, he's the hell-emerged philosopher with a tried soul and a sound mind, the one I see before me, the one I'm attempting to comfort.

Alexander's Perspective

Cordella knows the gnarls of Lizbeth's heart and so do I. We have both been tortured by her, the fiend possessing her making itself apparent in her eyes. I was alone, collapsed beside my deceased brother. As the moments of quiet drained away, an unfamiliar hush settled over my mind. For once, thoughts weren't plaguing every aspect of my being. I was free as a bird, yet horribly confined, pasted to the spot on which I sat. I put a name to the face, resignation was what I felt. During the first moment after his eyes became glassy and his soul faded, I believed I could continue, if only for a while longer. But as the blizzard battered and chewed at the building, I gave up. I pondered the way Lizbeth's eyes would look with that awful, glassy tint to them and I just couldn't endure it any longer. Every emotion I had felt so potently before, such as despising Lizbeth, had become dull beside the soulless eyes of my brother. The eyes are windows to the soul indeed, but not when the window isn't attached to anything at all. I was defeated, irrevocably, undeniably so, yet my mission still lay ahead of me.

Cordella brought me back from the dead. Her eyes have a way of reviving me when I most need them to. When she careened through the door, I thought she was Lizbeth. Ha, Lizbeth indeed. Cordella is far more divine and superior to the demoness. I found that I couldn't move to stand. I would just allow her to take her victory, let her steal my kingdom from beneath me. I was too tired. But then, she turned and her ebony curls twirled into my view. My heart stopped. Her perfect, heart-shaped face came into view along with her eyes. Oh, the cosmos before me. Life and death, beauty and peril. I would traverse the entire universe just to be able to gaze at her eyes forever. My heart began to beat again and warm, jovial blood caressed my veins.

"Alexander," She whispered, her gaze lovingly indignant. "You're crying."

"I lack any dignity. I've killed with my own hands. I've cried. I've loved. I'm not solid anymore," I said, shame catching in my throat. All she could do is stare for a moment. There I was, displaying weakness before Cordella, the one I care for most. We both reflected on our changes in that moment, our eyes glimmering as if trapped in recollection of past times. I again asked myself; how did we get here? An all-encompassing strength coursed through me, a godly zeal overtaking my figure. My hand reached for my brother's cutlass. It was mine now. A pang of guilt washed over me as I pulled myself to my feet. "Get behind me," I commanded.

"No, I've come here to help you, save you." Her tone was heartsick and desperate, as if pleading with me. All I wanted to do was win this miniature war and take her home with me, yet I feared we wouldn't make it through the fight. Lizbeth was a formidable nemesis, formidable indeed. And now I'm back in the present moment.

"Alright. Come, we're stronger beside each other." I hear an offensive cry from Lizbeth and my shoulders stiffen. I wipe my tears on my muddied sleeve. I would clean my face on my collar, but I left that behind when my brother strung me up on that cursed tree. His cutlass feels a bit weightier in my hand than before. I'm in agony. My side burns, my face bleeds, but Cordella's here with me, my anchor is a deluge of turmoil.

"I wish I got to tell you I love you more than once," I whisper to her as Lizbeth's footsteps grow louder.

"Oh, be quiet. You'll get sick of saying it so many times after we win this thing." Her words are encouraging, yet her voice quivers. I grasp onto every thread of her voice, a good, viable thread amidst the lot.

"I love you. I love you, I love you, I love you." Lizbeth climbs the top step, her head turning very slowly toward the opening. Her gaze is so sinister that my mouth hangs open and I can no longer speak.

"You don't love her Alexander. You love me!" her voice is far off, but her tone is incredulous. Each word gnaws at my remaining stamina. Now I truly believe she's possessed by a demon. I whisper a silent prayer, my lips creating friction against one another.

"No, I don't. I hate you. In fact, I don't even hate you. I despise you." My words register surprisingly strong and brash. Cordella doesn't speak at all. Lizbeth stares daggers at her though, as if she's the reason I despise her.

"And I suppose you actually love her then, do you not?" Lizbeth asks, her tone frighteningly playful. Her head hangs so limply on her neck, almost like a ghost. I'm afraid it'll snap off.

"Yes," I breathe. Fury circles her luminous pupils. She releases a shriek so terrible, so spine-bending that my ears feel as if they're about to shrivel up, turn black, and fall off. Her battle cry has been released, signaling the beginning of the immediate peril.

She throws herself through the door, her knives slashing through the wood. Cordella holds the sword, her arm unwavering. I find my feet backing away, my body's natural reaction to the danger. Cordella's instinct is to fight, though, her distinct form clashing against Lizbeth's. I find I'm unable to move, trapped in a state of paralysis. I'm frozen as I was in that horrid dream. I relived my mother's death and now, I'm observing something far worse in my own time. The amount of cowardice I possess is shame-worthy. I can't move, I can't help.

Lizbeth hits first. Cordella's shoulder bursts open, her purple blood spattering my face. I let out a gasp, but still can't compel myself to move. She admits a strangled cry, the sound piercing my ears. It only seems to empower her. She advances on Lizbeth, her shoulder ignored. She jabs, and parries blows, her form straight from the guide book. Lizbeth's suave confidence is daunting as well. She's just as deft as Cordella, if not more so. Lizbeth's crude street style is more viscous than Cordella's poised classroom swordsmanship.

Cordella makes contact with Lizbeth, her sword burrowing deep into the flesh of Lizbeth's knee. I cringe as I hear a sickening crunch. Lizbeth grits her teeth, her focus unwavering. How could she endure such pain, such agony? I've cried out over worse.

"If you wish to play dirty, so be it. An eye for an eye, a tooth for a tooth," Lizbeth shouts as she makes a slit in Cordella's thigh. Now both combatants are crippled in competition, both disabled by the other's blade. I roar against my invisible restraints. How dare she harm Cordella?

"I thought we already were, seeing you entered the duel illegally and all that." Cordella earns a slice to the nose, the blood dribbling down across her lips. This is a horrid amalgamation of love and obsession, two of the greatest influencers. Yet I can't make myself move. I curse myself again.

Suddenly, Lizbeth's legs lock together. The afflicted leg snaps inward and she crumples beside my brother. Oh Lord, a row of corpses. Or at least, soon to be corpses. Lizbeth heaves and shakes with pain, her eyes rolling back in her head as the pale white of the bone sticks from her leg. "Blast!" She seethes as her eyes roll forward again.

Cordella edges towards her, her stance poised and ready to kill. Both awe and horror register in my mind as I view the woebegone scene. Good against evil, the underlying plot to any story. Cordella is extraordinary, beautiful. Her hair slithers against her throat as she takes another step. Her pupils are narrowed in on Lizbeth. I should move, assist Cordella so that she wouldn't have to bear the burden of another's death. It would be the moral thing to do. I can't collect enough will within me to do so. In the same way one's eyes are drawn to a tragic accident, my eyes are drawn to the woeful occurrence before me.

"So y-you're just g-going to kill me now? After all w-we've been through? I thought worse of you. At least y-you're persistent in your endeavors to make me h-hate you," Lizbeth mutters. Cordella shows no weakness, save the slight tremble of her rosy lower lip. An eye less trained on human weakness would never notice it.

"This is how your life ends," Cordella affirms with intent. She glances toward me and I'm again taken aback by her beauty. Her curves fit against her gown, her figure wide and voluptuous. Blood trickles down her brazen skin, the contrast making her singularity more evident. I love her more than words can describe, yet words are all the description I'm allowed. It's cruel. There are too few words in the dictionary. If I was given the perfect words, the words that fit along her curves and nuances, I could write an entire book about my teenage lust-impassioned love. The awe and the agony penultimate death can instill in one is astonishing.

"Please Alexander, y-you won't let her d-do this, w-will you?" Lizbeth implores pleadingly. Her phrases sound all too painful and her eyes have just the right cocktail of angst and self-pity to make me want to act based on my separate, Christian morality. Yet I can't find it within me yet again, even after an audible plea. I want to. I should want to. But my lover is about to save us from the turmoil that has been plaguing us for so very long. It'll be over. My heart cracks slightly for Lizbeth. I remember how I loved her, but that too will die with her.

I remember how she saved me from myself. I remember many, many things. But she took the lives of people right out from under then, lives that I know aren't mine to bear any longer. Yes, indeed she has committed many woeful crimes for me, yet I am not responsible. I'm free from the burden, a stallion cut loose. As she said, an eye for an eye, a tooth for a tooth. *A life for the many.* The fractured bit of my heart reserved for Lizbeth blackens and crumbles to dust as I stare into her eyes, verdigris, the color bronze turns with time. As green as the sky on an Easter Sunday. As green as the grass in spring. As green as the world turns when I'm far away from myself. Green.

"I promised I'd never be like my father, yet here I am," Cordella laments, her eyes welling up with tears. She holds the dull, weighted sword above her head in an executioner's stance. An edge of starlight breaks through the raging gale fatefully as the blade falls, a single stream of cosmos entering the room in the final moments of a demoness.

"Don't worry love, you'll never get to be like your father," Lizbeth whispers, her voice suddenly a stalwart sing-song. She grabs at my brother's arm and allows the blade to chop the limb cleanly, a devilish smile gracing her features. I finally find myself the will to move and to speak.

"You beast!" I cry, stumbling backwards at the sight of the mutilation. His severed arm drops to the ground with a sickening squelch. I double over and vomit, my stomach not able to handle such an awful display. I'm not prepared for what happens next. I would never be, even after thousands of years. Even if I was sure and true in all my acts. Even if I was dead. It appears to happen more haltingly than the previous moments as all the worst things tend to do. Lizbeth kicks Cordella in the gut with her good leg, causing Cordella to bend over from the acute pain. Bend over right into...

I no longer despise Lizbeth. No, I don't despise her at all.

I want death for her. Is there a word for that? Cordella bent over from the blow right into the blade of her own goddamned sword, for Lizbeth held it erect for her to fall onto.

Cordella grasps at her throat. History repeats itself again and again. The cycle is tiresome and destructive, distorting every gilded painting to ever come into existence. I can't tell reality from memory. My mother's body, blood covering her gown and her neck. Cordella, blood collecting into a blade-forged rivulet in her neck. Her eyes glow brightly as if all the life she was ever meant to live is escaping her, the zeal diminished entirely. The stars in her eyes collapse in on themselves and the planets break apart and crumble. The celestial lights fade away and... It's all gone. She gasps and gasps, her hands clasping and clasping. But to no avail.

"Oh, be quiet. Boo-hoo. You're dying. You'll see him again. In hell, that is." Lizbeth bends over Cordella as if she's a child. Pure fear raptures within her eyes.

She's going to die.

The only one I have left in this world is about to die before me. I'm a waste of a life.

Suddenly, I'm able. Instead of going directly to her, I stand here for a moment, allowing the righteous rage to fully take over my mind. All my senses disappear and I'm left with only the need for revenge, the need for closure, to kill her. I make my footsteps soft as I approach her. My gaze falls on Cordella and I nod, silent tears collecting in my eyes. I hold the cutlass over Lizbeth's head, the inscription all too true. I don't wish to use it, yet I will. I close my eyes and shake, shake like the ground would during the rapture. And then, *slice.* Her red-haired head, on the floor. I drop the cutlass in resignation. It's done.

Third Person Perspective

They lay beside each other on the floor, his right hand in hers, the other holding the little leather notebook. He read the words aloud as she sunk deeper into an inky black pool, his melodious voice lulling her into an everlasting sleep. She always did love his voice, she always would. And even as her fingers grew cold in his and her pulse ceased, he kept reading the phrases over and over until they made no sense to him and he was numbed, her penned words no consolation any longer, for he was alone, this time truly, his greatest wish from the beginning. A shining image, given a terrible, dark demise.

EPILOGUE

Alexander, king of cravats. That is what they called him. Every day he wore different cravats in the most uproariously bright colors. None in vermillion, though. That color was forbidden throughout the great kingdom of Andria.

Alexander, wed to a Hyvernian noble's daughter. Her name was Victoria. Her skin was milky and her eyes light, but her temperament was cruel and her mind was lacking. He couldn't hold a conversation with her, nor could she hold a tune. However, she loved music and singing. Alexander hated both of those mindless pastimes. He was a good husband though, so he learned to play the harp for her. His deft fingers flitted mindlessly over the gilded strings whenever she wished. She, in return, listened to him whenever he recited his poetry and quoted it back to him verbatim. They had a mutually beneficial relationship, only enough love between the pair to someday create heirs. At best, they were begrudging friends.

Alexander the extrovert. No longer did he spend hours in silence. There was always sound, whether it be that of a banquet, or that of his wife's shrill voice. As he suspected in the beginning, only his thoughts would be his own in marriage. He had grown tall, cumbersomely so. He grew to be only a half-inch beneath his late brother.

One thing that hadn't changed about Alexander was the fact that he was a bastard and would forever be one. He didn't belong in this new identity, this position of power destined to be possessed by evil people and those without souls. He could see beyond his own iris.

In the end, he was a heed-worthy tale. In the end, he was alone. In the end, he still missed her, the queen from Walsia. His summer romance in the dead of winter. Her eyes and the worlds contained within them. He would forever long to reside in them. She had not died in vain. She sacrificed herself so nobody else would have to endure what she had. That invisible hand that had guided him all along had ended her life to save the many. Sometimes he wished it were him who had perished at Lizbeth's blade. Sometimes he wished he had kept her alive so that he could torture her for what she had done. Sometimes he was angry. Sometimes, sad. Sometimes, very rarely, a bitter-sweet happiness filled him.

He, with his newfound faith, restored Andria to its former glory. He cut off backward things at their sources and made new, wonderful additions to each city. He was a good ruler and a just king. All was replenished and all was made right at his hand. He was good.

Never would he lose his darkness or his scars. Cordella would always be in his mind. Edward would always be in his mind. Peter would always be in his mind. Lizbeth, however, would always be in his chest. She would always be that triangle of angst within him, her edges scraping away at his heart until the day he died. Yes, those brief months in winter would always haunt him. Forever and always until the day he returned to his lost loved ones. God bless the people.

ABOOKS

ALIVE Book Publishing and ALIVE Publishing Group
are imprints of Advanced Publishing LLC,
3200 A Danville Blvd., Suite 204, Alamo, California 94507

Telephone: 925.837.7303
alivebookpublishing.com